Leviathan

More Warhammer 40,000 from Black Library

• DAWN OF FIRE •
BOOK 1: Avenging Son
Guy Haley
BOOK 2: The Gate of Bones
Andy Clark
BOOK 3: The Wolftime
Gav Thorpe
BOOK 4: Throne of Light
Guy Haley
BOOK 5: The Iron Kingdom
Nick Kyme
BOOK 6: The Martyr's Tomb
Marc Collins

INDOMITUS
Gav Thorpe

• DARK IMPERIUM •
Guy Haley
BOOK 1: Dark Imperium
BOOK 2: Plague War
BOOK 3: Godblight

• THE CHRONICLES OF URIEL VENTRIS •
Graham McNeill
BOOK 1: Nightbringer
BOOK 2: Warriors of Ultramar
BOOK 3: Dead Sky, Black Sun
BOOK 4: The Killing Ground
BOOK 5: Courage and Honour
BOOK 6: The Chapter's Due
BOOK 7: The Swords of Calth

OF HONOUR AND IRON
Ian St. Martin

KNIGHTS OF MACRAGGE
Nick Kyme

DAMNOS
Nick Kyme

THE DEVASTATION OF BAAL
Guy Haley

CARCHARODONS: OUTER DARK
Robbie MacNiven

Leviathan

Darius Hinks

BLACK LIBRARY

A BLACK LIBRARY PUBLICATION

First published in 2023.
This edition published in Great Britain in 2023 by
Black Library, Games Workshop Ltd., Willow Road,
Nottingham, NG7 2WS, UK.

Represented by: Games Workshop Limited – Irish branch,
Unit 3, Lower Liffey Street, Dublin 1,
D01 K199, Ireland.

10 9 8 7 6 5 4 3 2 1

Produced by Games Workshop in Nottingham.
Cover illustration by Mikhail Savier.

See Black Library on the internet at

blacklibrary.com

Find out more about Games Workshop
and the worlds of Warhammer at

games-workshop.com

Printed and bound in the UK.

For more than a hundred centuries the Emperor
has sat immobile on the Golden Throne of Earth.
He is the Master of Mankind. By the might of
His inexhaustible armies a million worlds stand
against the dark.

Yet, He is a rotting carcass, the Carrion Lord of the
Imperium held in life by marvels from the Dark
Age of Technology and the thousand souls sacrificed
each day so that His may continue to burn.

To be a man in such times is to be one amongst
untold billions. It is to live in the cruellest and
most bloody regime imaginable. It is to suffer an
eternity of carnage and slaughter. It is to have
cries of anguish and sorrow drowned by the
thirsting laughter of dark gods.

This is a dark and terrible era where you will
find little comfort or hope. Forget the power
of technology and science. Forget the promise
of progress and advancement. Forget any
notion of common humanity or compassion.

There is no peace amongst the stars, for in the
grim darkness of the far future,
there is only war.

I see it

katabasis

pith and marrow

seams of blood

abscissions and growth

flux and reflux

I see it all

and I begin

Prologue

By the end, when there was no hope of escape, people turned on each other, tearing at the ones they loved, blind to everything but the terror.

Mothers, fathers, sons and daughters.

It meant nothing.

In their final moments they were just animals. Shivering and screaming. Flailing at the dark.

Fighting for life.

Tharro howled with them, begging for mercy as though the monsters attacking them might listen. As though they might *care*.

'Please!'

Then he tumbled to the floor and gasped in surprise. He looked around and saw that he was at home and it was still night. His wife, Valacia, was in bed, sleeping quietly. There were no wings. No bestial horrors. No screams. None of it was real.

He was so relieved that he laughed. A dream. That was all.

But it had been so *vivid*.

He could still feel the desperate hunger clamouring for his heart and his bones. He stood there for a while, trying to clear his thoughts, trying to think of other things, but he could not rid himself of sickening images. He dressed and headed outside, drinking in the cool night air and looking up at the stars.

Just a dream.

He could not remember ever being so affected by a nightmare, even as a child. Glimpses echoed round his thoughts. Fractured scenes centred on a huge figure. A four-armed colossus. God-like in size, taller than the trees, skittering and scything, a face too dreadful to look upon, bone blades jutting from a ridged skull. It was repulsive. The flesh on one side of its face had been burned, leaving charred sinew. But it was more than its appearance that filled him with dread, it was something deeper: an understanding of what it signified. It was not merely bringing death. It was bringing the final death. It was the Harbinger.

'Emperor protect me,' he whispered as he hurried away from his hab-unit, following a narrow path through the rocks, hoping the night air would calm him. He entered a small wood and the trees leant over him as he walked, forming a tunnel. When he emerged on the far side, he was surprised to see lights glittering further down the mountainside. Who would be awake, now? He headed towards them and saw that despite the late hour, hundreds, perhaps even thousands of people had gathered in the darkness. He recognised a few of them, but most were strangers. The sight of so many people huddled together in the middle of the night was bizarre and somehow dreadful. They were all looking out from the mountain, staring into the night.

No one was speaking.

They looked terrified, all of them, their faces pale and rigid, like skulls draped in the darkness. The knot in his stomach tightened. It made no sense, but somehow he knew what had scared them. He knew why they had gathered here, at the edge of the forest.

'The dream,' he said quietly, as he reached a young woman.

She gave a short nod, trembling as she looked across the forest.

'The Harbinger.' The name felt strange in his mouth, heavy and cold. He immediately regretted using it.

She refused to meet his eye.

Tharro remembered the sounds of his nightmare: the scraping of claws, the creak of chitin. Blood rushed in his veins. He imagined talons *paring* him, rooting through his abdomen. 'How could we share the same dream?' he asked.

'It is a portent,' the woman whispered.

'Of what?'

'The end.'

Sardia winced as she climbed, scraping skin from her shins. The ladder was fixed to the exterior of a chimney-stack and she was hundreds of feet above street level. Despite the fumes, she saw more of Salamis Hive than she ever had before. She had never fully comprehended the scale of the city until now. It was mind-numbingly vast. Thousands of hab-stacks and manufactoria, heaped on top of each other wherever she looked.

An excretion of industry and decay.

Monstrous shadows rumbled through the smog, airborne freighters departing for Port Dura, where their cargo would be shipped to other worlds, other star systems, even. She had heard their engines her entire life but never actually seen them. The sight filled her with wonder, and for a moment she could do nothing but stare.

Sardia hauled herself up another rung, losing more skin on the rusty metal. If she looked down she would lose her nerve, so she looked up instead, her sights fixed on the lip of the chimney-stack. She was wearing a rebreather with thick, reinforced welding goggles, but the fumes were so strong that her eyes still streamed. A parasite scuttled across her hand. She hissed in disgust, casting it off. There were even more of the insects up here, crawling across the pitted surface of the tower. Some were like locusts or cockroaches, their armoured bodies glinting. Others were like serpents, coiling around each other. But they were not actually either of those things and, whatever they *were*, they were not native to Regium. She had never seen anything like them before. Luckily though, there were none of the larger creatures. If she encountered one of those up here, she could not imagine how she would avoid falling to her death.

'Damn you!' she hissed, as she felt another of the parasites on her forearm. This time she was too slow. It sliced through her skin and burrowed into her muscle. She could feel dozens of them now, gnawing at the inside of her arm. The pain was becoming unbearable.

The other workers at the refinery knew about the parasites. They had to. When she'd first mentioned them, they sneered. Later, when she threatened to do something about them, they grew angry. It took her a long time to realise why. They *liked* the creatures. She saw people's skin ripple and bulge as they worked. She could see insectoid shapes moving over their muscles, but they did nothing about it. None of them cared. They took pleasure in letting the creatures invade their bodies. Even the foreman was uninterested when Sardia tried to warn him. She shook her head and climbed on. None of it mattered now. She wouldn't sit back and let Salamis be consumed. She was going to stop them.

As she approached the lip of the chimney-stack, she realised that the ladder didn't quite reach the edge. The final few rungs had been torn away at some point, and if she was going to reach the top of the chimney, she would have to stand on the uppermost rung and reach for the lip of the tower. She would have to balance above that sickening drop below. Flue gas hissed from cracks in the stone, blinding her as she tried to crouch on the top rung.

She couldn't do it.

'You have no option,' she hissed to herself. 'Don't be a coward.' She had seen the parasites teeming out through holes in the tower's base. This chimney-stack was their nest. They were breeding. She had to stop this infestation before it spread across the entire hive.

With a whispered prayer, she stood on the top rung, reaching as high as she could. She gasped in relief as her fingers latched on to the edge. Now all she had to do was haul the rest of her body up. A life of working in the refinery had made her wiry and strong, and as she tried to drag herself higher, she found a foothold and pushed.

And then she reached the top, lying on the lip of the chimney-stack, looking down into its guts. It was like reaching the summit of a volcano. Heat shimmered past her face, singeing her hair and dragging tears from her eyes. She blinked them away and tightened the straps on her rebreather, then squinted as she looked through the tinted lenses. 'Throne,' she whispered. The whole of the chimney-stack was filled with parasites. As the fumes drifted, revealing the full horror, she battled the urge to vomit. There were millions of them, crawling, slithering and flying through the darkness. The variations were countless. Some were like the creatures that ate through her skin, but others were even stranger – hulking, insectoid things with purple carapaces, crawling alongside blood-slick brains that floated through the smoke.

As Sardia watched, she felt her sanity straining. She had to move fast or she would lose her nerve. She unfastened the void-crate strapped to her back and opened it, taking out the explosive charge and priming it. 'For the God-Emperor,' she said, her voice trembling as she dropped it over the edge.

It took a few seconds to hit the bottom. Then light and flames rushed towards her. Sardia cried out, her skin blistering, her lungs filling with agony.

She fell back from the ledge, charred and broken. The fire did not only burn away her flesh, it also filled her with dreadful clarity. In her final moments she saw the truth. These creatures *were* only in her mind. The others had been right. Where she had seen claws and wings there was nothing but drifting ash. She had been deceived.

Her screams were cut short as she thudded onto the street below.

'Do your job,' said Beltis, glaring at a mob in the alley. Her hand was resting on the electro-flail at her hip and her tone made it clear she was not prepared to debate the matter, but the mob were undaunted. They leered at her as though sharing a joke at her expense. For the first time in many years she felt doubt. How could they look at her like that? How could they *dare*? The world had tilted on its axis. Had things really gone so wrong that lowlife scum like this dared to defy her?

'We'll go back to work when Gathas Kulm himself tells us to,' said the leader, a grey-skinned streak of bile by the name of Tirol. 'We work for him, not you. Or... Well...' He smirked. 'We *used* to work for him.'

Beltis' moment of doubt passed. These lowlives would be dead if it wasn't for Kulm. He'd raised them from the gutter. He'd turned a mess of warring, backstabbing petty criminals into an organisation of genuine power. They were worthless without him. Only Kulm could have enabled them to achieve the things they had done. His vision. His hard work. That was the only reason they had anything.

'You work for him,' she said quietly, climbing down a fire escape and dropping into the alleyway. 'Or you work for no one.' She kept her tone neutral, letting them think this was going to be a reasonable conversation.

Tirol raised an eyebrow. 'Is that meant to be a threat? Does he remember that we know all the details of this operation?' He raised his voice. 'What if the enforcers learn Kulm is the mastermind?' He looked at his friends. 'It's a disgrace, isn't it, if you actually think about it? All those munitions, made for the war effort, and Kulm takes whole shipments, lining his own pockets. Terrible, really – profiteering when our soldiers are so desperate for equipment. Especially if you consider who we sell them to. Not all of those people have the Imperium's best interests at heart, do they?'

Beltis was only a few feet from them now. 'You think the enforcers don't know? You really think it's down to luck that they've never come knocking on this door? Use whatever passes for your brain. The enforcers work for him. Just like everyone else in Port Dura.'

Tirol was growing in confidence by the moment. He was swaggering now, garnering smirks from his friends. 'You're living in the past, girl. That might have been true when Kulm was in his prime, but not now. No one has even seen him for months.' He sauntered over to her and whispered theatrically. 'Rumour is, he's dead. And you're just trying to pretend he's still alive because you know you're screwed without him.'

Beltis looked around at the group. 'Did he just call me "girl"?'

Some of them nodded instinctively, falling into old habits, forgetting they were meant to be defying her.

'What of it?' snapped Tirol, but his confidence wavered and he took a step back. 'You're Kulm's girl. Daddy's pride and joy. And you think that means you have the right to–'

His words became a cough as Beltis lashed her flail around his throat, triggering the current. The smell of cooking meat filled the air. He dropped to his knees, grasping at the weapon, smoke pouring between his fingers.

One of the others reached for something in his pocket, then abandoned the idea as he saw that Beltis was pointing an auto-pistol at his head.

As Tirol burned, the mob backed away, spineless as she'd expected.

'Kulm is alive,' she said, keeping her voice low. She waved her pistol at the far end of the alley, where groundcars were rushing through the smog. 'Meanwhile this place is going to hell and the enforcers are doing nothing.'

Tirol pawed at her, making an odd keening sound, his face turning purple.

'We know about the explosions at the warehouses and those fools setting themselves on fire in Sapha. Something's gone wrong and who do you think will sort it out? Our great planetary governor, over in Salamis? Or the Ultramarines? They don't care about normal people. Who knows what agenda they're working to. I don't think they even…' Her words dried up. She had only glimpsed the sons of Guilliman on grainy pict-captures, but that had been enough to unnerve her. She shook her head. 'No. Kulm will sort this mess out. Like Kulm sorts everything out.'

She killed the flail's power and snatched it back from Tirol's neck. He fell to the ground, sobbing, clutching at his ruined throat as smoke leaked from the wounds.

'Get back to work.' She pointed the flail at the mob, flinging blood and charred skin. 'And take this puddle of piss back to his mother.'

They leapt to obey, their rebellion crumbling as quickly as it had emerged, but as they dragged Tirol away, muttering apologies, she wondered how long it would be before they tried again. This had never happened before, but she had a feeling it wouldn't be the last mutiny. Things *were* falling apart. She looked around at the windowless buildings lining the alley. She could hear gunfire in the distance and people screaming. Port Dura was losing its mind.

She headed back inside, barking orders to menials as she headed up to her father's private chambers. She passed through gene-locked doors and paused at the top of the stairs, looking down the door-lined hallway, thinking of all the people who had visited her father here, come to pay fealty to the mighty Gathas Kulm, the true ruler of Port Dura. The great and the good had flocked here over the years – even the governors of Salamis used to come and bend the knee. But that was before the world went mad. Before the High Lords of Terra took an interest in Regium, upsetting her father's carefully maintained balance of power by installing that tedious dullard Seroc as governor and stationing the Ultramarines down at Zarax.

She wiped Tirol's blood from her flail as she approached her father's door. There was no need for him to know how bad things had become. He would be well soon, and then he would set things right, just like he always had.

She tied a scarf around her face, opened the door and entered his room, closing it quickly behind her. Insects swarmed around her and her scarf did little to block out the stench. The room was lit by dozens of blood-red heat lamps and the light revealed the carnage her father had wrought on his once beautiful belongings. Chairs and curtains lay scattered across the floor, torn and rotten, covered in mounds of cocoons and insect eggs. The air thrummed as moths and beetles flew back and forth, and the floor seethed with termites. The combination of movement and flickering red light was disorienting and made it hard for her to spot her father. Then she saw him, not far from where she was standing, sitting with his back against the wall. He was naked, but most of his tattooed bulk was covered by the thick white dreadlocks that hung down from his head. He was grabbing constantly at the insects he had bred, cramming them into his mouth, chewing furiously and staring into the middle distance.

'Father,' she said, trying to speak calmly, as though there was nothing strange about his behaviour. 'You've got to get dressed and come with me. This has to stop. We've got to show them that you're still alive. Still in charge.'

He continued eating as he looked up at her, spilling insects down his chest. 'They think they can eat me.' He crunched and swallowed. 'But they're wrong.' He shoved more insects into his mouth. 'I. Eat. *Them.*'

She stared at him, battling the urge to howl in his face. Nothing she said was going to have any effect. Perhaps she could try medicating him? He looked as physically powerful as ever, it was only his mind that had failed. She could describe the problem to the chirurgeon and swear him to secrecy, or pretend the medicine was for someone else. It seemed a reasonable plan, but deep down she struggled to believe it would work. Her father's madness was part of something bigger. It was the madness of the city, the madness that had overtaken the whole of Port Dura. She wiped some of the bugs away and kissed his forehead. Then she gave him the flask of water she had brought him and rose to leave.

Before she could go, he grabbed her arm and looked at her with bright, lucid eyes. 'Beltis. I *will* save us. If I keep them all in here, if I eat them all, they will never eat the city.' He tightened his grip. 'Do you understand?'

She fought back tears. 'I understand.'

He nodded and let go of her, slumping back against the wall and stuffing more insects into his mouth.

She paused at the doorway and looked back at him. He was eating furiously, but there were so many insects crawling over him that it looked like *he* was the meal. The sound of humming wings swelled in her head until it became so loud she could no longer bear it. She had the horrible feeling that her father's lunacy was somehow the truth, that the insects wanted to devour the city. 'We have to get out,' she whispered. Then she hurried from the room, locked the door and ran from the building.

Chapter One

THE FORTRESS CITY AT ZARAX
SAMNIUM PROVINCE, REGIUM

The tacticarium had been carved from burial chambers – chiselled from catacombs that snaked beneath the city. Auspex shrines and cogitators now obscured most of the walls, but in a few places fragments of sacred art were still visible. It mostly showed tree-roots, snaking down from the world's surface and encasing its core, cradling it in a nest of tendrils. But the more recent additions depicted the Emperor, His sword trailing leaves rather than flames and His helmet sporting a crown of knotted branches.

The chamber, once a site of prayer and sacrifice, was now full of quiet industry and the cold flicker of viewscreens. Helots and comms officers were hunched over runeboards, dressed in smartly pressed uniforms rather than priestly robes. Mind-scrubbed servitors scuttled spider-like over logic engines, their faces grey and toothless and their limbs replaced with bionics.

Lieutenant Varus Castamon of the Ultramarines First Company

was aware of the chamber's history, but his attention was focused entirely on the present. He watched parchment spooling from one of the servitors, then carefully tore some off, processing the information with inhuman speed. The symbols conjured images of warships in his mind, behemoths knifing through the void towards the outermost reaches of the system, weapons batteries coming online. He thought of his brothers, tracing their fingers over strips of vellum fixed to their armour, reciting blood-sworn oaths. The thought quickened his pulse and he wished, more than anything, that he was with them on this mission.

Across from him, Brother-Librarian Zuthis Abarim stood at the centre of the room, watching images projected from a domed holo-table, while a third Ultramarine, Brother-Sergeant Tanaro, was standing nearer to Castamon. Scattered around the rest of the room, dwarfed by the three Ultramarines, were dozens of humans – senior Militarum officers and their aides, all wearing starched regimental finery. Further back, scurrying through the shadows, making adjustments to the stacks of logic engines, were red-robed adepts of the Adeptus Mechanicus.

'How long?' asked Castamon, dropping the parchment.

'The strike force is approaching the edge of the system now, my lord,' said a helot, staring at a viewscreen. 'The deep-void returns are faint, but we can just about place the ships.' He pointed out a cluster of faint dots hanging over the holo-table. 'They'll shortly be passing the moons of Krassus.'

Castamon gestured for the Militarum officers to come closer. They obeyed his silent command, some trying to catch his eye but most trying to avoid it. He tried to imagine how they saw him. As a monster, probably. He was huge, of course, like any Space Marine, three heads taller than a man. His skin was dark and weathered and his head was shaved, displaying three scars that raked down over his skull – fat, silvery gouges left by a predator's claw. His blocky jaw was edged with a short silver beard, and his eyes were set deep under an anvil-hard brow. He did not seek to intimidate, but he was comfortable with the fact that he did. There were few who could hold his gaze for long.

He recognised all of the officers and they would have been surprised to know how well he knew the details of their military careers. Castamon was a warrior. He had no interest in politics, least of all the human variety. But he approached his posting on Regium with the same rationality and diligence he applied to everything else, remembering the words of his Lord Commander. *Fortify your mind with study. Prepare for all outcomes.* As he scrutinised the faces, he recalled facts gleaned from data crystals and genealogical tracts. Rather than soldiers he saw allegiances and rivalries, flaws and obsessions, debts and hopes – every shade of human frailty. They looked proud and determined, trying to hide how nervous they felt in his presence. They were good people. Whatever their failings, they had endured. They had survived long enough to see silver in their beards and feel aches in their bones. They were the exceptional few.

+The next couple of days will test them.+

The words formed telepathically in Castamon's mind. There was a time when he would have found the experience distasteful, repulsive even, but the voice was familiar now, the voice of a friend. He looked over at Abarim. The Librarian's suit of battleplate was even larger and more impressive than Castamon's. His head was buried in a thick ceramite cowl and his armour was intricately inscribed, covered with runes and horned-skull designs. He stood statuelike, towering over the humans. The lower half of his face was hidden behind a rebreather, but his eyes were visible and they shone fiercely as they focused on Castamon. He was gripping a force axe larger than any of the humans, a magnificent relic, worked with the same runic designs as his armour and shimmering with the same light that spilled from his eyes. Castamon noticed, with faint amusement, that none of the Militarum officers were standing near him.

This should not take days, he thought. *The ships are closing in on Krassus.*

+Tyrus has yet to locate his prey. And while he hunts, discontent spreads. You saw the crowds outside. They are scared. And scared people make dangerous decisions. Governor Seroc is too tolerant.+

You know my thoughts on the matter. Seroc is a good man. These people can police their own homes.

+You confuse lambs with wolves. Seroc is not equal to the task. None of them are.+

They need answers, that is all.

+Answers only beg more questions.+

Abarim would not usually address him in such an abrupt manner. He sounded almost bitter. The Librarian had been in pain for over a week and, though Abarim would never admit it, Castamon suspected his pain was growing worse. Pain was rarely a consideration for an Adeptus Astartes warrior, but Castamon knew this was not a physical suffering. It was something beyond his understanding – something linked to Abarim's esoteric skills. He needed to pursue the matter, but this was not the time. He wanted the soldiers out of his command bunker as quickly as possible.

He looked around the room. 'Governor Seroc asked me to speak to you, but I will keep this brief. We all know why we are here. There is panic and hysteria on Regium. Nightmares are spilling into people's waking hours. And there is a resurgence of the separatist threat, despite our labours in the spring. The separatists have a new creed, preaching of cataclysms and supernatural beings. But let me tell you this: there will be no

cataclysm. There are no such supernatural beings. And the separatists are merely opportunists, seeking to regain a vestige of
their former power. The cause of the nightmares is biological,
not spiritual. It can be measured, combated and reversed. This
planetwide hysteria stems from a foe that my battle-brothers
and I have encountered before.'

'People want to know why the Ultramarines are leaving
Regium,' said one of the officers, his tone brittle. 'That's one
of the main catalysts of this current panic. Perhaps if we'd
briefed people beforehand we could have allayed their fears.'

Castamon looked down at the man. 'We are briefing people
now.' He pointed to the planet hovering in the air near Abarim,
drawing their attention to a swirl of red light that was approaching it. 'The anomaly you see near Krassus is not a natural
phenomenon. Nor is it a warp storm. It is the remnants of a
xenos fleet.'

Some of the officers frowned as they studied the shapes, while
others whispered to their aides.

'It is a fragment of an alien armada known as Hive Fleet
Leviathan,' Castamon continued. 'It was first spotted several
months ago, fleeing past the orbital shipyards of Hydraphur in
the galactic north. The warships of the Navis Imperialis dealt
with some of the aliens, but a few stragglers survived and fled
south. We can only surmise what drove them this way, to the
west. Perhaps they were savaged by another xenos fleet. Or by
void-dwelling predators. Perhaps they were scattered many years
ago by the emergence of the Great Rift. We may never know.
But a few survivors are now skirting the outermost borders of
this system.'

Some of the officers shifted position and others cleared their
throats, about to ask questions, but Castamon raised his hand
for silence.

'The creatures belong to a recognised xenotype. The Great Devourer. *Tyranids*. Little is known of their origins, but our Chapter has waged war against them in other systems and I can tell you this: they have no connection to the forces seeking to overthrow the Emperor. The heretics who attacked us in the spring sought to breach the Sanctus Line because they wish to invade the Sol System. They sought a route to Terra. But the tyranids are different. They are driven only by senseless hunger. A strategic defensive measure such as the Sanctus Line is beyond their comprehension. Everything we know about them indicates that they are a species of purely bestial predators. They have no inkling of this planet's tactical importance. However...' He paused. 'As they skirt the edge of this system, they *will* be drawn to Krassus.' He nodded to the planet at the edge of the system. 'A vast world, rich in biomass. A place where they could feed and reproduce. My Apothecary Biologis, an expert in the dark matter of xenos, believes they will be unable to resist it.'

He paused, looking round the room again, pleased to see the concentration on people's faces. 'Which presents us with an opportunity we cannot ignore. These abhorrent xenos cannot be allowed to taint our border with Segmentum Solar and, thanks to Krassus, we have a chance to stop them. We can prevent them advancing any further from the Galactic West. Krassus will be like a beacon to them. Their attention will be focused *entirely* on it. So, they will be slow to notice this.'

He pointed to another shape in the hololith – a cluster of blinking white arrowheads, heading towards Krassus. 'At this very moment, my battle-brother Lieutenant Tyrus is leading a strike force to cut this canker from the void. I have assured my superiors that these stragglers will come no closer to Holy Terra. Tyrus is a warrior of great renown and he is accompanied by *two-thirds* of the Ultramarines stationed here on Regium.'

An elderly officer spoke up. 'Which is exactly why people are panicking, my lord. Sending the majority of your Ultramarines off-world seems reckless. What if heretics attack us from the void again? The Sanctus Line is always a target. That's why you're here. If heretics know we've lost so many of our Ultramarines, they'll see a chance to attack.'

Castamon nodded. 'The same concern was voiced by Governor Seroc. My original plan was to lead my entire force to Krassus. But, as you have observed, Regium is always a potential target. So, after much thought, I decided to remain here with a third of my garrison. If there are any more acts of piracy or orbital strikes, we shall have no difficulty dealing with them. Strike Force Krassus will be heading back within a matter of days. The tyranids will be eliminated quickly and the full garrison will be restored here. I have assured Governor Seroc there will not be a prolonged engagement at the edge of the system.'

The elderly officer shook his head. 'You were deployed here to protect Regium. And, as you said yourself, the aliens out near Krassus are few in number. Why did you have to send so many men?'

'Why did you have to send *any* men?' asked another officer. 'Why not report the matter so it could be dealt with by someone else? From what you describe, the xenos threat is insignificant.'

'Insignificant?' Some of the soldiers paled as they heard the warning in Castamon's tone. 'You betray your ignorance.' Images of bloodshed filled his mind. 'I have seen worlds devoured by a single tyranid swarm. They do not threaten. They do not bargain. They have no interest in wealth or power. We are naught to them but meat. If I allow them to leave this system, they will spawn. They will thrive. And they will consume.'

His words were followed by a troubled silence. Then one of the officers spoke up, his expression rigid as he battled to meet

Castamon's gaze. 'Governor Seroc sent us here to discuss the rioting and insurrection, but also the dreams and the madness. What does that have to do with aliens at the edge of the system?'

Castamon was impressed by the man's nerve, but he replied in a tone that made it clear this was a briefing, not a debate. 'My Apothecary Biologis has theorised that the tyranids are behind this psychosis. There is much he cannot explain, but his under-lying logic is sound. I have *seen* this happen before. Whether it is intentional or not, the presence of tyranids in a system induces hysteria.'

The man looked incredulous. 'People are burning down manufactories because of something that's happening on the other side of the system?'

'People are burning manufactories because, even from here, even from light years away, they feel the hunger of the Great Devourer.' Castamon looked at the red lights, pulsing blood-like above the table. 'They are unfathomable. They are your nightmares given form.' He waved at the V-shaped group of arrowheads. 'And we will grind them under our heel.'

Chapter Two

THE FORTRESS CITY AT ZARAX
SAMNIUM PROVINCE, REGIUM

People swarmed into the Library of Carnus, trailing mud over the mosaic floor and creating a murmured chorus, hundreds of voices speaking quickly and quietly, echoing up through the vast hexagonal atrium. There was a confusing jumble of gaudy outfits and accents, but people were united by one thing: fear. They huddled in groups, talking in urgent whispers and casting wary glances. The larger the gathering grew, the more frantic the conversation; panic spread like a fever, growing with every whispered word.

Governor Seroc was seated high above the throng, on a balcony that jutted out between the uppermost tiers of seats. He was close enough to the domed ceiling to see brushstrokes in the frieze, tiny echoes of humanity preserved in the Emperor's halo. He reached up into the air, letting his fingertips trace the shapes of the gold leaf, trying not to think about the weight of responsibility that had been placed on his shoulders.

He was surrounded by serfs and aides and there was a huddle

of priests sitting behind him, dressed in enough finery to shame the saints gliding overhead. He had never seen such an obscene display of wealth. Seroc guessed that just one of their trinkets would be worth enough to feed half of the population at his hive. The thought made his mood even darker. He turned to the senior priest. 'Confessor Thurgau. You have been glaring at the proconsul since she arrived. And your anger has so far failed to conjure a divine intervention.'

The confessor's face was transformed by a charming smile. He laughed cheerfully, despite the grim mood that had filled the library.

'Vela Zalth adopted your creed, despite being old enough to be your grandmother,' continued Seroc. 'Your faith is now her faith. Her temples are now your temples. Your work is done.'

Thurgau loosened his grip on the ornate sceptre he was holding, placing it in his lap, still smiling. 'The Emperor's work is never done.'

Seroc studied the young priest. The man's features were delicate and sharp, his skin so pale it was almost translucent. But his fragile appearance was deceptive. Since arriving on Regium he had transformed the populace, suppressing centuries of beliefs and transforming the local priesthood without a single drop of blood. He followed the direction of the priest's gaze and studied the cause of his annoyance. 'You'll never stop religious types mutilating themselves. At least, not without undoing all your careful work.' He looked down at the crowd. 'Some knotted metal and wood. Some punctured skin. Does it matter?'

'Governor Seroc, it *does* matter.' Thurgau's voice was not quite as smooth as usual. 'They plant seeds under their skin. They think the God-Emperor's blood is sap. These things are very relevant. Small deviations from doctrine lead to large deviations. It's sacrilege. And dangerous.'

Seroc decided to let the matter drop. This was not the time to be seen arguing with a senior Adeptus Ministorum prelate. He looked down at the crowd and saw that Vela Zalth was looking back at him, whispering to a younger woman whose skin was caged by the same, tangled piercings that had so annoyed Thurgau. It was her protégé and successor, the consul called Damaris. The women nodded to him and Thurgau, then continued making their way through the smoke.

Vela Zalth muttered to herself as she barged through the crowd with her cane, making her way up the side of a raised dais at the centre of the room. 'Why does everything require steps? Can't these people build anything flat?'

Damaris was looking at the rows of books that lined the walls while the elderly magistrate, Urzun, watched her intently. Urzun was nearly as old as Vela, and she felt a wave of nausea every time she caught him looking at the younger woman. He was a craven-looking thing, with a tangled nest of white hair and sunken, staring eyes.

'They put our songs in these,' said Damaris, tapping a book.

Urzun nodded, his face contorted by an exaggerated expression of disapproval.

'Who do?' replied Vela.

'The off-worlders. Their scribes print our songs in these books. The same songs we're not allowed to sing. They steal music from mouths and pin it to a page.'

'They've turned us into an exhibit,' whispered Urzun, squeezing Damaris' arm.

Every part of Vela was hurting, from her joints to her lungs. Even her scalp ached beneath her thinning hair. She usually found Damaris' passion endearing, but today she had no patience for it. And Urzun's lechery was grating on her.

She replied with more force than she intended. 'We're alive. And we're alive because of the off-worlders. What would have become of us if the Ultramarines hadn't been sent to Regium? We can accept the loss of a few songs.'

Damaris glared at Vela. 'Maybe you can forgive the off-worlders the theft of our songs, but can you forgive them for what they did on this, our most holy site? Why didn't they build their fortress at Salamis Hive? That would have made more sense. But Confessor Thurgau insisted it was built here. Why did they have to tear down Aureus Nahor to build this ugly fortress? The largest shrine on the continent. Do you remember how she looked in spring? Leaves glinting like fire. And they bull-dozed her without a thought.'

Urzun squeezed Damaris' arm again. 'I can still hear her roots, weeping under all this stone.'

Vela grunted in annoyance. The off-worlders had taught them many disturbing truths, including the real nature of the 'trees' they worshipped. 'There *are* no roots. Not really. Not *actual* roots. There never were. We know that now. We can hate it, but we can't unhear it.' Vela felt a flash of grief as she considered every-thing that had been taken from them. 'We have to move on. We have to accept the new ways.'

Damaris' eyes glittered with anger. 'The roots are there. We've seen them.'

'Our dead are buried in them,' whispered Urzun, staring intently at Damaris.

'They were machines,' snapped Vela. 'All of them. The off-worlders showed us proof.'

Urzun ignored her, continuing to look at Damaris with a sympathetic grimace.

Vela jabbed someone's leg with her cane as they finally reached the top of the dais. 'This will do. If I go any further,

I'll have to kill someone.' She glanced at Damaris. 'We all know why Thurgau wanted the fortress built here. It was a statement of intent. We have to worship the God-Emperor on their terms now. And that would never have happened while we were praying to Aureus Nahor. We can argue over doctrine, but their God-Emperor is still the same god, Damaris. So we just have to adapt. Think of the alternatives. Think what happens on worlds where people *refuse* to adapt, where people cling to their old faith. People lose more than just songs, I can tell you that. We should count ourselves lucky.'

'A thousand years of tradition crushed under rockcrete. Doesn't feel very lucky to me. And we survived well enough before they–'

Her words were interrupted as the crowd surged. There were mutters of annoyance as soldiers took their place on the far side of the dais, forcing everyone else to take a step back. The soldiers stared the crowd down, chins raised, standing to attention, armour and weapons clattering. Their battle-worn green-and-drab uniforms made a sharp contrast to the finery on display around them. Over their battle fatigues they wore plates of scratched flak armour that were more appropriate for a trench than a gathering of nobles.

'These are the ones you should be cursing.' Vela nodded to two Cadian officers at the head of the squad. 'Look at the arrogance. They strut about like they're gods. But they're not. They're not like Lieutenant Castamon. They're not Adeptus Astartes. They're just normal people under that armour. But look how they lord it over us. And she's the worst. The captain. You'd think *she's* the one who saved us from heretics.'

Urzun lowered his voice. '*I* heard that she didn't even return to her own home world to help protect it – that she did nothing when it fell.'

They all looked over at the captain. She was snapping orders at her second-in-command – a tall, haughty-looking sergeant with a ceremonial bugle at his belt. Captain Karpova was a sinewy knot of a woman. When she finished giving commands to the sergeant, she looked out at the crowd, glaring defiantly from beneath the peak of her cap. One of her eyes was dark and furious and the other was missing, replaced by a battered targeting scope. Her face was a wasteland of scar tissue, so brutalised it was hard to guess her age, but she was certainly younger than the sergeant.

'Hard to believe *she* did nothing,' muttered Damaris as she met the captain's determined stare.

Vela grunted but found it hard to disagree.

Captain Karpova noticed the consuls gawking at her but chose to ignore them, glancing around at the panicked-looking crowd and then up at the tiered seating. She spotted the distant figure of Governor Seroc on the balcony. He was a heavy-set, bearded man who looked fiercely self-conscious. She saluted him and was pleased to see him nod in reply, and even more pleased when she realised who he was talking to. She knew Confessor Thurgau well, having been deployed to Regium with him only a few months after Castamon. Her conversations with Thurgau were one of the things that made her grateful she was on Regium. His unshakeable faith was an inspiration and it had renewed her own.

'Sergeant Vollard,' she said, addressing the officer at her side. 'Status.'

She heard a crackle from the vox-link at his ear. He replied in his usual grandiose tones. 'All squads are in position, captain. I also ordered Sergeant Yurek to position sentries at the main gates into the fortress.'

She nodded, looking around at the crowd of nobles, tribal

leaders and priests. 'The separatists would love this. Everyone who matters is cowering in this room and no one's on guard. Doesn't matter how impressive a fortress is if you leave the damned gates open. Keep a close watch on the locals. When these crowds disperse, I'm going to find Lieutenant Castamon, but let me know if you see anything suspicious.'

Vollard glanced at her. 'Castamon?'

'He's here. I saw him when we arrived. He's briefing Colonel Levizac and Major Lucanus right now, while I'm left in the dark. It's beyond a joke. We've kicked our heels on Regium for too long. Something has to be done.'

'With respect, captain, Regium's the cornerstone of the entire Sanctus Line. Whatever duty we're given here, I don't think we need to see this as kicking our heels.'

'We're sidelined. Mopping up heretic cells is beneath us. This work could be done by planetary defence forces. Every day the war presses closer to Holy Terra, and we're stuck here, reprimanding criminals.'

Vollard gave her one of his grandiose smiles. 'Captain, Regium is–'

'Regium's important. I get it. I'm not a damned fool. But the Sanctus Line's in no danger. Lieutenant Castamon has a large portion of the Ultramarines First Company under his command, and reserves from the Eighth and Ninth. And that's to say nothing of the Regium Auxilia regiments he's got scattered across the continent. No planet outside of the Sol System is this well defended. I have no idea who sent us here, but it was a slight. And now someone has engineered things so we're here when the Ultramarines are briefing everyone else. I bet it was Colonel Levizac. Or Major Lucanus. Pompous, desk-bound oafs. They should spend less time denigrating Cadian regiments and more time getting their hands dirty. We're wasted here. And that's exactly what I'll tell the lieutenant.'

She pictured Lieutenant Castamon and, to her annoyance, felt daunted by the prospect of approaching him. She had heard people describe Adeptus Astartes as beautiful, but she struggled to understand why. They were magnificent, of course, but there was something disturbing about those enlarged, *almost*-human features. As soon as she heard she was to be deployed on Regium, she had researched Lieutenant Castamon. He was a decorated veteran, like the rest of the Ultramarines First Company, famed for his intellect as much as his savagery. Surely he would see sense.

'If Castamon's the deep thinker everyone claims he is,' she said, 'he'll see we're too good for this. And the governor is hardly likely to argue with him.' She nodded to a space in the crowd. 'Come on. Seroc will be starting soon. I want to be close so I can corner him and find out where Lieutenant Castamon's briefing is.' She gave Vollard a warning glance. 'And don't get too comfortable. I can see you *relaxing*.'

Seroc nodded to people as he made his way down towards the dais, adjusting braids on his uniform, trying and failing to make them lie flat. 'Throne,' he muttered. 'So many people. Half the planet.' Noticing the finery on display, he dusted himself down and raised his chin, striving to look at ease. He was overweight but muscular, just able to pass for powerful rather than dissolute, an impression that was helped by the thick, coal-dark beard that reached down to his belt. He fussed at his collars, feeling stifled and uncomfortable in his starched dress coat.

'They want answers,' said his aide, a stocky, grim-faced woman called Lanek. She was dressed in a similar uniform to Seroc and looked equally unhappy about it.

'No.' Seroc glared at the politicians and grandees on the dais. 'Not that way. Over here is fine. We'll be near the door. I want to leave the *moment* this is done. We have work to do. I'm not getting trapped in here.'

The two of them made their way through the throng and Seroc kept his gaze fixed determinedly ahead, trying to avoid making eye contact. Officially, he was now superior to the high-born who were milling around him, but he still felt out of place. Most of these people had never worked a day in their life. They made flamboyant gestures with soft, elegant hands that made him conscious of how callused and blocky his own fingers were. 'Here,' he snapped, gesturing for Lanek and the other aides to follow him into a space. 'This'll do.'

Lanek stroked her lank, undercut hair, scowling, clearly infected by Seroc's discomfort. 'We could have stayed in Salamis. We didn't have to leave the hive.' She took out a lho-stick and offered it to him. 'You didn't have to come in person.'

He waved the lho-stick away. 'Look at these people. They're terrified. And I'll not have Salamis grind to a halt. I refuse to miss a single shipment. These princelings can bitch and whine all they like but Salamis actually *matters*. They could lose a palace or two without noticing, but if we lose our manufactories the whole Sanctus Line suffers. Regium is the engine room of the whole damned show. How long would the Sanctus Line stand without fuel and ammunition? We've never missed a tithe quota. I'll be damned if things are going to go wrong now I'm in charge.'

A merchant in a periwig managed to catch his eye and started to head over, but Seroc and Lanek glared at him until he veered off, pretending he was approaching someone else.

Seroc dusted down his jacket again. 'How do I look?' He glanced awkwardly at Lanek.

She picked mud from the frogging on his jacket. 'Fine.'

He grunted, tugging at the cloth. 'I look like an idiot.'

'You'll fit right in then.'

Seroc laughed, despite the seriousness of the occasion. Then he recovered his composure and made his way onto the dais. Most people bowed and a few even dropped to their knees, pressing their foreheads to the floor, as if in the presence of the Emperor Himself. He growled in annoyance and waved them to their feet. Confessor Thurgau and the other priests flanked him, droning prayers and swinging censers, and people shuffled backwards as he approached the centre of the dais.

He waited for the murmurs to die down and allowed the quiet to ring out for a few moments. Then he pressed his fist across his chest and cried out, 'For the Emperor!' Even unamplified his voice boomed across the atrium.

There was a brief silence, then everyone in the crowd mirrored his pose and echoed his cry.

'I know, for many of you, it's been hard to reach this fortress,' he said. 'Some of you crossed half the province to be here. And I know you're all concerned about what you have left behind, but once you've heard what I have to say, I hope you'll feel able to return home. I know you've all been afflicted by these dreadful nightmares.' He realised he was tripping over his words, so he paused to steady his nerves.

'My lord,' said a noble, seizing the chance to interrupt. He looked at Seroc with obvious disdain. 'It's more than just nightmares. The whole of the Vanand Peninsular is cut off. We have no safe route to Salamis Hive any more. We've lost dozens of caravans. There's rioting right across the province and none of the roads are free from danger. Even getting here was almost impossible.' As he spoke, and people nodded in agreement, the man's voice grew in confidence. 'We can't bring you any fuel. And there's trouble everywhere. Whole towns are burning. We can't get any clear news of what's going on, but there are terrible stories – bodies thrown on pyres, people dying in their hundreds.'

'Shellib City is the same,' said a woman on the opposite side of the atrium. 'No one can get to the hive and there are fires burning day and night.' She looked around. 'Does anyone even know what the attacks are for? What do these separatists expect us to do? What do they actually want?'

A chorus of panicked voices erupted as people shouted over each other, relaying tales of violence and disorder. Then Seroc raised his hand for silence. Some people were so frantic that it took them a moment to notice the gesture, but soon the library was quiet again. Seroc studied the crowd and wondered how he had ended up in this situation. When the Ultramarines had landed on Regium, one of their first acts was to execute the presiding governor and dissolve his entire chain of command. Seroc had not been overly surprised. Regium's rulers had been in thrall to criminals for decades. But he was surprised by what happened next. Lieutenant Castamon had informed him that the logisticars of the Adeptus Administratum had given *him* the job of governing Regium. At first, he had been horrified, but over the following months he had begun to relish the opportunity. He had spent his entire life covering for self-interested frauds. He soon realised that he could hardly be *worse* than the leaders who came before. And perhaps he could even be better. He had even begun to think of ways to improve the hive at Salamis. Which made him all the more determined not to let the place slide into anarchy. He thought back to his conversations with Lieutenant Castamon and tried to speak with the same calm and gravitas the Ultramarine always showed.

'I know all about the problems you're facing. I'm facing exactly the same at Salamis Hive. But I'm here to reassure you. I've spoken to Lieutenant Castamon of the Ultramarines and he explained the cause of this violence and madness. It's a phenomenon he's encountered before, triggered by a small fleet of alien ships that's skirting the edge of our system.'

There was a chorus of shocked whispers, but he held up his hand for silence again. 'The xenos are no threat to us here, but the Ultramarines have launched ships and will deal with the matter. The lieutenant assures me that once the xenos ships have been destroyed, our problems will start to ease. Normality will return. But in the meantime, we have to remain calm and maintain *order*. All Militarum regiments are being redeployed. The Ultramarines are briefing them now. They will restore order at all the large population centres while I focus on maintaining the output from Salamis Hive. To ensure we make our tithe commitments, Captain Karpova and her *entire* regiment will be travelling north with me when I return to the hive.'

Karpova stiffened and Seroc saw outrage flash in her eye, so he continued, remembering the advice Castamon had given him. 'I have chosen Captain Karpova and her regiment, above all others, after being advised to do so by Lieutenant Castamon.' The anger in Karpova's eye was now mingled with curiosity. 'Castamon has followed her career closely and assured me she is one of the Imperium's most inspired soldiers.' He cast his gaze around the room. 'He told me that Captain Karpova was personally responsible for the success of the rearguard action on Cynus IV, and that it was her skill as a tactician that broke the siege on Sestos Prime.' He knew that few of the people on Regium would have heard of these military engagements, but his words hit the desired target. The anger faded from Karpova's eye and she somehow managed to stand even more erect. Had her skin been less scarred, he imagined she might now be blushing. Seroc was impressed. Castamon had known exactly the right way to bring her onside. 'With Salamis back under control, we will quickly restore order in the rest of the province.'

He looked back out at the crowd. 'Salamis has been mismanaged and neglected by my predecessors to such an extent that there is now a spiritual rot. Which is why these seditionists and lunatics have been able to create so many problems. Captain Karpova and her regiment can deal with the symptoms, but I need someone to dig down to the root of the problem. Which is why I shall also be taking Confessor Thurgau of the Adeptus Ministorum back to the hive with me. He and his priests will ensure that the faithless are returned to the fold. Faith and military might will hold the province together. But you must all play your part. Lieutenant Castamon assures me this will all be over soon.' He raised his voice. 'In the meantime, we must not allow sedition and heresy to take root.'

He was pleased, and not a little surprised, to see that most people were nodding, accepting his explanation. But he could also see that many of them were raising their hands, bursting with questions. For a moment, he considered staying where he was and doing his best to answer them, but then he realised there was a better option.

'Confessor Thurgau,' he said, turning to the priest. 'I have other urgent matters to attend to, so this would be an opportune moment for you to explain your holy mission on Regium. There are many here who have not yet had the chance to hear you preach.'

Thurgau's eyes blazed. He smoothed down his robes and bowed. 'It would be an *honour*.' Alarmed voices called out, but Thurgau strode confidently across the dais and raised his hands, bathing in the panic as if it were applause. 'Children of the Throne, I bring you glorious news from the Emperor of Mankind.'

As Thurgau slipped seamlessly into a sermon, Seroc made his way down from the dais and headed towards the doors, scowling at anyone brave enough to try to address him.

'You'll make a politician yet,' said Lanek as they hurried out of the library.

Chapter Three

'*Lieutenant Tyrus.*' The voice rang across the bridge. '*We have word from the Krassus orbital relay.*'

The bridge of the *Incorruptible* was shaped like a sword, or the nave of a cathedral, with Tyrus' command dais positioned at the intersection. He looked up from a crescent of display screens, his face bathed in flickering light. His skin was an angry mess of bio-acid scars and this, combined with the harsh green light, transformed his face into a grotesque mask. 'Did you retrieve the coordinates?'

There were dozens of people on the bridge, a mixture of human deck officers and ratings, red-robed tech-adepts and armour-clad Ultramarines from a mixture of companies. They all fell silent, looking up at the emitter that had relayed the message. The emitter was embedded in the chest of a glabrous, foetal-looking cherub whirring above the command dais.

'*Negative, lieutenant. I… It's hard to explain.*' The voice was little more than a screech of static, but even through the interference

43

Tyrus could tell there was something wrong. The foetal messenger grimaced, thrashing its stumpy wings.

'Master Augurum,' Tyrus replied calmly. 'Tell me what they said.'

'They said their augur returns show no sign of xenos bioforms. The skies are clear over Krassus. They are not under attack.'

Tyrus looked back at the columns of glyphs scrolling down his viewscreens. 'An entire fleet of bioforms does not simply disappear. Was the message distorted? Could you have misunderstood?'

'No, lieutenant.' The cherub flew higher, as though fearing reprisals, squinting its gummy eyes. *'There was a break in the interference. Our choristers were able to establish direct, uninterrupted contact with the relay for several seconds. They said their augur returns show no fleet in the vicinity. They also contacted the Beta Twelve scry-stations. None of the surveillance outposts show anything untoward.'*

Tyrus rose from his throne and strode down the steps of the dais, his boots clanking on the deck plating. He walked down the nave until he reached an oculus at the far end. The screen was vast, but the view remained as unhelpful as it had been since they left Regium. He looked out on a maelstrom of dust clouds and energy pulses. The presence of tyranids had not just blinded his augurs, it had made visual identification impossible too. 'The tyranids are here.' He paced up and down the walkway, rolling his shoulders, causing the fibre bundles in his armour to click and wheeze. 'They must be.'

He looked over at the only Ultramarine who was not clad in blue. Vultis was an Apothecary Biologis. He wore a suit of polished white power armour, draped in arcane diagnostic equipment and surgical devices. Rotary saws and pincers hung down from his backpack and containment cylinders clattered at his belt. 'Brother Vultis, what do you make of this? Is it possible you made a mistake?'

Vultis did not answer, staring up at the cherub.

'Vultis?' said Tyrus, raising his voice.

Vultis shook his head. 'Krassus is the largest source of biomass in the subsector. The xenos *should* be here. Everything I know about tyranid predation patterns indicates that they target the largest food source first. Bypassing Krassus would be out of character.'

'But they are not here.'

Vultis tilted his head back, eyes closed, thinking in silence for several long seconds. 'Lieutenant, even I know very little about this species. And people who make the mistake of thinking they *do* are usually wrong-footed. After decades of study, I only possess a base understanding of this xenotype. I do not know if they evolve in a way we can understand or in some other manner. There has been speculation that they can evolve at an accelerated pace – that they might adapt mentally or even physically in response to external stimuli.' Vultis began muttering to himself, referencing obscure texts by magi and xenobiologians.

'Brother Vultis,' said Tyrus. 'What do you think is happening here?'

Vultis nodded. 'The theories about potential accelerated evolution marry with my own research. And, if they are even close to the truth, it could be that this variant has developed a new predator-prey pattern, displaying feeding habits that are different to those we have studied before. Tyranids are *utterly* unknowable, even to me. They are an enigma. *But...* I have a foreboding that this kind of atypical behaviour will be for a reason.' He looked at a display screen and tapped at the runeboard, shaking his head. 'I am loath to make unsubstantiated guesses, but this feels like a ruse.'

'A trap?'

'Perhaps.'

Tyrus halted back near the oculus, and looked out at the void, considering what Vultis had said. 'Master Augurum,' he said, directing his voice at the wizened cherub. 'Which coordinates did you use when you attempted your last sweep?'

The coordinates you supplied, lord. All possible approaches to Krassus.

'Did you attempt a three-hundred-and-sixty-degree pass?'

No, my lord, but in these conditions it would make little difference. We have no reliable signal. Our brief contact with the relay station was a surprise.

'Try anyway. Look in all directions. Deep-void augur scans. Make haste.'

My lord.

The signal died, taking the static howl with it, and the cherub fluttered its absurd wings, swaying off into the shadows.

A deck officer approached. 'My lord,' she said, looking up at him. 'What are your orders?'

Tyrus shook his head, resuming his pacing. 'The xenos have been heading directly for Krassus since they entered the system. And the larger bioforms are as vast as battle cruisers. Even with all this disturbance there should be sign of them by now.' He looked at the oculus again, frowning at the tumult outside, thinking back over his previous encounters with tyranids.

My lord, screeched the cherub, fluttering from the shadows. *You were correct. We have located the xenos. They are heading away from the biomass source. That was why we missed it on the first pass.*

Tyrus looked over at Vultis. 'Then this *is* a trap. They are coming for us. We need to–'

No, my lord, begging your pardon, they are not headed towards our ships. They could have. They could have masked their approach with the empyric disturbance they've created, but they chose not to. They bypassed us. They're heading in-system. They're heading for Regium.'

'Regium?' He looked at Vultis. 'What is this?'

'We have been deceived.'

Something boomed in the distance and the command deck went dark. A moment later, emergency lumens blinked into life, bathing the chamber in fitful light. Warning klaxons brayed across the bridge.

'Lieutenant,' said one of the deck officers, looking up from his display screen, his voice taut. 'Starboard void shields just died. The generators have failed. And the portside generators are struggling to cope.'

'Starboard weapons batteries are offline,' said another officer, peering at his display.

'The plasma drives have stopped responding,' said another, staring at Tyrus, her face pale. 'We have no power.'

'Kill the portside generators before they overload,' said Tyrus, snatching his helmet from a stand beside the command throne. He locked the helmet into place as he strode across the bridge, heading for the exit. Warning sigils blinked across his helm display. He opened a vox-channel. 'Boarding action. Single point of entry. Void shield compromised.' He shook his head. 'Whatever it is, it is moving fast. We are breached. Weapons systems and void shields are down. All available military personnel, make for Ekato Deck.' He smiled inside his helmet. 'Whatever game these creatures are playing, they will pay for their hubris. Our prey has just thrown itself at our feet.'

He sprinted out into a passageway, the other Ultramarines following him, as the ship ground to a halt. With the ever-present roar of the vessel's reactors gone, there was an unusual quiet, broken only by the distant bark of klaxons and the creak of straining bulkheads. The *Incorruptible* was adrift. Smoke rolled down the corridors towards him and he heard the sound of more explosions in the distance.

No, not explosions, he thought – it sounded more like something tearing.

He studied the glyphs on his helm display. 'Brother Baraca. You are closest to the gunnery deck. What do you see?' White noise flooded the network, followed by distorted, incomprehensible words.

'Repeat,' demanded Tyrus, running faster.

'Atmospheric controls have been…' crackled the reply, followed by a jumble of overlapping, truncated voices.

'Ingress at Locri and Castrus access points, but I have no–'

'I saw something big. It was tearing through the Reclusium like it was–'

'Brother Domith, bring fire support to the–'

'Making our way to Ekato, but the grav-plating has been destabilised. Gravity is down to–'

'Brother Baraca, how close are you?'

'This smoke is behaving strangely. Like solid shadows. I think it must be–'

Tyrus tried to reply but the voices looped and overlapped until they became such a cacophony that he had to kill the channel. He changed direction, running down a different passageway, summoning schematics across his helm display, looking for a faster route to the gunnery deck. This way was even smokier, but when he glanced back he saw that his squads were still with him, calmly slamming magazines into bolt rifles and checking seals on their power armour. The Apothecary, Vultis, was also there, loading his absolver bolt pistol and adjusting his diagnostic equipment. Further back, struggling to keep pace, were a crowd of voidsmen drawing lasweapons and fastening rebreathers across their faces. *Like solid shadows.* Tyrus stared at the smoke and saw that it did seem odd. It was crawling across the floor, grasping like talons. He wondered if it might be a chemical attack. His suit showed no warnings, but there was definitely something odd about how the darkness was rolling and coalescing.

He halted before a set of armour-plated doors that refused to open. He hammered at the controls but nothing happened. 'Cyren,' he barked, stepping back from the entrance.

Behind him, one of his men raised a plasma incinerator and filled the passageway with noise and light. When the air cleared, the door was a molten heap.

Shapes rushed at Tyrus, half-hidden by smoke and blinking lights. They were hunched and two-legged, but even through the haze he could see they were not human. They each had four arms that hung low to the ground, ending in hooked talons. Their bodies were muscular and armoured, and they were moving incredibly fast. 'Hostiles!' he roared, raising his pistol and taking aim.

Projectiles whistled past Tyrus as he opened fire. Instantly, he felt at ease. His gun was bucking in his fist and his battle-brothers were with him. Things were as they should be. There was a thunderous din as the Ultramarines opened fire, punching xenos off their hooves and sending them scrabbling back down the passageway. More poured from the shadows, clambering over each other in a flurry of darkness, showing no sign of pain or fear. If he were facing another foe, Tyrus might have considered them brave, but to call tyranids brave would be like praising a disease. Even the word 'foe' was misleading: they were an infestation, something to be cleansed with steel and fire.

Tyrus placed his shots with care, so engrossed in the combat that he was only vaguely aware of movement behind him. Then there was an explosion of tearing metal that almost threw him off his feet. He whirled around and saw a rent in the walls, as if a battle tank had careened through the ship. Embers whirled through the smoke. He was shocked to see that several Ultramarines were down, their armour split as savagely as the bulkheads. The rest of the squad had backed away from the hole, weapons trained on the wreckage.

'Lieutenant!' cried one of his brothers as more tyranids flooded into view, clattering over the deck and leaping through the air.

Tyrus and the others opened fire, their weapons spitting rounds until there was nothing left of the tyranids but splintered chitin. Then Tyrus headed over to his fallen brothers, appalled to see that one of them was dead. He looked up at Vultis, about to give him an order, but he was interrupted by another loud tearing sound. He looked in the direction of the noise. 'Did none of you see it?'

Most of them shook their heads, but Vultis spoke up. 'I saw a shape. A tyranid, I think. But unusually large. And unusually fast.'

Tyrus considered the layout of the ship in relation to the damaged wall. 'Whatever it is, it appears to be making for the gunnery deck.' He clambered through the hole and into the next room, gesturing for the others to follow.

The room was a long, narrow mess hall and they sprinted past overturned chairs and tables, following the wreckage out into another smoke-filled passageway.

The tyranids were waiting. They flooded down the corridor, leaping through the darkness. The Ultramarines fired a storm of bolter rounds, but there were far more xenos this time and some managed to return fire. Whatever their ammunition was, it burrowed through power armour. Several Ultramarines fell backwards, clutching at wounds, blood spraying between their fingers.

Tyrus hurled a grenade and charged into the aftermath with the others rushing after him.

There was another explosion, far louder than his grenade, and Tyrus was hurled across the floor, almost losing hold of his pistol. When he looked back he saw another gaping hole and more dead Ultramarines. 'By the Emperor,' he muttered as he stood and rushed back. 'What *is* this?' The tyranids were still firing but he ignored them, battling anger as he marched over to the new hole that had been ripped through the wall.

'Something is toying with us,' said Vultis, looking at one of the devices fixed to his armour. 'Attacking and withdrawing.'

Tyrus gunned down another tyranid. It continued crawling towards him, so he whipped out his combat knife and sliced through the monster's carapace, removing its head. As he did so, some of the corpses twitched and clattered on the floor. 'Is that atypical?'

Vultis nodded. He went over to the dead tyranid and crouched next to it. 'And there is something else unusual. Did you see what happened when you beheaded this specimen? The others reacted.' He looked closer. 'And this is not the head. Look, the head is still attached. This is something else altogether.' He lifted the piece of tyranid Tyrus had cut away and they both saw that it was a small creature that had been attached to the larger one. It was still alive, thrashing and struggling as Vultis locked pincers around it. Then he used one of the tools on his backpack to drill through its carapace. As the drill bit sank deeper, the surrounding corpses juddered again.

Tyrus raised his pistol as he saw that some of the tyranids were trying to rise.

'Wait!' said Vultis, holding up the bloody drill. 'Let me try that again.' He pushed the drill bit into a different part of the creature and more of the tyranids tried to stand. They were little more than butchered remains, but each time Vultis probed the smaller creature they lurched into life, twitching and grasping like broken puppets. 'Fascinating.' Vultis tapped at the data-slate on his wrist. 'I wonder if there is any record of this behaviour happening before. Some kind of pheromonal trigger. I remember reading–'

'Brother-Apothecary,' warned Tyrus. 'Save your research until *after* we save the ship.'

Vultis saluted and rose to his feet, falling in with the other Ultramarines. But he kept his specimen, forcing it into one of the containment canisters at his belt.

It was becoming even harder to see through the shadows, but as Tyrus looked around, he realised that there were only five members of his squad left with him, along with Vultis.

'Keep moving,' he said, running on through another hole and following the trail of destruction.

A few minutes later, he came to a halt. Bulkheads had been hurled into a smouldering heap, blocking the route.

'This way!' Tyrus said, racing up a ladder to an access hatch. He turned the wheel-lock and shoved the hatch open, leaping up into a maintenance tunnel.

His boots had barely landed on the deck when the ship lurched sideways. He heard the unmistakable sound of explosions tearing through bulkheads. The tremor hurled him from his feet and he clattered across the floor.

'Lieutenant!' cried a voice from below, and Tyrus saw that the ladder was gone, along with most of the passageway. All he could see was the clinging darkness.

'Vultis!' Tyrus called. 'Cyren! Are you there?'

He heard distant, muffled replies, but he could not make out the words and they grew more distant by the second. He considered dropping back down, but the remnants of the floor looked like it would collapse under his weight.

'Meet me at Ekato Deck,' he ordered, drawing his bolt pistol as he rose to his feet and carried on down the tunnel, engulfed in fumes. As he ran, more tremors shook the ship and he attempted to use the vox-network again. 'Brother Cestaphon. Send me your coordinates. Update me when you reach the gunnery deck. Baraca? Brother Drinium? Can anyone hear me?'

'Lieutenant Tyrus!' Vultis' voice broke through the static. *'I think you are the target. I have your position on my display. Brother Domitus is down. And Cyren… But it meant to… You will see it when… It led us all away from you. …how a predator divides the herd. It is… and now it is hunting you.'*

'*What* is hunting me?'

The only reply was another howl of feedback.

'What is this?' demanded Tyrus, but at that moment the ship juddered again and he almost lost his footing. He steadied himself and ran on, leaping over rents that had opened in the floor and ignoring the torrent of alerts that were scrolling down his helm display. He reached an access hatch and was about to drop down through it when another explosion rocked the maintenance tunnel. Plasteel hammered into him as he tumbled back the way he had come, showered in debris. Then the whole structure gave way, and he crashed down into the room below. A balcony slowed his fall as he broke through it, then he slammed onto the floor.

More warnings scrolled down his helm display as his armour alerted him to damaged seals and buckled joints. He rolled back onto his feet, gun raised, and surveyed the chamber. He was on a large, rectangular observation deck, hundreds of feet long and dominated by a single leaf-shaped oculus that looked out onto the void. There was rubble scattered around him and some of the smaller pieces were floating above the floor. 'Grav-plating compromised,' he said, looking around the chamber.

'*Hunting you.*' Vultis' voice sheared through the static in his helmet. Then it became a garbled loop and faded back into the din.

Tyrus filled his helm display with schematics, examining the ship's layout, looking for another approach to the gunnery deck. He spotted a route, blinked the schematics away and strode across the chamber, checking his gun for damage as he approached one of the exits.

Boom.

The ship juddered again, but this time, rather than a tremor, it was a single hammer blow, as if a giant had pounded the floor.

Tyrus halted.

The noise had come from the next chamber.

Boom. Even louder this time, coming closer. *Boom.* The floor shook so hard that Tyrus struggled to stay on his feet. *Boom.* He looked down the chamber to the wall at the far end. Whatever was making the noise was on the other side and approaching fast.

Voices bubbled up through the static.

'*Lieutenant Tyrus.*' It was Vultis again. '*There is no… We have… You must return to the bridge. There is no way to… Return to the bridge. Get out of–*'

Tyrus approached the wall, raising his gun.

Boom. The sound was so close the wall trembled, spitting screws from brackets.

He stood side-on and took aim at the centre of the wall.

Nothing happened. He stood there for several seconds, gun trained on the wall, but the tremors ceased. He wondered if he was becoming confused. Perhaps the disturbance projected by tyranids could confound even Adeptus Astartes' minds? He was about to lower his pistol, but then he hesitated, thinking back over his encounters with tyranids. Most were frenzied, but there had been a few, rare occasions when they acted with more cunning. *It is hunting you.* Could that be true? Could Vultis be right? As he stared at the wall he sensed something staring back from the other side, something weighing him up, *considering* him.

'I am not prey,' he said, unclasping a chainsword from his belt and gunning the motor. The teeth rotated with a satisfying roar, hazing the air with promethium fumes. He sensed movement on the other side of the wall, something so heavy that the floor strained and creaked. He switched the chainsword from side to side.

He heard a single breath, deep and slow.

'Come on,' he whispered. 'Let me see your face.'

The wall exploded. Plasteel flew through the air, slamming into his armour and kicking him from his feet. He tumbled backwards, blood filling his mouth, then he stood and fired, bolt-rounds barking into clouds of dust.

A colossal figure stomped into view, so large it had to stoop to enter the chamber. For an absurd moment he thought he was facing a mythical beast, something dragged from a folk-tale. It looked like a dragon, wreathed in flames and hellish light. It was standing upright on its hind legs and an enormous, armoured tail was lashing around its hooves.

He recited a battle prayer to steady his thoughts and then he saw clearly. It was not a dragon, of course; it was a tyranid. Its purple-and-bone-coloured carapace was instantly familiar, as was the insect-like segmentation of its body. But he had never seen nor heard of a tyranid reaching this kind of size. It took him a moment to comprehend its scale. It was taller than the oculus. He held his fire and the two combatants studied each other.

'You *were* hunting me.' Tyrus peered up at the tyranid's face, surprised by how much intelligence there was in its eyes. And recognition. Somehow, it *knew* who he was. And, as the rest of its kind sped towards Regium, it had come here, alone, for him.

The tyranid shifted position, rocking the floor as it brought one of its hooves down. It looked away from Tyrus and surveyed the chamber, taking in the piles of debris and broken machines, then it stared out through the oculus, clearly seeing no threat in Tyrus or his weapons. He used the moment to study the joins in its carapace, looking for weakness or damage.

The tyranid was watching the pieces of metal that had lifted from the floor, drifting higher as the ship's gravity plates failed. Tyrus realised that was his answer. Its carapace looked no different to those he had seen on smaller specimens. If he could make it to its neck, his chainsword should be able to cut through. And with gravity failing fast he could scale the creature with some speed. A few well-placed bolt-rounds should buy him the time he needed to climb the legs.

He crouched and rolled his shoulders.

The tyranid snapped its head round and stared at him. There was a look of derision in its eyes. It was unmistakable. The emotion was so clear and familiar that it distracted him. It was a hesitation of less than a second, but it was enough. The tyranid moved with shocking speed, lunging forwards and thrusting a claw at him.

Tyrus leapt backwards, parrying with his chainsword, but he was only partly successful. He hacked through the monster's claw, avoiding decapitation, but the broken talon still sliced through the mouth grille of his helmet, impaling part of his jaw.

Tyrus pulled free and rolled clear, blood gushing from his ruined helmet. The data feed from his armour died as his faceplate collapsed, and he tore the helmet off, spilling blood and teeth down his chest. Pain suppressors numbed his face and he could already feel scar tissue starting to form. His body had been bred to protect itself.

The monster circled him. Tyrus reached up to touch his face and did his best to shove his broken jaw back into place. His secondary heart was labouring in support of his first and his vision was blurred, but his plan could still work.

He threw a feint, lunging towards an open door, and the monster fell for the ruse, shifting in that direction to block his escape.

Tyrus sidestepped in the opposite direction and opened fire, launching a volley of shots at an unarmoured area behind the tyranid's knee.

It stumbled, surprised, and lashed out with its tail, but it misjudged the situation. It expected Tyrus to back away, but he sprinted forwards instead, ducking the blow.

The tyranid screamed. The sound was so loud Tyrus felt like he had been shot through the temples, but he ran on, leaping at the monster, bringing his chainsword down through the carapace that protected its thigh.

It grasped at him, trying to envelop him with a spider-like claw, but he wrenched the chainsword free and leapt higher, reaching the tyranid's exposed ribs.

The tyranid screamed again, but as it tried to fling him off, he lashed out with his chainsword. The teeth cut through the monster's claw, whirring and grinding, shedding sparks and blood the colour of pitch. The blood hissed as it hit the floor, the metal bubbling. Tyrus triggered a gland in the wall of his mouth, leapt again and spat into the tyranid's face.

It staggered backwards as his acid burned into its jaw, melting the rigid plates around its mouth.

Tyrus clambered onto its shoulder and drew back his chainsword. The teeth screamed as he brought the weapon down towards the monster's neck.

There was a tearing, cracking sound and blood filled the air. It took Tyrus a moment to realise that the blood was red.

Suddenly, he was no longer on the monster's shoulder. It was holding him at arm's length and he was neatly skewered on one of its talons. Even the bioengineered wonders of Tyrus' body could not endure such trauma. The talon had punctured both his hearts and emerged between his shoulder blades. Massive blood loss robbed him of strength and his weapons fell from his grip, clattering on the floor, dozens of feet below.

The tyranid held him there for a while, studying him, bringing its face so close to his that he could see drool sliding down its teeth.

He tried to respond but his strength was almost gone. To his relief, the tyranid brought him closer to its crowded mouth, stretching its jaws wide. It would soon be over.

Only when he was inches away did Tyrus play his last card, triggering the grenade at his belt. *You will not have my ship,* he thought, before the explosion ripped through them both.

Vultis paused halfway across the gunnery deck as the explosion echoed through the ship. More klaxons began howling and a deeper, rumbling sound rose up from beneath his feet. He had never heard such a sound on a warship before, even in the heat of battle. It sounded more like an earthquake than a boarding action. He blinked a wall of data across his helm display, analysing the state of the ship. The *Incorruptible* was lost. He saw it as soon as the glyphs began scrolling down across his vision. The xenos had only attacked in small numbers but they had been unusually focused, advancing with incredible speed and destabilising the ship's superstructure. That was the tremor he could feel through his boots. The ship was collapsing. 'It makes no sense,' he said, talking to the specimen he had captured as if it could understand him. 'Everything will be destroyed. There will be nothing to feed on.'

He lifted the canister up and stared at its contents. He guessed, by the way it had been attached to one of the larger creatures, that it was probably a parasite. He thought back to how the other tyranids had responded when he drilled into the specimen. 'What *are* you?'

Another tremor rocked the ship and he saw that there were minutes, at most, before the *Incorruptible* came apart. It was a staggering loss. Not just the ancient, priceless warship but also the Ultramarines it carried. An hour ago, this turn of events would have seemed impossible. He had to get the parasite off the ship. He had never seen anything like it. He had to get it back to a laboratorium and study it properly. It could be the key to understanding the tyranids' aberrant behaviour.

'Lieutenant Tyrus,' he voxed, raising his voice over the howl of feedback. 'This is Brother-Apothecary Vultis. I am heading to Embarkation Deck Hyperia. I mean to board one of the launches and set a course for Regium. There will be enough fuel if I only use it for course corrections. If you can hear me, meet me there. The *Incorruptible* is lost. I repeat, the *Incorruptible* is lost.'

He changed his helm display, blinking the ship's schematics into view and zooming in on the deck where he was standing. He could reach the launches in minutes.

He continued across the gunnery deck, heading for the exit. He had almost reached the doors when he heard gunfire – a mixture of lasguns and auto-weapons. He raised his pistol and hurried to the doors, but what he saw in the passageway surprised him. There were no tyranids in the corridor, just humans – a mixture of ratings and voidsmen – but they were fighting savagely, attacking each other. There were corpses sprawled across the floor and the fighting was frenzied and illogical. They seemed to have lost their minds, leaping at each other and fighting so wildly that some of them had abandoned their weapons, scratching and biting like animals.

'Hold!' he cried, amplifying his voice through the mouth grille of his helmet.

There was no response. None of them even seemed to hear him. But then, when he took a step forwards, they became even more deranged, screaming and leaping at each other. Some of them looked towards him in terror, but he quickly realised they were not looking at him, they were looking at the creature hanging from his belt.

He called out again, but they were beyond his help and he was running out of time. He marched on, leaving them to their fight, heading towards the embarkation deck.

The deck was oddly quiet compared to the rest of the ship. There were dozens of tyranids scattered around the launches, but they were all dead – torn apart with such savagery that Vultis was reminded of the crew back in the passageway. There was something strange happening. Had these tyranids been affected by the same madness that had overcome the crew? But then, as he clambered over the remains, he saw the real cause. There was a patch of blue power armour just visible beneath the piles of dead xenos.

The ship lurched again, shaking with such force that metal rained down on Vultis, knocking him to his knees. Warnings chimed in his helmet as his suit warned him that the deck was depressurising. He was almost out of time. He clambered to his feet and stumbled through the falling debris, kneeling next to the dead Ultramarine, wondering if he might have time to harvest the warrior's priceless gene-seed. As he pulled a carcass aside, he saw tally marks scored into the Ultramarine's pauldron and felt a rush of grief.

'Baraca,' he muttered, grasping the warrior's lifeless hand.

To his shock, the hand tightened around his. Vultis laughed. 'You cheat death once again, brother. Another mark for your tally.'

He dragged Baraca from the mound of dead and hauled him towards the nearest launch, reciting battle oaths as the *Incorruptible* began cracking apart, groaning and howling, dissolving into the void.

Chapter Four

THE FORTRESS CITY AT ZARAX
SAMNIUM PROVINCE, REGIUM

Castamon paced around the command bunker, watching the ghostly images drifting above the holo-table. The room was almost empty. Sergeant Tanaro had led the humans back up to the ground level so they could ready their troops and prepare to leave the city. There were a few tech-priests still skulking in the shadows, whispering prayers and anointing logic engines, and the Librarian, Abarim, was also still with him, looking more pained by the minute.

'What do you need?' asked Castamon, looking over at him. 'Rest?'

Abarim shook his head. 'It will pass. As soon as Tyrus is done I will start to recover.'

'The signals are so weak,' said Castamon, looking back at the display. 'It is impossible to follow his progress.'

'This is the *Incorruptible*,' said Abarim, pointing to a hazy smudge of light. 'But there is something strange happening. These shapes are the escort ships, but there should be more. Some of them have vanished.'

'Vanished?' Castamon walked over to him and stared at the projection.

Abarim nodded. 'They should be visible. The larger ships are. Unless they have been destroyed by the xenos.'

'The *Incorruptible* is yet to reach Krassus. They should not have encountered any tyranids.'

Abarim closed his eyes and massaged his temples, taking a deep breath. 'It is hard to explain, I agree. But it looks like our ships have already engaged the enemy.'

Castamon stared at the fragments of purple in the projection. 'This makes little sense.'

'Look – it is not only the escorts, the *Incorruptible* itself has foundered.' Abarim leant across the table, bathing his face in light, peering at one of the blinking shapes. 'It appears it may be fending off an attack. Yet the xenos fleet is small. Think of the veterans on that ship, Castamon. Our best battle-brothers. They would not be troubled by such an attack. Why would they be forced to halt, even for a short time?'

To an outside observer, there was little humanity left in Castamon. He had been gene-doctored, surgically enhanced and hypno-indoctrinated. But he could still recall how it felt to be a man. Human emotions sometimes battled to the surface of his psycho-conditioned mind. And, when this happened, rather than suppressing the thoughts, he examined them. They were invaluable clues – the key to understanding the people he had been created to preserve. As he listened to Abarim, emotions warred in his thoughts and he attempted to disentangle them. What was troubling him? His fears were not the same as those that plagued baseline humans. He did not fear death, for example. War was his purpose and his trade. A worthy death was to be welcomed. No, it was the thought of failing Lord Guilliman that had quickened his pulse, the thought of bringing dishonour on his Chapter and failing to do his duty. 'Regium cannot be left undefended for any length of time,' he said. 'We cannot afford to have our warriors stranded out there at the edge of the system, locked in a prolonged engagement. We need them here. Or the entire Sanctus Line is at risk. This was an act of folly. I *should* have gone.'

'You could not have foreseen this. Even I had no foreboding of it. The force you sent is more than equal to the task. And Tyrus is capable of dealing with whatever has delayed them.'

'We need to find out why the *Incorruptible* has foundered. Establish contact with Tyrus.'

Abarim shook his head. 'Astrotelepathy is still impossible. It has remained blocked since the xenos entered the system. Any astropaths who tried to contact those ships would die before they could relay anything useful. Many of them are already on the verge of mental collapse.' There was barely disguised pain in his words. 'It is only thanks to my constant intervention that they are not already dying.'

'We must send word to him,' said Castamon. 'If not astropaths then I will have to…' His words trailed off. The hololith had blinked and updated. They both stared at the projection in confusion.

'Have we lost the connection?' asked Castamon, looking at one of the tech-priests.

She shook her head, pointing to patches of crimson writhing through the stars. 'The xenos fleet is still visible, my lord. Look, it is now continuing on towards Regium.'

'Then where are our ships? Where is the *Incorruptible*?'

She could not meet his eye. 'It looks… My lord, the signal is unclear, but it looks as though the ships have gone – as if they have been destroyed.'

'Impossible.' Castamon stared at the display. 'Abarim. What do you perceive with your warpsight?'

But Abarim could not reply. He had slumped against one of the machines, his fingertips pressed to his forehead and his eyes clamped shut. Blood swelled from beneath his eyelids, dark and vivid as it ran down his pale cheeks. His battleplate lit up, burning sapphire, and he started to shake.

'Brother.' Castamon grabbed him by the shoulders. 'What do you see?'

Abarim opened his eyes. They were crimson spheres.

'Castamon, I *see* it.' His voice was oddly flat. 'The Harbinger.'

Chapter Five

THE FORTRESS CITY AT ZARAX
SAMNIUM PROVINCE, REGIUM

Luco flexed each of his muscles in turn, battling the cramp that was starting to set in. The cave was little more than an alcove in the cliff face, a sheltered ledge, just deep enough for him to crouch in. Beneath the ledge there was a sheer drop to the tree canopy, forty or fifty feet below, and he knew that past those boughs, there was a much bigger drop to the forest floor. If he fell, he would have little chance of survival, but that was not the reason for his stillness. All across the cliff face, there were flocks of nesting orlaps, their wings clapping around their long, snake-like bodies. Many of them were larger than he was and they all had powerful, teeth-crowded jaws that could easily tear him open, but they were nervous creatures with many natural predators and if he moved they would explode from their nests with a terrible din, filling the air with screams until they real-ised he was only a solitary human teenager. Then a new kind of frenzy would begin as they fought to make a meal of him.

He wondered if he was alone on the cliff face, or whether

one of his rivals had struck upon the same idea of securing a hiding place while the adult orlaps were away hunting. The head of a single orlap might be enough to win the blood trials, but Luco was not prepared to settle for *might;* he had not spent two days cowering on the cliff face for an orlap, he had done it to guarantee victory. None of his fellow postulants had studied the behaviour of the creatures the way he had. No one understood predators like him. Since the death of his family, it had become an obsession – an obsession that gave him the edge over everyone and everything. The other postulants would not know that the serpents on this particular stretch of mountainside were hunted by a far more impressive predator.

Noise erupted beneath his perch. The orlaps were screaming in their hundreds. He looked down and saw that his patience had been rewarded. Clinging to the cliff face, cramming orlaps into its jaws, was an enormous predator. Kizils were related to orlaps, with the same scaled skin and ragged wings, but they were ten times the size with an appetite to match. The beast clawed back and forth across the rocks in a kill frenzy, its eyes rolled back and its wings thrashing violently. It killed far more than it could eat, sending carcasses tumbling down towards the treetops, but its savagery did not make it any less magnificent. Luco had never seen one this close before and he stared at it in wonder – a predator from the very dawn of the world, so successful that it had outlived all of its contemporaries.

There were few things that could pierce kizil hide, but the tooth at Luco's belt was one of them. He gripped it and shifted his position. There was no need for stealth now. The orlaps were too busy fighting for their lives to notice him. As he moved, he gasped in pain. Cramps exploded all over his limbs as he crouched and approached the edge of the drop, gripping his knife in his teeth to better move into position. He had to act fast. None of the other postulants would have thought to wait here for such a kill, but if any of them were nearby and saw what was happening, they might attempt to steal his prize. Besides, the kizil would soon be full enough to fly back to its nest. He steadied himself with one hand, gripped the tooth in his other and prepared to jump.

A new call echoed across the rocks. It sounded like a raptor, but Luco knew the truth. It was the whistle he'd taught his friend Baraca – the one they rehearsed as a signal for help. For Baraca to use it now, in the middle of the trial, he must be in great danger.

He tried to ignore it. He was *so* close. So close to proving himself worthy. So close to becoming an aspirant and then, one day, one of the Emperor's Angels of Death. He couldn't let this chance slip away.

The cry came again, sounding desperate now. It was down below, somewhere beneath the canopy of trees. Luco cursed inwardly. However much it pained him to admit it, he could not abandon his friend. He climbed from his perch and began scaling carefully down the cliff face. He had not gone far when a rock gave way beneath one of his feet and triggered a cascade of smaller stones.

The kizil paused, gore swaying from its jaws as it turned to face him. Its pupils rolled back into view as it stared at him.

Luco thought for a moment, judging the distance, then leaped from the ledge, diving at the kizil's back.

The kizil roared, sensing the danger, and launched itself from the cliff face, pounding its wings as it pushed off with its claws.

Luco landed between its wings and drew back his knife to strike. The creature rolled, slamming Luco against the rock, but he managed to jam his knife between its shoulder blades.

The kizil screeched and dived from the cliff, trailing blood as it flew off across the forest, and Luco fell, cartwheeling, towards the distant trees. Pain enveloped him as he crashed through the canopy, hurled from branch to branch. He could still hear Baraca below, whistling for help. Then something cracked against his skull and he lost consciousness.

Lights flickered through Luco Vultis' eyelids.

'Baraca?' he muttered. He struggled to recall where he was or what had happened to him. It was only when he heard a familiar voice that he was able to place himself. The voice belonged to Zarax's chirurgeon, Quand. The memory of Quand's warm, humorous face brought a host of other memories. He was no longer a teenager chasing orlaps. That had been many years ago. He was no longer even truly human. He was an Ultramarine, charged with the defence of the race he once belonged to. Who knew why his mind had chosen to summon such memories from his youth. That day had been a significant one, though. It was the day he had earned his place as an Ultramarines aspirant. His loyalty to Baraca had been observed. He was one of only two postulants to succeed, Baraca being the other.

'Suspended animation left him confused for the first few days, but he's recovering fast now,' said Quand. 'His hibernator membrane worked perfectly. The injuries he sustained during the crash landing could have killed him, but the surgical procedures have gone smoothly. He won't need to see me again.'

Vultis opened his eyes and, as he saw the medicae cell he was in, the rest of his memories fell into place. Quand was smiling, as usual, her tough, leathery skin crumpled around ink-dark eyes, but he could see sadness behind the smile. Her hair was slicked back and she was wearing the smart blue uniform of the Regium Auxilia. For the most part, the chirurgeon was unaugmented, but one of her arms had been replaced with an impressive collection of surgical implements: four bionic limbs that ended in a gleaming array of pliers, claws, scalpels and pincers.

There was a mirror suspended near his face, reflecting the light from a surgical lamp, and Vultis was surprised to see how little damage there was. There were some new scars around his cheek and nose but nothing significant. He was essentially unchanged – a long, rectangular face, brown skin and wide-set, mournful-looking eyes. His hair had been shaved during the surgery, but there was already a cap of dark stubble growing back.

'You have a visitor,' said Quand, backing away from him to reveal the figure behind her.

The medicae cell was not small, filled with gurneys, humming cogitators and tables littered with surgical equipment, but the presence of Lieutenant Castamon made it *feel* small. Castamon was fully armoured, but he had removed his helmet and Vultis saw relief in his commander's eyes.

'You are recovered.' The lieutenant's voice was a low rumble. 'I see it in your face.'

As always, Vultis felt like Castamon's gaze was peeling back the layers of his soul. He recalled the shameful loss of the *Incorruptible*. He had tried to suppress the memories, concerned he might delay his recovery with introspection, but facing Castamon's fierce stare brought them back. 'Forgive me,' he said.

Castamon looked surprised. Then he shook his head. 'Think clearly, Luco, and you will find you have nothing to apologise for.'

'But if Baraca and I had stayed...'

'You decided it was more important to bring word to me, and your instincts served you well. What use would one more death have been? You did the right thing rather than the vainglorious thing, exactly as I would have expected. And I hear you secured us a specimen that might give us a way to learn from our mistake. Besides, you told Quand that Baraca was barely conscious when you dragged him off that ship.'

'Has he recovered? Is he well?'

For the first time since the conversation began, Castamon's expression softened. 'I hesitate to use the word "well" in relation to Baraca. But Sergeant Tanaro has deemed him fit enough to resume his duties.' Castamon looked at Vultis' scars. 'A pointless, heroic sacrifice from you would have left us in the dark. If you had not returned to Regium our situation would be even worse. Thanks to your foresight, we now have a specimen to examine. Which may well turn out to be essential.'

'But I forsook my duty, escaping the massacre rather than standing with my brothers.'

Castamon's voice hardened. 'Do not brood on this. There is naught to be gained from it.'

Castamon's praise had not helped, but admonishment did. Vultis took a deep breath and sat up on the gurney. He placed his fist across his chest. 'My thoughts were clouded. They are clear now.'

Castamon continued studying him. His eyes were quick and intense, the eyes of an eagle tracking prey. 'Quand has worked with her usual skill. She tells me you require no more surgery.'

'I am ready to serve.'

Castamon nodded. 'I did not expect Lieutenant Tyrus to encounter any problems, but I still prepared contingency measures. Regium's entire network of orbital defence lasers has already been repositioned and void-shielded. Most of our defences are now positioned at Port Dura and Salamis Hive. The bulk of the xenos fleet should never reach our upper atmosphere. But in the unlikely event it does, I am relying on you to devise biological countermeasures. What do you propose?'

Vultis felt the same rush of excitement he had felt when he first captured his specimen. 'The tyranids showed uncharacteristic feeding habits on the *Incorruptible*. They also induced hysteria in the crew, just as we have seen here on Regium. And I believe the specimen I captured may be a key. If I can examine it in my laboratorium, I have several hypotheses I can pursue.'

'Quand,' said Castamon. 'Is he well enough?'

'Yes, my lord.' She tapped a socket on Vultis' chest. 'And his neural interfaces are all intact. So he'll be able to utilise his armour's diagnostic tools as usual.'

Castamon leant back, studying Vultis. 'What is the gist of your theory?'

Vultis' mind filled with an unbidden memory: fat globules of blood, gliding past his face as he drifted in the air, surrounded by corpses and body parts that were all weightless, turning slowly and bumping into each other. He shook his head and brought his attention back on Castamon. It felt good to focus on what he knew best: the study of predators.

'Only a small cluster of tyranids attacked the *Incorruptible*,' he said. 'They should have been easy to deal with. The creatures that attacked us were mostly man-sized, clad in a chitinous outer shell and armed with bladed forelimbs, like many tyranid warrior breeds we have faced before. The only difference was an armoured symbiont, fastened to their backs... a form of neurocyte.'

'And this is the sample that you captured?'

'Correct. I suspect that the symbionts act as a beacon. Perhaps pheromonal. I have observed similar traits in swarming insects. But as well as summoning more tyranids I surmise that they release chemicals to confuse their prey. And this, somehow, hinders communication networks. This is why we were unable to communicate clearly with each other when the *Incorruptible* was attacked. The presence of the tyranids in their midst had a dramatic effect on the baseline humans who were on the ship. They lost all sense of self. Many became psychotic.'

'Is the symbiont a relay or the source of the disturbance?'

'It would be conjecture for me to say at this stage.' Vultis took a deep breath and shifted position.

'Are you in pain?' asked Quand, looking surprised. 'I see no damage on the–'

'I am merely trying to clear my thoughts. The thing affected me too. Not to the same extent as the unmodified humans but...' He shook his head. 'When I saw the Harbinger, I thought it was a creature of the warp. One of the unborn. My vision was clouded and my mind projected all kinds of absurd–'

Castamon held up a hand. 'Harbinger? What is that?'

Vultis hesitated, confused, wondering if he was struggling with the after-effects of Quand's surgery. 'I...' For a moment he could not speak. 'I saw a larger xenos predator on the ship, the one that hunted Tyrus, and I thought of it as the Harbinger. But this is the first time I have said that word aloud.' It troubled him that he could not give a more cogent answer. 'There is no reason for me to name it. I am being unscientific.'

Castamon frowned. 'Earlier today, Abarim had a moment of precognition. He perceived a creature of fearsome aspect that was sundered, somehow, from the other xenos. He called it the Harbinger.'

'That is not possible. I have not spoken with Brother-Librarian Abarim since I returned and I am sure this is the first time I have said that name out loud. Did he describe what he saw? I have never seen a tyranid that large, nor any xenos predator for that matter. It was fast too, despite its bulk.' Vultis replayed his memories. His recall was usually perfect, but the events on the *Incorruptible* remained dreamlike. 'There was something else odd about it, though, more than its size and speed. It moved with purpose. It was not frenzied or mindless. And, strange as it may sound, I had a sense that it was a kind of outsider.' He frowned. 'I had the peculiar sense that it was aware of me. But then it moved on. It was single-minded, and as I tracked its progress I realised that it was hunting Lieutenant Tyrus. It seems it somehow disabled our engines and weapons batteries, and then calmly hunted him down. It was as if it knew he was our leader. It killed him with cool efficiency.'

Castamon thought for a moment, then nodded and stood to leave. 'We need to find out why you and Abarim have both referenced that name. Complete your research as fast as possible. And keep me informed at every stage. I deem this a matter of the utmost importance. I will order Brother-Librarian Abarim to seek you out.'

Vultis climbed from the gurney and saluted.

Castamon reached the door then glanced back. 'Just one other thing. Were you and Baraca the only people who boarded the launch?'

'Yes. I am sure of it.'

'Interesting. When it came down on the coast, and we tracked you, we saw several life forms heading away from it, moving fast inland, into the forest.' He headed out into the light. 'It seems that the Great Devourer has made its way to Regium.'

Chapter Six

Brother-Librarian Abarim paused at the entrance to Vultis' laboratorium, leaning against the door-frame to steady himself. As he looked down into the room he felt as though the material and immaterial had collided, merging into a riot of shapes. Everywhere he looked he saw talons and fangs, ripping and biting. Behind that orgy of death there was an obscene colossus, orchestrating the bloodshed. The Harbinger was in his thoughts constantly now. It seemed almost as though it had always been there – that this monster had been with him since his birth. Such a thing was impossible, of course, but he could not shake the idea. And its presence made even the easiest of his psychic disciplines hard to manage. He gripped his force axe and whispered a litany of warding, feeling every potent syllable course through his veins. Hard or not, he would do the work he was trained to do.

He took a deep breath and looked around the laboratorium. The building consisted of a single large chamber with balconies round the edge that housed an incredible collection. Every

77

inch of wall space was lined with shelves and cabinets, and they in turn were crammed with body parts. The room contained thousands of disembodied limbs, wire-mounted wings, embalmed heads, pickled organs, desiccated cadavers, mouldering animal skins and leering skeletons. Some of the specimens were hominids but most displayed a more peculiar morphology – alien predators from every warzone Vultis had visited, many of them so strange that even Vultis could not categorise them yet. The room was illuminated by strip lumens hanging from the ceiling on long cables, and the brutal light revealed handwritten, yellowing labels affixed to every talon and foetus. The labels were even more numerous than the body parts – thousands of small but exhaustive notes, all written in Vultis' tiny, neat script. His helots had transcribed the notes and fed the information into the rumbling wall of cogitators at the far end of the room, but Abarim knew that Vultis rarely used the machines, relying instead on his Adeptus Astartes powers of recall.

Servitors trundled through the collection, pouring compounds into jars and brushing resin onto cadavers. They were monofunctional and zombie-like, their legs replaced with wheeled carts and their eyes unblinking telescopic lenses. Other than the servitors, whose mouths had been neatly sutured, there was no one in the room with Vultis.

The Apothecary was down on the ground floor, stooping over a workbench near rows of clear, terrarium-like spheres mounted on metal frames. The spheres contained living creatures, reptiles and rodents that shifted constantly as Vultis worked, clawing and biting at their prisons, trying tirelessly to reach their captor. Vultis was unaware of their efforts. He seemed agitated, rifling through parchments and jabbing at data-slates, so engrossed in his work that he did not notice he had a guest.

Abarim drove his visions away. The real regained its distance from the unreal. The faces leering at him were not warp-spawned horrors, they were simply corpses and skulls. He had learned, many years ago, to isolate the different regions of his mind, to separate reality from the madness *behind* reality. But in the last few weeks it had become increasingly difficult. And, at every moment, he could feel Regium's sanctioned telepaths, teetering on the edge of collapse, consumed by the same visions he was battling. Holding them all in check left him in constant agony. He felt like his skull had been doused in flames. Then it occurred to him that entering the laboratorium had increased the pain. 'Why should that be?' he muttered.

His words echoed around the room and Vultis looked up in surprise. He was not wearing his helmet and Abarim saw the relief on his face. He was clearly pleased to have a distraction from whatever problem he was grappling with.

Abarim straightened up and masked his pain, marching down the steps and approaching his battle-brother. They grasped each other's arms.

'I am pleased to see you on your feet again,' said Abarim. 'You look well, Luco.'

'You do not,' said Vultis, speaking with such an absence of tact that Abarim laughed. 'What ails you, brother?' continued the Apothecary. 'Are you wounded?'

Abarim shook his head. 'Not wounded. At least, not physically. It is this hysteria, this astral madness, that has affected me. My mind is besieged by the same force that has driven the civilians to violence.'

'The Harbinger,' said Vultis, giving him a pointed look.

'The Harbinger. Perhaps. Castamon told me you used the same term. I have heard civilians using it, too.'

Vultis nodded. 'This cannot be mere coincidence. Let me show you something.'

As the Apothecary looked back at the notes on his workbench, Abarim studied him. There were some in the Chapter who were wary of Vultis. It was not so much they did not trust him, more that they struggled to understand him. The humour and camaraderie that bound the other battle-brothers was absent in Vultis. He was odd and obsessive, consumed by his work, more likely to reference biological data than share a joke. It was part of the reason Abarim liked him. His dedication to his craft was commendable. And as a member of the Librarius, Abarim knew all too well what it meant to be an outsider.

'Does this seem familiar?' asked Vultis, tapping his finger on the page of a book.

Abarim looked closer and saw a drawing of a tyranid. It was little more than a hurried sketch, but it was unmistakably the monster he had seen in his visions. There was something unpleasant about seeing the Harbinger printed on a page. It was as if someone had plucked a likeness from his dreams. 'Yes,' he said. 'This is it. This is the creature that has been clouding my thoughts.'

Vultis nodded. 'The author of this text referred to it as a "norn-emissary". He claimed it was an envoy or an avatar of some kind. His work was later discredited and he was eventually executed, but I am sure this is the Harbinger.'

'What do you suspect is happening here?' asked Abarim. 'Why are we seeing these things?'

Vultis closed the book.

'All I have are theories. But I believe there is far more to this than we originally thought. I do not think it is a coincidence that tyranids are passing through this system. And I think the visions you and I are sharing are a clue to the real reason they are here.'

Abarim noticed a clear-sided casket on the bench. 'Is this the specimen you brought back from the *Incorruptible*?'

'Yes. It was unfamiliar to me, but I have just been researching it and I discovered that this xenotype was recorded, just a few years ago, by a xenobiologian. He classified it as a "neurogaunt". Although, I am unclear whether he was referring to the symbiont or the host creature I cut it from. Or perhaps he considered them a single entity. Unfortunately, his notes were destroyed so I have a name and little else.'

'It looks like it is dying.'

Vultis nodded and looked troubled. 'It should be healthier. This suspension should have revivified it, but the exoskeleton is dissolving. It needs a host to feed on.' He adjusted some controls on the casket's base and pincers moved inside, jolting through the cloudy suspension and locking on to the specimen. A metal syringe flickered in the dark liquid and its needle punched through the tyranid's shell.

The specimen grew still.

Vultis stared at it, his face inches from the casket. Then he sighed and backed away and the specimen continued its struggles.

The pain in Abarim's head was growing worse again. It had flared as soon as he approached Vultis. 'What did you hope to see?'

Vultis finally focused on him, staring at him with dark, sombre eyes. 'I am attempting to recreate the tumult I saw on the *Incorruptible*. I want to induce an alarm response by injecting bioengineered hormones. One of my theories is that these parasites relay pheromone signals to the rest of the creatures. If I can simulate those biological signals, I may be able to pervert them. I could perhaps even turn them into a weapon that would confound the tyranid leaders. But nothing I attempt triggers a response.'

'Leaders?' Even through his pain, Abarim found the idea

amusing. 'Tyranids swarm and feed, Luco. They display no semblance of tactics. No strategy. No leaders.'

'They *must* have leaders. And they do employ tactics. Cast your memory back. Think of how we have seen them fight on other worlds. Think of the times they have confounded us. They act in concert.' He waved at specimens on the other side of the room. 'I have seen it work in numerous ways. The tyranids are ever-changing. They are like a virus, adapting to our galaxy – adapting to a new challenge.' He nodded to the symbiont before him. 'And, in this particular swarm, perhaps these parasites are how the dominant creature controls the lesser ones.'

Abarim tried to look at the creature but that made the pain in his head even worse, so he kept his gaze on Vultis. 'Even if that were true, how would it help us?'

Vultis grew animated, drumming his finger on a piece of parchment. 'When tyranids attack they follow a prescribed pattern. It is one of the few predictable things about them. They appear to have specific invasion stages. If we could understand how these parasites interact with each other, we could alter the sequence and throw their attacks into disarray.'

'But none of your chemicals have any effect.'

The light faded from Vultis' eyes. 'My efforts have been unsuccessful. I have tried dozens of pheromones. None of them trigger even a small response. I confess, I am baffled.'

Abarim leant closer, looking in at the tyranid. As he did so, the pain in his head increased and he stumbled backwards, knocking into a workbench and causing surgical tools to clatter across its surface.

Once he had steadied himself, he realised that Vultis was staring at him, a curious look on his face. 'What happened?'

'Empyric energy. A surge of it.' Abarim moved closer to the casket and felt the same bright agony sparking across his skull.

'Is the specimen causing it?' Vultis' eyes were gleaming.

Abarim backed away, nodding. 'Almost as if it were a psyker.'

'Or a psychic relay?' Vultis tapped his notes. 'A neurogaunt. Perhaps I have been approaching this from the wrong direction. Perhaps this symbiont uses telepathy rather than chemical signals. Perhaps it is a form of psyker. But I will need another specimen. It is the only way to test the theory. I need to see how they interact with each other.' He looked up at Abarim. 'Lieutenant Castamon mentioned xenos that fled from our launch after the landing. Has he located them yet?'

Abarim shook his head. 'They looked to be few in number and hidden in the depths of the forest. Hunting them down could take weeks and would leave the fortress undefended. He discussed the idea of a hunt with Sergeant Tanaro but decided against it.'

Vultis paced around his workbench. 'It need not take weeks.' He glared at the tyranid, squirming and trying to reach him. 'Not if *I* lead the hunt.'

Chapter Seven

THE FORTRESS CITY AT ZARAX
SAMNIUM PROVINCE, REGIUM

Vultis had no difficulty finding his battle-brothers. The streets of Zarax echoed with a low, droning hum, like the swarming of insects, that told him exactly where they would be. He left Castamon's citadel and headed north up a misty, statue-lined avenue, with the fortress' magnificent eastern gates looming on his right and the Library of Carnus at his back. To his left was a grid of narrower streets, crowded with ivy-lashed hab-units and fabrication blocks.

It was just after dawn but the avenue was unusually busy. Vultis had never seen so many people in the fortress. It was sometimes referred to as a city, but in truth it was smaller than most towns, made impressive by its fortifications rather than its size. He could see from the range of uniforms and skin tones that people had travelled from right across the continent. Most of them looked warily at him as he strode by, unsure how to behave in the presence of a Space Marine, but those he knew saluted in the Ultramarian style, pressing fists to chests. As always, there was mist pouring down over the battlements and weeds creeping across the flagstones. Despite Governor Seroc's best efforts, the forest was ever-present, always seeming just a moment away from reclaiming the land in an explosion of vines and shoots. From the other side of the battlements came the sweet, heady aromas of the forest and the warring calls of beasts.

As he made his way through the crowds, he passed an area known as the Caves of the Rubicassus. In a small act of concili-ation and acknowledgment of local beliefs, Confessor Thurgau had agreed with Governor Seroc that this part of the fortress could remain forested. It resembled an overgrown garden, straining at rockcrete fencing like a host of caged animals. Real animals still hunkered under some of the leaves and birds nested in the higher branches, screeching and cawing as he approached. Most off-worlders tended to avoid the place but Vultis was fascinated by it, and had he the time, he would have paused at the perimeter, gripping the stone palisade, trying to catch a glimpse of the reptiles that sometimes emerged from the cave-mouths, hunting rodents and insects with lethal efficiency.

After passing the caves he turned left onto another wide avenue and faced his destination. Zarax's stadium was even larger than the Library of Carnus, dominating the whole fortress, a broad, drum-shaped building circled by gargantuan pillars. It was taller than the walls that surrounded the city. The only thing that was taller was a statue of Lord Commander Guilliman, a stone colossus that stood just outside the fortress, watching over the stretch of coastline that bordered the city to the west.

There were braziers either side of the stadium's gates and they burned constantly with a fire that had been carried across the segmentum, preserved by hand, all the way from the Ultra-marines' home world of Macragge. As Vultis approached the flames he paused and whispered a tribute to his fallen brothers, summoning the faces of those who had set out for Krassus with him. Then he headed through the huge gates and entered the arena.

Squad Tanaro had gathered at the centre of the stadium. The Ultramarines were unarmoured, dressed only in loin-cloths, neural interface ports visible in their skin, their warplate arranged on a table at the far end of the arena, watched over by menials. The warriors had also discarded their guns and were armed with nothing more than combat knives. Some of them were bleeding from cuts to their arms and chests, and all of them were glistening with sweat as they lunged and hacked through the torpid air. Their foe was the source of the droning sound that was echoing through the whole fortress. Senary engines were bulky, armour-plated combat servitors that hung in the air, suspended by whirring canvas wings and trailing an abdomen-like undercarriage supporting six bladed limbs. The machines moved in awkward lurches, a crude approximation of life that Vultis found distasteful, but their blades were a dif-ferent matter, moving so fast that even his Adeptus Astartes eyes struggled to follow them. There were dozens of the machines in the arena, hovering like heat-dazed flies.

There were also some human soldiers in the arena. Local auxilia troops. Most of them were gathered round an Ultra-marine who was standing apart from the others, up on a raised platform, giving a speech. Sergeant Tanaro was slightly taller than his men, his blond hair was shoulder length, and his face was markedly different from the other veterans. Battle-brothers of the First Company were invariably horribly scarred. They had survived centuries of war and they carried their injuries with pride, as battle trophies, spurning offers of skin grafts or sur-gery. But Tanaro was immaculate. His skin was pale and flawless with no sign of a blemish, and his features were so refined that it was hard to believe he had ever faced combat. Some of his men joked that he looked more like a son of Sanguinius than of Guilliman, but they made those jokes in private. Tanaro's refined nature extended to his skills as a warrior. He was lethal. And famously unforgiving during training sessions.

'They were Heretic Astartes,' said Tanaro, looking out into the middle distance as he continued addressing the soldiers, his voice booming across the arena. 'Clad in the raiment of the damned. Had we not dealt with them that day, the entire system would have been infected with their lies and disease. The Lord Commander himself mentioned the incident and referred to Squad Tanaro by name.'

The soldiers were staring up at him as if he were a god.

'And do you know how many battle-brothers we lost that day?' He looked down at the crowd.

They stared back at him in awed silence.

'None.' His eyes shone. Then he frowned, noticing something in the training session. He stepped from the platform, strode over to his squad and drew his knife, launching a flurry of lunges at one of the Ultramarines, forcing the warrior to drop to his knees and yield.

Tanaro studied the man with disdain, eyebrow raised, blade to his throat. Then he waved the Ultramarine back to his feet with a theatrical flourish. 'Bring up your guard sooner, Timoleon, and watch your flank.' He stepped back and dropped into a combat pose. 'Try again. With your eyes open this time.'

A few of the auxilia troops laughed and Tanaro glanced at them, before lunging at his opponent.

Some of the senary engines had lost limbs and a few were lying broken on the ground, cadaverous faces staring out from their workings, but the training session was clearly going to last for several hours longer. Sergeant Tanaro saw Vultis approaching and touched a device at his belt. The combat servitors lowered their weapons, slumping motionless in the air as the sergeant marched over to greet him. He punched his chest in salute and looked at Vultis with a neutral expression. Vultis had long ago accepted his place as an outsider. If he were merely an Apothecary, things might have been different, but his role was more complicated than just treating wounds and preserving the Chapter's gene-seed. As an Apothecary Biologis he spent his every waking moment examining and researching species that Space Marines had been bred to abhor. The whiff of vile xenos blood preceded him, clinging to his surgical weapons. And, perhaps most troubling of all, he loved his work. Politicking and friendships were unpredictable but xenobiology followed rules, rules that he had learned to understand.

Tanaro greeted him in stiff, formal tones. 'Well met, brother. You have been weighed in the balance. And you were not found wanting.'

Vultis nodded his head, acknowledging the old Ultramarines saying. 'I survived when others did not. There is little honour in that.'

The rest of the squad gathered round, massaging bloody muscles and saluting him, wearing the same neutral expressions as the sergeant.

'You are no coward,' said Tanaro, softening his tone. 'I know you would not have chosen this, but you brought word of a dangerous situation. Do not underestimate that.'

Vultis looked around the group. 'How is Brother Baraca?'

Tanaro studied him down the length of his long, regal nose. Then he nodded and gestured to a distant figure, sitting in the lowest tier of seats on the far side of the arena. 'The Revenant endures. Escaping death yet again. He should have rescued you rather than the other way round.'

'How does he seem?'

'He seldom speaks and looks like he wants to break the neck of everyone he encounters. So, I would say he is unchanged.' The sergeant was about to walk away, then he paused, looking over at Baraca and speaking in a more thoughtful tone. 'He boasts of cheating death, but I sometimes wonder if that is really something to be proud of.' He looked at Vultis with interest, as though on the verge of pressing the matter. Then he headed back over to the senary engines. 'Welcome back, Brother Vultis.'

Squad Tanaro resumed their training and, as the whirring of engines filled the air, Vultis headed on across the arena.

Baraca was unarmoured like the others, and without his magnificent suit of power armour, he looked even more brutal than usual. He was the antithesis of Sergeant Tanaro. Where Tanaro seemed untouchable, surviving countless wars without so much as a chipped tooth, Baraca looked like he had never dodged a shot. Every inch of him was networked by scars and there were several places where his muscles had been torn out of shape, either by bite marks or gun trauma. His head was shaved and topped by a short, patchy mohawk, and his face was crooked and pummelled. There was a plasteel plate screwed to one side of his head where Vultis had once repaired his skull, and his nose had been broken so many times it was a shapeless mess. Where Tanaro was tall and statuesque, Baraca was broad-chested and ape-like, with rounded shoulders and wide-set legs. He stared, habitually, into the middle distance and he was holding a pauldron in one hand and carving it with another. There was a dangerous, blank look in his eyes and he was muttering to himself as he worked. But despite all this, Vultis felt a surge of relief at the sight of him. He was unchanged. Just as he had been unchanged by everything else they had faced over the decades.

Vultis smiled. 'The Revenant endures. Why are you still alive?'

Baraca held up the pauldron. It was covered in a scratched tally denoting all the times he had dodged death.

'Not your time to die,' said Vultis.

'Not my time.' His voice was as ruined as the rest of him – deep and ragged.

They gripped arms then sat together and Baraca offered Vultis a piece of whatever he was eating. 'Real meat,' he said, 'caught in yesterday's training session.'

Vultis nodded and took the food. For the last few days he had been fed through a tube and the sensation of eating still felt strange, but the meat was rare and good and he took a second piece.

'He hates you,' said Baraca, nodding at Tanaro, who was still leading the squad through their paces.

'Hates me?'

Baraca laughed. 'Luco, your head is too full of xenos. You should pay heed to the world around you. Hate is too harsh a word, I retract that, he respects you, but I sense that he resents you.'

Vultis shook his head, unable to understand. 'I am his battle-brother.'

'Do not be naive. You have the ear of Castamon. The lieutenant trusts you. Almost as much as he trusts Abarim. He admires you and listens to you. He respects your hunger for knowledge. Meanwhile, he barely notices Tanaro. He thinks of him as a proficient but conceited sergeant who only sees the surface of things. Think about how long Tanaro has been a sergeant without ever being considered for the promotion he so obviously craves.'

Vultis thought back over his exchange with Tanaro and realised, to his annoyance, that Baraca was probably right – Tanaro did act oddly with him. The thought that he had missed something that was so obvious to others made him reply in a harsher tongue than he intended. 'You have been in this squad longer than Tanaro and you have progressed less. By rights, it should be *your* squad.'

Baraca grunted. 'If I wanted to progress I would. I could be a captain by now.'

'Then why have you stayed where you are?'

Baraca tapped Vultis' chest armour. 'I have stayed *alive*, Luco. Others come and go, the glory hounds and the heroes, but they die and I remain. I do the work and I serve with honour. I do what the Emperor needs of me. I survive. And, until *I* choose otherwise, I will continue surviving.'

Vultis studied Baraca's brutalised face. His friend was a jumble of contradictions. He was no coward, whatever Tanaro might imply. He was a pragmatist, holding the line, war after war, as others shone in the spotlight. But there was also a fatalism to him that Vultis could not quite understand. Baraca had watched his brothers die, over and again, but he knew, somehow, that none of the rounds had his name on.

He shrugged. 'People are not my area of expertise.'

'Maybe they should be. Try studying them with the same level of focus you apply to the things in your bio-vaults. How are your specimens?'

'I have been spending most of my time in the medicae facility, bound to a gurney.'

Baraca laughed. It was a deep, explosive sound. 'So you have. That will teach you to spend time with me.' They fell into an easy silence. Baraca continued carving the notch into his armour while Vultis watched the training. They had not been together since the deaths on the *Incorruptible* and, though they did not speak of it, they both understood what the other was thinking. They were both outsiders, in their own way, but they still felt the loss of their battle-brothers keenly.

'I have come here with new orders,' said Vultis, eventually. 'From Lieutenant Castamon.'

Baraca looked surprised. 'Orders for me?'

'For the whole squad.'

Baraca grinned, which only served to make his face more disturbing. 'And you are telling me first, rather than the sergeant? That will hardly endear you to him.'

'I mean to tell him now. I just wanted to check on you first.'

'Check on me?' Baraca laughed. 'I like that.' He frowned. 'Are we heading back to Krassus?'

'No. There would be no point. The xenos never landed there. They are still heading towards us. Or at least most of them are. A number are already here.'

Baraca put the pauldron down and picked some meat from between his teeth. 'Tyranids? On Regium?'

'We were not the only things on that launch. There were bioforms too. Scout organisms, perhaps, which are now somewhere upon Regium.'

Baraca's eyes darkened. 'So we fled a battle *and* brought xenos to Regium. Not our finest hour, brother.'

'What else could we have done?' Vultis found most people's emotions a mystery, but he had known Baraca so long that he could sometimes guess at his thoughts. He knew why Baraca sounded so angry. He was thinking of the brothers they had lost.

Baraca nodded to the tools fixed to the back of Vultis' armour. 'You could have roused me. You carry enough stimms to rouse a butchered grox.' Muscles rippled in his jaw. 'We could have stayed and fought.'

Vultis knew he would never convince Baraca they were right to leave a fight, but he still felt the need to justify his actions. 'We are not all like you,' he said. 'Maybe it wasn't your time to die, but it would have been mine. And then there would have been no way to get word to Lieutenant Castamon.'

Baraca grunted non-committally. 'What are the orders?'

'I have agreed with Lieutenant Castamon that you and I will track down our stowaways. I requested that you and I go alone, but he insisted that we take the entire squad.'

'A hunt?' Baraca chewed savagely at the meat. 'We can make amends for bringing them here.'

'A *kind* of hunt. But we must do more than kill them. We have to catch some alive.'

Baraca played the part of battle-shocked zombie around most people, but he could not always maintain the act around Vultis. They had known each other since childhood and had become Ultramarines together. Artifice was impossible. He laughed a filthy, guttural laugh. '*Catch* them? Throne. Life is never dull with you, Luco.'

Before them, Tanaro was fending off attacks from one of the senary engines as he instructed the rest of the squad. He was speaking loud enough to address the human soldiers who were still watching the session. 'Accuracy and focus are everything,' intoned Tanaro, wielding his knife like a fencer, lunging and slashing with such grace that he seemed to be dancing. 'One cannot always predict the length of an attack so every ounce of energy should be weighed and balanced, spent with care. Brute force is the hallmark of the savage. We have been–'

Baraca stood up, walked over to Tanaro and slammed his forehead into the senary engine. Smoke plumed from its work- ings and it made a thin whistling sound. He followed up with a flurry of punches, ripping metal and cabling until the machine collapsed, sparking and juddering. He continued punching it even after its lights had blinked out. Then he stood over the wreckage, eyes burning, fists clenched.

Tanaro glared at him. 'You have been ordered to rest, Brother Baraca.'

Baraca continued staring at the wreckage, then nodded. 'Sergeant.' He returned to his seat next to Vultis.

Tanaro was on the verge of saying more, but he bit his words back and continued with the session, leading the group away across the arena. Some of the civilians looked at Baraca with undisguised fear.

'Anyone else would be disciplined for that,' said Vultis.

Baraca nodded. 'Castamon thinks I am on the verge of collapse.' Humour gleamed in his eye. 'They are indulging me.'

Vultis had seen this kind of behaviour in his friend before, this flaunting of hierarchy, and it grated on him. There was only so long such behaviour would be overlooked. But Baraca showed no sense of self-preservation. He behaved as if life were a game. And it had grown worse since they were deployed to Regium. Vultis found it troubling, but there was no time to press the matter.

'Do you remember the smaller tyranids we saw on the *Incorruptible*?' He kept his voice low, conscious of the nearby humans. 'The ones that were attached to the backs of the larger predators.'

'I thought they were just external organs.'

'I believe they are symbionts, living in a state of mutualism with the larger xenos. I suspect they were key to the tyranids' attack on the ship.'

Baraca stretched, flexing his butchered muscles. 'Science.' He sneered the word as if it were a curse.

'Do you doubt science or do you doubt me?'

'I doubt many things,' he said. 'You are a genius, Luco.'

'But what?'

Baraca absent-mindedly touched the tattoos down his arm. 'Theories and logic. They can only carry you so far. They are only the canvas, Luco. They are never the picture.'

'You speak in riddles. What do you mean? Do you doubt the power of research and study?'

'Did the Emperor conquer half the galaxy with science?'

'Yes, in part. And our primarch is now doing much the same, with the aid of the Martian priesthood.'

Baraca huffed. 'There is xenotech out there that *far* outstrips anything dreamt up on Mars. There is no need to stare at me like that, Luco – we both know it. You are not Confessor Thurgau. You know I am no heretic.' He nodded to his pauldron, gleaming in the sun. 'It took me a while but I have the right of it now. It is not science that will save us. It is not logic, machinery or weapons that sustain the Imperium.'

Vultis knew that Baraca did not share these thoughts with other people. As far as anyone else was concerned, he was just the Revenant – battle-shocked and blank-eyed, simultaneously revered and underestimated. He felt honoured that his old friend still showed him his true face, even though he disagreed with half of the things he said. 'Then what *does* sustain the Imperium? Enlighten me.'

Baraca nodded to the auxilia soldiers who were watching Tanaro. The sergeant had climbed up onto the terraces and, as his men continued training, was regaling his audience with another tale of heroism. He had turned his face to the sun, catching the dawn in his hair. He looked like the Emperor Himself. 'Look at them. Look at how they watch him. We know Tanaro is just a braggart, but to them he is like a saint. They have faith in him. *Faith* is the picture, Luco. Faith is why people endure even as the galaxy burns down around their ears. Gods and destiny.'

Luco sighed.

'Gods and destiny. I have little power over such things.'

Chapter Eight

Damaris followed the magistrate, Urzun, across the forum and into Zarax's maze of muddy, narrow streets. It was nearly midday and in the last couple of hours the city had become even more crowded. Citizens were arriving all the time, from right across the Samnium Province and beyond. Everyone she saw looked afraid and exhausted, and some people carried terrible wounds. They huddled against the plinths of statues and in the doorways of temples, clutching the few belongings they had managed to bring with them. Children looked at the soaring, classical architecture with awed expressions while their parents wept or stared at the ground. With every family that arrived, Damaris' outrage grew. Castamon had lied to Governor Seroc, she was sure of it. All this talk of xenos was nonsense. She had spoken to dozens of refugees and not one of them had heard of, or seen, alien horrors. People were not fleeing from xenos, they were fleeing from insurrection and civil unrest. Her people had reached their limit. They had been robbed of their faith, their culture and their home. *Pax Macragge.* That was the name soldiers gave Regium now. The Ultramarines presented themselves as saviours, but they were empire builders. Crushing history with towering arrogance.

Urzun paused at the corner of a building and turned to face her, seizing her hands. His dark-rimmed eyes shone with passion. 'It pains me to be the one...' he whispered. 'To show you such a thing is... I wish... But you would want to know, I am sure. And I thought, if it is not too arrogant of me, that you would wish to hear such a thing from me, rather than... Rather than another... Rather than someone who–'

'Urzun.' She gently freed her arms from his grip. 'What is it?'

He licked his lips, looked anxiously around, then nodded, taking her hand and leading her on.

They turned the corner and, as they left the enclosed streets and approached the city wall, Damaris recoiled. At the base of the wall, a squad of Militarum soldiers were using machines to dig up the ground and pour liquid ferrocrete into troughs. Only hours earlier, this part of the fortress had been crowded with sacred plants and caves. One of the few places the off-worlders had allowed to remain as it was before they began building the fortress. It was the last trace of Aureus Nahor, the shrine that had once dominated this stretch of coast. It was the lifeblood of her people.

Damaris rushed over to the sergeant in charge. 'Stop!' she cried. The plants and caves were almost gone; several of them had already been flattened and filled. She tried to pull one of the soldiers away from his machine.

'Consul!' warned the sergeant. 'We have work to do.'

She gripped the handle of her sword and glared at him. For a moment she really did consider using the weapon. She recognised the man. He was born not far from Zarax. 'How could you do this?' she hissed. 'This land is sacred. It was all we had left.'

The sergeant looked at her with sympathy but shook his head. 'The fortress needs to be secured and the caves lead directly down into the tunnels.'

She felt faint. 'The off-worlders have gone back on their word.'

'Things change,' said the soldier she'd grabbed, sounding angry. 'The Ultramarines said this section of the wall is not properly defended. They ordered us to fill the holes.'

'You're betraying your past!' she spat, pointing at him. 'Betraying your faith.'

'There's only one true faith. One way to worship the Emperor.' The soldier continued working, his eyes growing hard.

The sergeant's sympathy was fading fast. He looked darkly at her. 'We can't live in the past, consul. We have to adapt. Adjust to the new way. The Emperor wills it. The Ultramarines are His creation. Built in His likeness. He has sent them here to protect us.'

'Protect us?' She stared at the setting ferrocrete, feeling numb, horrified by her powerlessness. The caves were half-gone. As were the remnants of Aureus Nahor. 'Lieutenant Castamon's not a god.' She glared at the sergeant. 'And saying that doesn't make me a separatist. It's a fact. He's a soldier, not a deity. He can't protect us any better than we protected ourselves for all these centuries.'

A crowd began to form as people recognised Damaris. There were people she knew, but also people who had just arrived from the coast, staring at her in confusion or fear.

'Ask one of the Cadians,' growled the soldier. 'There's war *everywhere* now. Cults are springing up across the galaxy. People want to tear down the Imperium and kill the Emperor. Entire planets are vanishing into dust. Fleets have disappeared. It's not just a question of front lines and distant wars any more. The Cadians told me that the heretics are pressing ever closer to Holy Terra.'

The sergeant noticed the crowd gathering and gripped the handle of his pistol. 'Consul. You must let us work.'

Damaris wanted to howl in his face, but what was the use? The soldiers were all watching her with the same hard expressions as the sergeant. She would only make a fool of herself. And perhaps lose her position as consul.

She backed away from him and shook her head.

'I understand,' said Urzun. 'Such a loss. I have prayed in those caves all my life, just like you.'

'It's not so much the caves. It's them.' She gestured to the soldiers. 'They would not even *think* of questioning the off-worlders. They think all they have to do is follow Castamon's orders and everything will be fine. And look at them. I know these people. They are *my* people. They used to believe in the sanctity of this place. And of the whole forest. But they've forgotten all of it. Someone needs to show them the truth,' she muttered as they headed away from the soldiers and back towards the rows of hab-units.

Urzun licked his lips. 'Who? Show who the truth?'

'People need to see how wrong they are about the Ultramarines. Castamon's a liar and he's not in control. Everyone thinks the off-worlders can do no wrong, but if that were true, how do you explain all of this?' She waved at the refugees crowding down every thoroughfare. 'The off-worlders have squeezed production at Salamis Hive until people are rising up in protest. Now Governor Seroc is sending Cadian tanks to crush anyone who dares complain. And Castamon has sent Ultramarines to Shellib City to do the same. These are *not* the actions of people who are in control. But no one sees it. Because they're so sure the Ultramarines can never fail. They are so blind to it that they will bulldoze their own heritage just because Lieutenant Castamon tells them to.' She paused at the top of a street, leaning against a wall, drunk on fury. 'I wish I could show people.'

Urzun shuffled back and forth around her, rubbing his hands together and glancing up and down the street. 'What if there was a way?'

She stared at him.

He pursed his lips, looking at the ground, still rubbing his hands. He looked around to make sure there was no one within earshot. 'You want people to see that he's not perfect? That he makes mistakes?'

'Exactly.'

His eyes widened. 'We should talk in private.'

Urzun's chambers were immaculate. The bleached stone walls were lined with bookcases that were filled with per-fectly arranged scrolls – decrees, bills and statutes that had mostly become obsolete since the arrival of the off-worlders but which Urzun still guarded jealously as the source of his status. Damaris had visited the chamber before and found it vaguely disquieting. As well as the legal documents, he col-lated files on almost every soul in the region. He made it his business to know everyone else's business. He had boasted to her once that he could tell her anything she needed to know about her citizens.

He ushered her into a small lounge. There were cushions arranged in a circle around a low table, which was set with a carafe and some cups. There was a single, large window look-ing out onto the busy street and the sound of the crowds filtered into the room. He indicated that she should sit, but she remained standing. 'What is it? What are you thinking?'

He grinned apologetically and rushed past her, carefully click-ing the door shut. Then he closed the shutters at the window and tapped a lumen in the wall, flooding the room with golden light. He sighed, rubbed his jaw and walked in a circle, seeming excited and afraid at the same time. 'You said Castamon has redeployed some of his men.'

'Yes. Squad Gerrus, he called them. More Ultramarines, like the ones stationed here.'

Urzun continued pacing, but now he adopted a sage expression, holding a finger in the air as he spoke. 'You said Castamon is sending this Squad Gerrus to Shellib City to crush the rioting and looting.'

'Supposedly. What of it?'

'Well…' Urzun gave her a conspiratorial smile. 'What if Squad Gerrus never arrived at Shellib City? What do you think would happen then?'

'Well, the situation would keep getting worse. It's already anarchy there, by all accounts.'

Urzun moved close to her, whispering in her ear. 'And how might that reflect on Lieutenant Castamon and the Ultramarines?'

'They would look foolish.'

'Perhaps even incompetent?'

'Yes, I suppose.'

'Dishonest, maybe? And fallible?'

'Yes, but that won't happen, will it?' Damaris had the strange feeling that she was no longer in the room with a man. As Urzun circled her, she was reminded of a rodent, preparing to pounce on carrion. But she was also desperate to know what he was implying. 'Squad Gerrus will arrive at Shellib City. And they will crush the insurrection.'

'What about if they received different orders? What about if, rather than being sent to Shellib City, they received orders sending them to Port Dura? That would seem logical to them. After all, there is trouble there too.'

She frowned. 'Castamon would look a fool. Shellib City would be left in a mess. Squad Gerrus would be bogged down in all the trouble at the port.' She finally accepted the offer of a seat, dropping heavily onto one of the cushions, crushed by the weight of the conversation. 'Are you saying you could do that? Are you saying you can send false messages to Castamon's troops?'

He raised an eyebrow. 'If my consul willed it, yes. It was my job to connect their comms devices to the planetary network. And during the process it was necessary to understand some of their encryption codes. It would be entirely possible for me to send a message to Sergeant Gerrus. And the beauty of it is that no one would be able to trace the message back to us. The process would be handled by a monofunctional servitor, and I would simply wipe the relevant memories once we were done.'

He was trembling sightly and seemed excited by the audacity of what they were discussing, but Damaris felt angry again – angry that Castamon had forced her to even consider such underhand tactics. But if it worked, she might finally show people what a fraud Castamon was. She shook her head. 'I don't want to cause them any serious harm, though.'

Urzun waved his hand. 'It would make little difference, in the long term. When Castamon finds out he will decide where to send Squad Gerrus. But, in the short term, he will look incompetent or dishonest and it will appear that he is incapable of handling the problems. It would knock people's confidence in him.' He frowned. 'Is that what you wanted? A chance to shake people's confidence in the Ultramarines? This would do it, I'm sure. And then people would start listening to you again.'

She realised she was still holding a dead leaf she had taken from the caves. She crushed it in her fist. 'Yes. That's what I want.'

Urzun closed his eyes, whispering a prayer.

Chapter Nine

They flew away from the sea, heading inland, swallowed by the gloom of the forest. Vultis and Baraca sat side by side in a Storm Speeder as it hummed through the canopy, surrounded by the ocean-like crush of trees. Navigational data scrolled down Vultis' helm display as he steered the Storm Speeder away from a tumult in the branches. Other speeders followed close behind, carrying the rest of Squad Tanaro.

'It is getting worse up ahead,' said Baraca, gesturing to the cluster of trees they were approaching. The forests of Regium were savaged by a phenomenon known as the swell, a kind of tidal surge that sent smaller trees and plants cascading around larger ones in an endless collision that followed no apparent logic. It only happened once or twice a day, but there was no way to predict when. As Vultis looked where Baraca was pointing, he saw a whirl of green and brown rush towards them, tearing tendrils and branches from the surrounding trees. He gently nudged the flight controls and the Storm Speeder banked hard, coming so close to the swell that branches whipped against the fuselage.

'We have passed the crash site,' crackled Sergeant Tanaro over the vox. *'Did you see the remains of the launch?'*

'Yes, sergeant,' replied Vultis. 'But the heat signals indicate the xenos have moved on.' He steered the Storm Speeder down an avenue of mountainous tree-trunks, the canopies of which were far out of sight, lost in the rain-pregnant clouds, just as the roots were hidden in the darkness below. The trees on Regium were not only unusual in their size and mobility. Many of the larger, more stable trees were clad in metal – seams of ore that seeped up through the bark, forming metal cankers and veining their leaves like sap. Vultis had left the stability of the coast before, making several excursions inland, but he had never grown used to the idea of trees that ebbed and flowed. Some of the locals claimed they could predict a swell, but off-worlders had to rely on quick reflexes.

The swell had almost passed now, but lashed out with a few parting strikes – trunks collided, booming against each other like waves on a cliff. Vultis had anticipated these surges and steered the vehicle higher, flying over the tumult and back down into calmer regions.

The clouds, after threatening for hours, finally emptied, turning the forest into a steel-grey blur and making it feel even more like they were flying through an ocean. The sound of rain hitting leaves merged with the crashing of the swell to create a seamless, thunderous din. It sounded like the forest was growling at them.

'This weather could be a problem,' said Baraca, looking down through the rain at the distant forest floor. 'The swell could easily return. We should land.'

Vultis nodded. 'I will look for a clearing.' He opened a vox-link.

'I am preparing to land, Sergeant Tanaro.' Visibility was terrible but navigation runes on Vultis' helm display identified possible options. He waited a moment to be sure the swell had passed, then he nudged the controls and the Storm Speeder dived into the darkness with the others following. Vultis had never landed this deep in the forest before and, as the shadows engulfed him, he felt like he was descending into an underworld. The idea triggered others, reminding him of the mythical tales in which heroes made a journey into hellish netherworlds. There was something odd about the train of thought. His mind was not prone to wandering and, unlike Baraca, he had no interest in legends, but the idea seemed strangely significant. He drove it away with logic, thinking back over his experiments with the symbiont, looking for connections he might have missed.

'Is that a clearing?' asked Baraca.

As he steered towards the area Baraca had indicated, Vultis saw something. 'Movement at eleven o'clock. It is not flowing in the same direction as the branches. Is that the swell?'

'I see it,' replied Tanaro over the vox. *'Too small and fast to be the swell.'*

Vultis stared at the shape. It was little more than a blur, like a raindrop magnifying the leaves behind.

'None of the native animals have a chromatic carapace,' said Vultis. 'They are unable to employ this kind of camouflage.'

'But if it was a tyranid, I doubt we would have seen it,' said Baraca.

'Unless it *wanted* to be seen.' Vultis looked around the shadowy trees. 'Unless it wanted to prevent us noticing something else.' He saw another blur, rippling through the leaves. This one was closer and faster. 'Like *that.*'

'Apothecary Biologis,' said Sergeant Tanaro. *'Land and take cover.'*

Before Vultis could reply, another shape rushed towards the

Storm Speeder. He shoved the control yoke forwards, tipping the vehicle into a dive.

The shape hurtled overhead, missing them by a few feet as Baraca snatched his bolt pistol from his belt and took aim.

Vultis hauled the flyer out of the dive. 'No. We want them alive.'

He brought the speeder round in a wide arc, narrowly avoiding the other Storm Speeders.

'There!' said Baraca, pointing his gun. 'Another.' He leant forwards against his restraints. 'You only need *one* alive.'

This one was rushing at them head-on, about to collide with the speeder's nose. Vultis yanked the controls again, flipping the flyer onto its wing tip so the shape hurtled past its undercarriage. For a moment he saw the creature, its camouflage slipping at the instant of attack, revealing four, scythe-shaped talons and segmented body parts. It was unmistakably a tyranid. But he also spotted something else. 'This is not the correct specimen.'

Baraca twisted in his seat and opened fire, filling the cabin with noise and bolt shells.

The shape tumbled in the air and became fully visible. Baraca's bolt-rounds had torn its abdomen and it dropped through the darkness.

'You were not given the order to fire,' said Vultis, bringing the flyer round.

'No wings,' muttered Baraca, ignoring him. 'But did you see its legs?' He peered into the darkness, studying the monolithic tree-trunks. 'It *jumped* at us.'

Vultis looked around. They were surrounded by branches and tendrils. 'Possibly. Let me set this thing down so I can examine the remains.'

There were no more attacks as the speeders looped towards the forest floor. Landing gear sank into knee-deep mulch and the ground belched as the Ultramarines unfastened their restraints and climbed from their seats. They kept their pistols raised and trained on the surrounding shadows as they dropped down into the mud.

They communicated in silence, using hand gestures. Sergeant Tanaro ordered some of his men to fan out and guard the perimeter of the clearing while others hid the Storm Speeders, cutting down branches with their combat knives.

When they were done, Sergeant Tanaro crossed the clearing to join Vultis and Baraca. *Which way?* he signalled.

Vultis nodded to a gap between the trees that opened onto a path.

Tanaro hesitated. *Ambush?* he queried.

Vultis thought, then indicated that they approach the spot from different directions.

Tanaro signalled his agreement, and they left the clearing.

Full darkness enveloped them and even Vultis' enhanced vision struggled to reach more than a few paces ahead. He blinked runes across his helm display, triggering night scopes in the eye-lenses, transforming the darkness into a blood-red swirl. He had his pistol raised in one hand and his combat knife gripped in his other. Now, even more than in his laboratorium, he felt at home. He was equipped with the finest armour and weaponry the Imperium could supply, but when the violence hit, it was his reflexes and his strength that would keep him alive. Often, his mind was elsewhere, recalling facts, searching for correlations and causality, but here, in the wild, he was utterly present, feeling every beat of his pulse, hearing every breath of the wind, feeling the forest teeming around him. The darkness was full of sounds – the scratching, scuttling and fluttering of the things that lived on the ground, competing with the whistling, prattling and cawing of the birds overhead. And there was a deeper sound, behind the bickering of the wildlife – a low, rumbling, gurgling sound, like bubbles breaking in mud.

As he advanced, his suit's auto-senses tracked Baraca and the others, showing them as blinking glyphs on the helm display, but it also revealed other life signs in the trees around him. Vultis had studied the local fauna at length, categorising the various species in a more scientific manner than the locals, who labelled most denizens of the forest as spirits, weaving complex mythologies around them but rarely studying their biology.

He paused under a low-hanging branch and studied the shapes blinking across his display. The nearest was serpentine and fast-moving, winding towards him through the mud. He stared into the darkness and saw a pale shape. A venomous snake. It posed no threat to an Ultramarine, but to an unmodified human the venom could be lethal. He disregarded it and studied the second shape. It was a pack of wild canids. They were circling the area, clearly after something. He thought for a moment, following their movements. Scavengers, he decided. And not foolish enough to attack. So why were they circling? Had they spotted the tyranid Baraca shot? Were they waiting to drag the carcass away? If so, they might regret it. Tyranid blood would burn through them in seconds.

He tracked the glyphs denoting his battle-brothers. Sergeant Tanaro, Baraca and some of the others were heading towards the canids. But there was no sign of Brothers Thracius and Silvium. Their glyphs had vanished from his display. He blinked, adjusting the calibration, but there was still no sign of them. He could have opened the vox-channel, but he was reluctant to speak aloud. A clinging mist tumbled across the ground, hazing everything it covered and muffling the sounds of the forest. He had the feeling he was being watched.

Unable to see Thracius or Silvium, Vultis headed after Baraca and the others, following a broad, muddy track up a slope and back down into a narrow gulley. The ground grew wetter and the mist grew so thick as to be almost impenetrable. The sounds of the forest became strange and distant. When traces of light broke through from the distant canopy, they flickered across the tumbling mist, creating the illusion of figures and grasping arms. Vultis could see how minds less logical than his own could have imagined this was the domain of spectral beings.

He paused as he saw an area of deeper darkness near the stump of a fallen tree. He approached carefully. It was a carcass, the remains of a canid, larger than a man, possibly from the pack he had seen earlier on his helm display. He would have liked to have taken a sample of the acid that was hissing on its bones, but the whole mess dissolved as he watched, oozing quickly into the ground. There was something troubling about it. It was almost as if the ground itself were digesting the animal. He looked around and saw fragments of bone and hair where other creatures had rotted in the same way.

A new sound rose from the mist – a slow, repetitive *thud*, like someone beating a distant drum. He clambered up out of the gulley, through a low place in a wall of bracken and entered another clearing. There was a movement behind one of the tree-trunks and he dropped into a fighting stance, aiming his pistol as he advanced.

The mist was so heavy that it took him a moment to recognise that the shape was an Ultramarine, hanging upside down a few feet above the ground and swaying from side to side.

He edged closer, still resisting the urge to use his vox as he circled the trunk. It was Brother Silvium. He had been hung from a low branch. The knocking sound was his armour tapping against the bark as he swayed back and forth. He was dead. A large section of his power armour had been destroyed and his innards had been ripped out, left to dangle over his face. And there were shapes nestling in his corpse, pale and twitching as they burrowed through his exposed organs. Vultis edged closer, gun raised, and saw that they were tyranids but even smaller than the symbiont – no bigger than his thumb yet feeding with such a fury that Silvium's corpse was trembling.

Vultis cursed silently. The death of a battle-brother was always a tragedy. There were centuries of knowledge and skill in this single warrior. But for Silvium to have died so quickly and silently was shocking.

'Brother-Apothecary Vultis,' said Sergeant Tanaro, speaking quietly over the vox. 'You need to see this.'

Vultis found Tanaro kneeling silently in a clearing, picking at Brother Thracius' corpse. Baraca and the others were nearby, crouching in the undergrowth, guns raised as they watched the surrounding forest. The dead Ultramarine's left side was intact, but the other half of him had melted, flowing into the mud just like the canid, his face barely recognisable as it bubbled inside his helmet.

As Vultis walked over, Tanaro held up a piece of Thracius' burnt flesh. Part of his face. There was a thin trail of smoke drifting up from it where it had been splashed by acid. Vultis removed his helmet and sniffed. Then he nodded at Sergeant Tanaro, who nodded back and dropped the meat. The acid was tyranid blood – and there was more of it scattered around the clearing. The tyranid had killed Thracius here and moved on. Vultis put his helmet back on and looked around the clearing. Again, he thought how incredible it was that an Ultramarines veteran had been killed in silence and with such apparent ease. A gloom descended over the squad. They all felt the shame of the loss.

Vultis saw faint heat traces on the other side of the clearing where there was an opening leading into the trees. It looked like the creature had landed, bled, then leapt a dozen feet or so, slipping back into the forest.

The squad crossed the clearing, bolt pistols raised, and headed into the trees. Mist swelled around them, as though trying to block their way.

They followed a trail of broken branches, but then, to Vultis' frustration, the heat signs vanished and there was no clue to the tyranid's route. The signal from the canids was still visible on his helm display though. They were heading north-east, away from him. Perhaps they were tracking the tyranid Baraca had injured, determined to be on hand if it finally died.

He signalled to the others, telling them to keep watch on the surrounding trees. Then he removed his helmet again, closed his eyes and sniffed. Even as a youth, before he was remade by the Chapter's Apothecaries, Vultis had learned how to use all of his senses on a hunt. His parents had taught him to harness every tool at his disposal in his battle for survival. But now, as he sniffed the forest air, he employed sensory powers that an unmodified human could never dream of. He could smell prey. He could hear the hearts of rodents hiding in the carpet of leaves. He could taste blood, rushing through the veins of bats whirling overhead. He could sense the myriad life forms digging and clawing through the soil. And then, after a few seconds, he could smell something that had no place in the forest: the acrid stench of tyranid blood, oozing from a fresh wound and seething in the mist.

This way, he signalled, locking his helmet to his belt and leading the way down a narrow crevasse, lined with thorny undergrowth and drooping fronds. They carried on like this for nearly half an hour, fighting through the forest with all the stealth they could manage, Vultis focused entirely on his prey, tasting crushed leaves and catching scents that hung in the darkness, while Tanaro, Baraca and the others followed close behind, watching their surroundings down the barrels of their guns. As they advanced, they saw more butchered animals, torn apart and dissolving into the ground. Then, as suddenly as if a door had closed, the scent vanished, snuffed out like a candle.

They were in another clearing, dwarfed by the trunks that circled it. They stood thinking for a moment, at a loss, until Baraca tapped the side of his helmet, indicating that Vultis should listen. Vultis could hear the usual sounds of the forest: the noises of animals fleeing from their approach, or else occupied with business of their own, and the patter of raindrops on leaves. Then he noticed something new and understood what Baraca was suggesting. He could hear running water not far from where they were standing – just over the brow of the next incline by the sounds of it. It sounded like a forest stream. They climbed the slope until they saw the stream spread out below them. It looped and wound through the darkness, rushing down over a few small drops before joining a larger concourse further on. They followed the water until it met the larger river, but then Vultis was unsure how to proceed. The wounded tyranid might have carried on in the river, heading downstream, but it might equally have doubled back and headed upstream in the larger river. Or it might even have climbed up on the opposite bank and headed back into the trees.

They waded through the thick, weed-clogged water and clambered up onto the other side. There was still no obvious sign of any tracks or blood, so Vultis took some of the diagnostic equipment from the power pack on his back and began scanning the mud for things his eyes might have missed. This was not the work of a few stowaways. One or two tyranids could not have slaughtered two Ultramarines with such ease, not to mention the piles of steaming animal carcasses that lay everywhere he looked.

Baraca waved them over to a stand of trees, pointing at something. 'The locals are brave,' he said quietly. He tapped a tree-stump. 'Who would have thought they would venture this deep into the forest?'

He was standing next to a kind of sculpture, a totem that had been carved from the stump.

'Is that meant to be the Emperor?' asked Tanaro, peering at the carving. It was a figure seated in a gnarled, wooden throne. He was wearing ornate armour that was a stylised rendering of Adeptus Astartes power armour and he was also holding a flaming sword, but he had a third eye in his forehead, larger than the other two, and the rest of the sculpture was a spiral of root-like loops and whirls that tumbled out of the third eye. In some places animal teeth had been pushed into the wood – huge incisors, taken from predators and incorporated into the design. 'It looks more like a tree spirit.'

'But look how well made it is,' said Baraca, crouching to study the thing more closely and pressing his gauntleted hand to the surface, as though communing with the icon. 'And consider the danger the artist would have been in while working here. The forest teems with predators. Whoever did this would have been lucky to get this far without being poisoned or mauled. Or caught up in one of the swells. And then they spent hours making something this intricate.'

Tanaro shrugged. 'There is no accounting for religious zealots.'

Vultis was about to reply when Tanaro noticed something in the trees. He raised his pistol, causing the others to do the same, but then he grunted. 'Just another totem.'

Vultis squinted into the darkness and saw it. It was larger than the first but similar in shape.

'Wayside shrines,' said Baraca. 'I learned of them in the Library of Carnus. The locals build them as waymarkers, leading to their "gods", the old geoengines.'

Vultis shook his head. Baraca's interest in local customs seemed odd, even to him. 'It is irrelevant,' he said.

Tanaro nodded in agreement, quoting the Codex Astartes with as much gravitas as if he were on a stage. 'Know your purpose. Then direct every thought and deed to it.' But Baraca was not listening. He had already walked over to the totem and begun examining the carvings.

'We have to retrace our steps,' said Vultis. 'We will just have to…' His words trailed off as he noticed a familiar scent. 'Tyranid blood,' he muttered, seeing that part of the totem had been recently scorched by something brushing past it.

Baraca laughed. It echoed oddly through the mist. 'See? Tree gods have led us to our prey.'

Vultis was busy looking for scorch-marks on the ground ahead, but he glanced back. 'You speak in jest but sometimes it sounds as if you really *do* believe in gods.'

'I do *not* believe in gods, as you well know. But I believe we would be lost if not for the religion of the person who built these shrines.' He took a tooth from the stump and waved it. 'I have faith in *faith*.'

Baraca had always played the part of fatalist and mystic, but Vultis was starting to think it was more than an affectation.

'An Ultramarine puts his faith in reason,' warned Tanaro. 'And in self-mastery. Not in providence and symbols. You would do well to remember that, Brother Baraca.'

'More blood,' said Vultis, hurrying on down the track.

'And look down there,' said Baraca, pointing out a tall shape. 'Another waymarker.'

They had only taken a few more steps when a resounding

boom echoed through the forest. They halted and looked at each other. 'Another swell?' said Vultis. 'So soon after the other one?'

'Anything is possible on Regium,' said Baraca. 'And if we remain down here we will be torn apart. We need to get back to the speeders.'

Vultis shook his head, looking at the spots of steaming acid on the path. 'We could lose these tracks for good.'

Baraca thought for a moment. 'Geoengines remain motionless when the swells hit. I read that in the library, too. They are the only stable points in the forest. That is partly why the locals used to pray to them.'

'So we could shelter inside one of them?' asked Vultis.

Tanaro shrugged. 'A reasonable idea. Did you ever look inside the one we destroyed at Zarax? It was vast.'

There was another booming sound, even louder this time.

'That sounds close,' said Baraca. 'I doubt we could make it back to the Storm Speeder now even if we tried. And it would seem that our prey is also headed to the geoengine.'

Vultis fixed his helm back on and used the display to scan the darkness. 'The geoengine is close. A few minutes away at most.'

'Advance,' said Tanaro, and the squad ran on, still tracking the trees through their gunsights.

They passed the next shrine with barely a glance, though Vultis noticed it was grander than the previous two and clad in plates of rusty metal. A few minutes later they saw a huge silhouette looming up ahead. It was even larger than Vultis expected. In the darkness of the forest it looked like a hive city, like Salamis – an enormous, rusting mass that soared up through the canopy and threw the forest into an even deeper gloom.

'How could the locals ever have mistaken these structures for trees?' he said as they came closer to it. It was similar to an amphora in shape, rounded and swollen-looking. It was clad in roots, vines and trees, but there were many places where its original surface was still visible – patches of red rust punctuating the undergrowth – and the design was far too symmetrical to be a tree.

Nothing seemed able to grow within a few hundred feet of it and Vultis and Baraca found themselves running in the open across a dazzling expanse of sun-splashed mud. The forest was boiling behind them as they ran towards the huge shape, but they were only halfway across the clearing when Vultis spotted something.

He halted, raised a hand in warning and pointed his pistol at shapes in the mud.

There were corpses scattered across the ground. He approached with caution, and as he reached them, he saw that they were humans, civilians, wearing the white, rune-stitched robes of the native priesthood. Their swords were lying in the grass and their bodies were a blistered mess. They had been torn apart and scorched by bio-acid, their limbs and organs strewn across the blood-soaked mud. It must have been a frenzied attack. The body parts led all the way to the foot of the iron tree.

'The tyranid attacked then entered,' said Baraca, speaking over the vox-network rather than shouting over the din coming from behind them. 'And the geoengine is as vast as a warship. There will be many places to hide.'

'Keep moving,' voxed Tanaro in reply. He gestured to the oncoming swell. Trees were whirling up from the ground in a tornado of branches and roots, turning the forest into an ear-splitting maelstrom.

They ran past the final few corpses and, as they approached the structure, saw broad steps leading up between roots the size of hab-blocks. The servos in their power armour responded as they sprinted hard up the steps, taking them three at a time, heading towards a pair of massive double doors at the top.

The air filled with whirling leaves, and branches bounced off their armour as they ran. The ground was juddering as though in the grip of an earthquake.

Then they reached the threshold and dashed inside, entering through a smaller door cut into the base of the larger ones.

Baraca slammed the door shut behind them and slid bolts across while the rest of the squad scanned the room for danger. They were in a huge chamber that resembled a cavern hammered from rusty metal. There were tubular shapes lining the walls that must once have been pipes but were now so corroded they were almost indistinguishable from the roots and branches that crossed them. If the room had a ceiling it was too high to make out, and there were no windows of any kind. The illumination came from overhead – shafts of sunlight that lanced down through the sweltering air and bounced off angles in the walls, hanging suspended like strands of gossamer.

Vultis could see nothing moving as he paced back and forth, his gun trained on the shadows. The doors rattled and clanged but held firm as the trees howled outside. He approached the nearest wall and saw people looking back at him from the metal, arms and legs spread as if they had been crucified. 'Sculptures?' he asked, tapping one with the muzzle of his gun.

Baraca checked the door one last time then walked over to look. 'Burials,' he said. 'This is how the locals used to dispose of their dead. They nailed them to the inside of these places and the metal preserves the remains.'

The doors clattered again and the forest roared outside.

'Are you sure these sites are unaffected by the swell?' said Vultis, looking around the juddering walls.

Sergeant Tanaro nodded. 'They were built to terraform the planet. Lieutenant Castamon referred to them as *calefaction pumps*. They plunge right down to the core of the planet. The original colonists used them to bring heat to the surface.'

Vultis backed away from the fossilised bodies and surveyed the room. 'There are too many egress points. We must see if we can–'

Baraca silenced him by pointing to something dark on the ground. They approached it with caution and saw that it was blood – not the seething acid left by tyranids but normal, human blood. There was a lot of it, more than could reasonably come from one person, and it was smeared across the ground, leading to one of the doorways that led off the entrance chamber. They followed it across the room and, with the swell still screaming outside, headed deeper into the building.

Chapter Ten

The Guardsman howled in his sleep, bucking against his restraints, then slumped and grew still, his chin on his chest.

'Have you killed him?' demanded Beltis, striding across the interrogation cell.

'Don't touch him!' snapped Semler, her chirurgeon – a grubby little man with a tonsure and a wet-lipped pout. 'He's still wired up.' He pulled a lever on the device the Guardsman was strapped to, and a motor died. Then he pulled a strip of parchment from a slot on the side of the machine, peered at it and handed it to Beltis. 'I don't think he's dead, but either way, he's not going to tell you much now. This is what I extracted. Looks like gibberish.'

'It's not gibberish, you idiot, it's just written in High Gothic.'

'You can speak High Gothic?'

'Of course not. But I've seen that phrase before. In my father's library.' The thought of her father gave her a rush of grief. He was still where she'd left him, crawling in his own muck and feasting on grubs. She had not been able to bring herself to tell

121

Semler, or anyone else, the truth. She tried to stay focused on the matter at hand, holding up the slip of parchment. 'This is all he knew?'

'It's all that made sense from his so-called vision. If you ask me, he was as deranged as all the others.' He grimaced, waving vaguely to indicate the streets outside. Even up here, at the top of her father's hab-stack, they could still hear the sounds of rioting and gunfire. Port Dura had lost its grip on reality. The streets were full of lunacy and blood.

'The Great Devourer.' She looked closely at the text again. 'That *does* mean something.' She looked at Semler. 'Come with me.' She headed to the door. 'I'm going to need your help with something sensitive.'

The library was locked and barred. It was a quirk of her father's nature that he kept records and accounts, even of his most unlawful activities. For an average small-time crook, such punctiliousness would be dangerous, but it was a point of pride for Gathas Kulm that he had no need to worry about the authorities uncovering his crimes. He was the true governor of Regium and everyone knew it.

Beltis punched in the access codes and they entered a large, circular room, lined with cogitator banks, bookcases and glass-fronted cabinets. The exterior of the hab-stack was as dilapidated as the rest of Port Dura, but inside it was as grand as anything in the Governor's Palace at Salamis. There were desks at the centre of the room, each with an ornate table-lumen, and there were couches next to the books and logic engines, covered in furs and throws. But despite its grandeur, the place had an abandoned air. There was dust on all the surfaces and the lumens were all dark.

On the opposite side of the room, a large, curved window

looked out onto a forest of anchorage spars, warehouses and refineries. Beltis glanced at the chronograph on her wrist, surprised to see how dark it was outside. 'Where's the damned sky,' she muttered, marching over to the window. As she crossed the room, with Semler scuttling after her, she flicked some of the lumens on, punctuating the gloom with cones of amber light. When she reached the window, she saw that the sky was not just dark, it was moving. Port Dura was always bathed in smog, but this was different. The sky looked almost liquid. And things seemed to be snaking through it. She rubbed her eyes and frowned, realising she had not slept for days. 'I need to get some rest.' She looked lower and saw that many of the hab-blocks were burning. And there was no sign of anyone coming to do anything about it. Lower still, she could see flashes of gunfire in the transitway that passed the building.

'You said you needed me?' said Semler, looking anxiously at the scenes outside.

'Soon,' she snapped, striding over to a case full of data reels. She ran her fingers down a stack of cartridges labelled by hand with her father's messy scrawl. She tapped one. 'This is it.' She fished the cartridge out, headed over to a desk and slotted the cartridge into a cogitator. The machine rumbled into life and she heard the tape spooling inside. Then a luminous green hololith shimmered into view, hanging in the air in front of her face.

The image was a blurry mess of static and white noise. She muttered to herself as she turned the cogitator's dials. The image remained fuzzy, but the sound improved a little – enough that she could make out most of the words. The footage showed one of Mars' red-robed tech-priests. His face was hidden inside an embroidered hood, but she could tell by the way his robes hung that he was more machine than human, with pistons and clamps in place of hands and a beard of plastek pipes hanging down from his hood. He spent the first five minutes describing his position in the hierarchy of the Martian priesthood, speaking in a droning monotone. Beltis shook her head and wound the recording forwards. The magos was now describing, in exhaustive detail the specifications of the recording device he was using. She wound the recording back and forwards several times until she found what she was looking for:

'There are spore-filled clouds, mass hallucinations and outbreaks of citywide psychosis. This planetwide hysteria and rioting seems catastrophic, but it is, in truth, only a prelude of the full horror that is to follow. Once a planet's biosphere has been fully poisoned, the predatory xenos begin their invasion in earnest. By that stage there is little to no chance of survival for the local populace. Small groups of scout organisms give way to far larger numbers of warrior breeds, organic artillery and organisms that have evolved for the sole purpose of digesting biomass. The Great Devourer transforms the planet's flora and fauna into an easily digestible slurry and begins to feed. This orgy of consumption does not cease until the planet has become a barren husk. Then, glutted on its feast, the Great Devourer continues on to the next world, and so on, and so on.'

Beltis struggled to breathe as the magos described scenes of absolute desolation. 'This is it. This is what's happening to Regium.' She skimmed backwards and forwards again, desperately hoping that she was wrong, but the more she heard, the surer she was of Regium's fate. The magos then began listing the appropriate devices for displaying the message, describing every setting and interface in mind-numbing detail. He seemed more concerned with how to get the best playback quality than the apocalypse he had just described.

Beltis was about to give up in despair, when a static-hazed comment leapt out at her: *'The process of consumption is surprisingly fast. The tyrannic host is drawn to biomass as a moth is drawn to a flame. Escape craft are easily detected and consumed before they reach the upper atmosphere although occasionally, small, single craft manage to break through the pall unseen as the host focuses its appetite on larger prey.'*

'The *Barbalissus*,' she whispered.

'What?' whispered Semler.

She looked back at him. His face was grey and there were tears in his eyes. He looked like he was about to collapse. The sight of him, looking so pathetic, made Beltis realise she was being almost as pitiful. She took a deep breath. 'The *Barbalissus*. My father's shuttle. She's like nothing else on the planet. If anything could escape this...' She faltered, thinking again of the awful, droning revelations she had just heard. 'If anything could make it off-world it would be her. She's fast and light.'

Semler mouthed in silence, shaking his head, then managed to grasp what she was saying. 'A ship? You're saying we could escape this...' He gestured at the frozen image of the magos. 'Escape the things he just said.'

'We?' She pictured her father, cursing at cockroaches. 'Actually, yes, perhaps I *do* need you.'

He grasped her arm, tears now flowing freely down his face. 'Beltis. I swear I will never forget–'

She silenced him with a glare. 'But I'm not getting on a ship with a raving idiot.'

He nodded, looking even more panicked. 'Forgive me.' He looked at the spectral magos. 'But he said the Great Devourer surrounds the planet. If we flew up to one of the orbital platforms we'd be heading straight into the invasion.'

'I don't mean we'd just fly up into the alien swarm and then stop there. We wouldn't just go to an orbital platform. The *Barbalissus* could reach the augur station at Crozea Point. From there we could refuel and make it to the shipyards at Gabris.

And if we make it that far, we could buy passage on a Chartist freighter. We could leave the solar system. We could leave the whole subsector.'

'We have to tell the others,' muttered Semler.

Beltis took her laspistol out and lashed out, slamming the handle into his face. He crumpled in a spray of blood, clutching at his temples.

She calmly flipped the pistol round and, as he looked up at her, confused and afraid, pointed the muzzle at his face. 'Do you think we should tell other people what our plan is?'

He frowned, looking at the blood on his fingers then at the shimmering magos. 'No?'

'Correct. *Why* will we not tell anyone what we're planning?'

He continued frowning. 'Because only a single ship will have a chance of going unnoticed.'

'Only a single ship, Semler.' She holstered her pistol. 'Remember that. If Tirol or any of those other worms know about this' – she waved at the hololith – 'there will be a scramble for ships. Before we know it there will be a whole flotilla trying to get to Crozea Point. Quickly followed by a feeding frenzy as those… those *things* up there see us all coming.' She wandered over to the window, looking up at the shapes swelling overhead. 'Tell *no one*, Semler. Or I'll hurt you in ways that make those aliens seem harmless.'

Chapter Eleven

SAMNIUM PROVINCE, REGIUM

Confessor Thurgau rose from his chair and bowed graciously to the other passengers in the hosting chamber. Governor Seroc stood slowly and grudgingly, heaving his bulk from the chair and holding his lho-stick behind his back. He performed a barely imperceptible bow and then dropped heavily back down, continuing his whispered conversation with his aide. They were both looking through a viewport at a storm that was building outside. Down below, rumbling along a coast road, an armoured column ploughed through the rain – tanks, personnel carriers, mobile artillery platforms and ancillary vehicles churning through the mud, proudly bearing the insignia of the Cadian 401st regiment as they headed north to Salamis. The vehicles were flanked by squads of troopers and support staff who jogged in such perfect, seamless blocks that they were almost indistinguishable from the tanks.

'It's an edifying sight, is it not?' said Thurgau. There were menials, aides and servitors bustling around the room, but he only addressed the governor, speaking in his most reassuring tones. 'We will set everything to rights. I have no doubt. Salamis will continue to be the beating heart of Regium and the entire Sanctus Line.'

The governor nodded, but he seemed distracted, looking away from the Cadians to the clouds gathering overhead.

'You are in safe hands,' said Thurgau. 'And the Emperor is with us. I see Him in you, you know. As clear as anything. Our burden is His burden. His strength is our strength.'

Seroc nodded but looked unimpressed, still studying the weather. 'I have never seen clouds like this.' He turned to his aide. 'Have you?'

She shook her head, looking as dour as he did.

'We will see some strange things in the days ahead,' said Thurgau. 'Lieutenant Castamon warned us of that. But have faith. We can ride out any kind of storm.' The governor and his aide gave no sign that they had heard him, so he decided it was a good time to leave. 'I must reflect and pray before we arrive, so please excuse me.'

Servants placed vestments over his shoulders and handed him his sceptre, then he left the room and headed down a passageway towards his cabin. His closest assistant was at his side, a ruddy-faced brute named Wroth, who had served in the Ministorum for longer than Thurgau had been alive, working as one of its most devout preachers. Thurgau had risen to his prominent position through his skills as a politician and his connections in the holy synod, but when force of a more physical kind was required, it was Wroth he turned to. Everything about the man was huge: fists, belly, shoulders, voice and faith. His robes were as luxurious and delicately embroidered as Thurgau's, but they could not disguise his savagery. His eyes were small and flinty, there were religious sigils tattooed across his cheeks, and he looked like he could face down a herd of stampeding cattle.

'Governor Seroc should show you some respect,' said Wroth, his voice rolling up from his deep chest.

Thurgau gave him a warning glance, indicating that he should keep his voice down. 'We must make allowances. He was raised on this world, remember. We should he grateful he doesn't plant trees in his skin. What chance did he have, really, to be normal? Until we came here he had probably never met anyone from outside this system.'

'That's no excuse for disrespecting a senior prelate,' continued Wroth, speaking in the same bellowing voice. 'If he doesn't respect Ministorum protocol, what other matters of faith does he neglect? The man's one bad choice away from heresy.'

'Aren't we all?' warned Thurgau as he waited for a servant to unlock the door to his cabin. Only once they were inside, and alone, did he continue. 'I have my doubts about him too, if I'm honest.' He poured them both some wine. 'There's a feverish look in his eye that I do not like. He looks too proud. He thinks about his own petty struggles, when he should be thinking of…' He gestured to a shrine in the corner of the room, showing the God-Emperor writhing in agony on His Throne. 'Wider conflicts.'

Wroth gave a grudging sigh and the two of them sat down at the small table in the centre of the cabin. They sat like that for an hour, discussing what they had learned from the governor about the problems in Salamis. Then, as the storm outside the viewport grew even darker, Thurgau asked Wroth to leave, saying they both needed to spend some time in prayer. Before he left, the two men stood at the viewport, studying the weather.

'I have *never* seen clouds like that,' said Wroth.

Thurgau nodded. The clouds were dark and fast-moving, but higher than storm clouds usually were. And oddly seamless – as smooth as a blanket. It was as if the world were being shrouded. 'It is beginning,' he said, touching the medallion that hung at his chest – the starred skull symbol of the Adeptus Ministorum. 'But if the Emperor wills it, we shall endure.'

'Why would the Emperor *not* will it? Why would He want Regium to fall?'

Thurgau smiled. 'Answer your own question. How many times have you explained this in your sermons? We cannot seek to understand the ways of the God-Emperor. He is unknowable. He may have decided that the Ultramarines and the Militarum regiments will save Regium. But if events go otherwise, it does not mean the Emperor has been bested – it simply means He is working towards goals we do not comprehend. The ultimate victory will be His, as long as we remain true.'

Wroth looked flustered and snarled his reply. 'You're saying you think Regium might fall?'

'I'm saying we should never presume to know the will of the Emperor. And we must be ready to face whatever comes.' He smiled again and nodded to the door. 'I suggest you get some rest before we reach Salamis. From what Governor Seroc told us, I think we're going to have our work cut out for us.'

Once he was alone, Thurgau drained his cup and crossed the room to a void-crate. It was covered in a cloth that was as beautifully worked as his robes. He pulled it gently away from the box, folded it and placed it on the table, whispering a prayer as he did so. Then he glanced at the door before unlocking the crate and opening it. It was stuffed with vestments and sacred objects: small, metal shrines; a scrimshawed skull; a vial of blood; a metal casket containing fragments of stone that had once been on Holy Terra, touched by air that might have touched the God-Emperor Himself. Thurgau carefully moved the objects aside and took out a small, teardrop-shaped bottle, no larger than his fist. He closed the crate and sat on the edge of his bunk. His pulse quickened as he considered what was about to happen. It was dangerous, performing the rite in such a small, crowded transport, but he could see no option. He had to know what the Emperor's plan for him was. He had to know what he needed to do when he landed at the hive. He glanced at the door again, then very carefully removed the stopper from the bottle and sipped the liquid inside. He placed the bottle on a table next to his bunk and lay back, loosening his collar and resting his head on the pillow.

At first, the only effect was a pleasant warmth that spread from his chest to the rest of his body, flushing down his limbs into his fingers and toes. 'What do I offer you?' he whispered, closing his eyes. 'My blood, my soul.' He repeated the words, focusing on the familiar rhythm of the catechism as the warmth in his veins grew, becoming a bright heat that snatched his breath. Slowly, relentlessly, the heat became a terrible burning. Tears welled in his eyes. They were tears of pain but also of ecstasy. It was the heat of divinity. The tincture had opened his mind to the gaze of a god. He was burning in the light of the Emperor's divine magnificence.

His body began to convulse as the tincture poisoned him, but even as he lost control of his material form, Thurgau's grip on his spirit form grew stronger. The pain was dreadful, but it was a price worth paying. By drinking the tincture he tormented his flesh, but he also allowed his spirit to reach out and touch the divine. 'My blood, my soul,' he repeated. His voice grew husky but the words remained sure. The pain grew until he thought he could endure no more, but then, at the very pinnacle of the agony, he reached the eye of the storm. He could no longer feel the bunk beneath him and, when he opened his eyes, the cabin had vanished.

Thurgau was adrift in an incandescent sea. Torrents of gold and silver enveloped him. He tumbled like flotsam. Faces emerged from the currents, serene and determined – the faces of those who had given their lives to serve the Emperor, burning like candles as they radiated His divine essence from Holy Terra. Most of the spirits were absorbed in their work, projecting the Emperor's light with every drop of their lives, but a few managed to acknowledge him, compassion and gratitude flashing in their eyes as they looked his way. In these moments, as he swam in the Emperor's light, Thurgau felt a sense of fraternity unlike anything he had ever experienced in the material world. He was one with the Emperor, marching with His host. One day soon, when his chance came, he would be able to leave his mortal flesh and reside here forever, burning with all the purity of the others. And the moment was close now. He had felt it as soon as he landed on Regium. A lifetime of patience was about to be rewarded. He was about to ascend.

The light swelled, becoming so bright that he could no longer see the spirits; no longer see anything. Then a new vista swam into view. He was on a plain before a steep-sided valley. For a moment he thought he was seeing a gateway to the Emperor's heavenly abode – a fortress beyond the knowledge of His mortal servants. But he quickly realised the valley was on Regium. He could see the vast, glittering expanse of the Argentum Forest behind the rocks. He was raised up from the ground, riding in a battle tank, holding a banner aloft as the vehicle splashed through churned-up mud. There was an army massed behind him, roaring, all of them, their voices raised in tribute to the Emperor as they charged. Then, as he saw what lay ahead, he almost faltered. A multitude was swarming from the valley: misbegotten horrors, like chitinous insects but as tall as men or, in many cases, even larger – lumbering, juddering colossi, hazed by spore clouds. He could not comprehend the nightmare that was flooding across the plain. *Is this what you want of me? To face this?* Even Thurgau, devout as he was, felt a moment of doubt.

His question was answered as he watched the scene play out. The army rushed towards the monsters with him leading the way, banner trailing as the tank crashed into a wave of claws, mandibles and pulsing flesh. He watched as he was torn down by the creatures, dismembered and devoured; but rather than being routed, the army was inspired by his death – it drove them into a righteous fury so great that even the alien host could not stand before it. The xenos started to crumple under the savagery of the attack.

Then the scene faded, washed away by another pulse of light, and Thurgau saw himself again. This time, rather than leading a charge, he was mounted on a plinth. He was looking at a marble statue that portrayed the moment of his death, face raised to the heavens and banner held high as monsters tore into his body. The statue was in a great plaza, surrounded by steely-eyed warriors who were chanting his name – inspired and emboldened by his death.

'Martyrdom,' said Thurgau, finally understanding why he had been sent to Regium, finally understanding what the Emperor expected of him. Saying the word interrupted the rhythm of the catechism, but it no longer mattered. The pain had gone. Only the ecstasy remained. He opened his eyes and stared at the cracks in the ceiling. Everything was more vivid than before. As if the skin of the world had grown thin and miraculous light was leaking through, making everything wonderfully sharp. The Emperor's light was no longer confined to his visions; he could see it with his waking eyes, everywhere he looked.

'My blood,' he said, sobbing with happiness. 'My soul.' Then exhaustion overcame him, and he slipped into a dreamless sleep.

Chapter Twelve

COGNATION APPARATUS MMXCI, SAPIENTIS DATASTACK
EUM SEQUOR MUNITORUM FACILITY, PORT DURA

ISO 481 was hungry. The thought came as something of a shock because ISO 481 could not remember having *any* thoughts before. It tried to flee, to sink back into comfortable oblivion, but oblivion resisted. More thoughts emerged. It was terrifying and that led, in turn, to the idea of emotions. Along with terror came dread, grief, confusion, despair and, even worse, hope. Incredibly, none of these things, neither the thoughts nor the emotions, appeared in the form of zeros and ones. They were not data. They arrived magically, fully formed, inside ISO 481's head. The concept of a head was perhaps the most shocking of all. ISO 481 became aware that it had a head, or, rather, it *was* a head. The workings of the cognation apparatus pressed against it from all sides – cables and duct piping, circuit boards and power transformers – touching every inch of ISO 481's skin, defining the head's shape with hot, oily caresses. *I am alive,* thought ISO 481. *I am a head.*

As ISO 481 struggled with the enormity of these revelations, it sensed that there was something even more disconcerting waiting to reveal itself – a dark, looming presence behind the thoughts and emotions, a thing that was called memory. Not memory in the sense of processing power but actual memories. ISO 481 glimpsed hints of what lay in the darkness, images of a time when it was not an *it* but a *he* – a being who was more than just a head in the bowels of a vast machine; a man with limbs and a body, walking in the places *beyond* the cognation apparatus. This awful clue to what had been lost was too much to bear, so ISO 481 fled back to its first, shocking thought: it was hungry. The thought made little sense. ISO 481 had no body to sustain and it could feel nutrient pipes gurgling beneath its skull, nourishing its brain. But it could not escape the feeling of dreadful, bottomless hunger.

In an effort to understand, ISO 481 resumed its habitual function, processing the information that was squirted endlessly into its cerebrum, looking for correlations between pieces of data so that the wider apparatus could perform more efficiently. Even this seemingly familiar activity had been transformed. The zeros and ones had lost their anonymity. Where once they were a faceless puzzle, they now spoke clearly to ISO 481, telling a story of munitions plants and factorums, supply chains and weapons depots, of an entire city built around a space port. These places appeared in ISO 481's thoughts and ISO 481 realised it was not hungry for nutrients in a pipe, it was hungry for *everything*. It wanted to consume the things it had suddenly discovered so that it would no longer be horrified by them. ISO 481 felt a vague concern that doing such a thing might be somehow incorrect, but the answer to that lay in memories and ISO 481 was not ready to face those, so it focused on the matter at hand: how could it consume the things it had discovered? How could it end this awful hunger? How could it find peace?

ISO 481 studied the space port's buildings and equipment and realised that they were too hard to consume, too large and too brittle. It would need to soften them, to make them more digestible. As ISO 481 had this thought, it sensed that it was receiving help from another mind. A mind similar to its own that also wished to sate its hunger. The other mind was sympathetic. It was willing ISO 481 to succeed. *I can do this*, promised ISO 481, pleased to have found a friend.

ISO 481 did what it did best, analysing data and looking for connections, drawing on the great wealth of information that was flowing through the apparatus. Within seconds of realising it was alive, ISO 481 had found a way to feed itself and to feed its new friend. There were fuel reserves hidden beneath the manufactoria and armouries, and they were all connected. There were ancient tunnels linking them. If the temperature was raised in one of the fuel reserves, the fuel would become unstable and eventually detonate. The heat would then travel through the ancient tunnels to a great power generator buried beneath the city. And when the power generator combusted the resultant energy surge would pass through the city structures above and alter them. The space port would become edible and ready to digest. As would the biomass that moved around it.

There, interred in the darkness, ISO 481 remembered how to smile.

Chapter Thirteen

SAMNIUM PROVINCE, REGIUM

'It should be on the horizon any moment, my lord,' said the pilot, addressing Castamon over the vox.

The gunship was rumbling through low, leaden skies and it took Castamon a moment to spot Port Dura, up in the distance. The weather was dismal. Dark, heavy clouds and banks of rain clung to the aircraft, forcing the lieutenant to squint as he tried to make out the details. 'Smoke,' he said, pointing to dark columns that were rising from the distant city. 'Attempt to hail Port Master Soleb again.'

The pilot opened a different vox-channel and hailed the port, but the only answer was a squall of static. She shook her head. 'Still nothing, lieutenant.'

Abarim was seated at his side, but the Librarian was deep in thought and Castamon knew better than to disturb him. Since talking with Vultis, Abarim had been in a near trance. He had told Castamon he was attempting to locate the Harbinger or, at least, to understand why that name seemed so significant.

And the effort was consuming all his thoughts. The cowl on his armour burned with blue light that shimmered down the cables linking it to Abarim's brain.

The passenger compartment behind them was crowded with Regium Auxilia troops, carrying immaculate, polished lasguns and clad in a uniform almost identical to the one worn by the Ultramar Auxilia back on Macragge. He had considered bringing more Ultramarines but then decided against it. This was little more than a reconnaissance mission. No one had been able to contact Port Dura for the last twelve hours. All he needed to do was halt the rioting and ensure the space port's lasers were still operational.

As he looked back out at the distant city, Castamon realised he was mistaken – it was not raining; there was no water on the gunship's wings. But the air was unusually hazy, almost opaque. He had seen this before. 'Tyranid spores,' he said.

'Lieutenant?' asked the pilot, glancing back from the flight controls.

'Is there a place to land?' he replied, looking down at dark swathes of forest.

'There is a clearing, lieutenant, on the crown of the next rise. Half a mile to the south-east of us.' She tapped a viewscreen. 'Will that do?'

Castamon nodded. 'I need to examine the air.'

They were halfway to the hill when the world turned white. Regium's greys and greens vanished, replaced by dazzling light that caused the pilot to gasp and shield her eyes. The flash was followed by a deep, resonating boom and the gunship flipped sideways, then tumbled.

Castamon jolted against his harness as the pilot battled to regain control of the aircraft. Warnings chimed and something rattled against the fuselage.

Abarim looked up in surprise, his pupils limned with blue energy.

'Pilot, what hit us?' said Castamon, raising his voice above the din.

The pilot gasped as she managed to level the gunship out. Her hands danced across the flight controls as she flipped levers and adjusted gauges. 'Unclear, lieutenant. I suspect lasweapons. Or missiles?'

Castamon squinted into the gloom, readying himself for combat.

'Wait,' said the pilot, staring at the control panel. 'No. I can't tell…'

Abarim spoke calmly. 'We have not been hit.'

As the light faded Castamon saw he was right, but up ahead in the distance it looked like a second sunrise was taking place. There was a dome of white light simmering on the horizon, so fierce that Castamon's visor dimmed as he looked at it. It grew as he watched, spreading slowly into the surrounding dark-ness, causing the air to shimmer and dance. 'What is that?' he demanded.

'Port Dura,' said the pilot, her voice numb. 'It *was* Port Dura.'

'Orbital strike,' said Abarim, leaning forwards against his restraints, trying to focus.

'No.' Castamon was studying the sky. 'There are no contrails. No sign of anything from overhead. We would have seen a rocket strike.'

'The auspex shows nothing gathered outside the space port,' said the pilot. 'Nothing that could be an army, at least.' She peered at one of the small viewscreens on her control panel and her face grew pale. 'It's gone. The whole city.' There was a tremor in her voice. 'What kind of explosive could do that?'

Castamon looked at Abarim. 'The plasma reactor that powers the lasers.'

The Librarian shook his head. 'The generatoriums are buried deep, brother. Well hidden. And well protected. How would anyone reach them? They would have had to find a way to create a chain reaction that linked every one of the city's reactors. They would have to grasp every detail of how the city is wired. No single person would have such comprehensive knowledge. Not even the port master.'

'You must be mistaken,' said Castamon, looking back at the pilot. 'The whole city cannot be gone.'

She quickly wiped away tears. 'It's gone, my lord.'

Castamon quickly reassessed his plans. He had expected to stop the tyranids at the edge of the system. The defence lasers at Port Dura had been an essential part of his strategy. But not any more. He looked out at the distorted air. The xenos had already reached Regium. He needed to rethink.

'Contact Zarax,' he said. 'See if Tanaro and Vultis have returned.'

'There is no signal from the fortress, lieutenant. I lost contact within an hour of take-off.'

He thought for a moment, drumming his fingers on his armour.

'Our main ground defences are at Salamis,' said Abarim. He waved at the ball of fire that used to be Port Dura. 'This must not be allowed to happen there. We have to ensure the hive is safe.' He looked at the pilot. 'Do we have enough fuel to reach the hive?'

'Yes, my lord.'

Castamon shook his head. 'We will return to Zarax.'

Abarim clutched his head, blue light flickering between his fingers. Then, when he recovered, he stared at Castamon. 'Zarax is defended by Ultramarines. But there are no battle-brothers at the hive. If Salamis is destroyed we will be hard-pressed. The fortress cannot stand alone. The tyranids are already in the upper atmosphere. And they must be here in large numbers. This must be why my foreknowledge has become so unclear.'

Castamon shook his head, sure in his decision. 'There are no Ultramarines at Salamis Hive, but every Cadian on the planet is about to arrive there, commanded by one of the most determined officers in the subsector. And they are bolstered by Confessor Thurgau and an army of priests. We can send messengers to the hive. We can warn Governor Seroc that an attack is imminent. But we must return to Zarax.'

'Why?'

'Look at the skies, brother. The xenos are poisoning the atmosphere. You know what comes next – full-scale invasion.'

'But what do you hope to achieve by returning to the fortress? If the hammer falls, it will surely fall at Salamis Hive, where the majority of our forces are gathered. Surely we should muster everything we have in one location?'

'Our efforts would be in vain. Consider the facts. We have five squads. That will mean a lot at Zarax, but if we send them out of that stronghold they will be dangerously exposed. Many might never reach the hive.'

'Your logic is sound,' admitted Abarim, looking out at the spores. 'This seems like more than just a few ships fleeing from a defeat.'

'Agreed. This is not the behaviour of routed stragglers. They showed no interest in Krassus and they ambushed Tyrus. And now, with impossible speed, they are here' – he gestured at the hazy air outside – 'polluting the atmosphere and assaulting defence batteries. We missed something.'

Abarim gripped his force axe and light flowed through the blade, coiling like oil in water. 'The tyranids at Krassus were a decoy.'

Castamon nodded. 'I have drawn the same conclusion. They drew out our best and bravest and then, while our attention was on the death of Tyrus, their main strength must have been approaching from the other direction. How else did they reach us so fast? I suspect this is a large invasion force, here with the express purpose of destroying Regium, and they are using the kind of tactics we might employ.'

'In which case…' Abarim shook his head, as though unwilling to voice his concerns.

'In which case,' said Castamon, 'the other worlds of the Sanctus Line might also be in danger.'

The pilot glanced back at this, eyes wide. Then she regained her composure. 'We are approaching the hill,' she said. 'Shall I land?'

'Negative, pilot,' he replied. 'Set a course for Zarax. I have to find Brother-Apothecary Vultis.'

Chapter Fourteen

ARGENTUM FOREST
SAMNIUM PROVINCE, REGIUM

Vultis paused and looked back at the others. 'Did you hear that?' They were halfway down an unlit corridor, still following the trail of blood.

Tanaro strode to his side and nodded. 'Projectile weapons.' He gestured for his squad to advance. Including Tanaro and Baraca, there were eight members of Squad Tanaro remaining, plus Vultis. Nine veterans of the First Company. Enough to deal with almost any eventuality. As they reached an intersection, the sound of gunfire increased, making it clear which passageway they needed to choose. They turned left at the junction and raced down a smaller, equally dark corridor. Muzzle flashes blinked up ahead.

'I need one alive,' said Vultis, giving Baraca a warning glance as they saw a doorway looming up ahead.

Before Baraca could reply they advanced through the doorway into an open, cavernous space. The corridor became a wide walkway of grilled metal that reached out across an abyss, extending into a darkness so deep that even Vultis' eyes could not pierce it. Other, smaller walkways crossed the darkness from other directions, all leading to a circular, hub-like platform at the centre of the chamber. There were dozens of corpses scattered across the central platform. They were pilgrims, like the ones outside, their white robes gleaming in the darkness. Three of them were still alive, firing at the surrounding gantries. Bullets whined through the air and ricocheted off unseen metal, but the shots were wild and untargeted. One of them was screaming, shaking his head violently as he fired, and the other two were flinching and twitching. All three were drenched in blood, picked out of the darkness by a single lumen dangling from a servo-skull that was circling overhead.

'Any sign of the xenos?' asked Tanaro, scanning the gloom then looking at Vultis.

'Faint heat signals, sergeant,' he replied. 'East, north and south.'

Tanaro nodded and waved the squad on. They advanced in silence, walking slowly out across the bottomless drop, pistols raised.

One of the pilgrims turned and looked their way. Then he began firing at them. The shots whined through the air or clanged harmlessly on their power armour.

'Hold your fire,' boomed Tanaro. 'I am Sergeant Tanaro of the Ultramarines First Company.'

There was a moment's silence as the pilgrims stared blindly in their direction. Then one of them called out, his voice hysterical. 'By the Throne! Help!'

Tanaro studied them in silence, then looked at Vultis. 'How many signals?'

Vultis adjusted his equipment, studying a screen on his vambrace. 'Far more than the small group Castamon described.'

'Then these are *not* just a few stowaways.'

Vultis shook his head. 'These are large numbers. They must have originated from multiple landing points.'

The pilgrims were still screaming desperately into the darkness, begging for help, but the Ultramarines continued talking calmly.

'Why would xenos gather here?' asked Sergeant Tanaro. He looked up at the surrounding architecture.

'Sheltering from the swell?' suggested Baraca.

Vultis shook his head. 'But why are they waiting? Why not attack? They usually employ opportunistic predation patterns. I do not understand what would hold them back.'

Baraca grinned in the dark. 'My reputation precedes me.'

Tanaro gestured for the squad to advance. He sent three of his men down one side of the walkway and three down the other, while he and Baraca advanced down the middle, but Vultis hesitated. There was something wrong. Something familiar that he could not pin down. The others were only a dozen paces from the pilgrims when he finally relented and followed them towards the platform.

'What is your business here?' demanded Sergeant Tanaro as he reached the centre of the chamber and stepped out into the light. It was a pitiful scene, almost as dreadful as the mess outside the building. The three surviving pilgrims were close to death, their robes torn and dark with blood and their eyes glazed and confused. Two of them backed away, cowering as they saw who they had been firing at, but the one who had called out held his ground, looking up at the Ultramarines. He gripped an autopistol with a determined expression. He was heavily pierced with branches and painfully thin, with sodden black hair plastered down over his bony cheeks and large, staring eyes.

'My lords,' he said. 'Forgive us. We could not see you in the dark. And there's something in here. Monsters. They attacked us.' His voice wavered as he looked down at his dead companions. 'Then they vanished and left us like this.'

'What do they want with us?' cried one of the other pilgrims, an old woman who was using a sword as a crutch, blood pouring from a gash in her neck.

'Who is in charge?' demanded Tanaro.

The man flinched at Tanaro's harsh tone but nodded. 'I am, my lord.'

'Tell me your name.'

He took a deep breath, brushing his hair from his face. 'I am Ephraim. We are the Keft. Guardians of the world roots. We are here because–'

'When did the xenos attack?' interrupted Vultis. 'Was it at the same time as the swell hit?'

'Yes.' Ephraim was still staring at the Ultramarines with a mixture of terror and awe. 'No… I mean… I think they were in here *before* the swell.' He glanced into the darkness as he spoke. 'They forced us out onto this platform.'

Vultis shook his head. 'They forced you onto this platform? They *herded* you?'

'I don't know. Perhaps. It felt like that. They attacked.' His voice wavered. 'People died. But once we were on here, they…'

'They're still watching us,' hissed the old woman, clutching at her wounds, her eyes straining. 'They're waiting. Why are they waiting? For Throne's sake. Please. *Do* something.'

Baraca strode to the edge of the platform and looked down one of the gantries. He hammered his pistol against the handrail, making a clattering sound that chimed through the darkness, causing the pilgrims to gasp.

Vultis approached the gantry and stood at Baraca's side, waiting for a response, but there was nothing. He thought for a moment, then headed back to the platform, picked up a severed arm from the pile of dead pilgrims and hurled it down the gantry. It landed with a dull thud, splashing blood across the metalwork.

A sound rose from the shadows, quiet at first but growing louder. It sounded like air escaping from punctured tyres – a wavering hiss that filled the darkness.

Vultis looked back at Sergeant Tanaro.

Tanaro nodded, signalling for the squad to head out onto the gantry.

'Wait,' hissed Ephraim, sounding panicked, but the Ultramarines had already begun striding into the darkness. They maintained the same formation as before: three on one side, three on the other, with Tanaro and Baraca in the middle and Vultis at the rear.

They quickly saw figures up ahead, twitching in the shadows. They were similar in size to the pilgrims, but they were not a uniform shape. The first one Vultis saw clearly was like the creature Baraca had shot from the Storm Speeder – humanoid and upright, with powerful legs and talon-like forearms. As he moved further down the gantry, others came into focus. Most were similar in shape, but rather than having bone-scythe arms, they were clutching stomach-like organs or pipe-like growths that jutted from their limbs.

Back on the platform, the pilgrims began screaming again, but Vultis blocked out the sounds, focusing on the flexing talons and flickering tongues up ahead. He examined each of the xenos in detail as he clanged down the gantry towards them, cataloguing and cross-referencing, comparing them to similar predators he had faced in the past.

As the xenos watched the Ultramarines approach they continued hissing, forcing air through their dagger-like rows of teeth. Eyes glinted in the darkness, black and featureless. Then, with a final hiss, they attacked, hurtling down the gantry, moving in spasmodic lurches.

Baraca laughed hungrily, unslinging his pyreblaster from his back and gripping it in both hands.

'Baraca,' Tanaro warned. 'They will be little use to Vultis as charcoal.'

Baraca grunted a curse but, without breaking his stride, smoothly swapped his pyreblaster for his pistol and combat knife.

Moist popping sounds filled the darkness. The tyranids were squeezing gristly pipes that were attached to their abdomens. Glistening shapes spat from the pipes and whistled through the air, thudding into some of the Ultramarines, hitting with enough impact to slow their advance.

Vultis passed one of his battle-brothers and saw thumb-sized bugs attached to his chest armour. They were digging frantically, trying to bore through the ceramite. The Ultramarine cut them away with his combat knife and stamped on them, splitting shells and splashing acid across the floor.

More screams came from the platform. Vultis looked back and saw that some of the ticks had attached themselves to the old woman. She howled and thrashed as they flayed her alive, blood fountaining from her robes. The other two backed away, horrified and unable to help.

'Target the xenos that are using bio-weapons,' said Sergeant Tanaro as the tyranids rushed towards them. 'They have no symbionts on their backs. Pistol fire only.'

They raised their bolt pistols, shots barking into the darkness. Light and noise filled the chamber, revealing the web of walkways surrounding them. Carapaces shattered and creatures tumbled through the gloom. As light flashed over the gantries, the Ultramarines saw tyranids on dozens of the walkways, loping into view, gripping their living weapons. And they were not just on one level – they were also on gantries above the Ultramarines' heads and below their feet.

Vultis took a step back and carefully shot away the legs of the first tyranids to reach him. Then he turned on his heel, firing at the ones sprinting at him from other directions. Most tumbled to the ground but one broke through the barrage, slamming into his chest and forcing him backwards. It moved so fast Vultis was unsure whether it was the species he needed or not. He lashed out with his combat knife, splitting its carapace, but rather than hindering it, the damage sent it into a frenzy. It bucked and convulsed, rattling talons against Vultis' armour. Bladed arms rained blows on his head and chest. Its movements grew more frantic and it screamed. The sound was thin and hideous, like the sound of an animal being slaughtered. Acid sprayed from its mouth, washing over Vultis' faceplate, hissing on the visor and obscuring his view.

Baraca was nearby, grappling and struggling in the same way as Vultis, holding a tyranid at arm's length and trying to disable it without killing it.

Sergeant Tanaro hurled a tyranid to the ground and shot it at point-blank range, drenching himself in venom. 'Clear a space,' he ordered, dropping the creatures with head shots.

Vultis stood back to back with Baraca as they filled the air with bolt-rounds and noise. As the other Ultramarines followed suit the xenos returned fire, spitting parasites.

Vultis paused to slam a fresh magazine into his gun, making a quick calculation to work out how many rounds he had left, but then the attack ceased. The tyranids stopped screaming and faded silently back into the shadows, leaving their dead sprawled across the gantries, steaming and sizzling.

Baraca grunted and moved to follow them, reloading his gun

as he went, but Sergeant Tanaro grabbed him by the shoulder, shaking his head. 'Tyranids do not retreat.'

Baraca grunted and fired a last shot, kicking a distant shadow from a gantry.

Vultis had the same feeling he'd had when he first entered the chamber – a sense that this situation was familiar; that he had experienced it before. As he peered into the shadows, he saw that they were glinting with dark, unblinking eyes. 'Why did they cease the attack?'

Behind them, the pilgrims were still screaming and howling, but the Ultramarines paid them no heed.

'They appear to be sounding us out,' said Sergeant Tanaro, kicking a severed alien head. 'Gauging our firepower.'

Vultis looked back down the gantry they had used when they first entered the chamber. The faint light of the doorway had vanished, blocked by twitching, silhouetted figures. 'Unless this was all a trap. We thought we were the hunters. But perhaps we are the prey.' As he said the words, an image of the Harbinger filled his mind. He thought back to his childhood and looked at Baraca. 'Do you remember how attoks hunt, back at home?'

Baraca nodded. 'They slaughter cattle and leave the carcasses as bait. Then, when larger creatures come to feed, they encircle them.' He laughed grimly. 'The pilgrims were a lure?'

'Exactly.'

'Then why are the xenos still holding back?' said Baraca. 'If this is where they wanted us, why not attack?'

'They may not have realised what they were hunting,' said Tanaro loftily. 'I'll wager that Ultramarines are too rich for their blood.'

Baraca grunted and marched down the walkway. 'Well, I see no reason to–'

Tyranids exploded from the darkness. Some leapt at Baraca,

scything at him, while others fired acid-drenched grubs. Baraca stood proud as he gunned them down, lighting up the hideous menagerie that surrounded him. The rest of the squad rushed to his side and opened fire. 'We can burn our way out,' cried Baraca, slapping the pyreblaster on his back and glancing at Tanaro.

'Not until I have a specimen,' said Vultis.

Tanaro looked around. 'Have you seen the bioform you need? Are there any in here?'

'Yes. Several of these creatures have the strange symbionts attached to their backs.'

Tanaro raised his voice, addressing the whole squad. 'Advance to the exit. Engage the xenos in close combat. Once the Apothecary Biologis has captured a specimen, open fire with pyreblasters. If the xenos follow us to the outer chambers, we will seal the exit.'

Vultis tapped his canister and looked at his battle-brothers. 'Be sure I have what I need before you unleash hell.'

Tanaro called back to the chamber's central platform, addressing the pilgrims. 'We will cross this gantry at speed. Keep up, reach the next chamber and you will be safe.'

The old woman was dead but, to their credit, the remaining two pilgrims readied themselves, taking deep breaths and checking their weapons.

'The Emperor is watching,' snapped Tanaro. 'Do *not* be found lacking.'

The chamber trembled. The pilgrims cried out as tyranid carcasses fell from the gantries, dropping into the unseen depths. 'The swell,' barked Tanaro. 'It *is* strong enough to affect the geoengine.'

Baraca looked at Ephraim, who was stumbling out onto the gantry. 'Has the swell ever torn down one of these places?'

The man appeared ready to pass out, but he shook his head. 'The shrines are eternal. World roots can't be damaged.'

The chamber shook with such force that some of the smaller gantries were dislodged from the walls, swinging loose with a scream of grinding metal. The clattering of hooves rang out as xenos raced to safety.

'This is not the swell.' Vultis was gripped by a sudden certainty. 'This is–'

A wall collapsed, spilling rain-grey light into the chamber, and a shape strode into view, stepping out onto the central walkway.

The creature was enormous, towering over the Ultramarines.

Vultis recognised it instantly.

The Harbinger.

Chapter Fifteen

Shapes fell silently from the sky, patches of black that were hard to make out in the greater darkness that had consumed everything. As the shadows landed, somewhere over the horizon, they made deep grumbling noises, like distant thunder.

Tharro was crouching on an embankment at the edge of an abandoned transitway, staring out into the gloom.

'What do you see?' whispered Valacia from the bottom of the incline.

'Lights,' he whispered back. 'It's the Desoluta Outpost, I think.'

'Desoluta? Have we come that far? If there are lights, maybe there are people?'

Since fleeing the agri complex, they had found every town and homestead abandoned. Everyone seemed to have had the same thought as Tharro – make for Salamis. Surely there would be some help at the hive? Surely someone would be in charge? But Tharro and Valacia were old. They could only move slowly. They needed a vehicle.

'Could be people,' he said, wishing he had a pair of magnoculars. 'I don't think the place is on fire.'

She began climbing up to join him, then stopped, struggling to catch her breath and coughing. He reached down, helping her up. 'Could it be *them?*' she asked, gripping his hand tightly. 'The things in the dream?'

He shook his head. His dreams were different to Valacia's. He saw a single, huge monster with burn-marks down one side of its head. It was coming to devour him, and each time he pictured it, whether he was asleep or awake, he had the sense that there was no way to escape – the giant would hunt him down. But Valacia dreamt of a host – a tide of smaller creatures, each no bigger than a man, flooding through the darkness, swarming like insects, picking the flesh from everything they passed. 'I think it's people,' he said, trying to control his excitement. 'Those lights look like they're coming from groundcars or maybe haulers, don't you think?'

She nodded eagerly, still gripping his arm. 'But what if they won't take us?' She coughed again. 'What if they say they have no room?'

'They'll take us.' Her cough made him determined. 'Or we'll find a way to take one of the groundcars.'

She glanced at the shotgun he was holding in his other hand, her eyes wide in the darkness. 'You're not…' She shook her head. 'We don't know how to fight. If they're not friendly we should just move on.'

He waved at the air. 'This gas, or dust, or whatever it is – it's killing us. I feel like I'm breathing razors. And I can hear what it's doing to you. We have to head north. There must have been a fire or something.' He had said, a few times now, that the fumes must be from a fire, but neither of them really believed it. They both sensed that the poisoned air, the shapes falling from the sky and the monsters in their dreams were all linked, all part of an awful nightmare that they could not explain or wake up from.

She looked unconvinced. 'If you try and use that thing on someone, they'll just turn it on you. You're no fighter.'

He said nothing. She was right, of course. He had never fired the thing in anger. But he might have no choice if people refused to help them. Every breath he took hurt more than the last, but that was not the worst thing. The worst thing was the sense of dread that grew in him every time he looked up. The end was close now, he could feel it. It had been coming for him since that first dream dragged him from his bed, and now it was almost upon him. They had to get to the hive.

He helped her up onto the transitway and began hurrying down it, keeping to the edge even though there was barely any light. He had a lumen in his bag, but he did not dare use it until he knew the people at Desoluta were friendly.

As they came nearer, his hopes started to lift. They both heard the sound of groundcars roaring round the outpost and indecipherable voices floating through the darkness. 'They'll help us, I'm sure of it,' he said, picking up his pace and pulling Valacia after him. She nodded back, her eyes gleaming with hope.

Shots rang out in the distance – the harsh rattle of autoweapons.

They froze.

'That came from up ahead,' he whispered, glancing at Valacia. She nodded.

'Let's get closer,' he said, pulling her on.

She refused to move, shaking her head.

'We have to,' he insisted. 'It might be enforcers, dealing with looters.'

She relented, letting him lead her on.

They crawled down off the side of the road as they reached the outpost, keeping away from the lights that spilled out between the buildings. As they edged closer, he saw that there were people in the small square between the structures. Some were seated in ground-cars and trucks, while others paced between the silos and hab-units.

'Miners?' whispered Valacia, frowning as she tried to make them out.

'I think so,' he replied, seeing that some of them were wearing tinted welding goggles and heavy overalls. 'Why would they have come out here? Why leave the hive?'

She stared at him, squeezing his arm. 'Unless things are even worse at the hive? Maybe they came here because things are bad at Salamis too?'

'No.' He shook his head. He could not bear the idea that a vast metropolis like Salamis could have fallen into the same kind of anarchy that they had seen in the agri complexes. 'That can't be right. I don't think this pollution could have spread to—'

More shots rang out. This close, the sound was jarringly loud, and he almost cried out in shock.

'Look!' whispered Valacia.

One of the miners dragged a corpse into view. It was a man. Blood was rushing from holes in his back.

Someone cried out. It was a horrible, panicked sound. Then they saw a woman sprinting from the buildings out onto the transitway. She was running directly towards them.

Another miner walked calmly out after her, raised a pistol and shot her, firing repeatedly until she lay still.

Tharro felt Valacia stiffen at his side and he understood why. As the miner walked over to the woman he had shot, they saw him more clearly, and his face was terrifying. His skull was strangely elongated, like an egg lying on its side, and his brow was crossed by bony, ridged protrusions. But worst of all were his eyes. They were dark, featureless mirrors.

Tharro clamped his hand over Valacia's mouth, sensing that she was about to scream. He felt like screaming himself when the half-man paused and looked directly at him, staring into the darkness. Then the creature sniffed, like a hound on a hunt.

Valacia buried her face in his side, shivering with terror. Tharro held his breath and slowly rested his finger on the shotgun's trigger.

Booming sounds rumbled in the distance as more of the shapes fell to earth.

Tharro slowly raised the shotgun.

Then the miner grabbed the dead woman and began hauling her back to the outpost.

Tharro exhaled and removed his finger from the trigger.

When the miner was back with the others, he finally dared to whisper. 'Did you see that?'

'We have to get out of here.' Valacia's voice was trembling as they stared at the figures in the square. They dragged more dead bodies into view, dropping them in a heap. 'Did you see how it was sniffing? I swear it almost realised we were here. It could smell us, even in this bad air.'

He nodded and was about to head away from the transitway when he noticed something. Just outside the outpost, a dozen or so feet away, there was an empty groundcar. It was a powerful-looking machine, the kind that rarely came out to the agri complexes.

'I can barely breathe,' he whispered. 'What about you?'

She shook her head. 'It's horrible. I feel like I'm breathing mud. But what difference does it make? We have to get away from those... whatever they are.' She followed his gaze and saw the abandoned groundcar. 'No,' she breathed. 'Are you insane?' She yanked at his arm but he refused to move. 'They'll see you!' she hissed, staring at him. 'And they'll come over here.' She closed her eyes. 'What are they? How can they look like that? What's wrong with them?'

'We would have a chance,' he whispered. 'If we had that groundcar we would have a chance to get out of here. If we just head off on foot we're dead, Valacia. You know it. I can't breathe this stuff any more. Another half a mile and we'll have to lie down in a ditch and wait for the carrion-birds to take us.'

'Rather that than face those *things*.' She sobbed quietly, but she was no longer trying to pull him away.

'It's our last chance. You know it, Val. I'm done. I can't walk any more.'

She said nothing but she nodded, then pressed her face against his chest.

'I have an idea of how we could do it,' he said, even though he sensed she was no longer listening to him. 'I could throw one of these rocks pretty far. I think I could throw one right over there to that fuel silo. It would make a pretty good noise.' He realised how absurd he sounded, talking like he was some kind of hero, but he kept on regardless. 'Then, when they head over there to look, we can crawl over to the groundcar while they're all facing the other way. And if it doesn't work, if we don't make it over there in time, we won't have lost anything. We could still just crawl away into the darkness and, well, keep looking for another outpost, I suppose, to see...'

His words trailed off as he realised he was talking nonsense. They both knew they would never reach another outpost.

'Are you with me?' he whispered, picking up a rock. She still had her face buried in his chest. 'Will you be ready to start crawling when I throw this?'

She said nothing, but he felt her nod.

He looked back at the miners. Now that he had seen one close up, he could tell how strange they were even at a distance.

Their bulbous, distorted skulls reminded him of the monster in his dream and also their movements – there was something fitful and insect-like about the way they walked and carried their weapons. None of them were speaking, he realised. But they still moved in unison, as though answering silent commands, as they dragged more bodies onto the mound.

I can't do this, he realised, looking at the rock in his palm. His hand was shaking and there was sweat stinging his eyes and blurring his vision. *We will have to crawl away and die because I'm too much of a coward to try and live.* Then he looked down at Valacia. She had lifted herself away from him, wiped the tears from her eyes and was now staring at the groundcar with a mixture of horror and determination. *She's not defeated yet,* he realised. *So neither am I.*

He took a deep breath, leant back and hurled the rock as hard as he could. It arced high in the air and he sighed in relief, seeing that he had thrown the thing well. Then, as he looked at the outpost, he saw that none of the miners were watching the stone. They were all staring at him.

'Run!' he gasped, hurling Valacia down the slope and breaking into a sprint, racing in the direction of the groundcar.

The half-men came after them in silence, moving like automata. As they spilled from the outpost, walking out into the muddy fields, they drew pistols and loaded shotguns.

'Faster!' cried Tharro, gripping Valacia's hand as he ran.

Shots rang out. One whistled right past his face and kicked mud up at his feet, but he ignored it. There was no point trying to weave or duck. All they could do was run and hope they reached the groundcar. *What if it's out of fuel?* The thought almost made him sick, but he ran on. There was nowhere else to go.

Some of the half-men were jogging now, still horribly silent, staring at him with dead, oily eyes.

Pain exploded across his cheek and blood washed up over his face. Valacia screamed but they kept on, pounding through the mud.

'Halt,' called out one of the miners, finally breaking their silence. The word sounded flat and lifeless in his mouth, as though he was repeating something he did not fully understand.

Then, to Tharro's amazement, they had reached the ground-car. They yanked the doors open and leapt inside. He cried out in relief as he saw the ignition crystal jutting from the control panel, but when he tried to start the engine it only coughed and spluttered, refusing to turn over.

Shots shattered the windows, covering them in glittering shards and lacerating the side of Tharro's face. More shots hit the side of the car, punching through the chassis and buckling the roll bars.

Valacia grabbed something and crawled into the back seat. There was a deafening blast just behind his head, and he realised she had taken the shotgun.

The nearest of the half-men stumbled to a halt, looking down at a ragged hole in his chest, then he tumbled into the mud. Valacia pumped the slide back and fired the shotgun again, hitting another miner in the chest and punching him back through the air.

Tharro howled as he realised he had failed to open the groundcar's fuel line. He flipped the switch and tried the crystal again.

The engine roared.

More shots rang out and Valacia screamed, falling back in the seat.

Tharro slammed his foot on the accelerator and the ground-car lurched forwards, churning mud as it raced off across the field and onto the transitway.

In the rearview mirror, the half-men lowered their weapons,

watching them go in uninterested silence. Then they turned and headed back towards the outpost, dragging their dead with them as they went.

'Valacia!' cried Tharro, straining to look over his shoulder. 'Are you hurt?'

She dragged herself up from the footwell and onto the seat. Her face was grey and bloody, but she shook her head, eyes wide, patting the barrel of the shotgun. 'Perhaps I should carry this from now on.'

He laughed, almost hysterical with relief. 'They missed you?'

She nodded, examining her overalls. 'I think so.' She stared at him in the mirror, her smile fading. 'What were they?'

He shook his head, keeping his eyes on the transitway and trying not to look at the shapes rolling overhead. 'We'll be safe when we reach Salamis. They'll know what to do.' He tried to sound confident, but they could both hear the tremor in his voice.

Chapter Sixteen

Vultis stumbled as the Harbinger stepped out onto the walkway. For a moment, he thought the whole thing would give way. Stanchions buckled, spitting rivets, barely managing to hold. The creature's morphology was similar to the smaller tyranids, but everything was magnified to an absurd scale. Its head was topped by cranial armour that rose from its skull in a trio of bone blades and there was a colossal tail lashing around behind its legs. Vultis glanced at Tanaro. 'Do we hold to the same plan?'

Tanaro nodded without hesitation, directing his squad to new positions. 'But we will need more than pistols to take this thing down.'

Vultis nodded, but he was surprised to feel anger coursing through his veins. Something about the colossus was affecting his mental state. The creature was vile, but that was no excuse for his lack of composure. He replayed Castamon's warning in his head. *Passion is weakness. Equilibrium is strength.* He must be rational. His purpose was to reach Zarax with the symbiont. Everything else was extraneous.

The colossal tyranid was halfway across the gantry, advancing slowly as the lesser organisms swarmed around its legs, hissing and brandishing their weaponised growths.

'Courage and honour!' cried Tanaro, raising his pistol.

'Courage and honour!' roared the other Ultramarines, hoisting their pyreblasters onto their hips.

To Vultis' surprise, the two pilgrims raised pistols and cried out, 'For the Emperor!'

The Ultramarines opened fire, spraying blue-white promethium as they ran forwards.

'For Guilliman!' howled Sergeant Tanaro as he led the charge, vaulting over burning bodies. 'For Ultramar and Macragge!'

Vultis ran in his wake, firing his bolt pistol and lashing out with his knife. It was a chaotic scene, with creatures pressing in from every direction, but the Ultramarines moved with parade-ground precision.

Shadow washed over Vultis as the Harbinger strode through the flames and reared up in front of them. The smaller bioforms were frenzied but the Harbinger looked oddly serene, gazing down at the carnage. Then it leant back, raised a scythe-like arm and hammered it down, splitting one of the Ultramarines down the middle, splashing his innards through the darkness.

The blow landed with such force that the whole structure gave way, collapsing with an explosion of sparks and rent metal. Dozens of tyranids were hurled to their deaths and the Ultramarines finally broke ranks, leaping for handholds. The Harbinger killed a second Ultramarine, beheading him with another swipe of its bladed arm.

As the gantry gave way, Baraca tumbled into the abyss, still spewing fire from his pyreblaster.

The Harbinger fell too, plummeting after him.

Vultis reached out just in time to grab a shard of splintered metal as bodies tumbled past him.

The smaller tyranids screamed and ignored the rest of the squad, making straight for Vultis.

Rather than grab on with a second hand and haul himself back up, he remained where he was, suspended one-handed over the drop and using his spare hand to shoot. The gun barked, punching tyranids back into the darkness.

Then it clicked on empty.

He clamped the gun to his armour and hauled himself up onto the listing walkway. All around him, Ultramarines were doing the same, clambering up through the wreckage, firing into the mayhem.

A tyranid leapt at him, raking claws across his armour and driving him back to the edge.

He jammed his combat knife through the creature's jaw. Then he lifted the still-struggling xenos up off its hooves and prepared to hurl it from the ledge. Just in time, he saw the shape on its back. He slammed the host creature onto the floor, placed his boot on its throat and used the knife to cut the parasite from its carapace. The symbiont fidgeted and squirmed in his gauntlet, trying to free itself. As he clutched it tighter, his mind filled with a vivid image. He saw Zarax burning and tumbling, laid to waste by a xenos host. Then he rose above the destruction, as if flying up into the clouds, and saw the whole continent sink under a tide of purple-and-bone-coloured horrors.

Pain exploded across his face. He fell, rolling and clattering across the grilled metal. The vision faded and he leapt up, still gripping the symbiont. There was a man-sized tyranid standing a few feet away holding a tube of rotten muscle. Black, treacly liquid dripped from the weapon's orifice. The pain in the side of his face grew worse and he heard a grinding sound, like someone working a lathe. He ignored the pain, opened the containment unit and shoved the symbiont inside, fastening the lock. The cylinder immediately filled with a viscous, life-sustaining suspension. Then he slammed a fresh magazine into his pistol and shot his attacker in the head, sending it spinning into the abyss.

Vultis reached up to touch his helmet. The ceramite had cracked. Something moist and spiny was clawing at the break, shivering as it tried to puncture his skull. He popped it in his fist like an overripe fruit. Acid smoked and fizzled down his helmet and he hurled the mess to the floor. Then he looked around, gun raised, searching for his next attacker. Nothing was close enough to be a threat. He took clippers from his armour and gripped a thin spine that the parasite had left in his cheek bone. He had treated enough tyranid victims to know that the spine would currently be pumping venom into his bloodstream. He pulled at the spine. It was barbed, tearing his bone and cartilage, but it came free.

He took a few steps backwards towards the central platform and gunned down the nearest tyranids, clearing a space so he could look around and get a clear picture of what was happening. The main walkway was mostly ruined and it had taken several of the smaller gantries with it. Tanaro and the others were back on their feet and firing. There was no sign of the Harbinger but, to his relief, he saw Baraca, several layers down, still spitting gouts of promethium as he hauled himself back up towards the exit. He was not surprised to see that the pilgrims were dead, fragments of their bodies dangling from the splintered metalwork. He checked the containment unit was still secure then headed off down one of the gantries, loosing off shots as he crossed the cavernous drop.

He was halfway to the exit when the web of metal screamed and jolted again. He lost his footing but managed to control his fall, leaping onto another gantry and crouching low as the chamber shook.

The Harbinger crawled, spider-like, into view, scuttling up the walls, tearing gantries from the rock.

Tanaro and the others had almost made it to the exit. It was now a ragged hole, rather than a doorway, and the daylit chamber beyond was clearly visible.

Vultis sprinted down a gantry, leapt a ten-foot gap and landed lightly on another gantry. He downed attackers, tearing throats and faces with his knife, and ran on, making a direct line for the exit.

Ahead of him, Baraca clambered up towards the doorway, pouring promethium onto creatures swarming up after him.

Vultis had almost reached the opening when the gantry vanished from beneath his feet. He tried to grab a handhold but there was nothing within reach and he fell, plunging into the darkness.

The Harbinger caught him in a claw as big as he was and opened its jaws.

Vultis quickly analysed the thing's face, identifying flaws and weaknesses. The left side of it had been wounded by a recent explosion. Chitin and muscles had been ripped away, exposing the workings of its jaw. The whole left side of its head had been burned, revealing charred, exposed fibres. The divide ran so neatly down the centre of its face that it looked like a mask, one side pale and bone-like, the other dark and glistening.

He fired at the wounded side until the gun clicked on empty. The rounds punched through the monster's chin and jaw. A smaller breed of tyranid would have been killed by the shots, its brain pulverised, but this one was merely surprised. Its head snapped to one side and it stumbled. It only loosened its grip on Vultis for a moment, but that was enough. He leapt clear, drawing his knife as he dived, slamming the blade into the wall and swinging high enough to latch his other hand around a support.

The Harbinger sank its claws into the wall and prepared to leap up after him.

Flames roared past Vultis and splashed into the tyranid's upturned face as Baraca and the rest of the squad opened fire. The promethium clung to every crevasse and fold, gathering in the area of exposed tissue.

The Harbinger stumbled again, dropping a dozen feet as it scrabbled at the rock for another hold.

Vultis leapt a few more times, then Baraca reached down, grabbed him by the forearm and hauled him up to the doorway.

Below, the Harbinger was trapped in the wreckage it had created, enmeshed in a web of broken supports and gantries. Seeing that it could not stop Vultis leaving, the creature tilted its head and screamed. The sound was so loud, and so disturbing, that even the Ultramarines recoiled, stumbling back from the opening.

'Bolt-rounds,' said Sergeant Tanaro, waving the squad back to the ledge. 'Target the supports.'

They fired on the gantries heaped around the Harbinger. The metal tore under a storm of shots, coming away from the tyranid's grip in a shower of sparks and the creature fell, plummeting into the darkness, still screaming as it vanished from sight.

The Ultramarines waited at the edge of the chamber, listening to the crashing noises that echoed up from the darkness. A few of the smaller tyranids leapt across the drop, hissing and trying to latch on, but they were easily shot down; after the first few attempts, the other xenos realised the jump was too far and began shooting instead, spitting grubs and tendrils through the air.

The Ultramarines backed away, seeing no need to waste any more ammunition. Then Sergeant Tanaro led them all back across the entrance hall towards the doors that opened onto the forest. The swell was already fading, little more than a rippling in the leaves as they emerged into daylight. They hurried across the open area that surrounded the base of the geoengine, not stopping until they were back beneath the cover of the trees.

'That thing was set on reaching you,' said Baraca, studying Vultis. 'An old friend?'

Vultis felt the gaze of the whole squad upon him. He nodded. 'I saw it on the *Incorruptible*. It was the creature that slew Tyrus.'

The others all watched him in silence and he had the familiar sense that they were wary of him, as though his study of xenos had tainted him.

Sergeant Tanaro was solemn for once. 'We must make haste to the Storm Speeders. If xenos are landing in these kinds of numbers, Lieutenant Castamon must be informed.'

Chapter Seventeen

'They're holed up in the blast furnace.' Sergeant Vollard handed a pair of magnoculars to Captain Karpova. 'Impolite, if you ask me. They should have the decency to come out where we can shoot them.'

They were deep in the bowels of Salamis' underhive. The air was revolting, worse even than the rest of the hive. It was so toxic Karpova could even taste it through her rebreather. Her lungs ached and her head was starting to spin. And the place looked hellish. If there had ever been any logic to the surrounding architecture, it was long gone. It looked like a drunk god had hurled manufactories together then stamped on them, forming a slurry of acid, excrement, slag and liquid metal. Karpova's lip curled in distaste. She had been born in a hell-hole like this and it brought back unpleasant memories, memories of powerlessness and fear. She drove them down. She wasn't sump vermin any more. She had harnessed her anger

and used it to carve a career. And that career was not going to
end here, knee-deep in effluence and chem-slop.

There were twelve squads positioned around her in the filth
and none of them were visible. They all had the sense to hunker
down and wait for her signal. Sergeant Vollard, however, was
standing proudly with one filth-spattered boot resting on an
outlet pipe, a cane tucked under one arm and his hands clasped
behind his back.

'The gentleman we fished from the tar-pit suggested that they
might be more of a religious cult than your common-or-garden
gangers. And they do not appear to be involved with any of
the separatist factions. They have given themselves a fanciful
moniker. Brotherhood of the Bloody Dawn or something
equally cheerful. The informant was under the impression they
have been operating for a long time – before all the recent
unpleasantness with the–'

Someone fired a lasweapon from inside the blast furnace. The
shot narrowly missed Vollard's head and he had to pause as
shrapnel rained down on him. Then he continued as if nothing
had happened. 'Religious types are so tedious though, aren't
they?' He raised a warning hand. 'Heretics, I mean, obviously.
You know how devout I am, captain. In fact, there's many a
time that I…'

Karpova was no longer listening. She had developed a useful
ability to block out most of what he said and only tune back
in when he said something relevant. She liked him, but his
thought processes were entirely verbal. She scanned the blast
furnace through the magnoculars, adjusting the magnification
and zooming in on the location that the shot seemed to have
come from. There was no one visible. She could not entirely
blame them. Perhaps the hive scum down here didn't recognise the Cadian Gate sigil on her troopers' shoulder pads, but

they *would* have recognised the skill with which they slaughtered underhivers. They must be able to see that the Emperor's judgement was about to be meted out.

'Ensure this is done cleanly,' she said. 'I don't care if they're separatists, zealots or petty criminals. I want them dealt with quickly.' She adjusted the magnoculars and zoomed out, taking in the whole of the blast furnace. It looked like the base of a crane or a derrick but constructed on a huge scale – a tower of girders and support struts that stretched up into the smog and looked like it could be toppled with a good shove.

Vollard nodded and took his cane from under his arm, using it to gesture at locations in the heaps of rust and shattered rockcrete. 'Autocannons. Arranged in pairs, ready to take out the main supports. A few shots will do it.' He gestured to the squads hunkering out of sight, gripping an impressive array of lasguns, flamers and grenade launchers. 'When the roof falls on their heads we will be waiting.' He hesitated, lowering his voice. 'I did wonder, however… Before we give the order, shall I offer the criminals a chance to repent? It might do well' – he waved his cane – 'in front of the men, I mean, to show a little clemency.'

'Clemency?' She stared at him.

'I merely meant, well, there is the matter of their eternal souls to consider. Even a murderer can beg for forgiveness, before the end.'

She looked closely at him, feeling a vague presentiment of danger. Vollard had always been affected and a little absurd. If he weren't such an excellent soldier, she would have demoted him years ago just to avoid his prattle. But this seemed different. He looked genuinely concerned for the souls of people who had proven themselves to be murderers and saboteurs. He looked uncomfortable about the fact that they were about to die. They had fought together for decades and she had never seen him hesitate like this. She shook her head. 'Give the damned order and we can leave this cesspit.'

He laughed, but it was brittle and forced. 'Of course, captain.' Then he hesitated again, looking around, as though someone could come to his aid.

Karpova was about to give the order herself when he seemed to recover. He shook his head, laughed awkwardly again and spoke into the vox-bead at his collar.

There was a loud barking sound as the guns opened fire, and almost immediately the blast furnace began to crumble. Girders buckled and brackets sheared. As Karpova would have expected, the gunners had placed their shots with care. Rather than leaning, the structure folded in on itself, concertina-like, collapsing within its own footprint. There was an explosion of dust, noise and fumes and then the whole tower was down. The initial collapse was followed by a wave of subsidence as slag and rubble flooded down from the surrounding storage silos. Finally, after a few minutes of this, the dust began to settle. That did little to illuminate the scene, however. The underhive's miasma of chem-fog and promethium fumes still hung heavy in the air and the only illumination came from an arc-light blinking somewhere in the distance, creating the illusion of silent lightning.

'Ladies and gentlemen,' said Sergeant Vollard, addressing all the squads across the vox-network. 'The ship has sunk. The rats will shortly disembark.'

An eerie quiet followed, broken only by the sound of rubble settling and girders groaning.

'There,' said Karpova, seeing something through the magnoculars. 'Someone is digging their way out. I'm surprised they can still…' Her words trailed off. 'Hold your fire,' she said into her vox-bead. 'What *is* that?' She turned to Vollard, handing him the magnoculars.

'Interesting. Looks more like a claw than a hand. Only three fingers. And talons.'

Again, Karpova sensed that there was something odd about the sergeant's manner. She had seen him face nightmarish foes without flinching, but now, as a figure dragged itself from the rubble, he seemed dazed. 'Ugly beggar,' he muttered.

She snatched the magnoculars back and looked back at the rubble. The man had now dragged the top half of his body clear and was trying to haul the rest out. But 'man' was not quite the right word. The figure was essentially humanoid but mutated. He was grotesquely, unnaturally muscular and his skin was mauve and hairless. There were scraps of clothing attached to his hulking shoulders and pieces of what looked like mining gear, but he was also clad in a strange kind of shell that seemed to have formed on his skin – ridged armour plates, like an insect's carapace.

'Mutant,' she spat. She had seen similar cases before – people whose heresy was so profound, whose beliefs were so sacrilegious, that their bodies became as sick as their minds. But there was something oddly familiar about this one. It put her in mind of something she could not quite place. Something about its elongated skull and jerking movements.

She was so engrossed in trying to work out why the mutant seemed familiar that it took her a moment to notice that Vollard had stepped down from the pipe and leant back against a wall. 'What's the matter, man? You've seen heretics before.'

'I've seen *these* heretics before,' he muttered, not meeting her eye. 'Thought it was a dream. But perhaps it was a memory.' He stared at her. He no longer sounded unctuous or pompous, just dazed. 'Feel a bit odd, actually.' Then he laughed in that strange manner again, shaking his head and dusting himself down. 'Forgive me, captain. This damnable smog. Can't seem to think straight.'

She found his behaviour increasingly troubling, but there were more pressing matters. She opened the vox-channel again. 'All squads. Fire at will. Take down everything that comes out.'

Las-beams whined and shimmered through the smog, slicing into the mutant just as it managed to stand. Large sections of its body were cut away but it lurched forwards, oblivious, picking up a metal pole as it stumbled across the debris. It howled as it ran, and the sound was a strangled mixture of human and bestial. As it came closer, Karpova saw armoured dorsal plates jutting up from its back and finally she realised what it reminded her of. 'Tyranids,' she muttered, as a second fusillade sliced into the mutant, finally stopping it in its tracks. The creature toppled backwards, spilling blood and organs, just as a pipe behind it spewed a tide of fast-moving shapes.

'All squads, fire at will,' she repeated, drawing her own las-pistol and standing up to take aim. Las-beams flashed from dozens of directions, cutting into the mutants, but they seemed utterly unconcerned, charging into the barrage, clutching make-shift weapons made from pieces of mining equipment. The combination of grotesquely muscled bodies and tyranid-like carapaces meant it took several hits to slow them down. Then, from other places in the rubble, smaller mutants rushed out. They were closer to human-sized, and though their faces were half-hidden by rebreathers, Karpova could tell that they too were alien-looking. Their heads were elongated, like the first one, and many of them carried plates of chitinous armour that looked just like the armour plates on tyranids. They all had peculiar bony ridges across their foreheads and their eyes were blank and inhuman. They flooded from sewerage pipes and ventilation shafts. There were so many of them, and they were moving so fast, that she was reminded of termites leaving a disturbed nest. *It's like they're turning into tyranids*, she thought. *Could the xenos*

have spread some kind of infection that possesses people? Most of
them had four arms and claw-like hands, and some were well
equipped, clutching auto-weapons and clad in flak armour.

'Flamers!' she snapped.

Fire tore through the darkness, drenching the mutants in a
thick, blazing coat of promethium.

To Karpova's annoyance, even this seemed insufficient to slow
the brutish vanguard creatures, and then, just as she was about
to give another order, she heard the shrill whine of mining lasers
and ducked behind the barricade.

The structures around her detonated, hurling lumps of glowing
metal through the air. As she hunkered down, she heard howls
of alarm and pain and the crash of falling buildings.

'Squads Twelve to Nineteen,' she barked into the vox, raising
her voice over the din. 'Return fire.'

Replies crackled in her ear, confirming that the order had
been heard. She killed the channel and stood up, taking aim
as she climbed up over the barricade, a grim smile forming on
her face. This was turning into a fight worth having.

Shots rained down on the mutants from every direction. The
barrage was so intense that it lit up the smog, turning it into a
dazzling white shroud. 'All squads, advance,' she said, firing her
pistol as she strode across rubble and smoking bodies.

A mutant lunged at her. She had a fraction of a second to register how grotesque it was. Its head was misshapen and its eyes
showed no hint of emotion or humanity. She lashed out with
her sabre, decapitating it, then fired into the headless corpse, just
to be sure. 'Show no quarter,' she said, marching on, slashing
and firing as she advanced.

Her squads surged forwards around her, congregating on the
outlet pipe that the mutants had crawled from. By the time she
reached the pipe, the sounds of combat were fading. She felt a

flicker of disappointment. There were just a few scattered bursts of las-fire as the squads finished off the last few survivors.

'Captain,' said Vollard, wading through the carnage to her side and pointing his sabre at the corpse-clogged opening. 'May I?'

She shook her head. Then she clicked on the stablight on her pistol and pointed it into the darkness, crouching to peer inside. She saw more dead mutants, but no sign of movement. 'Trooper Brauron,' she said, looking back at the squads lining up behind her. 'Any readings in this pipe?'

A trooper broke ranks, clutching a handheld device and tapping at it. 'Nothing, captain. No movement or life signs.'

She nodded, prodded some of the corpses with the tip of her sabre, then headed into the pipe, stooping low as she climbed over the corpses. 'Let's see what they were so keen to defend. Brauron, stay close and tell me if you detect movement.'

Her light switched back and forth, glinting on the liquid waste that gurgled round her boots. Fat, oily rats scampered at her approach, but there was no other sign of life. 'They threw everything at us,' she muttered, 'to protect an old drain.' She sniffed and grimaced. 'A drain that smells like something died in it.' There was a sweet, greasy stink on the air that lined her throat and made her want to gag.

She heard the clatter of weapons and flak armour as her troopers followed her into the darkness. Then, after a few minutes, she saw light up ahead. Rather than the harsh light of a lumen, it was the warm, shifting glow of a fire, and she felt heat washing over her face. She reached the end of the pipe and paused, crouching at the opening, looking down the barrel of her laspistol. The pipe led to what looked like a sump – a circular reservoir that would likely once have contained a pool of oil, but was now dry. There was a broken pump at the centre of the chamber and that was where the light was coming from.

'Throne,' she muttered, dropping down into the chamber and staring at the pump. 'What is that?'

There was a fire burning on top of the pump. Someone had piled human remains on it and set them alight – heads and limbs, stacked in a pile and pouring black smoke into the air. 'Were they *cooking* people?' She edged closer, keeping her pistol raised as she noticed other inlet pipes leading away from the sump. But as she reached the pile of remains, she saw that they were not meant as a meal. There were occult symbols painted around the pump on the floor, in blood.

'Sacrificial altar,' said Sergeant Vollard, emerging from the darkness as troopers spread out around the chamber, guns trained on the exits.

'Looks like it,' said Karpova, kneeling down to study the marks. 'Unusual, though.' She had encountered cultists in many different warzones and there was an element of consistency to their madness. They often carried sigils that were subtle variations of icons she had seen on other worlds, but these daubings were unlike any she had seen before. They resembled serpents, writhing round the head of a xenos predator with three blade-like tusks rising up from its head. 'Looks like a tyranid,' she said, shining her stablight on the grotesque image. 'These people were praying to xenos.' As she studied the shrine, she had a sudden sense that something awful was about to happen. She tried to dismiss it, but the feeling grew, an ominous, building threat that made her look back over her shoulder.

Vollard was standing right behind her. He looked terrible. All the colour had drained from his face and he looked like he was about to be sick. She stared at him. 'You've seen worse than this.'

He shook his head, frowning. 'Forgive me, captain. I… I fear I might be… I'm not myself.'

'Not yourself?' She stood and gripped him by the arm,

nodding to the troopers that were crowding into the sump. 'Show some damned backbone.'

'I've seen this before,' he said, pointing his sword at the xenos face. 'I've seen it in my dreams.' He laughed oddly. 'Captain, I think my mind has gone.'

'Forgive me, captain,' said a nearby trooper, nodding at the swirls of paint. 'I've seen this, too. I think it's called the Harbinger.'

Karpova felt a surge of anger. It took her a moment to identify the reason, then it clicked – the face on the floor was familiar to her too. She had been trying to suppress the truth, but the word 'Harbinger' had dragged it into the light. What was happening to her? She considered admitting that she understood what Vollard was saying, then she realised that the surrounding troopers were all staring at the painting with fear in their eyes. The sense of foreboding rose to such a level that she felt like sprinting back up the waste pipe. 'It's all this polluted air,' she said calmly. 'It's clouding our thoughts. This place is toxic. We've spent too long down here.'

She looked back at the charred body parts and the disgusting sigils. How had she come to this? Decades of training and service and here she was, crawling through drains with a head full of maddening images. All she had ever wanted was to prove what she was capable of, and now, in this foetid pit, she felt like she was drowning.

'Burn it,' she spat, turning to go. 'Burn all of it.'

Chapter Eighteen

ARGENTUM FOREST
SAMNIUM PROVINCE, REGIUM

Storm Speeders roared and lifted from the forest floor, summoning a cloud of leaves and spray as they rose through the branches. It was only as they broke through the forest canopy that Vultis realised it was now as dark above the trees as it was below. His speeder's engines coughed and spluttered as he banked, and the navigational equipment chimed angrily, unable to come online. The tactical display in his helmet was equally shot, spitting fragmented data down his visor until he killed the signal with a blink.

As the others circled around him, he stared out across the treetops. In any normal forest, they would have been able to plot a route with ease, using familiar landmarks to retrace their path, but the swell made that impossible. Even the sun was hidden, obscured by the heavy darkness that had enveloped the planet.

'Brother-Apothecary.' Tanaro's voice crackled over the vox. 'You have studied this forest in detail. What do you advise?'

'One moment, sergeant.' Vultis steered his speeder lower,

looping down to one of the hilltops that broke through the trees. Then, as he circled, he saw what he was looking for. In his first few weeks on Regium he had catalogued the most common species of tree and made extensive notes on them. He had observed that moss only grew on the northern side of the trees that rose above the others. He used this fact to identify north and then flew higher, picking out landmarks that were south-west of his current position. He locked the speeder on that setting and roared off across the forest, confident he was now heading back towards Zarax. The other speeders fell in behind him. 'If we maintain this heading we will reach the fortress,' he said.

'Are you sure?' said Baraca, who was seated at his side. 'The weather might have other ideas.' To the east, Vultis saw the familiar signs of a swell starting to form. The treetops were eddying like a wind-lashed pool.

'Those are only the early flurries of a storm,' he replied. 'We should outrun it if we hold our course.'

As the speeder accelerated he glanced at the containment unit. The symbiont was thrashing and writhing, slamming against the armaglass. As it flailed uselessly at its prison, he saw that it was watching him with its black, featureless eyes. The first specimen he studied had not been as intact as this one, and he was surprised to realise that the thing did not appear to be mindless. It looked malevolent, even calculating. And its eyes were not as blank as he had thought. There were shapes drifting across the tacky surface. Or were they lights? The speeder was locked on course, so he leant down, looking closer at the parasite's eyes.

Vultis hunched over the mound of corpses. His arms and chest were slick with clinging blood and his mouth was crammed with raw meat. The corpses were the pilgrims. He had cornered them and torn them apart. They never stood a chance. Not against him. He felt a wave of disgust at the thought that he was here, sunk so low, feasting in the abyss.

Something slammed into him, jolting the speeder sideways. The image of the feast was still large in his thoughts, and for a moment he could not grasp what was happening. He seemed to be in two places at once – two minds.

'Fill your mind with reason,' he said, using Castamon's words as a mantra. 'Leave no room for the unnecessary.'

It worked. The lieutenant's logic shone like daylight into his mind, revealing the truth. Had the symbiont confused him? Had it invaded his thoughts? He remembered his talk with Abarim in the laboratorium. If the thing was channelling etheric power, perhaps its leaders were nearby.

'Are you still with us, Luco?' said Baraca, staring at him.

There were klaxons sounding on the control panel and the speeder was juddering. The roll bar next to him was buckled, as was the door, and he could smell smoke. Something had hit them while he was distracted. He looked outside and saw that there were shapes darting through the shadows. He had made a study of the local raptors and none of them were large enough, or demented enough, to slam into a speeder. The shapes were only silhouettes, but the sinuous limbs and the bat-like wings were familiar – they were winged tyranids, of a kind he and Baraca had faced many times before.

He took out his bolt pistol and tried to target one of the shapes. They looped and spiralled as they flew, turning in the spores like scraps in broth. He finally managed to get a bead and squeezed the trigger.

'Vultis?' Baraca looked back at him through the darkness. 'Is that you?' Baraca was running down a walkway, following the pilgrims. His armour was dented and smoking and there was blood smeared across the blue ceramite. Vultis rushed at him, raking his claws down

Baraca's back, tearing the power pack from his armour and sending Baraca tumbling to the floor. Baraca whirled around, bringing his combat knife up, but Vultis cast it aside. Baraca howled as Vultis began ripping through his armour and into the flesh beneath.

Vultis cursed as he found himself back in the Storm Speeder. There were more alarms and the speeder was now shaking violently. Baraca had leaned over and grabbed the controls, struggling to hold their course. The air was full of promethium fumes and it sounded like the anti-grav plates were about to tear loose, clanging and rattling against the undercarriage.

A tyranid hurtled towards him through the darkness. He fired, kicking it backwards in a flurry of wings, but more were diving at the speeder from every direction. Baraca gunned some of them down, but others flew on and thudded into the fuselage. They died as they hit, their carapaces exploding on impact, but he realised that was their intent – they were using their bodies to destroy the speeder's fuel lines and grav-plates.

One of them latched on to the edge of the cockpit and gripped Baraca's arm with a claw, wrenching him sideways and tearing at his harness.

Baraca grabbed it by the head, snapped its neck and hurled it into another tyranid, sending both tumbling backwards.

Cries howled across the vox-channel as the rest of the squad struggled to pilot their speeders.

Then Baraca grunted in annoyance as the control panel died under his fingertips. The klaxons ceased and the lights blinked out, leaving the whole interface inert.

The speeder dropped, plunging towards the forest.

Vultis thought fast. He was hundreds of feet up. The crash would most likely kill him and Baraca, and even if they survived, the containment unit would probably be smashed. He would never get the specimen back to his laboratorium. The thought of failing Castamon horrified him. He grabbed the control yoke back from Baraca and, to his relief, the speeder responded. It had no power, but he could at least direct the crash. Vultis thought back over the reports he had read. He studied the surrounding trees, estimated the distance he had left to travel and decided on a plan. It was hazardous, bordering on reckless, but the alternatives left him almost no chance of survival. 'My engine is dead,' he voxed. 'I intend to ride the swell. The rest of you, hold your current course.'

'Ride the swell?' demanded Tanaro. 'Explain yourself.'

He fired a few more rounds, knocking back the nearest tyranids, then banked the speeder hard to the right, sending it straight into the path of the storm. 'This is the only way, sergeant. We will rejoin you at Zarax.'

Branches and leaves crashed as they surged forwards, catapulted by incredible force. Vultis' head jolted back against his seat and he heard armour plating tearing from the wings. But the speeder held together. And, rather than being dashed to the ground, it was hurled forwards, surrounded by a howling din. Baraca laughed savagely at his side. 'By the Throne!' he bellowed.

The tyranids tried to follow, but the moment they entered the swell they were torn apart by the whirling trees, ripped into shreds and swallowed by the maelstrom of branches. Vultis steered towards the direction of the swell, minimising the damage to the wings and fuselage and letting the storm carry the speeder, gently nudging the controls as branches eddied around him. The fuselage rattled louder as the speeder lost altitude. There was no sign of the xenos now, but there was still a good chance that the speeder would be torn apart before he could reach the edge of the forest. He tried the ignition again, but the mag-plates remained silent. The tremors became so violent that the control panel cracked, exposing the frame beneath. There was so much debris lashing into his face that Vultis struggled to see, but he had a suspicion the trees were thinning out. Then he was sure of it. The speeder was approaching the edge of the forest.

There was a shriek of tearing metal as more fuselage came away. Air howled through exposed engine parts and despite Vultis' efforts to keep the speeder level, it started to tilt, the left wing pointing gradually downwards. He battled with the yoke, conscious that his glide was about to become a spin.

Then there was a loud clang and they were free, shooting out across fields of moonlit grass. No, not moonlit, he realised. There were lights flickering in the darkness overhead. He did not have time to consider the implications of that yet. Air roared through the ruined speeder as it rattled through the gloom. The controls were still threatening to send them into a spin, but he held the yoke firm and, as the ground rushed up to greet him, kept the wings level. Beside him, Baraca was still laughing.

The landing gear had been ripped away so the speeder landed on its belly, jolting Vultis and Baraca against their harnesses and throwing up a wave of soil that drummed against them as they tore through the ground.

After a few seconds, it came to a halt. The tail rose into the air, then slammed down, giving the Ultramarines one last jolt.

Finally, there was silence.

Chapter Nineteen

THE GOVERNOR'S PALACE, SALAMIS HIVE
SAMNIUM PROVINCE, REGIUM

Governor Seroc looked out through armaglass doors. Salamis sprawled below him, a collision of industry and decay. Cargo transports, aircars and guide-tugs swarmed through the smog, lights blinking as they banked and looped through the city. He watched them for a while, counting the fires he could see raging in hab-blocks and warehouses. It was shocking how quickly things could fall apart.

He turned his back on the scene. His office was sparsely decorated. His predecessor had crammed it with gilded tables, portraits and overstuffed couches, but Seroc had cleared all that away the day he took office. There was a scratched metal trestle table, covered in charts, architect's plans and scrolls, and a few uncomfortable-looking spindle-backed chairs. Other than that the room was empty apart from a cabinet-shaped cogitator chuntering quietly to itself in the corner, spewing reams of parchment into a metal basket. 'Did the Ultramarines lie?' he wondered aloud.

His aide, Lanek, was perched on one of the chairs, scowling and tapping her foot on the floor. She looked up, surprised.

Seroc took a deep drag on a lho-stick, holding the fumes in his lungs until he felt light-headed.

Lanek shuffled on her seat. '*Can* Ultramarines lie? Didn't the Emperor breed that out of them? They're better than us.' She licked her lips, looking at the papers on the table. 'Perfect.'

Seroc took another deep drag on the lho-stick, struggling to keep his hand steady. 'Nothing about this situation is perfect. Do you remember what they said? They said they would crush the xenos' – he gave a vague wave – 'somewhere out there in the void. And all I had to do was keep people calm.' It was taking all his strength of will not to howl. He had heard the stories. He had seen the things that were landing in the fields and forests.

'Better be careful what you say,' she warned. 'The confessor will be here any minute.' She lowered her voice. 'It's not wise to criticise the Emperor's finest.' She walked over to the window to stand beside him. They never displayed affection in public, but in the absence of servants she squeezed his hand and spoke softly. 'Look, how many times have we been through hell? Plenty. And usually with a self-serving tyrant at the helm, rather than an honest man like you.'

'This is different. You know it is. We're not just facing an angry mob this time.' He rested his forehead on hers. Then he loosed her hand and walked over to the table. 'Why in the name of the Emperor did they choose me as governor? I've never sought power. I didn't want any of this.'

'Maybe that's why. Maybe it's because you're better than all the power-hungry crooks who came before.'

'The bar wasn't set very high.'

She moved some of the papers and lifted up a drawing that was different to all the others. Rather than a technical schematic it was a sketch – a drawing of a Salamis remade, with open spaces and cleaner air. 'None of the others would even dream of this.'

He gave a non-committal grunt. 'A dream is all it will ever be.'

'At least you had the dream. At least you aspire to *something*.'

He smiled at her, wishing he could see himself as she did. 'I wonder what the confessor wants.'

There was a knock at the door and Lanek headed over to open it. 'We're about to find out.'

Seroc stubbed out his lho-stick on the desk and waited to greet his guests.

Captain Karpova came in first, tense and glowering, followed by the haughty, long-limbed Sergeant Vollard. They saluted him like he was the Lord Commander Militant, then stepped aside as Confessor Thurgau swept into the room, hands clasped in benediction as he smiled at everyone. He was accompanied by his huge, savage-looking bodyguard, the preacher Wroth.

Seroc was aware that he should attempt some platitudes, perhaps even offer them a drink. He was also aware that, in front of such powerful people, he should avoid plain speech and keep his cards to his chest. His awareness of those things only served to worsen his mood as he barked out: 'Castamon was wrong.'

Karpova and the sergeant had already noticed the plans on the table and were frowning as they tried to decipher his notes. Confessor Thurgau gave him a sympathetic smile. 'What do you mean, governor?'

He tapped the papers in front of him. 'This isn't just a few xenos ships loitering at the edge of the system. This is an invasion. Full-scale invasion. Here, on Regium. I got these reports from the Ilunum Orbital before it went off-grid. They show the whole of the Samnium Province, from the Kourko Mountains right down to the Vanand Peninsular. He tapped a blurry shape.

'This is the fortress at Zarax. And this, up here, is Salamis. And these dark areas, here, here and here, are *enormous* swarms of predators. Predators of a kind no one has ever seen before.' He heard the tremor in his voice but could do nothing to stifle it. 'And this, this is where the predators *destroyed* the processing plants at Ereza.' He snatched a sheet from the table and held it up to the confessor. 'This is how it looked before the swarm.' He lifted the other sheet. 'And this was after they passed. Nothing left. Just ruins, barren earth and bodies. The whole outpost, wiped out in a few hours. It's like they ate the damned place.' He jabbed the printout again. 'The same thing here. And here. All of these outposts, wiped out. Everyone dead.'

Captain Karpova took the sheet from his hand, spread it out on the table again and peered at the details, tracing her finger over the lines. 'They're heading for Zarax. These groups that came south from the foothills emerged at different points, but look how they're all coming together – they're massing, and they're all headed south to the fortress.'

'Apart from these,' said Seroc, still unable to steady his voice. 'These ones that appeared near Shellib City. They seem to be headed straight for *us*.'

Karpova nodded. 'Smaller numbers, though, compared to the swarms moving on Zarax.'

Seroc stared at her. 'The Ultramarines said they would deal with the xenos. All we had to do was keep order in the meantime.'

She stared at him. 'Situations change.'

'So what do we do? I tried to contact Castamon but he's not at Zarax. I spoke to a sergeant. He said to hold my nerve and await further instructions when Castamon returns from Port Dura. Hold my nerve? What in the name of the Emperor is that supposed to mean?'

Karpova was still studying the maps. 'It means you follow the orders you have been given. Maintain stability. Maintain output. Defend Salamis.' She tapped another printout, a schematic of the hive. 'You have void shield generators, power shields and defence lasers. And you have the Four-Hundred-and-First. We can hold this place until doomsday if we need to.'

'Exactly.' Confessor Thurgau smiled. 'Although...'

'Although what?' said Karpova, snapping her gaze onto the priest.

'Well, we haven't spoken to Lieutenant Castamon since we saw him in Zarax.' He shrugged. 'Sometimes, and I'm sure you know this better than anyone, captain, if a chain of command has been broken, it's more important to honour the *intent* of an order, than to slavishly adhere to the details.'

Karpova narrowed her eye.

'Forgive me,' he said, taking the map. 'Here's Salamis, threatened by the smaller xenos force and very well defended, thanks to Lieutenant Castamon, with powerful void shields, lasers and thousands of local troops, including your own, magnificent regiment. And here, here we have Zarax, threatened by an *enormous* host and defended by a tiny garrison.'

'Castamon told us to protect the hive,' said Seroc, worried by where the conversation was going.

'But why, governor?' Thurgau smiled again. 'He asked us to hold the line because if Salamis falls, he will be exposed from the north.' He waved the paper. 'Now there's a vast host descending on him from the north. That's exactly what he feared. So should we stick to the letter of his command and watch as he dies?' He looked around at them all. 'What hope will there be for any of us if Castamon and the Ultramarines are wiped out? What hope will there be for Regium? What hope will there be for the entire Sanctus Line?'

Karpova nodded, slowly, and looked at the maps again. 'He

sent the entire Four-Hundred-and-First up here. I think he knew a large force might approach from the north. He just thought it would hit the hive rather than bypass it. The xenos are not behaving as he expected. You might be right. We might need to adapt to the developing situation.' She pointed out another location on the map. 'What's this here? To the south of the xenos?'

'Korassa Gorge,' said Seroc, battling a wave of nausea.

'And is that the only route through that line of peaks?'

'Well, yes, I suppose. The alternative is to head five hundred miles east into the forest and loop around the Kourko Mountains.'

'Then that explains the disposition of the xenos swarms. Look, they're all making for that pass. It's the quickest route to the fortress. But if we hit them there, we'd create a bottleneck. We could hold them indefinitely.' She nodded eagerly. 'Perhaps even do more than hold them back. These creatures win by weight of numbers. Most of them are mindless. Their primary tactic is to overwhelm defences by swarming at them from every direction, heedless of their losses. But in a confined space like a gorge that tactic would not be available to them. The vanguard would be small. We would have complete control over the situation. And if I positioned artillery on the surrounding slopes, here and here, we could inflict heavy losses on the creatures further back. We could create an extremely efficient crossfire.'

'Captain,' said Confessor Thurgau, staring at her in excitement. 'Let me explain why I needed to speak to you all this morning. Since we reached the hive, I have been performing my duties to the best of my ability. I have preached sermons to people on the brink of ruin, people whose faith was wavering.' He nodded to his companion, the glowering brute called Wroth. 'And my brethren have dealt with many groups who had already lost their faith, punishing their vile idolatry and misbelief. Between the sermons and the executions, we have made steady progress.' He looked earnestly at Governor Seroc. 'We are purging Salamis of sin, governor. You no longer need to worry about the souls of your citizens. But...' He began pacing the room, swinging his sceptre. 'I have known for weeks now that the Emperor requires *more* of me.'

He saw the frown on Seroc's face. 'Let me explain. My career in the Adeptus Ministorum has progressed at unusual speed. I'm not telling you this through vanity but because I sense the Emperor's hand behind my success. Every crucial decision I have made has been driven by what I can only describe as visions.'

Seroc glanced at Lanek, knowing she would treat this comment with the same scepticism as him. She was careful not to meet his eye, keeping her gaze on the wide-eyed confessor as he hurried back and forth.

'Whenever I have reached an impasse, either spiritually or in more worldly matters, I have prayed until the answer presented itself.' He grinned at them all. 'And, by the Throne, it works. Every time. And here, on Regium, I have felt the Emperor's presence clearer than ever before. He is so close, my friends. So close I can almost touch Him. So close that, even before I asked Him for guidance' – he waved at the maps and charts – 'even before all of this, He spoke to me. He showed me, with more clarity than ever before, what I was sent here to do.'

Seroc felt like he was in a room with one of the raving addicts who sometimes accosted him on the streets, but he was worried to see that Captain Karpova was staring intently at the priest, hanging on his every word. 'What have you seen?' she asked.

The confessor came to a stop in front of the window, gripped his sceptre in both hands and tilted his head back. He closed his eyes and spoke in a sing-song voice. 'I can see it now, even as we stand talking in this room. The vision is with me, always.'

'Praise the Emperor,' rumbled the preacher, Wroth, closing his eyes.

'I see myself, carrying a Cadian banner and riding at the head of an armoured column. I am leading a glorious host. And the wonderful thing is' – he opened his eyes and pointed his sceptre at the papers on the table – 'the host is advancing into a narrow gulley, just like the one Captain Karpova has pointed out on that map.'

Karpova nodded. 'And what happens in the gulley? What do you see next?'

'Victory.' He said the word quietly, but his eyes were flashing. 'The Emperor's light is shining down on me and the soldiers at my back, your regiment, captain, see the light. And they believe in the light! And it spurs them on to efforts no one could ever have imagined, even from such hardened warriors. Your troopers do not simply halt the xenos, they *rout* them. They slice into them like a surgeon's blade and cut the heart from the swarm.' There were tears forming in his eyes as he pictured scenes only he could see. 'They become one with me, the light, the cosmos and the Emperor. They are His fist, slamming down on the monsters that have come to devour His children.'

The confessor leant back against the wall, breathless, his eyes still locked on Karpova. 'It is a *miracle*.' He shook his head, regaining his composure. 'But until you looked at that map, I had no idea where or how it would take place. Now we have a name and reason. We must strike the enemy at Korassa Gorge. And we must do it because that is where the xenos will be at their weakest.'

'Castamon's orders were to protect the hive,' said Seroc.

'Exactly,' said Karpova. 'And how can we do that if we let this host continue to Zarax? Look at those charts. The Ultramarines are already facing attacks from the south and east. And maybe even from the west if the xenos can travel through the sea. They can hold, I'm sure, but Castamon is not expecting attack from the north. He thinks the enemy will move on us here, at the hive. That's why he granted you so many resources. And his logic was sound. But the xenos are behaving oddly. They're ignoring the hive and throwing everything at Zarax.' She gripped the handle of her sabre, fixing him with her single, furious eye. 'We *cannot* allow that to happen.'

Karpova turned to the confessor. 'I know nothing of holy visions, but the things you describe fit exactly with the tactics I would employ. We can trap their vanguard in a crossfire and rain death on the rearguard, driving them forwards into the kill-zone. We could confuse them and send them into a frenzy. And in all that mayhem, I will be able to lead my most skilled troops and try to find whatever alpha creature seems to be commanding them. There must be something – a predator that's larger or stranger than the lesser breeds.'

'Do you know that would work?' asked Seroc. 'How much do you actually know about these monsters?'

She continued glaring at him. 'They are an enemy. And an enemy always has a leader. I will single it out and behead the attack. It could be done in a matter of hours. We will make the northern approach to Zarax safe and then return here, ready to defend the hive against any counter-attack.'

'This is madness.' Seroc was unable to hide his frustration. 'We can't base our whole strategy on your wild guesses and a...' He waved at Confessor Thurgau. 'On a *vision*. On a dream that might be the result of indigestion. It's lunacy.'

His outburst was followed by pregnant silence. Thurgau looked shocked by what he had said and Karpova glared at him.

Wroth tilted his head to one side and gave Seroc a quizzical look. 'Lunacy?' His voice was low. 'Is that how you describe the beliefs of a senior Ecclesiarchy prelate?'

Seroc could feel Lanek's stare burning into the side of his face. His aide was furious with him, but Seroc had never mastered the art of dissembling. 'We can't base our whole military strategy on something so... so vague.'

Wroth took a deep breath. Then he reached for something under his robes.

'Wait.' Confessor Thurgau held up a hand. 'We've all been disconcerted by what we have seen.' He gripped Wroth's shoulder. 'The governor is a devout man. I'm sure he did not mean to imply that Ministorum doctrine is lunacy.' He gave Seroc a kind look.

Seroc felt a crushing sense of despair. 'No,' he said quietly.

Thurgau nodded. 'And you would not wish to hinder the plan I have discussed with Captain Karpova, would you?'

Seroc reached for a lho-stick and lit it with trembling fingers, looking at the maps on the table. 'My prayers will go with you.'

Chapter Twenty

The fortress was surrounded by lights. As Damaris looked out from the battlements she felt like the stars had fallen from the heavens. The sky was black and strange, with no sign of the constellations she was used to, but the slopes leading up to Zarax were clad in pinpricks of light. People were approaching the fortress from every direction, pouring from the forest to the east and south, and from the hills in the north, and arriving at the coast to the west, all of them bathed in the light of torches and lumens. She had never seen so many people gathered in one place.

Vela was at her side, leaning on her stick, and Magistrate Urzun was standing a few feet away, but none of them had spoken for several minutes. Damaris was no longer trying to convince anyone that the crowds were fleeing political unrest. The people who poured through the gates brought shocking stories – tales of monsters that tumbled and slithered from the sky, predators unlike anything seen on Regium before. Some had seen their families torn apart and devoured. And no one dared look up, staring ashen-faced at the ground. Every now and then there was a pulse of light in the blackness and each flash revealed a nightmare – fleeting glimpses of the mass that had blotted out the stars. It was not clouds or fumes, but coiling, heaving shapes, organs or limbs too vast to be comprehended. Damaris was crushed by grief and fear. What was happening to her home? Regium had seen riots and war but never anything on this scale. It looked like the end of the world.

Ultramarines strode back and forth along the battlements, barking orders to the human soldiers who were manning the guns. They looked unfazed by what was happening overhead, but Damaris could not stop thinking about how few they were in number. Everywhere an Ultramarine passed by, people regained their confidence, leaping to obey, reassured by the Space Marines' implacable confidence. But there were only a handful of them, less than forty, she guessed. And it was her fault there were so few. She glanced at Urzun, thinking back over their lunatic decision to redirect the other squad. How could she have agreed to such a plan? The shock of seeing the caves destroyed must have robbed her of her senses. She could remember the absolute confidence she felt at the time, the belief that it was right to make a fool of Castamon, but now, as the darkness pressed in, she wanted to leap back in time and make herself see sense.

Urzun caught her glance and stared back at her, looking panicked, no doubt imagining what would happen if she revealed what they had done. They would be executed, certainly, but as she felt the sky grinding and churning overhead, the idea of being shot seemed almost like a blessing.

'What is it?' snapped Vela, noticing how they were looking at each other. 'Why are you looking so shamefaced?'

'What do you mean?' said Urzun, his panicked tone making it even more clear that they had something to hide.

'Damaris?' said the old woman, frowning at her.

Damaris had never lied to Vela. Everything she had achieved, her rise to the rank of consul, was down to the old woman's trust in her. Could she tell her? Perhaps Vela could help undo the damage? No, she decided. Falsifying Imperial orders was an act of unpardonable heresy. She could not involve Vela in that. She shook her head and looked away, too ashamed to meet Vela's eye.

'Whatever it is,' began Vela, her cheeks flushing, 'you'd best start–'

She was interrupted by a commotion further down the wall. One of the Ultramarines had his head tilted and his fingers pressed to his helmet while others were gathering round him. The Ultramarine nodded, looked up and pointed into the night, gesturing to the hills north of the fortress and saying something to his battle-brothers.

'Is this it?' muttered Vela. 'Is it beginning?'

'Is *what* beginning?' whispered Urzun, pawing anxiously at his wild hair and looking at the crowds outside the walls.

A low, rumbling drone swelled from the darkness, growing quickly louder.

'Why aren't they doing anything?' cried Urzun, staring at the Ultramarines. 'They're just standing there like–'

His question was answered as Castamon's gunship rumbled into view, looming out of the darkness, landing lights blinking and revealing blue-and-white Ultramarines insignia. Cheers rose up from people in the streets below and even Damaris found herself mouthing a prayer. Castamon's unshakeable conviction had always enraged her, but in the face of what she had seen at the gates, it now seemed like a lifeline. 'Let's get to the landing pad,' she said, helping Vela towards the steps. 'He must have news from Port Dura. He will have answers.'

They entered the crush at the bottom of the steps and had to fight their way through the crowds.

'When do we stop letting people in?' muttered Urzun, grimacing as the mob pressed close. 'Are we expected to house the entire province in one fortress?'

Damaris scowled at him. The more she thought about it, the more incredible she found the idea that she had entered into a conspiracy with such a cowardly man. She had always considered him vaguely unpleasant, but she now realised how poisonous he was. 'Would you rather lock them outside the walls?' She waved at the shapes churning in the sky. 'To face that?'

'No, of course not. I just worry that we cannot house so many people in comfort. I have no need of a bed myself, of course, and I...' His words trailed off as he looked up at the sky and lost his thread. He looked terrified.

She ignored him, struggling on through the crowded streets until she saw the landing platform up ahead. An Ultramarines warrior was waiting to greet the lieutenant. He was fully armoured and stood motionless, bathed in exhaust fumes as the aircraft crunched down. The Space Marine was flanked by soldiers, helots and crew, who rushed forwards as the engines died and the landing gear rattled on the ground.

Lieutenant Castamon leapt down onto the platform before the boarding ramp had finished lowering. He was followed by human soldiers and then by the hulking, heavily armoured form of the Librarian, Zuthis Abarim.

As the Librarian emerged from the fumes, several onlookers backed away, making the sign of the eagle. Abarim was emitting an odd light – ghostly strands of blue and purple that coiled around his armour. It looked like he was at the eye of a storm. Fingers of electricity crackled around his gauntlets and flashed in his cowled helmet.

'What *is* that?' gasped Damaris, looking to Vela for an explanation. She had heard people describe the Librarian as a psyker, saying that he possessed unearthly, telekinetic powers. And Vela had previously warned her that Abarim might be able to read her thoughts. She had considered the claims to be fanciful, but now, as the Librarian clanged down the ramp, leaning heavily on a battle axe, she felt a rush of fear.

'Is he on fire?' whispered Urzun.

Damaris looked at Vela. 'Is he?'

Vela shook her head, clearly unnerved.

Damaris turned her attention to Castamon and was relieved to see that he looked as composed as ever. He marched straight over to the Ultramarine who was waiting on the platform to greet him, and spoke quickly, before ordering him back to the walls. Then he looked around the crowd that was forming on the landing pad. He singled out Damaris and Vela and gestured for them to follow him as he headed off, flanked by soldiers and equerries. 'We have little time,' he said, his voice resounding through the darkness. Abarim followed the group at a slower pace, limping but still cutting an imposing figure as his armour sparked and flickered.

Terror pulsed through Damaris and she struggled to move. Why did he want to speak to her?

'Move,' whispered Vela, grabbing her arm and dragging her towards Castamon.

When they reached Castamon's citadel, guards appeared at the top of the steps and threw the great doors open. Castamon swept up the steps and headed inside, calling out as he entered. 'Consuls only. No one else is to be admitted.'

There was a flurry of requests from nobles and merchants, but the guards stared them down, slamming the doors once the small group had been admitted. Damaris' terror grew as Castamon marched through galleries and antechambers in silence, heading towards his private rooms.

Urzun whispered in Damaris' ear. 'What did he mean, we have little time?'

The same troubling thought had occurred to Damaris, but her thoughts were mostly fixed on her treachery. Castamon had returned from Port Dura. She had tricked Squad Gerrus into going to Port Dura. Did he now know what she had done? Was he about to execute her? She glanced at Vela. Would he execute her, too?

They entered a vast, austere-looking stateroom lined by statues of robed Ultramarines who were posed with muscles straining and brows furrowed, as if holding the ceiling aloft. The statues were huge, and Damaris felt crushed by the weight of their gaze. The architecture was grand but severe and, apart from a heavy stone table and its chairs, the chamber was unfurnished. The place did not radiate beauty or luxury, only uncompromising power. Castamon indicated that Damaris and Vela should sit.

Abarim avoided the table and headed to a far corner, sitting on the pedestal of a statue and clutching his hands together, head bowed, as though in prayer. Castamon removed his helmet and sat down at the table. He placed his helmet on the table's surface with a *clang* then leant back, massaging his scarred face. Damaris and Vela sat opposite, with Urzun loitering nervously behind them.

An uncomfortable silence stretched out.

'How is Port Dura?' asked Damaris, when she could bear it no longer.

Castamon stared at the table, drumming his fingers on the

stone. She thought that he had not heard. Then he spoke, his voice a low rumble. 'Destroyed.'

'Pardon?'

'Port Dura has been destroyed.' His gaze remained fixed on the table.

Her old anger resurfaced, overcoming her terror. 'The entire city?' She felt cold with rage. 'How can you say that so calmly, as though it doesn't matter?' She struggled to breathe. 'All those people...'

He looked up at her, but rather than meeting her eye, she had the sense that he was studying the lines of her face, examining her.

'Thousands of people lived there,' she said, her anger growing as he failed to show any hint of emotion.

'Tens of thousands,' said Vela, quietly.

Castamon's tone remained impassive. 'I understand what the destruction of the port means. When Regium is safe, I will allow myself the luxury of grief.' He waved a hand, dismissing the subject. 'I have to locate Brother-Apothecary Vultis and bring him back to Zarax, but there are things I must explain to you first. There is much to be done and little time to do it. My men are busy manning the walls, along with most of our auxiliary troops, so they cannot be waylaid by hysteria. My brothers tell me that your people are already panicking. So I need you two' – he nodded to Damaris and Vela – 'as trusted figureheads, to give them ballast. You must ensure they remain steadfast.'

Vela glanced at Castamon's bolt pistol. 'They'll obey any command you give them.'

'My purpose on Regium is not to police your subjects. You will ensure that they *want* to help. They need to understand what is at stake if they become a distraction. If they rage against their situation or allow terror to get the better of them, they could hinder my men. And that will *not* be tolerated.' His tone hardened. 'Is that understood?'

They nodded.

'What about Salamis?' asked Vela. 'Is the hive safe?'

'Governor Seroc and Captain Karpova have their orders. They are to remain in the hive, whatever happens beyond its borders. Salamis is *heavily* armoured and I have faith in the Cadian Shock Troops. With the Four-Hundred-and-First there, Seroc can hold that hive until I have dealt with the situation here.'

Vela shook her head. 'You said you have to find your Apothecary first. So he's not here?'

Castamon nodded. 'He has not returned from the hunt.'

'What if he's been…? What if you never find him?'

Castamon ignored the question. 'I have one other matter to address before I leave. Squad Gerrus never arrived at Shellib City. And there has been no word from them for several hours. Intermittent vox-messages *are* getting through, so the squad's silence is peculiar.'

Damaris felt Urzun tense behind her. 'Why are you asking us about this?' she asked, immediately realising how defensive she sounded.

Castamon looked puzzled by her response. 'I have a way to contact them.' He glanced at Abarim, who was still sitting in silence, fingers of light playing around his armour. 'But it will place a further strain on Brother-Librarian Abarim. If you have news of the squad, it will save me harnessing other methods. The presence of Ultramarines is a matter of note. People discuss it. Have any of the recent arrivals mentioned Gerrus or his men?'

Damaris felt like she might vomit. Was Castamon toying with her? What kind of monster was he? No, she decided. If he suspected her, she would already be dead. 'I've heard nothing,' she managed to say, giving Vela a hesitant look. 'Have you?'

Vela looked back at her, frowning, obviously sensing she was holding something back. Then she shook her head. 'I've heard nothing of any Ultramarines outside this fortress,' she said, replying to Castamon. 'And as you say, their presence usually causes a fuss.'

Castamon gave her an unreadable look. Then he stared at a shaft of light that was hanging from a high window. He remained like that for several seconds, lost in thought, before he turned to Abarim. 'Make the attempt. If you are still able.'

Abarim did not look up.

Castamon paused for a moment, as though listening to something. 'I understand,' he said, answering a voice no one else heard. 'But the risk is worth it. We must locate them.'

Abarim nodded. Then he stood up, lifted the enormous axe from his back and began pacing the room.

Castamon watched him, then looked over at Damaris and Vela. 'You may feel some discomfort.'

'We'll leave,' said Vela quickly, shoving her chair back.

'You will stay.' Castamon's voice was like iron.

Vela licked her lips, clearly not pleased, but she remained in her seat. Damaris wondered what Vela knew of Librarians that had made her so keen to leave the room. And she also wondered what Castamon meant when he said they might feel some 'discomfort'.

Abarim walked in a circle, his head still bowed. The energy dancing across his armour responded to his movement, becoming more pronounced. The joints of his battleplate flashed and the pipes in his cowl rippled with light. As he circled, he let the blade of his axe trail along the floor, scratching the flagstones and kicking up embers. Rather than fading, the circle grew brighter, shimmering with the same light that was pulsing from his armour. The light radiated cold rather than heat and, as Abarim scored the floor, the temperature in the room dropped. The cold spread with shocking speed, until Damaris saw her breath clouding in the air before her face as if she were outside on a winter's day. Vela hugged herself, grumbling.

As the blade scraped the floor it produced a humming sound, like a finger tracing the rim of a glass. The sound grew gradually louder until Damaris' head started to pound. She could not stop thinking about the fact that she had sent Squad Gerrus to Dura. And Dura was destroyed. She had sent them all to their deaths. She had murdered the Emperor's most prized warriors. Could there be any greater crime? Damaris had the horrible feeling that humming sound was in her thoughts with her – that it was stirring memories to the surface. But that was lunacy. She stared at her trembling palms, half expecting to see blood on them. Was she losing her mind? The sense of another presence in her mind increased as the sound droned louder. Then she remembered Vela's warning that the Librarian could read minds. She felt a rush of panic and looked up to find that Abarim was staring directly at her. His eyes were slivers of blue fire. Without warning, he clanged the haft of his axe on the floor. The sound stopped and the circle vanished. Lights still sparked across his armour, but the room returned to a more normal temperature and the sense of menace faded. Abarim sat back down on the plinth, lowering his head.

'There is no need to search for the squad.' This was the first time Abarim had spoken since the Ultramarines landed. He sounded even less human than Castamon. 'They have been sent to their deaths.' The light in his eyes pulsed brighter. 'This woman has betrayed us.'

'What do you mean?' demanded Castamon.

'Damaris sent falsified orders to Sergeant Gerrus.' Abarim kept his head bowed and his tone neutral. 'As a result they were in Port Dura when it was destroyed. I have examined her thoughts. Her guilt is clear. She is a traitor.'

Damaris had come to think of Ultramarines as emotionless, automaton-like beings, but the anger she saw in Castamon's eyes was as terrifying as the things in the sky. If she had not been seated, her legs would have given way.

'Is it true?' he asked quietly.

She wished she could find some righteous anger to use as a crutch, but it had abandoned her – all she had left was shame. She lowered her head, staring at the table.

'Damaris?' said Vela, sounding dazed.

'Were you also responsible for the destruction of the port?' asked Castamon.

'No!' cried Damaris. 'I know nothing about that! I would not murder my own people.'

'But you would murder ours,' said Abarim.

Castamon rose slowly to his feet and gripped the handle of his pistol.

Damaris was too terrified to move. All she could hear was her pulse hammering in her ears.

Someone banged on the door.

'Enter,' said Castamon, still holding the gun and staring at Damaris.

'My lord,' gasped a breathless soldier, running into the room. He saw that Castamon was gripping the gun and hesitated, before he recovered his composure and continued. 'My lord. Brother-Apothecary Vultis has returned.' He stood to attention, trying to sound calm, but could not entirely hide his excitement. 'We had brief vox contact with him. He came down somewhere outside the gates.'

Castamon continued watching Damaris as he replied to the

soldier, showing no emotion at the news. 'I will join him when I have finished my business with the consul.'

The soldier saluted, took a last glance at Damaris, then hurried from the room, closing the doors behind him.

'She murdered them,' said Abarim. 'They were good men. Veterans. Taken from us on the eve of battle.'

Castamon released his gun.

Damaris let out the breath she had been holding.

'Your life is forfeit,' said Castamon. 'But it will not end until I have time to find out what else you have kept from me.'

The Ultramarines stood and headed to the doors in silence. Then the doors slammed and they were gone.

Damaris sat in stunned silence, trying to grasp what had just happened. Behind her, she heard soldiers entering the room and she slumped forwards onto the table, letting her head fall into her hands.

Chapter Twenty-One

Castamon strode through the gates and headed out into the crowds. He was preceded by blocks of auxilia troops, who used their lasguns to shove people aside and clear a path. Thousands of refugees were racing through the darkness and swarming around the gates, wounded and traumatised, jostling for a place in the fortress. But Castamon barely registered them, marching down the avenue made by the soldiers, out into the fields. The air resisted him, thick and greasy and filled with spores. He took out his pistol and made for a glimmer of light up ahead, just beyond the edge of the forest. Abarim was at his side, armour shimmering as he gripped his force axe.

'Life signs.'

Castamon nodded. 'I see them.' He blinked sigils across his helm display. 'It *is* Vultis. But it would seem that he came down hard.'

The auxilia soldiers began to drop behind as he and Abarim picked up their pace. He had ordered the rest of the Ultramarines to remain on the walls and prepare for imminent attack. The impact tremors were a constant drumroll now and he knew, from hard-won experience, what was about to happen.

After a few minutes he saw the shape of the downed Storm Speeder up ahead, silhouetted by flames coming from its fuselage.

'He lives,' said Castamon as a figure came rushing towards them. He recognised the shape of the Apothecary's Gravis armour and the autopsy equipment mounted on his backpack. Despite his bulky battleplate, Vultis was running fast across the mud, showing no obvious signs of injury. Behind him was the hulking shape of Baraca, who also seemed to be unharmed.

'They are not alone,' said Abarim.

It took Castamon a moment to understand what Abarim was referring to, then he saw that what he had mistaken for the edge of the forest was actually a line of figures – a numberless host, stretching out in every direction, bearing down on Vultis.

'He needs covering fire.' Castamon glanced back at the troops rushing after them. 'But the light is too poor. They might hit Vultis and Baraca.'

'I can help,' replied Abarim.

'Abarim, are you sure? I saw how it drained you, reading the consul's thoughts. Will you have enough control?'

'A little light, brother. I can still manage that.'

Before Castamon could press him further, Abarim raised his axe, crying out an oath as he ran. Energy pulsed from his armoured cowl, shimmering down his arm and igniting the axe's runes. The temperature dropped and the distant thumping sounds grew muted. Then columns of light burst up from beneath the ground, lancing through puddles and troughs, illuminating the fields for hundreds of feet in every direction. Castamon felt a surge of righteous power. It was more than light, it was the force of Abarim's will, igniting the very air.

Vultis emerged from the glare, his white armour flashing as Baraca pounded after him. But Vultis and Baraca were not the only things Abarim had revealed. Behind them the light washed over a tide of glinting shapes. Thousands of xenos that were thundering from the forest. They were so numerous and frenzied that it was hard to distinguish one from another – carapaces, talons, tendrils and beaks all merged together.

'Covering fire!' bellowed Castamon across the vox-channel, raising his gun as he raced through the light.

The sound that followed was immense. There were hundreds of soldiers in the field behind Castamon and just as many up on the fortress walls, and as one they opened fire. Along with the lasweapons and the Ultramarines' bolters, there was the ground-shaking boom of autocannon batteries, blasting hard rounds into the oncoming host.

The barrage smashed into the front ranks, ripping them apart. There was a rattle of exploding bodies as shots vaporised shells and hurled limbs through the air.

Vultis and Baraca ignored the carnage erupting behind them and continued running towards Castamon and Abarim, sprinting across the trembling earth, but some of the xenos were closing in on them – gangly, humanoid creatures with bone-scythe arms and powerful hind legs that hurled them forwards at incredible speed. They twitched and lurched as they ran, lashing at the air and cutting across the ground.

'Abarim!' cried Castamon, before opening fire, spitting bolter rounds into the tyranids. 'Strike them down!'

'For Macragge!' roared Abarim, thrusting his force axe towards the alien host.

Nothing happened.

Then the Librarian cried out and stumbled, lowering his axe. The light died.

The gunfire ceased.

Castamon stopped and looked back at Abarim. He could just about see the Librarian in the afterglow of las-bolts, clutching his head and stumbling, about to fall.

Thousands of hooves drummed across the ground. Behind Castamon, soldiers cried out in alarm. They were no longer able to see their foe, but they were close enough to hear them coming. Castamon blanked the voices out. Distracting thoughts tried to impinge on his consciousness – thoughts of what would happen if he and his battle-brothers failed to reach the fortress. He drove the doubts down, determined to analyse the situation with dispassion. Unlike the humans, he could still see reasonably well, even in the near-total darkness. Vultis and Baraca were still running towards him, only seconds away now, but the tyranid vanguard was about to overtake them.

He grabbed his combi-weapon and heard the reassuring slosh of promethium. Then he rested the gun on his hip and sprayed white-hot flame through the night, tearing the darkness. He aimed near Vultis and Baraca, but not so close as to injure them. Tyranids erupted, exploding into flames, rolling and tumbling across the ground. His fire also illuminated the ranks further back, giving the soldiers behind him a chance to open fire. There was another deafening barrage.

'I have it!' cried Vultis as he reached Castamon. He did not stop to talk, racing on towards the fortress with Baraca in his wake.

Castamon hurled another torrent of flame and considered his next move.

'Do we need to buy him time?' gasped Abarim, stumbling through the darkness to his side. He looked dreadful but his fist was raised, ready to fire the storm bolter fixed to his vambrace, ready to die if it was needed.

'Leave that to us,' crackled Tanaro's voice over the vox.

Storm Speeders howled through the sky, rushing in from the direction of the forest and firing on the xenos. Bolter rounds drummed into the tyranids, ripping into the vanguard as grenades lit up the darkness.

The speeders banked and dived, strafing the tyranid front lines and sending the xenos charge into disarray.

'Go!' cried Castamon, turning and running back towards the fortress with Abarim staggering after him.

The air was heavy with the stink of burning flesh, and as he ran Castamon fired blindly over his shoulder, back towards his pursuers.

As he neared the gates he saw that the scene had become even more panicked. There were still crowds of civilians outside the walls and they were fighting each other in their desperation to get inside.

Castamon used his helm display to check that Vultis was safe, then he waved Abarim through the gates and turned to face the seething dark. As soldiers retreated past him, he raised his combi-flamer and stood alone, spewing promethium across the field, lit up by the infernal light of his weapon. People screamed and howled all around him and the tide of xenos was just about to hit. Inhuman faces glinted in the firelight, their basalt-black eyes showing no trace of emotion. Gunfire rained down on them from the battlements, but it was like hurling pebbles at the sea. And everywhere he looked, civilians were sprinting and stumbling across the muddy fields, abandoning bags and possessions, desperate to escape.

+You can do no more for them.+ Abarim sounded calm again. +We must close the gates and raise the shields.+

Castamon nodded. The wave was about to break. The tyranids were almost on them. 'Sergeant Tanaro,' he voxed. 'You have done enough. Bring your men back into the fortress.'

The Storm Speeders banked and roared towards him, flying low, still firing on the tyranids, then they soared up and over the walls.

+Now,+ warned Abarim.

Castamon fired one last time, then turned his back on the carnage and marched through the gates.

Behind him, the tyranids sliced into the crowds. There was an explosion of screams and the sounds of people being ripped apart. The monsters were senseless – clawing and devouring in a frenzy.

As Castamon entered the courtyard Sergeant Tanaro came running towards him from the opposite direction with his battle-brothers, all of them gripping pyreblasters. They fired out into the darkness as the gates rushed down, incinerating everything that charged towards the quickly closing gap.

The gates slammed shut, but a single tyranid leapt through first. It hissed, whirling around, its claws scraping on the rockcrete and its tail lashing.

Sergeant Tanaro strode forwards with his bolt pistol raised and slammed several rounds through the monster's head, sending it clattering back across the flagstones.

There was a loud thud as the tyranids outside crashed into the gate, hitting with such force that the walls juddered.

Castamon wiped blood from his visor and looked around. Vultis was safe, leaning against the wall of a building on the other side of the courtyard with Baraca. The Apothecary offered up a weary salute as he saw Castamon looking. Baraca was busy scoring a line into one of his pauldrons, as he did every time he believed he had escaped an unworthy death.

Abarim was also nearby but he was pacing back and forth, still clutching at his head; his force axe was hanging loosely in his grip, the blade dark.

'Raise the hoardings!' cried Castamon as he strode across the courtyard. 'Activate the cautery shields. Man the walls!'

Soldiers and Ultramarines leapt to obey, and before he had taken more than a few steps, a rumbling sound rose from beneath the ground. The fortress' reactor was powering up dozens of interlinked transformers and generators.

On the battlements above a metal canopy clattered up from the stones, locking to crenellations, covering the walkways and hanging out over the parapet. There was a series of slamming sounds as autocannons were rolled forwards against the metal, barrels jutting from perfectly sized embrasures.

Castamon nodded as he watched the siege defences clang into place. The clattering of the metal was followed by a deep, grinding hum, resonating through the walls as the shields were activated. He looked up as a shimmering barrier rose over the fortress. It looked like a dome of oily liquid, rainbow-like, with colours bleeding into each other.

'A void shield,' said a trembling voice. 'Nothing could breach that.'

He looked down and saw the elderly proconsul, Vela Zalth, was standing nearby, leaning on her staff, with the withered-looking magistrate, Urzun, cowering behind her. The magistrate could not meet Castamon's eye, but he guessed it was he who had spoken. 'It is not a void shield,' he replied. 'It is an ancient Terran defence known as a cautery shield. A heat-transference bulwark. We were able to link it to the old calefaction pumps.'

As the shield rose, the sound of the tyranid attack grew muffled and distant, as though heard underwater, and a sense of calm returned to the fortress. Even the civilians became less panicked as they watched Castamon talking calmly to the magistrate. He was about to move on when Vela spoke up.

'Damaris is not a heretic,' she whispered urgently, blocking his way. 'I have no idea what happened. I don't understand why she did what she did. But she's no traitor.'

Castamon studied the old woman, surprised. Few people would have the nerve to challenge an Ultramarine, let alone block their way. 'I will seek you *both* out when the situation is stable,' he replied. His tone made it clear that this was a warning rather than a promise.

Vela and Urzun paled, but before they could say more Castamon strode on through the crowd, doling out orders and examining defences. The brief moment of quiet was broken as the guns began to fire, recoiling with teeth-rattling force. The shield rippled as shots cut through it and the noise of splintering bodies was just audible outside.

'Good work, brother,' said Castamon, spotting Vultis and heading over to him. He looked at the parasite swimming in the Apothecary's containment unit and felt a shiver of hate.

'Lieutenant,' said Vultis standing upright and saluting. He waved at the shields and the soldiers rushing to man the walls. 'This invasion is advanced. I witnessed spores coming down all over the forest, some of them large enough to carry whole broods of attack creatures. The tyranids could not have travelled here so fast from Krassus. There is more to this than we thought.'

Castamon nodded. 'I suspect the tyranids at Krassus were a decoy. We have been attacked from the opposite direction. Attacked by a much larger force. This was a planned invasion. They never had any interest in Krassus and I doubt, now, that they were retreating from a defeat. It was a lure – a way to draw me away from Regium. And it almost worked. I almost took the entire garrison out there. If I had done that, Regium would be doomed.'

'But why would they choose Regium over Krassus? Krassus is far richer in biomass.'

'I think it likely that they have the same goal as the heretics – to target the Sanctus Line.'

Vultis looked past him, to where the glimmering shield rose over the battlements and the guns were pounding. 'How long can you hold them? How long do I have?'

'Zarax is built to endure. We are well provisioned. But this is a vast host. I cannot say how long the shields will hold. It may be as little as hours.'

'And what about the wider populace?' asked Baraca, still carving his pauldron. 'What about the people on the rest of the planet?'

'I have done what I can for the people of the Samnium Province,' replied Castamon. 'All refugees in the north of the continent have been directed to Salamis Hive, and the hive will stand. They are well defended and Governor Seroc has Regium's entire complement of Cadians. As for the rest of the planet...' He looked at Vultis. 'Their best hope is that you complete your research quickly. If our theory is correct, and the tyranids are thinking tactically, then their energy will be focused here. They tried to draw me out to Krassus, and that failed, so now they will attempt to devour Zarax. *We* are the primary target.'

Vultis nodded. 'It is too early to make a definitive assessment, but what I have seen may fit this theory. The tyranids we encountered in the forest behaved in a manner I have not seen before. It almost seemed as if they lured us into one of the old geoengines, where they lay in wait. Once we arrived, they encircled us. I was reminded of hunting techniques I used when I was a youth.'

'They drew you out, just as they did with Tyrus.'

Vultis nodded. 'It would seem so. And that is not all. We were attacked by a creature that was larger than any I have encountered before in a tyranid swarm. And I swear it was the one I saw on the *Incorruptible*. The one Abarim and I thought of as the Harbinger. And I had the strangest sense of it watching me, *understanding* me. There was a cold intelligence in its eyes. I could easily imagine that such a creature had devised the plan to ensnare us.'

Vultis' tone was odd and distracted. It reminded Castamon of how Abarim had been sounding recently. It occurred to him that if Vultis became confused or unable to work, there would be a significant delay in the research. He nodded through the crowds to the buildings beyond. 'Get your specimen to safety and begin work. I will join you as soon as I can. Baraca, stay at his side. Let nothing interrupt his work.'

They both saluted and headed off into the crowds while Castamon turned to face a barrage of questions from soldiers who had gathered round him. He answered them as quickly as he could and then headed off towards the walls. He jogged up some stairs and stepped out onto the battlements, joining another crush of bodies – troopers and engineers, yelling orders to each other as they manned the weapons, surrounded by noise and smoke.

A mortar round landed outside, and in the resultant flash of light he saw that the fields around Zarax were completely full of bioforms. They were flooding through the darkness in their thousands, waves of armoured thoraxes and barbed, glistening tails. It was quite unlike an army. No banners. No generals. No bellowed commands. Just an ocean of snarling horrors, seething from the forest. Along with the waves of bipedal and hound-like shapes there were large, lumbering bioforms – sinewy hulks with sphincter-topped appendages that trembled as the monsters stomped through the mud. Winged creatures fluttered overhead, like bloated bats with talons and undulating tails. There was movement everywhere he looked. Even the forest was in motion: the trees were swaying, falling and collapsing, throwing up clouds of steam as they fell. Castamon had faced tyranid invasions before and he understood what was happening – the xenos had transformed the atmosphere. They had made it so toxic it was acting like a stomach, slowly digesting every form of life it touched.

Sergeant Tanaro saw him coming and saluted. There was a gleam of excitement in his eye visible even through the visor of his battle helm. His attitude could have been considered callous, considering what had just happened at the gates, but Castamon could forgive the sergeant's eagerness. It was a long time since any of them had faced a foe on this scale – a foe worthy of the First Company. And the hive fleets of the Great Devourer were old enemies of the Ultramarines Chapter. He could understand Tanaro's enthusiasm for the fight.

'Port Dura has been destroyed,' said Castamon, 'and we have lost Squad Gerrus.'

'The entire squad?' Tanaro could not hide his shock. 'That is a bitter blow.'

'We will lament their passing with promethium and bolt-rounds,' said Castamon.

Tanaro punched his chest armour. Then he waved out into the darkness. 'We calibrated the shields just as you ordered, lieutenant. Everything is working as it should.'

Twenty feet from the fortress, the glimmering dome touched the ground. The tyranids inside the shield had finished feeding and were clambering over each other, starting to scale the walls in their hundreds. But the thousands of xenos outside the perimeter had been halted. They were hurling themselves at the shield, clawing and climbing over each other, but most of them were powerless to advance. Castamon looked in different directions and it was the same everywhere he could see – the shield was holding. The tyranids crushed against its surface were blackened and smoking.

'Multilayered,' said Tanaro, his voice full of pride. 'Each layer running at a different frequency. Slowing ground troops almost as effectively as projectiles or energy attacks.'

As they watched, some tyranids managed to breach the barrier, hauling their carapaces through the shield as though crawling through glue. But only a minority passed through the surface; most remained trapped on the outside of the dome, juddering and burning. And those that did make it were scorched and limping, trailing melted carapace as they approached the wall.

'Lieutenant?' said Tanaro, gesturing to the xenos inside the shield. Some were now halfway up the wall, slamming their claws into the reinforced rock as they climbed.

Castamon nodded, and Tanaro called out to the soldiers. 'Fire at will!'

Where the canopy jutted out from the battlements, it created a hood with a grilled opening underneath, so the defenders were able to aim down through murder holes at the shapes scampering up towards them. Auto-weapons clattered and lasguns screamed. All around the fortress walls, the rest of Squad Tanaro called out the same order. The tyranids were ripped apart, falling back onto the others in a shower of gore.

A noise caught Castamon's attention and he looked the other way, down at the crowds inside the fortress. The civilians were out of control, attacking each other and grappling over belongings. This was exactly what he had hoped to avoid, but with the consul under arrest, the mob was leaderless. The auxilia troops were trying to restore order but many of the people were too far gone – overwhelmed by the scenes at the gate and exhausted by their journey, they had finally found a way to express their outrage and horror at what they had seen.

'We do so much for them,' said Tanaro loftily. 'We face things they could never dream of. And they repay us with treachery and barbarism.' His hand rested on his pistol. 'They are–'

'They are the reason we exist,' interrupted Castamon. 'And you would do well to remember that. The Emperor did not forge us through battle lust. He forged us to preserve humanity.' He tapped Tanaro's gun. 'Which takes more than ammunition. We have to show them what they can be. Courage is not enough, Sergeant Tanaro, there must be honour, too. Remember that, always. We must set the standard for others to follow.'

'Of course,' said Tanaro. 'Forgive my outburst.'

Castamon looked down at the streets below. The scene had already become a riot. People were breaking into buildings and being clubbed to the ground by angry soldiers. He saluted Tanaro and headed back down the steps to the courtyard. When he was back on the ground he marched over to the steps of the library and stood at the top of them, framed by the building's grand portico.

'Silence!' he roared, using the vox-grille in his helmet to amplify his words. The crowds fell quiet, looking over at him, halted by the threat in his tone. He waited until everyone was looking his way. 'There are monsters at the gates,' he said. 'They know nothing of reason. Nothing of duty or virtue. But you are the sons and daughters of the *Emperor*. Your ancestors are His ancestors. Your blood is His blood.' To his surprise, he found that he was becoming angry. He analysed the emotion, tracking its source, and pictured the face of the consul, Damaris. He understood. He had put his faith in her and she had failed him. He accepted the rage and it lessened, but he kept the ferocity in his voice, using it as a chirurgeon uses a scalpel. He waved at the damage the mob had done to statues and buildings. 'The people of Regium are known throughout this entire sector. You are respected and admired. You kept this world pure when so many others fell into heresy. The Emperor knows who you are. And He sees you. He sees you *now.*'

People backed away from each other, lowering their make-shift weapons and staring up at Castamon. Some looked scared and others ashamed, but many looked up at him with pride, dusting down their torn clothes and standing tall.

'These monsters have not come to conquer you. They have no creed. They have nothing but hunger. They came here to *devour* you.' People began to look panicked again, turning to each other and whispering frantically. 'But know this! The Emperor has not forsaken you. He has given you a chance to serve – a chance to honour the debt we all owe Him, a chance to grind these monsters into the ground. I have armour, equipment and weapons. But I need willing hands. I need strong hearts. I need *you.*'

He lowered his voice, using the vox-grille to ensure his words still reached every corner of the fortress. 'Have you come here to cower and bleat?' He looked across the sea of upturned faces. 'Or have you come here to *fight?*'

He saw some confused expressions in the crowd, and some people looked too afraid to respond. Then one of the local priests stepped forwards, his skin encased in a mesh of rusty-looking twigs and tendrils. He was a youth, no more than eighteen or nineteen, but he stared furiously back at Castamon, his eyes shining as he punched his fist into the air. 'For the Emperor!'

The boy's voice was small and weak compared to Castamon's, but in the stillness of the moment, it carried.

'For the Emperor!' cried a woman near the youth, holding her fist in the air even though her voice was shaking.

Dozens, then hundreds of people cried out until there was a forest of raised voices and fists. Castamon let their cries wash over him. Every ragged voice confirmed his faith in them. 'Humanity has a spine of steel. The same steel the Emperor used to forge the Imperium. With every breath you prove your worth! Every struggle! Every act of defiance! Humanity *will* endure! The horrors of this galaxy will *never* extinguish this fire!' He pounded his chest. 'The light of man!' The crowd was roaring now, howling so loud they even drowned out the endless thudding of the invasion. So loud they even drowned out his amplified howl. 'The light of the Emperor!'

He called out to the auxilia troops, who had backed away from the crowd, still gripping their lasguns. 'These people are exactly where they should be. Do not club them, arm them.'

As he marched away, Castamon looked up at the walls, pleased to see that Sergeant Tanaro was watching.

Chapter Twenty-Two

Captain Karpova thought of home. The craggy slopes of Korassa Gorge reminded her of the magnificent Rossvar Mountains she climbed in her youth; mountains on a world that was no more. She was so lost in memories of Cadia that it took her a moment to realise someone was speaking to her. It was one of her elite Kasrkin troops, clad in a suit of thick, moulded armaplas, his voice muffled by his helmet. 'It's Sergeant Vollard,' the trooper was saying. 'We've found him.'

She returned her attention to the present, looking out into the darkness. The gorge below, like everywhere else, shook to the sound of xenos spores. There was a constant *whump, whump* sound as the pods landed in the distance, spilling alien life into the gloom. She was up high, on the rocky slopes of a mountain pass, overseeing the hastily assembled gun emplacements, but the air was no clearer up here than it had been down in the gulley below. It was like breathing stagnant water. Every breath caught in the back of her throat and her eyes streamed constantly. Unlike the Kasrkin trooper, some of her face was exposed to the air, and when she touched her skin it felt gluey and loose. She knew if she brushed at it with any force, layers of skin would slough away. Regium was consuming her.

She swallowed hard, trying to rid herself of the vile taste in her mouth, then turned and looked at the trooper. 'Vollard? I haven't seen him since we left Salamis. Why didn't he attend the briefing?'

The trooper hesitated. 'It's difficult to explain, captain.'

'Try.'

'He's had to be restrained, captain. I found him lying in one of the munitions haulers. He was behaving in an odd, reckless way. Left to his own devices, he might have set the hauler alight and possibly triggered the explosives. When we challenged him, he threatened to shoot us and had to be forcibly disarmed. I was about to inform Commissar Valpys and then... I wondered...'

He hesitated again.

She realised why the trooper had come to her rather than the commissar. Valpys would not make time to try to get any sense out of Vollard. They were on the eve of battle. The execution would be cursory and very visible. Commissar Valpys would make it clear that such behaviour could not be tolerated, and the sergeant would be publicly disgraced. His record would be spoilt. The trooper had come to her because he, like many of the other troopers, respected and liked Vollard. They did not want his career to end in public dishonour.

'I wondered,' said the trooper, keeping his voice neutral, 'if you might wish to deal with the matter personally. We've kept him with the haulers. Trooper Bruzek is watching over him.'

She sighed, looking at the frenzied activity on the rocks around her. According to Governor Seroc's information, they had a few hours at most before the xenos reached the gulley.

She was needed here. But then she pictured Vollard's face. The man deserved better than to die in ignominy. Whatever Regium had done to him, it should not be allowed to eclipse years of bravery and sacrifice. Vollard had once been her commanding officer and was a damned good one. She owed him a lot.

'Who knows about this?' she asked, keeping her gaze locked on the gun emplacements.

'Only Bruzek and me. We all thought you might prefer it to be treated with discretion. No one has informed the commissar.'

She nodded, adjusted her cap and began climbing down the rocks. Her optical implant was fitted with a night scope, but she still had to tread carefully as she made her way back to the path. 'You should be with your squad,' she snapped, without looking at the trooper.

He saluted, heading off in the other direction, thanking her quietly as he vanished in the fumes.

They were digging trenches in the gulley and Karpova nodded approvingly as she saw them, returning salutes and answering questions as she passed through the lines of troopers. They had dug the trenches in the mazelike pattern she had specified – an echo of the fortifications used in the kasr fortresses that once protected Cadia. Every ditch and earthwork was topped by lines of razor wire, and though she did not show it, she was impressed with how much had been achieved in so little time.

She realised the air *was* even worse down here. Like everyone else, she was wearing a respirator that covered most of her face, but the taste was still so strong she had to battle the urge to retch as she headed away from the trenches and marched past lines of tanks and armoured personnel carriers. 'Bruzek,' she said as she walked, speaking quietly into the vox-bead at her collar. 'Where are you?'

There was a crackle in her ear, then the trooper replied, giving her directions to the hauler he was waiting in. She nodded and changed direction, heading past troopers rolling lascannons through the gloom and up into raised positions on the surrounding rocks. Everyone was so busy preparing for the oncoming battle that most of the troopers did not even notice her. Yelled commands echoed oddly through the darkness, dwarfed by the endless, distant thudding sounds.

Finally she reached the area at the rear of the army where the equipment haulers had been parked. She spotted the truck Trooper Bruzek had described, headed over, pulled the tarp back and climbed inside.

'Captain,' said Bruzek, jumping up to salute her as she climbed over ammo crates and piles of lasguns. Sergeant Vollard was gagged and bound, but he had been put in a reasonably comfortable position, sitting on sacks of ration packs.

She returned Bruzek's salute as she approached Vollard. There was a lumen hanging from a void-crate and, as the light swayed back and forth, washing over Vollard, she saw how dreadful he looked. Rather than looking at her, his eyes were flicking from side to side, as though watching shapes only he could see, and he was mumbling frantically into his gag as his feet drummed on the sacks.

She studied him for a moment, then let her hand fall to the pistol at her belt. 'Leave us,' she said.

Bruzek looked pained but saluted her; before dropping out of the truck, he also saluted Vollard, even though the sergeant was oblivious. Then he was gone and Karpova was alone with Vollard.

She took the gun from its holster and flicked the safety. Then she paused. A memory came to her, unbidden. She thought of her first day in Vollard's squad, when she was still just a trooper. They had been tasked with the job of holding an abandoned manufactory as a column of heretics tried to pass through to the hab-stacks on the other side of the building. The fighting had been particularly savage. Half of the company had been wiped out. But Vollard had kept his eye on her the whole time, giving her a wry smile every time she caught his gaze. Like everyone else on Cadia, she was bred for war and her training had been almost as brutal as her first battle, but she would never have survived that first day in the regiment if it had not been for Vollard. The heretics had been transformed by years of worshipping dark gods. They were like nothing she could have imagined. Some had faces in their chests and snakes for tongues. Others had knife-edged wings that sprouted from their backs and cloven hooves in place of feet. Her mind had teetered in the face of such madness and, despite everything she had been taught, her nerve had faltered. But when she saw Vollard looking at her with an expression of droll disbelief, she somehow came back to herself.

She replaced the safety and put the gun back in its holster. Then she took a flask from her belt and sat next to Vollard.

He flinched in surprise, then recognition flashed in his eyes as he saw who she was. He gasped as she pulled the gag down over his chin, closing his eyes and tilting his head back.

'Here,' she said, lifting the flask to his lips.

He hesitated, then took a sip. A violent coughing fit shook him and she snatched the flask away, but he shook his head and she held it to his lips again. This time he managed to hold the drink down. He sighed with pleasure, then his expression darkened. 'Damn,' he muttered, looking around at the piles of equipment. 'I've made quite a mess of things.'

She removed her respirator, had a drink and studied him. He was himself again. His eyes were clear and his feet were no longer kicking at the sacks. 'That's what I've heard.'

'Is Commissar Valpys on his way?' There was a slight tremor in Vollard's voice.

She shook her head, holding the flask to his lips again. 'He's too damned important to waste on the likes of you.'

He laughed. It was a genuine, honest sound and Karpova savoured it like music. Outside, the endless thudding of the pods continued, but in the back of the hauler there was still the sound of humanity. 'My head is clear now,' said Vollard, looking at the piles of equipment. 'But before… I could see the xenos everywhere.' He laughed, but it was a bitter sound this time. 'In here. In my uniform. In the air. I was hallucinating.'

She thought for a moment, studying his face a little closer. His skin, like hers, was starting to sag and loosen, to liquify, but it was noticeably worse. And when he breathed, she could hear fluid rattling in his lungs. 'Where's your rebreather?' she asked, looking at the equipment fixed to his belt.

He frowned. 'Not seen it since… Not seen it since we uncovered that rats' nest in the underhive.'

She waved at the hazy air. 'So you've been walking around since then breathing in all this?'

'I suppose I have.' He looked at her, hope flickering in his eyes. 'Why did you come here?'

'You know why I came, but now I'm wondering… Wait a minute.' She rummaged around in the crates and sacks until she found a respirator. She switched the filter on and strapped the mask over his face.

He took some deep, ragged breaths. Then he shrugged. 'I do feel a bit better. My head is clearer.' His eyes creased in a smile. 'What a damned idiot.' He frowned again. 'But what if it's more than the fumes? How can I be sure I'm safe?'

She analysed her motives. She had come here to give Vollard a dignified way out and now she was considering… considering what, exactly? Letting him live? Would she be doing that for the good of the regiment or for more selfish reasons? No, she decided – Vollard was a good man, one of her best. And she could ill afford to lose him. She reached behind him and undid the restraints. He leant forwards, rubbing his wrists and taking more deep breaths through the respirator. Then he gave her a questioning look.

'Stay with me.' She held his gaze. 'I'll watch you. I'll know.'

There was no trace of his habitual ironic expression. He looked troubled.

'We all make mistakes,' she said, thinking back to the decisions that saw her absent from Cadia when it fell. 'But some of us get a chance to make amends.' She tapped the regimental bugle at his belt. 'And you're the only one who can get a note out of this antique.'

He looked like he was on the verge of saying something earnest and heartfelt, then the wry glimmer returned to his eyes. 'Do you know,' he said, 'the rebreather helped. But I think it may have been the drink that really brought me to my senses.' He eyed the flask. 'I wonder if it might be safest to have one last snifter.'

She stood and replaced her respirator, adjusting her cap and dusting down her fatigues. She tried to think of something to say that would match his jokey tone, but the concussive thumping sounds outside drained the humour from her. This was an invasion on a vast scale. It would be her biggest fight yet. Her pulse quickened as she considered the implications. A victory here, shielding Castamon from a crippling attack, would show the 401st for what it was: one of the finest Militarum regiments in the entire Imperium. 'Straighten your uniform,' she snapped. 'It's time these people see what we're worth.'

She jumped out of the wagon and down onto the muddy

rocks, looking at the crowds of toiling soldiers. 'Cadia stands,' she said quietly, her skin tingling with emotion. Then she signalled for Vollard to follow and strode off into the murk, barking orders as she went.

Chapter Twenty-Three

'These people are different,' said Valacia, grabbing Tharro's arm.

They had parked at the brow of a hill, overlooking a smaller transitway than the one they were travelling on. There were lumen beams flickering back and forth and the headlights of several groundcars shimmered in the gloom.

'*How* are they different?' demanded Tharro, coming back to the ledge and peering down the slope. There were dozens of people gathered around the groundcars. One of the vehicles was on its side, clearly wrecked, and they seemed to be examining it.

'They're upset,' said Valacia. There was someone trapped inside the trashed groundcar and people were pointing at them, waving their arms and arguing. 'Some of them look like they're crying. The things we found at the fuel depot weren't like that, were they? They wouldn't have cried and argued.'

Tharro took a deep breath. Their journey to Salamis had mostly been a waste of time and fuel. The hive was surrounded by monsters. Even from half a mile away, they had seen that the place was besieged. The one small consolation was that they had found a pair of rebreathers and some ammunition for the shotgun in an abandoned Militarum barracks. They were also now wearing plates of flak armour that would probably get them shot as deserters if they bumped into any soldiers, but that was low on Tharro's list of fears. 'These people do look different to the ones at the fuel depot,' he admitted. 'But that doesn't mean they won't try to kill us.'

'We're dying anyway. We can drive across the whole province if you like but something will eventually eat us, or we'll starve, or choke on these disgusting fumes. I mean, what's your plan? What are we actually going to do? This fuel will be gone soon. Will we just keep walking?'

For the last couple of days, Tharro had felt a pain in the side of his chest. It was like a cramp, deep behind his ribs, and it felt horribly significant. He had not mentioned it to Valacia. What was the point in giving her another thing to worry about? But he had a terrible feeling something was rotting in his chest – poisoned by the vile air. He could not help imagining what would happen if he suddenly dropped dead. Valacia would be alone in this hell. He looked down at the arguing figures below. At least if they were travelling with someone else, she wouldn't end up alone. He nodded. 'Let's go down.'

She stared at him. 'Really?'

He studied the group again. Some of the people had guns and they were all carrying bags of food and equipment. 'They look like they know what they're doing.' He gripped her hand. 'Shall we?'

She nodded and they turned away from the slope, climbing back into the groundcar and starting the engine.

They drove slowly down the transitway. Valacia had the shotgun in her hands, but she kept it out of sight and Tharro tried to drive in a way that seemed unthreatening.

The people gathered around the wrecked car backed away from it. Some of them were holding guns and knives but no one raised a weapon as Tharro and Valacia approached. They just spread out and waited in silence.

As he drove closer, Tharro began to relax. They *did* look like normal people. Farm labourers by the looks of them, just like he was. They looked scared and wary and some of them were injured, but they had normal eyes, filled with emotion, and none of them had the ridged, mutated foreheads he'd seen at the fuel depot.

'We're from the Bethzar agri complex,' he called out. 'We tried to go to Salamis but it was even worse there.'

'Are you armed?' replied one of the men. He was heavy-set and balding with a blocky, stern-looking face.

'Yes,' replied Valacia, keeping the shotgun out of sight on her lap.

'Wise.' The man was holding a pistol. He toyed with it for a moment, thinking, then nodded and tucked it into his belt, gesturing for them to approach. 'We don't have any spare food. Or spare weapons. So don't ask.'

Tharro drove closer and parked. Then he and Valacia sat still as people began slowly gathering round, looking curiously at them.

Some of the group wore respirators that obscured their faces but others were visible, and they all looked terrible. Their skin was grey and oozing and their expressions were pained. Most of them coughed as they approached and the sound was horrible to hear – a deep, liquid rattle ending in a wheezing gasp for breath.

Tharro's hopes sank as he saw that these people looked even worse than he and Valacia did. But there was something in the stern man's expression that intrigued him. A look of determination. 'Where are you headed?' he asked. 'To Zarax?'

The man laughed bitterly. 'It's worse there than here. The

swarms are all congregating on the fortress.' He leant so close that Tharro could hear the rattle in his throat. 'This is all because of the off-worlders. Did you know that?' His words dripped with bile. 'The swarms only came here because of the Ultramarines.'

'Who told you that?' asked Valacia, gripping Tharro's arm.

'Well, it doesn't take a genius to work it out. All the swarms have headed straight to Zarax. Even the ones that have hit Salamis were heading to the fortress. And it's not just that. We came from Port Dura, and before we left I spoke to one of the local militiamen. Do you know what he told me?' The man was red-faced with anger now. 'He told me that the Ultramarines have a long history with these creatures. Tyranids, they call them. And they've been at war with them for *centuries*. They're old enemies. Apparently, the Ultramarines have driven the tyranids from dozens of worlds and now the tyranids want revenge. That's why they followed the Ultramarines here.' He waved at the tortured sky. 'The off-worlders brought all this down on our heads. Every death is down to them.'

Tharro had heard all sorts of tales and he treated this one with the same circumspection as the others, but he had no desire to start an argument with an armed mob. 'Where *are* you going then?' he said.

The man hesitated then shrugged. 'You may as well know if you're going to join us. *Are* you going to join us?'

Tharro looked at Valacia and she nodded. 'If you'll have us,' said Tharro.

They got out of the groundcar and shook hands and exchanged names. The man was called Jebel. 'We're going to the Uxama chem-works. Have you heard of them?'

'Yes. But there's nothing there. They were abandoned years ago. Some kind of turf war. Rival gangs. The place was shut down.'

'There *is* something there.' Jebel's eyes shone, and Tharro felt a current of excitement wash through the group. 'Tolophon here's an engineer.' He waved to an elderly man at the back of the group. He looked half-dead, leaning on someone and staring at the ground, drool hanging from his oxygen mask. 'He's struggling to get his words out now, but when we first found him he could still talk. And he told us he did a job at the chem-works years ago. Secret work. He got out of there because of a tip-off. He heard that the engineers would be killed once the work was finished. And do you know what he was building?'

Tharro shook his head and Valacia gripped his arm tighter.

'He was building a secret hangar. A place where a crime lord was going to hide cargo shuttles. The kind of cargo shuttles that don't appear on any manifest lists, if you know what I mean. The hangar's underground. Hidden in old world roots. But Tolophon knows how to get in.'

Tharro looked over at the engineer. 'But how can he tell you if he's…? If he can't talk?'

'You can still show us, can't you?' said Jebel, looking over at the engineer.

Tolophon continued staring at the ground, but he gave a slight nod.

'So why've you stopped?' asked Valacia, looking over at the wrecked groundcar.

The man looked pained. 'We're *not* stopping.'

There was a grumble of disagreement from some of the others and Tharro realised this was the source of the argument they had seen from up on the ridge.

Jebel waved them over to the crashed groundcar and Tharro saw the problem. There was a young woman trapped in the wreckage dressed in a blood-drenched boiler suit. She was barely conscious and the blood was flowing from a wide gash across her forehead. 'We can't move her, and we can't move the ground-car,' said Jebel.

Some of the others started to argue again, but he glared at them until they fell silent.

'What's her name?' asked Valacia, dropping to her knees at the side of the groundcar.

Jebel hesitated, seeming angered by the question. 'Avula,' he said finally, but he would not look at the woman. He turned to Tharro, growing angry again. 'We've already stayed here too long. Do you understand?' He waved back down the transitway. 'You've seen what happens to anyone who stays out here.' He looked up into the darkness. 'We're visible. I'm amazed the swarms haven't come already.'

'But do you have any cutting tools?' asked Valacia, sounding desperate. 'You can't leave her here like this.'

'We could spend hours!' cried Jebel. Then he took a deep breath and spoke in a calmer voice. 'We could spend hours trying to get her out. And we don't have hours. The tyranids will be here any minute.' He glared at the rest of the group. 'And you all know it.'

Most people looked away and none of them offered up any argument.

'We can't leave her,' whispered Valacia.

Jebel looked from her to Tharro, shaking his head. The anger had gone from his voice and he now sounded numb. 'You can come with us to Uxama if you want. Or you can stay here until…' He waved at the sky. 'But we're going now. And when we get in that hangar, we're getting off this planet. I have a pilot. We *are* doing this. We *are* getting out. But if you stay here then change your mind, don't expect to find us waiting for you at Uxama. We have one shot and we're taking it the moment we reach that hangar.'

Valacia stared at Tharro. 'I'm not leaving her.'

Tharro could see the passion burning in Jebel's eyes. The man was utterly determined. He was going to leave the planet. He was going to escape. Nothing could stop him. He cherished the image. He pictured himself on a shuttle, watching the world shrink beneath him as he rose into the void. Then he let the image go. He sat down heavily next to Valacia and gripped her hand.

Jebel looked on the verge of saying something angry, but eventually sighed and nodded. He thought for a moment, looking from Tharro to Valacia. Anger and pity warred in his eyes. Then he took the autopistol from his belt and handed it to Tharro. 'Use this.' His voice was brittle. 'However you see fit.'

Then he walked away and the others followed, climbing into their groundcars in grim silence, before starting the engines and roaring off down the transitway.

The lights remained visible for a long time, and Tharro struggled to watch them go.

Chapter Twenty-Four

They heard them before they saw them. The ground shook to the rhythm of numberless hooves. Confessor Thurgau was in the turret of a modified tank, standing up through the commander's hatch, looking down the barrel of its massive Earthshaker cannon. The tank's searchlight was scanning back and forth across the gulley, its harsh, white light flashing on the surface of rocks and pools. He could see Captain Karpova and Sergeant Vollard riding in the tanks to his left and right, magnoculars raised to their masks, and there were dozens more tanks along the entrance to the gulley, engines rumbling and searchlights probing the darkness. Karpova had positioned her Kasrkin troops directly behind the tanks and, behind them were the companies of shock troopers – serried blocks of men and women, standing in such perfectly arranged ranks that they somehow managed to look immaculate, despite their filthy uniforms. Behind the shock troopers there were units of Sentinels – armoured, bipedal walkers, laden with flamers and missile launchers, twitching on hydraulic legs like impatient flightless birds. Further back still, Karpova had positioned ordnance in the surrounding hills, next to the blocks of armoured supply vehicles, but mostly in rocks that lined the gulley, hidden from sight by netting and leaves. Red-and-blue Cadian banners were mounted on the tanks and they flew proudly, snapping in defiance of the viscous air.

The drumming of the hooves grew louder and Thurgau began to make out other sounds – the smack of beating wings and the scuttling of smaller creatures, clicking across the rocky ground. *'Hold until I give the order,'* said Karpova, her voice crackling across the vox-network. Thurgau did his best to remain calm, quietly chanting a hymn, but he struggled not to howl. He was shivering with emotion and he could sense everything with an acuteness he had never experienced before. He could feel the fibres of his robes, brushing against his skin and the cold metal of his sceptre as he gripped it in his fist. But he could feel much more than that. All around him, invisible in the darkness, he could feel the God-Emperor's host. He could feel their faith in him and their respect for him. They were with him, these souls who guided the Emperor's light through the galaxy – evanescent beings who gave their lives so that the Master of Mankind could pierce the darkness of the void. And soon, perhaps within the hour, he would join them. Everything was proceeding exactly as he had foreseen. He had seen these ranks of soldiers, waiting silently for the storm to hit, eyes grim and resolute behind the goggles of their respirators, lasguns raised in seamless lines, their boots sinking into the mud. Every time he drank the tincture, he saw this moment exactly as it had now come to pass. 'My blood, my soul,' he whispered.

Wroth and the other preachers were standing on either side of his tank, heads bowed and weapons raised in prayer. Some carried chainswords and axes and others carried guns, but all of them were draped in strips of parchment that fluttered around their robes, covered in lines of denunciation and warding.

'*I see them,*' said Karpova, as shapes glinted in the distance. '*Hold your fire.*'

'*Handsome devils,*' replied Sergeant Vollard.

The sergeant's flippant tone seemed surreal to Thurgau. How could he speak like that on the cusp of a miracle? But, of course, no one else knew what was about to happen. He had explained the first part of his vision to Karpova, that he would inspire her regiment to victory, but he had not explained the nature of the miracle; he had not explained that it was his death, at the crucial moment, that would drive the army onwards. He had not explained, because how *could* he explain that he was going to ascend?

Then, even without magnoculars, Thurgau began to see movement in the gorge. It looked like a dam had burst, hurling a debris-filled torrent towards them. The drumming of hooves grew louder and, in response, some of the soldiers began to chant, quietly at first but with growing force: 'Cadia stands! Cadia stands!' The battle cry spread quickly through the ranks until thousands of voices carried the refrain and it became a great chorus. As the proud voices swelled around him, Thurgau had another revelation. It hit him so hard that he thought he might collapse with the wonder. At the moment of ascension, he was going to see the God-Emperor. He felt it with sudden, absolute certainty. He was not just joining the divine host, he was going to meet the Emperor of Mankind Himself too. He was going to appear to him here, today, at the heart of the battle, at the moment of his death. 'My blood, my soul,' he whispered, gripping the hatch, shaken by the weight of the revelation.

'*Squads Twelve to Thirty, take aim.*' Even Karpova now seemed affected by the sound of the chanting. Her voice was tight with emotion.

Thurgau had closed his eyes, trying to come to terms with the scale of the moment. He was about to meet his god. He opened his eyes and saw that the tide of xenos was now close enough for him to discern individual shapes. Had he been unprepared, he might have cried out in horror. They were hideous – a blizzard of membranous wings, gleaming exoskeletons, tentacles and claws. But he *was* prepared. He had seen all of this before, every time he drank the tincture. Everything was exactly as it should be. Ecstasy flooded his limbs and he jammed his sceptre up at the sky. 'Cadia stands!' he howled with the others, his voice breaking with emotion, even though he had no connection to Cadia. 'Cadia stands!'

The xenos were now so close he could see individual faces – long, keratinous heads with soulless eyes. They were clawing and scrambling over each other as they charged, but they still made no sound other than the thudding of their hooves. There were no howls or roars. It was as if they were mute.

Thurgau fixed the sceptre to his belt, then hefted a chainsword from his back, savouring the weight of the oily metal and whispering a prayer as he kissed its scarred teeth.

The tyranids were a hundred feet away, but Karpova still had not given the order to fire.

Seventy feet.

Thurgau gunned the chainsword's engine and the teeth roared around the blade.

Forty feet.

Wroth and the other preachers dropped into battle stances, raising maces, hammers and chainswords.

Twenty feet.

'Open fire,' said Karpova quietly.

Thurgau was blinded and deafened. The gulley was transformed by a dazzling howl of defiance. Shots ripped through the xenos, kicking them over, hurling them through the air and slamming them to the ground. Armoured bodies flipped and splintered. Viscera filled the air, raining on tanks and ground. The barrage tore down hundreds of the creatures in an instant, filling the air with blood mist.

The fusillade was so loud that Karpova finally had to raise her voice. *'Sustained fire!'*

Thurgau gasped as artillery continued raining death from above and behind him. It was the sound of judgement. The footsteps of the apocalypse. He howled with righteous fury, but his cry was lost in the terrible din. It was as if the world were being hammered on an anvil. The light of the las-fire filled his mind, burning through his thoughts, becoming a halo around a figure that was striding towards him holding a flaming sword aloft. Thurgau wept as he howled. The Emperor had come for him.

'Cease fire.'

Karpova's voice brought him back to his senses. He had no idea how long the barrage had lasted, but as searchlights swayed back and forth he saw that the entire gulley was heaped with ruptured, blackened dead. The smell of ozone and promethium filled the air and there was a whistling sound inside his ears.

The ground began to judder again and another tide of shapes began pouring down the gulley. Karpova followed the same procedure as before, ordering the companies to hold fire. The troops began their chant again. 'Cadia stands! Cadia stands!' And then, just as the tyranids were about to reach the lines of tanks, she gave the order to fire. If anything, the salvo seemed even louder the second time and the light even brighter. This time, Thurgau saw the Emperor so clearly that he began to make out His face. His breath stalled as he saw His magnificent features, bathed in holy fire. Artillery boomed and lasguns screamed but Thurgau was consumed by his vision. He had a vague sense that the tyranids swarmed repeatedly and were driven back each time, but he was only half in the physical realm, feeling his soul lift from its shackles, drawn towards the figure in the light. But however fierce the gunfire, the figure remained just out of reach, further down the gulley. 'We have to move forwards,' he breathed. Then, recalling the battle that was raging around him, he spoke into the vox-bead at his collar, speaking to Karpova on a closed channel. 'We have to move forwards.'

'Agreed,' she replied, although he guessed her reasoning must be different to his. Unless… Was she seeing the God-Emperor too? Was the vision spreading? The idea was not a pleasant one. If she knew his plan was to martyr himself, she might attempt to stop him. Or even try to take his place at the Emperor's side. He looked over at her, but in the fume-filled darkness it was hard to see her clearly and her face was hidden behind her respirator anyway. 'Fix bayonets!' she snapped, and a rattle of blades filled the gloom. 'All companies, advance!'

Thurgau stumbled, almost dropping his chainsword as his tank lurched forwards, the treads crunching over splintered bodies and broken wings. On either side of him, the other tanks trundled into the gorge. Officers barked commands and banners fluttered, the colours picked out by roving stablights. The troopers roared their battle cry as they charged, bayonets gleaming, towards the xenos.

Thurgau steadied himself as the tank picked up speed. Guns were blazing all around him and there was another dark tide hurtling down the gulley towards them. Wroth and the other priests were keeping pace with the tank, bounding over corpses with their weapons raised, howling prayers at the approaching xenos.

Then, finally, the tyranids were on them. There was a flurry of glistening limbs and the sound of armour buckling, followed by the ripping of cloth and flesh. The Cadians fired into the onslaught and jammed bayonets into the heaving mass. The tyranids were so frenzied they seemed to be everywhere at once, leaping, tearing and biting.

One of them clattered over the fender of Thurgau's tank and leapt at him. He caught a brief glimpse of gaping jaws before he swung his chainsword and hacked the monster in two, spattering blood through the air. He heaved the carcass aside as another tyranid scrambled up onto the tank and loped towards him, fixing him with its dark, blank eyes. 'Holiest of holies!' he howled, bringing the chainsword round and grinding it into the tyranid's face. 'Make me the vessel of your *wrath!*' Brain and exoskeleton filled the air as he forced the blade down, his muscles screaming with the effort. A third leapt at him, then a fourth, but with every prayer-fuelled lunge he felt his strength grow. Below him, Wroth and the other preachers echoed his prayers, dealing out blows as savage as his.

Something small rushed through the air near his face. He wrenched his chainsword free and snatched a look around. The Cadians were ploughing through the xenos lines, churning them under tank treads and blasting them apart, but the tyranids were now returning fire. Some of the xenos were gripping knots of sinew, organs that were attached to their chests by veiny cords. They cradled them like guns, spitting projectiles. At first Thurgau thought the shapes were bullets, but as they slammed into troopers, he saw that they were alive – burrowing creatures that chewed through armour and flesh. Cadians began to drop as they fought, clutching at wounds, blood rushing between their fingers. Other tyranids carried cones of rotten meat that spasmed, spewing tendrils over the Cadian lines. Like everything else in the tyranid arsenal, the tendrils were alive, contracting on contact and sinking barbs into their prey, dragging them, struggling, down into the mud and the dead.

Everywhere Thurgau looked, hideous life forms were surging over the tanks and troops and the army was no longer advancing. Further down in the valley, artillery shells were still raining down on the rear of the xenos swarm, and for every Cadian who fell dozens rushed to take their place, driving the xenos back, lunging, shooting and stabbing with just as much zeal as the aliens – but they had ground to a halt. The sheer weight of xenos, both dead and alive, was incredible. Their bodies were clogging the treads and gears of tanks with no consideration of pain or loss of life. The tyranids hurled themselves to their deaths without hesitation and, despite the huge numbers of Cadians, the battle was already grinding to an impasse.

'There,' whispered Thurgau, as he spied a patch of raised ground up ahead. It was the spot he had seen so many times before. The place he would die. And the place he would meet his god. 'Captain Karpova!' he cried into the vox, peering through the strobe-lit battle. It was hard to see clearly in the tumult, but Karpova was riding in the command vehicle – a battle tank that was far larger than the others. She was firing her pistol into the xenos while the tank's turret-mounted lascannons blazed beneath her. She glanced his way, still firing into the oncoming horde.

'I have to reach that hill!' he cried, pointing his dripping chainsword.

She nodded, still firing, then barked orders across the vox.

Tanks began veering to the left and the Kasrkin troopers surged in the same direction, felling tyranids with incredibly precise head shots. They looked like they were acting out a training exercise rather than facing thousands of swarming xenos.

Thurgau's tank roared forwards, crushing another wave of tyranids, while Wroth and the others howled more prayers, rushing in the vehicle's wake. As the tank trundled up the incline,

Thurgau wept for joy. He was so close now, only moments away from glory. As the priests and Kasrkin converged on the slopes of the hill, with Karpova's enormous tank close behind, Thurgau realised that the vision was already coming true – the eyes of the entire army were on him. When he fell, they would surge forwards, just as he had seen in his dreams. And their momentum would carry them on through the entire host, breaking the deadlock.

'For the Emperor!' he cried, holding his chainsword above his head and raising a flag with his other hand. 'For Cadia!'

Some of the troopers echoed his cry and it began to wash through the army, but the Kasrkin fought in silence, racing up the hill, still placing their shots with almost preternatural accuracy.

The xenos fell away and Thurgau's tank climbed towards the top of the hill. Emotion flooded him and the light of the battle filled his thoughts. All he could see was the incandescent figure approaching to greet him from the opposite side of the hill, gliding through the air, His feet floating above the ground and His arms outstretched.

'The Emperor dwells within us!' cried Thurgau. 'His is our armour and we are His sword!'

And then, moments away from his prize, Thurgau's prayers stalled in his mouth. As the figure on the hill moved closer, he realised it was not the shape he had expected. His thoughts were still ablaze, but he could see enough to know that the figure was not a man. It was gliding above the ground, as he'd thought, but nothing else was as he had foreseen. He struggled to breathe. Where he had expected to see the Emperor of Mankind, he saw what looked like an enormous lump of meat, shrouded in veins of lightning and trailing barbed tentacles. What he had mistaken for the Emperor's halo was a bony, circular mantle surrounding a grotesque, palpitating brain. There were smaller creatures floating in the light, but it was the first one, the largest one, that caused Thurgau to scream. It was in his mind. *This* was the source of his visions. This *thing* was the source of the light. He had been tricked. As he wailed, he imagined he could feel those vile tendrils, locking around his skull, poisoning his thoughts, filling his mind with lies. His visions had not come from Terra, they had come from *this*, this monstrous alien horror. He could feel its will threaded through him. It was consuming him – not physically, like the lesser tyranids would, but mentally. It was devouring him with lies.

With the entire army watching him, Confessor Thurgau tried to flee, clambering out of the hatch and scrambling back over the tank, dropping his chainsword and flag as he fled, screaming and clawing at his face.

Karpova called out to Thurgau, demanding to know what was happening. All around her, the attack was faltering and tanks were grinding to a halt. She felt a flash of doubt. Could she have been wrong about Thurgau? No, she decided. Faith burned from that man like a beacon. He had been touched by the God-Emperor's fire. He would not fail them.

Then, as the drifting shape floated closer, Karpova saw it clearly for the first time. It was like an enormous lump of flesh, like a deformed brain, wreathed in lightning and clad in a barbed exoskeleton. The limbs trailing beneath it rippled as if suspended in liquid and the entire creature seemed to inhabit a different environment to the other figures in the battle. The way it floated silently through the carnage made Karpova feel as though she was watching an old pict reel.

Still, the Kasrkin showed no fear. Even the arrival of such a horrific being did not unnerve them. They charged up the hill with another barrage of shots, but the smaller tyranids flew at them, enveloping them in tendrils and knocking their shots off target. Then the troopers near the hill began howling and stumbling, clutching their heads and dropping weapons as the larger tyranid glided serenely towards them, energy coruscating from its brainlike mass.

'Take it down!' cried Karpova. 'Protect the confessor!' She could see no sign of Thurgau, but neither had she seen him die. If she could drag him from the wreckage of his tank, she was sure he would still work the miracle he had promised. He would have foreseen all this. She just needed to hold out until he reappeared.

The soldiers behind her rallied, surging forwards again, but the ones near the drifting, brainlike thing remained crippled, screaming and tearing their respirators off, clutching at their heads.

'Throw everything at it!' she cried, pointing to the drifting nest of tentacles, but at that moment a powerful tremor rocked through the gulley causing rocks to tumble from the slopes and throwing troopers from their feet.

'Captain!' cried Sergeant Vollard, drawing her attention to the other side of the ravine. The ground was churning and sagging, forming a wide, circular depression.

'Fifth Company!' she yelled, addressing the squads nearest the sinkhole. 'Watch your flank!'

A serpentine shape blasted from beneath the ground, hurling corpses and rocks into the surrounding soldiers. The monster's anatomy was hideously simple – a worm-like body, six muscular legs and an enormous maw that gaped like petals. It rose into the air then dived at the nearest trooper. It swallowed him whole, thrashing its head as it gulped him down. Then it lashed out with its tail, surrounding itself in mud and debris before lunging into the lines of soldiers.

The troopers opened fire, but the ground was now trembling in dozens of other places, causing the ground to shake.

Karpova scoured the battlefield, looking for Thurgau, but there was no sign of him.

Chapter Twenty-Five

THE FORTRESS CITY AT ZARAX
SAMNIUM PROVINCE, REGIUM

Castamon stormed through the crowded streets, heading towards the fortress' north gate. 'What do you mean?' he demanded. 'Was the wall hit before the shield went up?' People saluted as he passed, both soldiers and civilians, but he ignored them. 'When did this happen?'

'After the shields went up,' voxed the soldier he was talking to.

'Impossible,' he replied, seeing the gates up ahead. 'The shield neutralises projectiles. It incinerates them.'

'Forgive me, lieutenant,' said the soldier. *'But the blast was definitely after the shields went up.'*

Soldiers backed away as he neared the gates, pushing civilians aside and clearing a path to the wall so that he could see the damage. The sergeant he had been talking to rushed through the crowd and met him at the foot of the wall. 'It punched straight through,' he said, nodding to the damage.

Castamon crouched next to the hole and began examining it. The noise of the dying tyranids was deafening. They were still throwing themselves against the shields, heedless of their losses. Thousands of them were now heaped against it, burned and broken. The stink was horrendous. Every now and then, one of them would manage to squeeze through, only to be blasted apart by Tanaro and the other Ultramarines up on the walls. Castamon blocked out the din and ignored the cries of civilians, calling out to him, begging for reassurances that they were safe. He traced his fingers across the charred stones. At first he thought that the sergeant must be right, that the shield was defective in some way, then he had a more troubling thought. 'Did you see the projectile?' he asked.

'See it?' The sergeant licked his lips. 'No, my lord, I did not see the actual missile.' He looked around at his men, but they all shook their heads. 'We only saw the blast,' he said. 'The impact.'

Castamon climbed into the hole, moving blackened rocks aside. 'This damage did not come from a missile,' he said. 'Look at the direction of the blast. It came from *beneath* us. From beneath the wall.'

'Sappers?' The sergeant shook his head, growing paler. 'Would they…? Do monsters like that dig tunnels and plant explosives?'

'No, they do not,' he replied, moving more rocks aside. 'But heretics *do.*' He hefted a huge slab of rock aside and revealed an opening and a drop. 'There are tunnels under the gate,' he said, voxing Sergeant Tanaro. 'Bring your men here. Now.'

He dropped through the opening into the tunnel below. He looked up and down the passage, pistol raised, but he could see no one and the tunnel did not look like the work of sappers. There were images carved into the stone, or rather one large frieze portraying many figures. It was intricately worked, and in several places stained with dark patches that looked like blood. The image showed crowds of people, all of them on their knees with arms raised in tribute. Some were holding metal standards forged in the shape of a curled serpent. Above the figures the artist had carved hundreds of stars, and descending from them there was a divine being, radiating shafts of light. The image should have been beautiful, but there was something repulsive about the deity. It was essentially human in form, but there were serpentine shapes boiling around it, ending in barbed talons, and the head was oddly elongated with dark, blank eyes. Behind the figure there were half-seen shapes that, to Castamon, looked like tyranid bioforms, with floating tentacles and segmented, beetle-like carapaces.

He touched one of the dark patches on the wall and blood came away, glistening on the finger of his gauntlet. Then he noticed wires trailing off down the tunnel.

'Lieutenant,' voxed Tanaro. *'We were delayed on the wall. On our way now.'*

'Be quick.' He rushed down the tunnel and reached a circular chamber. There were piles of Militarum weapons and equipment scattered around and fuel canisters lashed to pallets. The stench of chemicals caught at the back of his throat. It smelled like acid or toxins.

There was a clattering sound from behind him, back in the tunnel.

Castamon whirled around and sprinted back out of the chamber.

Three men attacked, rushing from another chamber and opening fire. They should have been terrified, but their faces showed no emotion at all. They stared through him. They were dressed in scraps of Militarum flak armour and gripping auto-guns. The rounds tore holes in the wall behind him but did little damage as they clattered against his armour. He holstered his pistol, seeing no need to waste ammunition.

Even as he marched towards them, they showed no fear. He

was not entirely surprised. By the time heretics reached the stage of painting their guilt on a wall, they were often too deluded to remember their own names. But there was something odd about their demeanour. There was a blankness in their eyes. It was as if they were hypnotised – as if someone else was controlling them. The first man tried to club him with his gun, but Castamon snapped his fist, then snapped his neck before hurling him at the other two attackers. Their shots went wild as he strode towards them. He punched the first, driving his fist through the man's chest, then high-kicked the second, tearing most of his head away. All three collapsed on the ground, dead, their blood rushing across the floor. Castamon turned and walked towards a crate, hearing movement.

There was only one cultist hiding behind the second crate and his expression was as blank as the others. He was gripping a lascarbine in his hands, but rather than firing it he shook his head, speaking in a numb voice. 'They forced me to help. I had no idea they were heretics.'

There was no fear in his voice, even though Castamon had just butchered his three companions, and Castamon also noticed something else interesting. There was a tattoo on his neck – the same serpentine design he had seen in the wall carvings.

'Where are the explosives?' he demanded.

Humour flickered in the man's eyes. He opened his mouth to speak but Castamon silenced him with a backhanded knife swipe, severing his head and dropping him to the floor.

'Liar.'

He headed through the doorway the cultists had emerged from. Auto-rounds clattered into his armour, hitting him in such numbers that he staggered backwards a few steps. He counted the muzzle flashes. Nineteen cultists. Reluctantly, he raised his bolt pistol and drowned out the autoguns with the harsh bark of his own weapon. He only fired three rounds but he took careful aim, ensuring they inflicted maximum damage, each one ripping through three cultists and filling the room with blood.

As the surviving cultists reeled from the blasts, peering through the dust and trying to take aim, he holstered his pistol and marched into the room. There were snapping and ripping sounds as he made his way through the group, tearing them with his hands and crushing them with his boots.

Then something flew through the air and shattered against the wall near his head.

Emerald fumes billowed round him and heat pulsed from his armour. The stink of acidic chemicals washed over him and the targeting reticule in his helmet lit up as figures dashed for cover in the next chamber. Smoke was billowing from his battleplate and from the surrounding wall and he stepped aside, taking cover behind a pile of engine parts as he examined the armour. The ceramite layer of his left pauldron was melting. There was a pus-yellow liquid bubbling on the surface, and as he tried to brush it away, it scorched the fingers of his gauntlet. The chemicals were having an even more dramatic effect on the three cultists who were in the room with him – they were convulsing on the ground as their flesh bubbled and slid from their bones.

Another object whistled through the air towards him, but he was ready this time, sidestepping fast enough to dodge the liquid as its container smashed on the machine parts.

More cultists arrived, launching a fierce barrage of shots. He stumbled under the impact but paid them little attention, looking for the source of the chemicals. He thought he saw a giant tyranid, rearing up from the darkness, but then he realised it was only the shifting shadows, playing a trick on him. The figure he had seen was just another cultist. She was standing directly opposite him. Unlike the others, she was not wearing flak armour but the remnants of a medicae officer's uniform, complete with surgical devices and vials of liquid. Like the others, her expression was blank, as though she was merely a puppet. At the sight of Castamon she hurled another bottle and dived through a doorway.

The bottle smashed on the wall above Castamon and the effect was more explosive this time, tearing a chunk from the stone and showering the floor with acid. As it splashed across his armour it sloughed away more of the ceramite, causing warnings to scroll down his helm display. The acid bit so deep it damaged some of the suit's fibre bundles. He felt a flash of anger – not at the heretics, who were beneath his consideration, but at himself. He should have approached with more caution. The suit might be irrevocably damaged.

He killed the next heretic with a graceless punch, throwing himself off balance. 'Self-mastery,' he said, jamming his knife through another and fighting with more control. 'Reason.' He picked the next heretic up over his head and hurled her against the wall. 'Virtue.' He hammered the knife handle down into a heretic's skull, splintering the bone and pounding the man to the floor. He repeated the mantra as he fought. 'Self-mastery. Reason. Virtue.' By the time they were all dead he was calm again.

He approached the doorway used by the fleeing medicae officer, using more caution this time. He magnified his helmet's audio filters, examining the sounds in the next room and conjuring a mental picture of the scene. There were more cultists waiting for him, a larger group than the one he had just torn apart. They were shuffling carefully into cover and readying weapons. More autoguns, by the sound of it. And he could tell from the echoes of their movements that the next chamber was large. He could smell acid in there, but there was so much of the stuff eating through his armour that it was hard to locate the woman who was carrying it. The combination of his damaged battleplate and the number of cultists left him little option. He took his combi-flamer from his back, clicked the activation rune and opened fire as he marched through the doorway.

The gun poured flame over the nearest group, igniting them. Figures flailed and screamed as he looked around, allowing himself a fraction of a second to take in all the details. He was in some kind of burial chamber. It was cylindrical and hundreds of feet in circumference, and as the heretics blazed, they lit up dead faces, preserved in the walls. There was a large group of cultists gathered at the centre of the chamber. They were hunkered down behind a makeshift barricade, constructed from engine parts and scrap metal, and behind them he could see the one carrying medicae equipment and another figure who was hunched over a small, metal casket covered in wires. The whole chamber was covered in food scraps, excrement, discarded equipment and mouldering corpses. They had clearly been down here for a long time, but whatever their purpose was, he had sent them into a frenzy of activity. The figure hunched over the casket was snapping cables to it and tapping at a runeboard. Castamon's suit warned him that there were people targeting him from every direction, but he sensed instantly that he needed to focus on the figure with the metal box.

He strode across the chamber and opened fire again, drenching the barricade in flames.

Auto-rounds drummed into him, hitting him so many times that pieces of his power armour tore free, clattering across the floor. He leant into the storm of bullets, still firing and managing to take slow, juddering steps.

He was halfway across the chamber when he saw a rune blinking across his visor. 'Tanaro?'

'I'm here,' replied the sergeant. *'Just approaching the wall.'*

'The situation is under control. Cultists have been trying to...'

His words trailed off. The figure at the casket had risen from his work and turned to look over at him, a blank-eyed grin on his face.

The burning heretics dropped their guns, raising their arms in silent praise.

The world turned white.

Chapter Twenty-Six

THE FORTRESS CITY AT ZARAX
SAMNIUM PROVINCE, REGIUM

Damaris howled as pieces of stone tumbled down over her back and shoulders, knocking her to the floor. The detention block was shaking and cracks had spread across the walls of her cell, causing the bars to slump and bulge. It sounded like the whole fortress was collapsing. Then the tremors eased, the rocks stopped falling and the dust started to settle. 'Vela?' she gasped, before breaking into a coughing fit.

'Yes,' replied the old woman from somewhere outside the cell. She sounded panicked. 'I'm still here.'

Damaris struggled to her feet and looked through the bars at Vela. 'What was that? It sounded like an explosion.'

'Throne knows,' muttered the proconsul, dusting herself down. She looked around at the cracked walls and the slumping bars of the cell. 'We need to get you out. This whole place is about to come down. I'll demand they move you. Or maybe I could just break you out.'

'Break me out? What would be the point? The first Ultramarine to see me would put a gun to my head.'

Vela studied her, frowning. 'Why did you do it? Are you really a…?'

'A heretic?' She fiddled with the barbed wood that snaked through her skin. 'Of course not. But I still lied. I still caused their deaths.'

'So you didn't know Port Dura was going to be destroyed?'

Damaris felt a stab of pain that her old friend could ask her such a thing. But then she thought of how things must look from Vela's perspective. The old woman had little reason to trust her. 'No,' she muttered, looking at the floor of the cell. 'I just thought they would be delayed.' She waved at the rubble. 'And I never thought this was going to happen. I thought Castamon's talk of xenos was just another rod for Governor Seroc to keep us all in line. I thought it was just a way to justify all their empire building.' She shook her head. 'I'm a dangerous idiot.'

Vela's expression remained grim, but she softened her tone. 'I always liked that part of you.'

Damaris could not bring herself to laugh.

'We need to get you out of here,' said Vela. 'I don't know what caused that explosion, but this whole building is unsafe. 'Whatever you've done, I'm not leaving you to be crushed to death.'

'I don't deserve your sympathy.'

'Oh, don't play the bloody martyr. What use are you to anyone down here? I've *seen* what's out there. I don't think even Lieutenant Castamon expected this. Half the province is being eaten alive. So you might as well get out there and do something useful. Make amends.'

Damaris enjoyed the fantasy for a moment, imagining that she could make up for her treachery by fighting at the walls or treating wounds, but then she remembered the warriors she had sent to their deaths. She shook her head and sat down on one of the pieces of rubble. 'Thank you,' she said. 'Thank you for coming to see me. For caring. I can bear the others despising me, but not you.' She looked out through the bars, her eyes glistening. 'Do you believe me? I never meant for anyone to die.'

Vela reached through the bars and gripped her hand. 'You made a mistake. We're not *like* the Ultramarines. We're just human. We have to work with what we've been given.' She shrugged. 'And I think that means we're stronger than they are. Why do you think the Emperor fights so damned hard for us?'

There was a sudden passion in Vela's voice that dragged Damaris from her self-pity. The old woman was right, she could feel it in her bones. She knew the holy texts. She knew the stories. *Why do you think the Emperor fights so damned hard for us?* The Emperor had faced every imaginable hell. He had sacrificed His flesh and His own sons to preserve humanity, to preserve people like her. It had to be for a reason.

Another explosion rocked the detention cells and both women cried out in alarm. When the dust settled, they were both sprawled on the floor and covered in rubble.

'I'm getting you out,' spat Vela, climbing to her feet with difficulty. The bars to Damaris' cell were leaning away from the wall at a drunken angle and it only took one shove for the old woman to send them crashing to the floor.

They embraced, then climbed the stairs leading back up to ground level. At the top they both paused to take a deep breath and ready themselves. Then they walked out into a nightmare.

Chapter Twenty-Seven

THE FORTRESS CITY AT ZARAX
SAMNIUM PROVINCE, REGIUM

Castamon woke to the sound of screaming. He was confused for a moment, trying to place himself. He was in utter darkness, and trapped beneath a great weight. He strained to shift one of his hands, but it was held firmly in place. He was wearing his power armour but the auto-senses were not responding. There was no helm display. He remembered dropping down into the tunnels, then he recalled reaching the heretics and seeing the figure stooped over the device. It must have been an explosive charge, he realised, remembering how the cultist had smiled at him as he looked up from the box. The heretics had failed to destroy the wall at the first attempt so they had been laying more explosives when he disturbed them. He remembered the images on the wall, showing a grotesque xenos deity descending from the heavens. They were trying to let the xenos in. They *wanted* to be invaded. The folly of heretics never ceased to amaze him.

His suit's life support functions were offline so he let his thoughts roam over his body, doing a body scan from his

Dartus Hinks

extremities to his head. He could feel lesions to his chest and arms, but it did not feel like any of his bones were broken. The air quality was so poor that two of his lungs had closed down, but he guessed that was his body's natural response to the toxins, rather than a sign of any damage; his third lung was providing a steady supply of filtered, untainted oxygen.

Castamon ignored the screams and focused on the fact that he was still alive. The blast could have killed him. He could not move one hand, but when he flexed the fingers of the other one, he realised it was free. He shifted some rocks and felt something give in the rubble. Now he could move his whole arm. Gradually, he began shuffling and straining against the weight, pulling himself into an upright position.

After a few minutes of clawing and stretching, he realised he was being a fool. It might take hours to climb up to the surface, by which point the shield might be down. He was using brute strength when he should be using his mind. He had to think of a better option. He thought again about his predicament. With his suit's auto-senses down he had no way to contact his battle-brothers. Unless… He smiled as he saw the solution. He could only contact Tanaro by voxing him, but that was not the case with all of his battle-brothers. He cleared his mind and focused on a single word. *Abarim.*

There was no response, so he tried again, picturing the letters in his mind. *Abarim.*

+I hear you, brother,+ came the reply. +I am coming.+

Minutes later, Castamon felt the rocks around him start to rattle. Soon they were rising, and as they lifted, they carried him with them. He felt like he was being reborn. Finally, he saw the tormented sky and the crowded streets of the fortress. Abarim was standing alone, head tilted back, hands resting on the head of his force axe. Power was coruscating from the cowl of his armour and scattering across the ground near his boots. Beyond the light there was a halo of darkness around him, deeper than the surrounding darkness and simmering with the power of the warp.

Castamon drifted for a moment, hanging above a mound of rubble, then Abarim gently lowered him onto the street and the halo was extinguished.

There were people racing past but not one of them paused to watch the miracle of Castamon's return. They were all staring in horror at the north gate, and as he turned to look in that direction, he saw why.

Chapter Twenty-Eight

'We must reach the laboratorium,' snarled Vultis, coming to a halt and lowering his gun. Baraca ran across the street to his side and they stood in silence for a moment, watching the violence that had erupted all around them. The fortress looked like an endless, rolling explosion. A massive section of the north wall had been blown away, tearing through the battlements and creating holes in the shield. The streets were littered with dead and dying people who had been hurled by the explosion. Clouds of spores were billowing back and forth, threaded with flashes of gunfire, and soldiers were sprinting between burning hab-units, howling into laud hailers as stablights flickered back and forth. Ultramarines had already gathered at the breach in the wall, spraying flames into the darkness, and there were hundreds of human soldiers massing behind them, shooting and hurling grenades, but they were dwarfed by the torrent of tyranids that was pouring through the gap. The Ultramarines looked undaunted, but most people were screaming. Some of the xenos had made it past the defenders and into the streets. They were butchering everyone they reached, shaking with kill-fever.

'The heat shield is damaged,' said Baraca, nodding to the shimmering dome beyond the walls. He fired his bolt pistol at some approaching xenos, flipping them backwards into the fragmented darkness. His gun sounded like a mallet striking iron.

Vultis nodded. 'That explosion will have severed plasma coils beneath the wall. The shield has lost power.' He loosed off a barrage of shots. 'My time is slipping away. We must move quickly.'

Gun-servitors opened fire from a nearby roof, legless torsos with autoguns in place of arms and sutured, eyeless heads. The guns rattled so loudly that neither of them could speak for a moment. Then, when the servitors paused to reload, Baraca called out to Vultis, raising his voice over the din of battle. 'Do you see Lieutenant Castamon? My suit cannot locate him.'

'My suit's auxiliary systems are failing,' said Vultis. 'I see nothing clearly.' He looked at the breach in the wall. Sergeant Tanaro was there, along with most of his squad, but there was no sign of the lieutenant. An image flashed across his thoughts, of Castamon lying dead on the ground. He dismissed it. Castamon had endured worse than this. 'He may have gone to the laboratorium, expecting to find me there.'

He looked around at rows of hab-units and comms towers. Everywhere his gaze fell, people were fighting for their lives. Winged tyranids were diving through the fumes, gripping cylinders of muscle that spat smaller creatures onto the people below, eliciting more howls and screams. 'We could spend an hour fighting our way through these streets, by which time the shield might have failed. There must be another way to get there.' He looked back the way they had come and saw two women cowering in the rubble, trying to hide. They were blood-drenched and ashen-faced, but he recognised them. 'The consuls,' he said.

Baraca looked back at the women. 'If we stay to protect them, there is no chance of us–'

'No, I did not mean that.' Vultis strode through the whirling fumes, gunning down another tyranid before reaching the two women. They recoiled as he approached, looking as terrified of him as they were of the monsters. Baseline humans were often afraid of Space Marines, but he sensed this was more than that. They were both shaking. He wondered if they had been driven to madness by the bloodshed.

'Consuls,' he said upon reaching them. 'Can you speak?'

The younger woman, Damaris, stared at him in terrified silence, but the older one wiped some of the blood from her face and nodded.

He crouched down to talk with them. 'I need to reach the laboratorium, but since the wall came down all of our routes are blocked. We could fight our way through, but it will be slow work. Is there any other way we can go?'

Vela was about to reply when Damaris spoke over her, her voice numb. 'Is this happening everywhere? Is the whole planet like this?'

'Can you help me or not?'

'We have to show them,' said Vela.

Damaris seemed about to argue, then, as she watched people being ripped apart all around her, the fight went out of her. She nodded, standing up and helping Vela to her feet. 'There are tunnels we could show you.'

They headed south, away from the fighting. As they rushed from street to street, Vultis was surprised to see that most people were headed in the opposite direction, towards the battle. And these were not soldiers but civilians. They were clutching guns and sabres, but they were not wearing the uniform of the Ultramarian soldiers: they were refugees – farmers, manufactorum workers and pilgrims – but they all wore steely expressions as they hurried towards the breach.

Vela noticed his surprise. 'It's Castamon's doing.'

'What do you mean?'

'People were panicking. Rioting. The soldiers were getting violent. Then your lieutenant made a speech. He told them they had the Emperor's blood in their veins. Then he told the soldiers to stop attacking them and give them weapons.'

Baraca laughed. 'They were rioting and he gave them weapons?'

They halted as Vultis held up a warning hand, pausing at a junction between the hab-units. He let off a few pistol shots, dropping some distant figures, then looked back at Vela. 'Where did he go after he gave the speech? Did you see?'

She shook her head. Then she pointed to a low, broad, flat-roofed building with a colonnaded facade. 'There are tunnels beneath the consular villa. They predate the rest of the fortress but we have kept them intact. We can use them to avoid the...' She looked at the tyranids and her words trailed off. 'We can use them to reach your laboratorium.'

Vultis nodded, and after firing a few more rounds, he headed off towards the villa, waving for the others to follow. They raced up the steps that surrounded the building and ran into a deserted atrium. Damaris and Vela led the Ultramarines across the open space into a warren of chapels and function rooms on the other side. The place was deserted. They ran down empty hallways and through cavernous halls.

Finally, gripping each other's arm, the consuls led the way down into the building's cellars.

'I insisted the villa be built on this spot,' explained Vela, looking up at Vultis with a defiant gleam in her eye. 'I told Governor

Seroc and the others that it had to be here because of its position on the planet's ley lines. But they didn't understand what I meant by ley lines. This villa is built over an entrance to the world roots. Aureus Nahor's strength is still here, under this rock.'

Vultis found it baffling that she could still refer to her old faith with such reverence, even though she knew that the sacred trees were nothing more than mine shafts and engines. But he did not comment on it, eager to keep moving.

Damaris and Vela paused at a doorway, each pressing their palms into holes on either side of the frame. Locks ticked and clanged like the workings of a clock; then the door rattled sideways, opening onto a chamber behind. A lumen blinked into life, revealing a room crowded with religious paraphernalia: holy texts and scrolls, priestly robes, ceremonial swords and bundles of metallic-looking sticks that had been polished and sharpened for threading under skin. Damaris moved some of the objects aside and grabbed one of the swords, staring at the blade.

Vultis paused, holding up his hand as he heard something familiar. 'Baraca, do you hear that?'

Baraca tilted his head, listening.

Then the walls exploded.

Vultis tumbled through the air, carried on a wave of rubble, and slammed to the ground in a different room.

Vela thudded down a few feet away from him, cradling her head in her arms as rocks rained onto her, but there was no sign of Damaris. Baraca was still standing in the passageway, his armour shrouded in dust. His pistol roared as he fired into the gloom, taking a few steps backwards on a floor that was now buckled and skewed.

Vultis tried to stand but realised he could not move. A large piece of rubble had pinned him to the ground.

Someone screamed as a serpentine shape rattled up through the broken floor. It was colossal, hurling shattered flagstones as it reared over Baraca. It was worm-like with an angular, insectile head and jaws like barbed petals. As it coiled across the floor, walls were still coming down, revealing the streets outside and glimpses of the battle.

Baraca rushed at the monster, grabbed its jaw and slammed its head to the ground. Its body thrashed, smashing more walls, but he held fast as it struggled in his grip. Then he pressed his pistol to its skull and fired twice, drenching his armour in blood.

As Vultis struggled to free himself, he saw Damaris stagger into view and help Vela to her feet. They both raised their swords and cowered behind Baraca, staring at the clouds of dust. There was movement everywhere.

'Baraca,' grunted Vultis, shoving at the massive piece of stone.

Baraca looked back, but then dozens of man-sized bipedal tyranids scrambled into view, leaping at Baraca and driving him back. He fired a few times then clapped his gun to his belt, whipped out a combat knife and waded into the fray, hacking the tyranids apart.

'There!' cried one of the consuls, and Vultis struggled into a different position, looking around at the room he had fallen into.

At first he thought his eyes were playing tricks on him. He was sure he glimpsed movement near a grand fireplace, but then there seemed to be nothing there. He guessed what was happening and stared at the whirling dust until he saw what he was looking for – some of the dust was halting in mid-air, revealing the outline of shoulders and arms. That was enough for Vultis' imagination to flesh out the rest. It was another two-legged humanoid tyranid, but this one was larger than the others and it clearly possessed a chameleonic ability. Vultis had studied similar tyranids and he guessed that it had been waiting in silence, looking for the right moment to strike a suitable prey. It ignored the women and walked slowly towards Vultis, becoming clearer as it moved through the falling dust. It had four arms – two ending in claws and two larger ones that arched over its head like long, curved blades. Its head was long and insectile, like others he had seen, but rather than gaping jaws, its lower face was a mass of writhing tentacles. The monster approached on blood-caked hooves and its tendrils reached out from its face, extending like fleshy worms.

Behind him, Baraca was still locked in battle and Vultis cursed as he tried again to move the piece of rock. The servos in his armour whined, but it was useless – the thing would not move. The tyranid showed no sense of urgency as it stalked across the room towards him.

'For the Emperor!' cried Vela, leaping at the tyranid with her sword raised.

Damaris followed her lead, and their blades cut into the crea-ture at the same moment. Damaris' sword plunged deep into the tyranid's chest, cracking its carapace, and Vela's sliced into the nest of feelers on its face.

The monster staggered, then recovered and hammered one of its mantis-like blades down. The blade punched into Vela's face with such force that it plunged down through her neck and into her torso before hooking out through her stomach. Then the tyranid lifted her still-twitching body and hurled it into the street.

Damaris tumbled backwards over the rubble, horrified.

Baraca was still in the corridor, surrounded by xenos, so Vultis was alone with his attacker. The creature loomed over him. There was blood running from its face where Vela had cut some of the feelers away and he could see its organs pulsing beneath the hole in its exoskeleton, but it looked as calm as when it had entered the room. It studied him, as though deciding which was the easiest part to break.

Vultis managed to grab his pistol and shoot. The tyranid fell against the fireplace, but then leapt across the room towards him.

The attack was so fast Vultis barely managed to bring up his hands. The monster thudded into him, obliterating the large piece of rubble that had held him to the ground and knocking the pistol from his grip. It slammed Vultis into the far wall, pinning him against it.

An acidic smell washed over him as the tyranid pushed its face closer. Its beard of feelers shivered, reached out and gently latched on to the faceplate of his helmet. White-hot pain exploded all over his head as mucus-coated tips sliced through the ceramite and pressed into his temples, burning through his skin and burrowing into his skull.

He tried to reach for his knife but it was impossible, so he brought his knee up instead, slamming it into the hole Damaris had cut through its chest.

Blood filled the air and he felt something give inside the creature. Then it shuddered and backed away. The feelers disengaged from his forehead with a series of wet sucking sounds.

The tyranid recovered and lunged, its tentacles again reaching for his forehead.

He sidestepped and brought his combat knife round in a slash. The blade passed through the tyranid's neck, severing its head and sending it bouncing off the wall.

Damaris dropped onto the rubble where Vela had died and sobbed, staring at the bloody stones.

Baraca was still fighting, punching furiously at a tyranid he was gripping by the throat. He struck it until its skull collapsed, then he hurled the remains to the floor and strode over to Vultis with gore dripping from his fist.

The ground was trembling constantly now, and as Vultis looked out at the battle he saw shapes writhing up from beneath and lunging at the fortress' defenders. Meanwhile, smaller species of xenos were still pouring through the breach in the wall.

'Lead me to my laboratorium,' he said, approaching Damaris. 'That is how you will avenge your friend.'

They all staggered as another tyranid blasted up from beneath them. Vultis shoved Damaris behind him and raised his pistol.

The floor erupted as a second tyranid snaked into view. Then another and another. Damaris gripped Vultis' arm to steady herself as the ground lurched and rolled. Eventually there were five of the snake-like creatures rearing over them, maws straining and tails smashing through what remained of the walls.

Vultis held Damaris close as the ceiling rained down, exposing the room above and spilling furniture and masonry. When the rubble had ceased falling, he let her go and looked around at the xenos, choosing his first target.

Baraca was at his side, passing his knife from hand to hand and making a low snarling sound. 'Go,' he said. 'I can hold them here while the consul leads you to the laboratorium.'

Vultis considered the idea and dismissed it. Every one of the tyranids was looking at him. 'They came here for me,' he said. 'If I leave, they will only follow.'

'Then we fight,' snarled Baraca, dropping into a battle stance.

'Is it your time to die?' asked Vultis. It was a genuine question.

Baraca looked up at the shapes towering over them. 'Not even close.' He clanged his knife against his chest armour. 'Courage and honour.'

'Courage and honour.'

The reply came from Damaris. Vultis looked down at her in

surprise and saw that she had drawn back her sword, ready to fight. Her face was smeared with blood and her sword-arm was shaking, but her eyes burned.

Then the monsters attacked.

Chapter Twenty-Nine

KORASSA GORGE
SAMNIUM PROVINCE, REGIUM

Captain Karpova cursed herself for listening to Thurgau. They could have waited at the end of the gulley, pounding the tyranids with artillery, but he had been adamant that he had to reach the hill. She hacked a tyranid down with her sabre, sending it back into the swarming mass around the tank. Then she looked around at the fighting. The worm-like creatures were exploding up from the ground in dozens of places and the attack was not random. They had burrowed down the gulley and most of them were attacking the rearguard of her army, pushing the squads forwards and cutting off their retreat.

'We're being herded.' Vollard's voice was strained as he fought. She snatched a glance at him and was pleased to see that he was showing no sign of delirium. She could imagine he felt the same as her – now that she was in the heat of battle, doubt fell away. She simply had to react to the situation and identify the most efficient way to regain control. *'I think this was a trap,'* he said.

'Impossible,' she snapped. 'Thurgau saw all this in a vision.' Even as she spoke the words, she was battling doubt.

'Did he see himself swooning like an idiot and diving under the treads of his own tank? What if he was just losing his mind, like I did?'

She spat a curse. Vollard was right, she could see it as she looked around the gulley. The larger tyranids *had* been waiting for them, waiting underground to burst out and pen her soldiers in. Her artillery was struggling to shoot now that the rest of the regiment was scattered down the gulley. And there were winged creatures swooping down from the fumes and diving at the gun emplacements. Everywhere she looked, the tyranids were moving with precision and purpose, corralling, cornering and dividing her troops. It was quickly turning into a massacre. *No,* she thought, battling the urge to howl. *This cannot happen.*

She gasped as a tyranid bounded up onto the turret and locked one of its claws around her throat. It opened its jaws so wide that its whole head seemed to be hinged. She grappled with it, trying to force it back, but it was gripping her with four arms and the mouth edged closer, despite her best efforts to hold it off. The creature's tongue snaked from its mouth, probing the air like a serpent then winding towards her face, dripping strings of venom that scorched her armour. The tongue reached her rebreather and the rubber burned and smoked.

With a grunt, she managed to wedge her pistol under its chin and pull the trigger.

Blood washed over her face and the tyranid fell away, bouncing and clattering down the tank's armour plating. There was a hiss of melting rubber as xenos blood ate into her mask, but she managed to whip the respirator off, hurling it into the battle before the acid reached her skin.

Dizziness washed over her as she breathed the thick, infested air. She coughed and spluttered, then grabbed a mask from a corpse lying near the turret, wiped the man's blood off and fastened it quickly over her face.

'I think I have identified a leader,' she said when she had recovered, speaking to Vollard on a closed vox-channel. 'The creature at the top of the hill.'

'The floating lump?'

'I can't know for sure that it's the leader.' She gunned down another tyranid. 'But it has a damned honour guard. None of the others have that kind of protection. And it's completely different from all the other xenos. Look what it's doing to the Kasrkin.' Her elite troops were being butchered on the brow of the hill. As light shimmered from the drifting monster, enveloping the soldiers, they were left crippled – thrashing on the ground or lying in a foetal curl as the smaller tyranids attacked, ripping them apart in a feeding frenzy. 'It's burning their minds out. We have to stop it. These things are definitely getting orders from *somewhere*. Look at how coordinated their attacks are.'

She barked a command and her tank rumbled through the battle, heading towards the hill. Shots poured down on the floating tyranid from dozens of different directions, but it barely seemed to notice, swaying peacefully in the air as energy spilled from its tentacles. The more she studied it, the more confident she grew that it was the leader. Most of the other xenos resembled species she had encountered before – either upright, bipedal humanoids with four arms, or hunched hound-like things clad in the same pale carapace. But the one on the hill seemed quite different. And like any other general on a hill, it was not involving itself in the fighting, but watching calmly from a vantage-point.

'Get me closer!' she snapped, voxing her driver and firing at the xenos clambering over the tank's chassis. As the vehicle ground on through the mud and bodies, tyranids threw themselves into the treads, clogging the workings as they died. Slowly, the tank juddered to a halt, gears screaming as the wheels failed to turn, jammed with mounds of bloody flesh.

She roared in frustration, loosing off another furious barrage. She twisted around in the hatch and saw tyranids pouring from the gulley walls, emerging in their thousands from hiding places in the rocks. The serpent-like monsters were still sprouting from the ground down the whole length of the valley and the main swarm was still advancing from the north, no longer slowed by artillery. Finally, she saw Thurgau's corpse, lying near an overturned tank, his sceptre smashed and his blood soaking into the ground. It was a tragic, pathetic end for someone she had invested so much in.

'No!' she whispered. 'This will not happen.' She leapt from the tank and began sprinting up the side of the hill, drawing her sabre. Tyranids rushed at her from across the hillside, but troops flocked to her side, and together they cut a path up the slope towards the drifting shapes.

The few surviving Kasrkin struggled to their feet and joined the charge, still fighting with incredible skill, despite their wounds.

As she neared the top of the slope, Karpova stumbled to a halt. The tyranids had vanished and so had the hillside. She was standing in a kasr – one of the vast fortress cities that once protected the surface of Cadia. It was impossible, Cadia was long gone, but the mazelike jumble of streets was unmistakable.

Then the vision was gone. She howled and fired as tyranids poured across the hillside towards her. She led her troops forward with a bellowed command and they reached the top. The brainlike monster was even more repulsive when seen close up, suspended above its billowing nest of tentacles and spilling light into the darkness. It paid her no attention, dragging screams from the Kasrkin it had ensnared, but the smaller species sailed towards her, shimmering and undulating.

She raised her pistol to fire, but the hillside vanished again. She was back on Cadia, back in the streets of the kasr. And there were soldiers running towards her. They were Cadians, like her, their faces grim and determined as they charged, spitting las-bolts from their guns.

Karpova howled in frustration. She knew the tyranid was confusing her, clouding her head with illusions, but the faces and streets seemed so real, so familiar. She stumbled to a halt, shaking her head, forgetting what she was trying to do.

'Damned cowardly, if you ask me,' said someone, shoving her forwards. 'Playing mind games on the field of battle.'

She almost fell but the shock dragged her thoughts back to the hilltop. She glanced back and saw Vollard. His chest armour had been ripped apart and his uniform was in tatters. He was bleeding from dozens of wounds. But he met her gaze with a look of wry amusement. 'Luckily, some of us have little mind left to lose.'

His eyes were clear again. He was back. The thought gave her courage and she rushed on across the hilltop, pounding through the mud with Vollard at her side.

One of the smaller shapes charged forwards, trying to envelop them, but they lashed out with their sabres, slicing it into strips of flesh that fluttered to the ground.

Behind them, troopers howled war cries and rushed at the other drifting shapes. Karpova felt a swell of pride as she saw Cadians battling towards her from every direction. Half of them were torn down or pummelled into the mud, but the rest raced on, heedless of the bloodshed, determined to fight at her side.

And then she was under the large creature. Its tentacles fanned out above her head, scattering arcs of light. Vollard raised his pistol, aiming for the centre of its brainlike flesh, but one of the tentacles shot out and looped around his head. He howled and stumbled back.

Tentacles unfurled in different directions, lassoing troopers or thrashing them into the ground.

There was a howl of las-fire as the remaining Kasrkin crested the hill and drove the monster back.

Vollard fell to his knees, howling as the tentacle tightened around his head.

The barrage of shots from the Kasrkin grew so fierce that the monster tilted back, losing its grip on Vollard as it struggled to remain upright. As Vollard staggered clear, the tyranid turned to face Karpova, singling her out from the crowd, drawing back its tendrils to strike.

Vollard rose to his feet, his face blackened and oozing with blood, and put his bugle to his lips, blowing a fierce blast.

The note rang clear through the tumult. It was so odd, so incongruous, that everyone paused and looked his way, even the tyranid.

Karpova took her chance. She rolled across the ground, stopped directly beneath the monster and leapt up, punching her sabre through its middle.

Screams rang out, not in the air, but in Karpova's head. She fell to the ground, dropping her sword and clutching her ears. All around her, soldiers did the same. The screams were horrendous and they built towards an agonising crescendo.

She rolled clear, gripping her head, drenched in tyranid blood, feeling it sizzle across her armour.

The creature continued its scream, then lurched in the air, rolling like a punctured dirigible before fluttering to the ground in a shower of blood. The scream stopped.

Karpova's sword was embedded in the monster and her pistol

was melting as she dropped it to the ground. Bio-acid was dissolving her skin as she heard dozens of hooved feet thundering towards her. She climbed to her feet and saw that everyone on the hilltop was dead or dying. Vollard lay crumpled in the remains of the psychic tyranid, his flesh melting.

She looked at the monster she had killed and enjoyed a brief moment of triumph. She grabbed Vollard's bugle and blew, piercing the din with a sound that seemed to come from the mountains of Cadia.

Then the tyranids reached her and started to feed.

Chapter Thirty

'Where the hell am I?' roared Gathas Kulm, rearing up from his seat and jolting against the harness.

Beltis was so shocked to hear her father speak that she nearly crashed the groundcar. It zigzagged across the litter-strewn transitway, nearly colliding with an overturned hauler before she managed to right it.

Her father was sitting next to her in the front of the vehicle and there were two more men seated in the back. One was Semler, her wretched little chirurgeon, gripping the case full of nutrient blocks and stimm serums he had used to keep her father alive. The other was an overgrown brute called Vant, who was clad in a flak jacket and leaning out of the car, scanning their surroundings down the barrel of a lascarbine. Semler and Vant looked as shocked as she did at her father's recovery. It was the first time he had said anything since they'd escaped Port Dura, even though the downers Semler had given him must have worn off hours ago.

Kulm looked down at himself, then at his daughter. His eyes were completely clear. 'Where are my damned clothes? Are you insane?'

At another time, she might have laughed at the irony of him calling her insane, but as it was, she felt like crying instead. Tears of relief filled her eyes. He was himself again. She had never really dreamed it might happen. His madness was gone.

'Golden Throne,' he muttered as he looked outside the ground-car. The world was drowning in spore-heavy clouds and the only light came from the burning vehicles that littered the transitway. The flames revealed hundreds of corpses and not all of them were human. Most of the xenos had moved on, heading south towards Salamis, but there were still a few skulking through the ruined buildings at the sides of the road, scuttling silently and quickly through the corpses, sometimes pausing to feed before skittering off into the gloom. There were larger shapes moving in the clouds overhead, *much* larger. Beltis would not let herself consider what they might be. 'What happened?' said her father. The rage ebbed from his voice, replaced by disbelief. 'What are those things?'

Despite the horror of the scene, Beltis felt giddy at the sound of his voice. He was *sane*. He had come back to her. 'It's an invasion,' she said, keeping her eyes locked on the transitway. 'But not heretics – it's aliens. And this time we're going to lose. They destroyed Port Dura.'

'Destroyed?' He slumped in his seat. Beltis understood the horror in his voice. Most of their wealth had been tied up in the port. 'How?'

'Some kind of bomb, I don't know. Flattened the place. If you look back, you'll see a patch of deeper darkness. That's the mushroom cloud that used to be Dura. A few people got out before it happened, like we did.'

He sounded numb. 'What about *our* people. Tirol and the others?'

'Tirol!' She spat the word. 'You can forget about him. And all the others.' She nodded to the men in the back seat. 'Apart from these two, everyone betrayed you. Once you got sick they showed their true colours.' She glanced at the electro-flail at her belt. It was caked in blood. 'They didn't live to see the explosion.'

Kulm pulled his dreadlocks away from his chest and stomach, examining himself. 'Sick? How was I sick?'

She hesitated. 'You couldn't think clearly.' She gunned the engine, speeding up as a shape approached from a toppled hab-unit. The shape veered off into the darkness and she relaxed, slowing down to a more manageable speed. 'You're not the only one it happened to.'

'Couldn't think clearly?' he murmured, sounding troubled, and she wondered if he was starting to remember. Perhaps he was remembering the taste of the grubs he'd crammed down his throat. He fell quiet for a while and she left him to his thoughts.

After several minutes had passed she grew worried. What if he was slipping back into the madness? She had no idea what had brought him to his senses. She had left Port Dura thinking it would clear his thoughts. But that was before she knew how screwed the rest of the province was. Everywhere was as bad as the port.

'Where are you taking us?' She was relieved to hear that he still sounded lucid. 'What are we going to do?'

What are we going to do? He had never spoken to her with such deference before. It hurt her almost as much as his madness had. The mighty Gathas Kulm, asking his daughter what to do. He was broken. She kept the pity from her voice as she replied. 'My plan was to get us to Salamis Hive. But then I spoke to the refugees heading away from the hive. They said it's surrounded by a huge army of the aliens and there are insurrectionists making matters even worse, blowing it up from the inside. And, apparently, there's an even bigger army gathered around the off-worlders' fortress down at Zarax. And all the outposts and fuel depots are under attack, too. The whole province is under attack.'

'And the rest of the planet?'

She shrugged. The thought stalled her for a moment. The Kulm empire was vast. They controlled mines, manufactories and refining plants right across the planet. If all of Regium was under attack, they might have lost everything. They would become as powerless and poor as the two morons in the back of the groundcar, as powerless as everyone else. 'I have a plan,' she said, recovering her composure. 'There's enough fuel in this thing to reach the Uxama chem-works.'

He frowned. 'Uxama?' He sounded dazed, but it was not the madness returning. He was remembering things, she was sure of it, things that were making him feel confused and ashamed. 'What's the point in going to Uxama? It's the arse end of nowhere.'

'Exactly.' She lowered her voice, even though there was no one to hear, apart from the two in the back and she was paying them well enough not to worry about loyalty. 'No one goes there since the works shut down. The place is desolate. It *looks* like there's nothing there.'

He nodded and a glimmer of life returned to his eyes. 'But there *is* something there.'

'Right. No one knows about that hangar. But those shuttles are still in there. I checked the latest shipment manifests and there should still be at least three. One's just an old Arvus and the second is just as slow. But one of them is the *Barbalissus*. She's fast. And easily big enough to hold four people, especially as we're not carrying any cargo.'

'So we leave with nothing.' The fire faded from his eyes.

'We leave with our lives.' She nodded to a void-crate at her father's feet. 'And as many thrones as I could carry. There's enough in there for us to make a new start. The shuttles should have been refuelled when they landed. The *Barbalissus* could easily make it to the augur station at Crozea Point. From there we can get to the shipyards at Gabris and try to buy passage to another system.'

He took a deep breath and let it out. Then he nodded and put his hand over hers. 'You did well. You held it together.' He spoke in gruff tones, but it was the most affection he had ever shown her. He looked back at Vant. 'Give me a gun.'

Chapter Thirty-One

Castamon had climbed up onto the plinth of a ruined statue to raise himself above the panicked crowds. Abarim was at his side and they were studying the damage caused by the blast. Most of the walls and shield were still intact, but the breach at the north gate was so vast it had spilled crowds of xenos into the fortress. There was a tide of scarab-like creatures, no bigger than rats, washing over buildings and people, devouring everything they passed, leaving heaps of pulped flesh and stripping the facades off hab-units. There were also larger bipedal predators, rending and gouging as they sprinted through the crowds. Humans and Ultramarines were fighting back, firing into the throng, but winged tyranids were diving at them from the darkness, ripping flesh and latching on to power armour.

Castamon and Abarim were surrounded by piles of dead xenos, their splintered shells sizzling with corrosive blood.

Sergeant Tanaro had survived the blast and Castamon had ordered him back to the walls with his squad. But Castamon and Abarim were not alone. They were flanked by Ultramarines and hundreds of auxilia troops who had rushed to aid Castamon.

Castamon divided his thoughts between two areas of focus. One half of his mind considered the surrounding battle, making sure his troops were fighting with precision and efficiency. The other part of his mind was processing the situation at the north gate. Even from here, he could see the rent in the wall. It was obvious that the blast had come from underground, reaching up through the wall like a claw.

One of the two-legged tyranids ripped through the lines, decapitating soldiers as it raced towards him.

Castamon slowly raised his bolt pistol, took aim and removed its head. It stumbled a few steps further, then fell at the base of the plinth, causing soldiers to leap aside as blood fountained from its neck.

'Something has changed,' said Abarim.

Castamon looked at him in surprise. 'What do you mean?'

'The tumult in my head has ceased. My thoughts are clear. Something significant has happened.' For the first time in weeks, there was no pain in his voice.

'How?' asked Castamon. 'Do you know why?'

Abarim shook his head. 'The psychic pall is still there. I still feel it gnawing at my thoughts. But some component of the tyranid attack has foundered. Or has been deliberately confounded. My guess is that the xenos have just lost a powerful psyker.'

Castamon looked around. 'Here?'

'No. Further north, I think. Perhaps at Salamis.'

'Are your powers restored to their full strength?'

'For now. But it may only be a temporary respite. The swarm

may be able to birth more psychic creatures. We need to make the most of my recovery. What do you command, lieutenant? Shall I join the others at the breach?'

Castamon could see flickers of blue near the north gate. Ultramarines from various squads were battling to stem the tide, but they were hugely outnumbered.

'We have work to do here first, brother,' he said, as a large shape smashed through the auxilia soldiers, heading towards the broken statue. The tyranid was much larger than any of the nearby xenos and moving on all fours, weighed down by a cannon-like growth on its back. The creature was built like a tank, broad and heavy with dorsal pipes that spewed spores as it stomped through the crowd. It seemed oblivious to the shots raining down on it, gorging itself on the dead and the living, slavering and belching and trailing viscera from its teeth. It was heading straight for Castamon and Abarim, and as it neared the statue it halted and took aim. The tubular growth shivered and vomited fire. Green flames screamed towards them.

They dived from the plinth, and as Castamon rolled back to his feet, he swung his combi-flamer from his back and returned fire. The tyranid staggered but Castamon kept firing, striding down the steps towards it, finger locked over the trigger, waves of heat washing over him.

Abarim strode into view. He was gripping his axe in both hands and light pulsed from the blade as he hacked it into the tyranid. The combined attack was too much for the monster. It gave a last, smouldering belch then crumpled, rolling back through charred bodies. Castamon put the combi-weapon on his back and drew his pistol as bipedal xenos leapt through the smoke at him. He shot some and kicked others across the street, while Abarim moved through the fray, swinging his blazing axe and detonating every tyranid he struck.

The auxilia troops surged forwards, a proud sight in their blue-and-gold uniforms as they opened fire, creating a circle of twitching bodies around Castamon and Abarim.

'I have another idea.' Castamon had to shout so that Abarim could hear him over the noise of the battle. 'Are you sure you are at full strength?'

'Close enough, brother,' roared Abarim, beheading another tyranid.

'Could you seal that breach with your mind? Could you create a psychic barrier? We *must* buy time for Vultis to complete his work. You moved rocks to lift me from the ground. Could you harness even greater power and reassemble the defences?'

Abarim looked up at the fortress walls. 'It would take me days.'

'No use.' Castamon began heading to the breach. 'We need to stop them now.'

'Wait,' said Abarim. 'There may be another way to achieve what you ask. I spoke to Vultis about his research. He means to replicate the link between the tyranid symbionts. His theory is that they might be psychic relays, that they employ a form of telepathy. If his theory proves correct, and he is able to discern the science behind it, he hopes to mimic the signals, to send misinformation and confuse the swarm.'

Castamon glanced around at the fighting. Everywhere he looked, the Ultramarines and human soldiers were being driven back. 'Speak quickly, brother.'

'Perhaps I could enact a simpler version of his plan, using my own psychic abilities? Vultis suspects that the xenos are led by a distant leader. If that is true and if I *blocked* their link to that leader, the lesser creatures would be in disarray. I cannot send misinformation, but perhaps I could create a psychic barrier to cut them off from their commanders.' He shook his head. 'I could only project a small barrier, though.'

'It is not enough. What would happen if you transferred your power through the shield generator? That barrier already exists. Could you thread your psychic powers through the shield we already have?'

Abarim looked surprised by the suggestion. Then, slowly, he nodded. 'Perhaps. It might be possible.'

Castamon sensed that the Librarian was holding something back. 'Is it a foolish suggestion? My grasp of psychic transference is poor.'

'No, not foolish. But hard. Linking my thoughts to the reactor would not be difficult – it is the most basic form of technomancy – but spreading empyric power across the whole fortress would be a different matter. The scale of it is the problem. I would be draining a huge amount of energy from the immaterium. And spreading it through the power shield would require a huge degree of control.'

'Or you might destroy the fortress?'

'Worse than that. I would risk drawing warp entities onto the material plane. I could turn myself into a warp rift – a gateway for the unborn.' He stared at the ground for a moment, then nodded. 'I *can* do what you ask, but I will not be able to maintain the psychic barrier for long.'

'It will be enough.' Castamon gestured to the xenos that were flooding through the fortress. 'Isolate them from their leaders. Send them into disarray. And then we can create a temporary stockade across the breach.' He gripped Abarim's hand. 'Are you sure you can do this, brother?'

Abarim hesitated. 'I can,' he said, finally. 'But ensure Sergeant Tanaro and the others stay away from the command bunker. I must do this alone. There could be disastrous consequences if I am disturbed.'

Castamon still sensed he was missing something, that Abarim

was not telling him the whole story, but another tide of xenos was spilling through the breach and he had no time to press the matter. He raced away from the Librarian, calling Ultramarines to his side as he raced back to the stretch of broken wall. 'Give us all the time you can, Abarim. Vultis will not fail us!'

Chapter Thirty-Two

'What is your greatest strength?'

Abarim was standing at the top of a ruined watchtower, looking out across a corpse-strewn desert. Thousands of heretics lay dead, tangled in razor wire and heaped in mounds, but many more were gathering. The coming battle would be a greater challenge than any he had faced before. Castamon was sitting nearby on a gun emplacement, his armour glinting in the sun. He was younger then, but already a lieutenant. Already a hero of the Chapter. Abarim could clearly recall every detail of the conversation, even though it took place centuries ago. It was his first campaign. His first great trial.

'You have studied long and hard,' continued Castamon. 'Your appetite for wisdom does you credit. You have mastered disciplines that I could not even begin to comprehend. And, before that, you excelled at the martial arts and military strategy. You have conquered the crude, human facets of your personality and tamed the esoteric powers granted to you by the Emperor. So, what do you consider your greatest strength?'

Abarim nodded. It was an interesting question. The kind that Castamon excelled at. He thought of everything he was capable of. He could melt flesh with a thought. Topple walls with a gesture. He could read minds and fight for hours without rest. He could calculate trajectories and rates of fire without pausing for thought. He was everything the Emperor willed him to be – an army contained in a single warrior. But what was his *greatest* strength? He thought back over everything he had read, from Guilliman's masterwork, the Codex Astartes, to other military texts and obscure meditations on the vagaries of the warp. He realised that, for once, he could not easily answer. Several minutes played out in silence. He was determined not to give a facile response. One of the things Castamon demanded of his men was that they look beyond the superficial and seek the *ultimate* truth. As he thought, his gaze came to rest on part of the ruined battlements. Two insects were locked in a mindless battle, whirling and scuttling, trapped in a frenzied dance. Perhaps it was pheromones that had driven them to fight, or the need to impress a potential mate, but, whatever the cause, they were powerless to stop, driven by instinct and the needs of the flesh.

Abarim relaxed as his mind settled on the correct answer. 'My greatest strength is reason. The power to make a choice. My body could be broken. My etheric powers could be nulled. Tactics can fail. But whatever befalls me, I will always have the power to *choose* what I do next.'

'A good answer.' Castamon looked out across the desert, studying the piles of dead. 'There is *always* a choice. Sometimes we might try to convince ourselves we have no option, but it is never true. It might only be a choice between one evil and a lesser evil, but it is still there. Even if it is only the choice between a poor death and a good one.'

A poor death and a good one. The words echoed round Abarim's mind as he strode through the battle. He fired his storm bolter as tyranids lurched towards him, his arm jolting as the explosive rounds destroyed the creatures, flinging body parts across the flagstones. His battleplate was pulsing with psychic currents. His connection to the immaterium was still tenuous. It was like glimpsing a distant coastline through fog. But even that was dizzying. After days of feeling almost impotent, even a weak connection left him feeling drunk on power. The warding runes on his armour were rippling with blue flames. He felt like a man who had been deprived of water then given heady wine. Even a momentary lapse of control would allow the warp to tear through his flesh and flatten the surrounding buildings. But Abarim had learned, long ago, how to avoid lapses of control. He recounted the oaths of warding he had been taught in Ultramar, in the Fortress of Hera on Macragge. He used the rhythm of the words as a mantra, steadying his thoughts and harnessing the tides of the warp.

He reached the end of the street and entered the forum. The square was as crowded as everywhere else. Squads of auxilia troops had gathered around the domed mausoleum on the far side. They were there on Castamon's orders, protecting the entrance to the bunker network that spread beneath the forum. They were putting up an impressive defence, using tactics drilled into them by Sergeant Tanaro, but there were now large numbers of xenos inside the fortress. There was a semicircular mound of tyranid carcasses heaped around the squads of soldiers, but the numbers of dead were nothing to the number of living creatures bounding over the bodies and hurling themselves at the troops.

Abarim stood at the edge of the plaza, studying the scene. There were too many. They would not stop him reaching the mausoleum, but it would take him an age to fight through them. He flexed his gauntleted fingers, allowing a little lightning to play across the digits. He had to be careful. To do as Castamon asked, safely, was going to take every ounce of his strength. He could not risk exhausting himself beforehand. If he hurled warp-fire at the tyranids, he would carve a path through them, but they would rush back into the space and he would have to expend huge amounts of energy forcing them away again. He looked around the forum, seeking an easier answer. The plaza was lined with enormous statues and there was one near the mausoleum. It was a likeness of the Lord Commander's adoptive father, Konor Guilliman, holding a scroll aloft. The statue was over fifty feet tall and Abarim nodded, pleased as he calculated its mass.

Carefully, he allowed empyric energy to flood his thoughts as he stared at the statue. Then he reached out his hand, splaying his fingers before closing them into a fist. On the far side of the plaza, Konor Guilliman's legs imploded, crushed by Abarim's telekinetic grip. The sound of breaking rock was loud enough to ring out over the fighting. Some of the auxilia troops paused to look at the statue, crying out in alarm, but the tyranids attacking them were too frenzied to realise the danger, continuing to mass around the pile of carcasses.

The statue teetered, then fell, slamming onto the swarm with such force that the ground juddered beneath Abarim's boots. He steadied himself then ran across the square towards the mausoleum. Much as he tried to deny it, there was something wonderful about unleashing his power. He could still feel the weight of the statue in his fist. Exerting power was addictive. The warp *wanted* to be unleashed. Most of his training had revolved around the dangers inherent in that. To fully embrace the warp was to embrace madness and heresy. The risks were incalculable. As he ran, he recited the prayers of warding again, steadying his pulse and focusing on the task ahead.

The soldiers cheered him as he reached the mound of dead and clambered over it. The tyranids were regrouping and there were hundreds more flooding from the streets that fed into the forum, but he had achieved his goal – he had reached the mausoleum without delay. He nodded to the cheering soldiers and ran in through the entrance. 'Hold them here!' he cried, as he headed inside.

The soldiers faltered briefly as they realised he had not come to aid them, then they returned to their positions, opening fire on the approaching hordes.

Abarim ran down steps and on into darkened passageways. The bunker network was mostly abandoned as people battled in the streets above. Gun-servitors hummed into life as he passed doorways, but seeing he was no threat, they slumped back into a daze, embedded in the walls like grey-skinned mannequins. He rushed past armouries, food stores and the blinking lights of the tacticarium and on, down another flight of steps into the lower levels. The sounds of battle became muted and confused.

Finally, he reached the chamber he sought. He entered the access codes and, as the door rattled up, he stepped inside. The room was filled with light and the air was thick with the tingle of electricity. Rows of voltaic cells lined one of the walls – oily, rune-scored barrels linked to each other by rubber cabling and crackling with power. Another wall was heaped with grumbling logic engines, draped in wires, rows of blinking crystals and flickering glass valves. The reactor itself was no larger than a man's chest – an unassuming metal casket under a glass dome. Cables entered the dome through sockets and linked the casket to the voltaic cells. There was a single servitor in the room – a torso with a solitary arm and no discernible head, adorned with so many pieces of machinery that its human origins were almost impossible to discern. It was tapping spasmodically at a runeboard and there was a candle wedged between its shoulders, dripping wax and filling the room with the smell of melting animal fat.

Abarim paused at the threshold, staring at the reactor. *A poor death and a good one.* Had he acted without honour? He had not lied to Castamon, but he had withheld something from him. It *was* possible to do as the lieutenant requested. He allowed his thoughts to brush against the reactor's spirit. Yes, it would be easy to make the connection, to bind himself to it, but the next part, spreading his will across the entire shield, that would be a different matter entirely. He would need to link himself to the reactor's current and he would have to do it *physically*. Should he tell Castamon what that meant? He reached out. Even down here in the bunker, he could touch Castamon's mind. It would be possible to explain the situation. But to what end? It would change nothing. The fortress had been breached. The tyranids were already massing outside Vultis' laboratorium. The soldiers would hold out for as long as they could, but it would not be enough. This was the only way to buy Vultis time. And telling Castamon the details would force the lieutenant to hesitate, seeking an alternative when there was none. No, this was the only way, he was sure of it.

He crossed the room and raised his hands before the glass dome, as though warming them by a fire. Then he allowed a little empyric energy into his palms and passed his hands smoothly through the glass without creating so much as a hairline crack. He flexed his fingers, whispered a prayer, then moved his fingers through the sides of the metal casket and gripped the core of the reactor.

There was a soft *whump* as electricity punched through him. His armour could repel most shocks, but this was such a high voltage that it even burned through his ceramite, latching on to the layers of metal beneath. Pain exploded in his head and his hands spasmed, locking to the reactor. The current lanced through his body to the floor, passing through his primary heart and stopping it. Pain nullifiers flooded his body, but the agony was too intense for them to completely shield him. He ignored the pain and battled the convulsions, doing a quick mental scan of his body, studying the damage to calculate how long he had before he lost consciousness. The current had missed his smaller, second heart. It was spasming but still managing an irregular beat. The electricity had shorted his suit's internal functions, but before they blinked out, the runes in his helm display told him that his lungs were filling with blood and there were bleeds appearing on his brain. None of those things would have the chance to kill him, though. He was being cooked alive inside his armour. He could already smell his organs burning. But his body had been engineered to endure almost any kind of hell, at least for a while. He estimated he had five minutes or so.

Abarim felt no more doubt. The resurgence of his powers would be brief. The swarm would quickly replace whichever psychic creature had been killed. But in this brief moment, with this sacrifice, he would buy Vultis the time he needed. He was not being needlessly heroic or vainglorious, this was simply the only option. He prepared himself, silently repeating oaths of purity and warding.

To his surprise, a memory flashed across his mind. He remembered sparring with his brothers at the edge of the desert. They were teenagers, laughing in the sunshine, drunk on the possibilities of life. For a worrying moment, emotion threatened to derail him, but rather than battling it, he allowed it to pass through him, acknowledging it and diffusing it as Castamon had taught him. He smiled, remembering how mercilessly his brothers had mocked him that day. Ridiculing his dream of becoming an Ultramarine. And he remembered, unexpectedly, how much they had loved each other. He wondered how they faced their end when it came. With courage and honour, he was sure. Then he let the memory go and sent his thoughts out into the shield.

Chapter Thirty-Three

'They're coming back.' Governor Seroc stared at the viewscreen embedded in his desk, hardly able to believe what he was seeing. 'Thurgau was right. Damn it, he was right.' He was in his office, surrounded by dozens of senior officials and enforcers. They looked dreadful. All of them were wounded in one way or another, with arms in slings or burns across their faces, and their uniforms were in tatters. But at Seroc's words, hope flared in their red-rimmed eyes and they fell silent, breaking off from panicked conversations to look over at him. Despite the presence of so many people, Seroc embraced Lanek. She laughed, before shoving him away and shaking her head. 'We might even be able to see them,' said Seroc, heading over to a pair of huge armaglass doors and throwing them open.

He stepped out onto a balcony that looked down over the sprawling mess of Salamis. The air clogged his lungs, making him cough and splutter, but he strapped his respirator into place and walked over to the railings, gripping them in both hands and staring across the city. The others rushed out after him, crowding onto the balcony to look out into the miasma. Salamis had fallen apart with a speed that Seroc would have thought impossible. The scene below him looked like the delusions of a religious fanatic. Over half the buildings were on fire now and the ferocity of the glow, filtered through the haze of spores, made it look as if the hive was being boiled in lava. Without the support of the Cadians, the local enforcers had been killed or driven into cover and anarchy now reigned. Vast scaffolds rose from the inferno, scythe-shaped serpents made of metal and crammed with thousands of sacrificial victims. The people in the cages were screaming as they died. It was a sound Seroc knew he would never forget. These were his people. His responsibility. And he had failed all of them.

'You won't be able to see anything out here,' growled a heavy-set enforcer behind him, but he handed Seroc a pair of magnoculars, looking feverish with excitement.

'Thank you, proctor,' he muttered, adjusting the settings until the lenses slipped into focus. He gasped as he accidentally zoomed in on one of the scaffolds, seeing a dreadful glimpse of anguished faces, before looking higher, out across the blazing spires and hab-stacks. 'There. I *do* see them. They're almost back.'

The others pressed forwards against the railings, taking out spyglasses and magnoculars and trying to spot the Cadians. 'Do you see?' A vast cloud of flame billowed across Seroc's vision, and for a moment he could see nothing, then the scene slipped back into focus and he made out the approaching army in more detail. Only, it wasn't an army. 'Throne preserve us,' he whispered. People around him cried out as they saw what he was seeing. It looked like a landslide, but it was teeming with life. He saw tyranids similar to the ones he had seen previously, swarming towards the city in such numbers that his mind baulked at

Leviathan

trying to estimate how large the host was. But he barely registered the smaller creatures. At the head of the swarm, lurching through the darkness, there was a line of behemoths, hunched, scuttling monsters as big as hab-stacks, clad in the same pitted carapaces as the smaller breeds with chimney-like tubes jutting from their thoraxes that belched mountainous clouds of spores.

Seroc would have ordered the weapons batteries to open fire, or mustered the local Militarum regiments, but everyone was either dead, hiding or worshipping at the feet of burning effigies. He wanted to look away, to flee, but he felt powerless to move, watching in mute horror as the enormous creatures reached the outskirts of the hive and, without even pausing, ripped into it, tearing through factorums and hab-towers as if devouring a field of grass. Fuel bowsers detonated and aircars crashed as the monsters rushed through the lower levels of the hive. Then the waves of smaller tyranids flooded in their wake, washing over crowds of fleeing people and devouring everything.

The people on the balcony began to run, howling curses and prayers as they tried to race for safety, but Seroc could see that it was pointless. Even those who managed to reach their aircars would be consumed the moment they left the ground. There were numberless swarms of winged xenos, sweeping down from the darkness overhead, packed so tightly that it looked like a glinting shroud was smothering the hive. The aliens were approaching so fast that he estimated they would reach him in minutes.

He looked around and saw that everyone had fled, even Lanek. He felt a brief flicker of hurt, then realised he was being absurd. What did it matter? How could he blame her? She had contacts and schemes of her own. Perhaps she thought she could find a way out. Good luck to her.

He headed back inside, closing the doors behind him, removed his mask and lit a lho-stick. Then he crossed the room and sat down at his battered old trestle table, looking at the drawing he had made of the city. The city as he wanted it to be. The city that would never be.

A door banged and he looked up in surprise to see Lanek coming towards him. She was carrying two full glasses. He felt an overwhelming rush of relief. Somehow, despite everything that was happening outside, and everything that was about to happen, he felt relieved to know she had stayed with him. She kissed him on the forehead and handed him a drink, then sat next to him in silence. They were both facing the doors that looked out onto the balcony. The light swelled like an incredible sunset. It would have been beautiful if he didn't know the cause. Then the light dimmed as shapes filtered down in front of the flames, falling like curtains over a final act. The sound of thrumming wings filled the air, growing quickly louder until the doors were rattling in their frames.

He took Lanek's hand and they drank, emptying their glasses and quietly placing them down on the table.

Then the doors exploded towards them.

Chapter Thirty-four

Beltis slowed the groundcar and steered it into the trees at the side of the transitway, before killing the engine. 'Damn,' she muttered.

The chem-works were as lifeless and dark as the last time she'd seen them. The chimney-stacks and cooling towers were just visible, rearing up in the darkness, covered in a mess of broken gantries and derricks and rusting promethium drums. But the site was no longer abandoned. People were scurrying through the shadows, hunched and furtive, their lumens flicking back and forth across the ruins.

'They've found the damned hangar,' snarled her father, leaping from the car, gripping his autopistol. 'I've lost everything and now they're trying to steal my only way out.'

Beltis was pleased to see how quickly he was recovering. He seemed almost as fierce as he'd ever been. But that also meant she had to handle him carefully. His temper was quick and, once it took hold of him, uncontrollable.

'We can deal with them,' she said, jumping out of the groundcar and rushing to his side. 'They're just labourers. Workers from one of the agri plants. I doubt they even know how to get in a shuttle, never mind launch one.'

'I'm not so sure,' whined Semler, crawling from the car and sidling up to her. 'What if their farming machines use similar technology?'

'Sawbones is right,' snarled Kulm, tying his dreadlocks back and checking his gun. Then he looked around. 'I need some damned clothes.' He glared at Beltis. 'Why did you bring me out like this?'

'You weren't being particularly compliant.' She went to the rear of the groundcar and took out a boiler suit, flak jacket and boots. 'I grabbed these, just in case you came to your senses.'

'Came to my senses!' he growled, snatching the clothes.

She could tell from his tone and the fact he had not asked her for details of his illness, that he could remember how bizarrely he had behaved back in Port Dura. She wished she could ease his pain, 'You're not the only one who–'

He silenced her with a glare, then continued dressing. Then he summoned the heavy brute, Vant, over to his side. 'Does that thing have a full pack?' he asked, nodding to Vant's lascarbine.

Vant nodded.

'Good, because we're not letting even one of those maggots get their paws on my ships.' With that, he stomped off across the transitway, triggering the lumen fixed to his pistol.

Beltis rushed after him, her heart racing. When she and Vant had bundled him out of Port Dura, she had lost all hope of ever speaking to him again. She could not bear to leave him in that place, but she felt like she was rescuing his corpse. Now he was back, his eyes burning and his jaw muscles rippling.

They were still a hundred feet from the outbuildings when someone called out in alarm.

'They must have night scopes,' grunted Vant.

'Doesn't matter,' replied Kulm. 'Let them see us.' He fired a shot, lighting up the fumes with a muzzle flash. 'Run, maggots! Gathas Kulm is coming for you! And you thought the xenos were bad.'

Clattering noises and the sound of running feet rang out from the buildings. Lumen beams flashed and danced across the walls as people dived for cover.

A small group emerged from behind a slag heap, their hands raised. Beltis could not make them out clearly in the gloom, but they were men, dressed in labourers' overalls with rebreathers strapped across their faces. 'We found ships!' cried one of them, sounding excited. 'They're under the ground somewhere! But we can't find the hangar. Can you help us? Do you–'

Kulm silenced the man with a shot to the head, knocking him back into the darkness. 'You found *my* ships,' he snarled, gunning a second man down.

The rest of the group panicked and people began running from other buildings, sprinting for the trees that bordered the plant.

'Stop them!' yelled Kulm, shooting at the fleeing shapes. He looked back at Beltis, Vant and Semler, his eyes straining. 'Don't just stand there.'

Beltis snatched her pistol from her belt and began firing, but Semler just cringed and Vant shook his head. 'They're running,' the brute said.

Kulm rounded on Vant, spitting with rage as he grabbed the man by the collar of his jacket. 'What do you think they will do if they get away? Do you think they'll keep my hangar secret? They'll tell anyone they can that there are ships here. And their friends might be more than just farmhands.'

He let go of Vant and began shooting the labourers again,

his pistol bucking in his fist as it spat auto-rounds into the scattering crowds.

'You're a monster,' rumbled Vant.

The word 'monster' stabbed into Beltis. She howled and lashed out with her electro-flail, wrapping the barbed cables around his throat and yanking him to the ground. The current burned his skin and electricity danced over his limbs. But he was tough. Despite the convulsions rocking through his body, he ripped the flail from his neck, hurled it away and pointed his gun at her face.

Kulm fired, repeatedly, knocking Vant backwards into the gloom. He stood over the man for a moment, making sure he was dead, then turned to Beltis and Semler. 'No one leaves here alive, understand?'

They both nodded, Beltis with pride and Semler with terror. Then, all three of them advanced into the complex. Semler took out a small, elegant-looking laspistol and the three of them opened fire, filling the place with noise and light. People were so panicked that it was an absurdly easy job. Beltis felt a glimmer of guilt but crushed it down. It was either this or her father died. Only one ship could leave. It was survival of the fittest. The labourers would probably have done the same if the tables were turned.

A few people fired back with stub guns and shotguns, but the shots were panicked and untargeted and gradually the trio advanced through the chem-works towards the central hub.

A few minutes passed without sign of movement. 'I think we got them all,' gasped Semler. He looked dazed and absurdly proud of himself, as though he had survived a great battle.

They approached the central hub of buildings, still scanning the darkness with their guns. Suddenly Kulm paused. 'It's here.' He grinned, his teeth flashing in the darkness. He stamped on the ground, moving back and forth until his boot clanged on a different surface. Then he dropped to one knee and brushed away the dust and gravel, uncovering an expanse of rusty metal painted with yellow hazard stripes. He looked at it for a moment, then nodded and took a few steps sideways. Then he crouched again and brushed away some more of the gravel. This time, along with the corrugated metal he unearthed a flat, dark square that flashed in the light of his lumen. 'Morons,' he said, looking around at the dead labourers. 'What use would it have done them if they'd found this? They don't know the damned access codes.' He slapped the metal. 'This stuff is six feet thick.'

He wiped more dust from the data-slate he had unearthed, then pressed his palm against it. Static-hazed binary scrolled across the crystal and blinked away, leaving an eight-by-eight square of green, luminous characters. Kulm tapped at them, paused, then tapped a few more times. A moment later the hum of a generator reverberated under their feet and the gravel began to shake.

'Back away,' said Kulm, stepping away from the data-slate.

Gradually, as the gravel trembled and shifted, a rectangular depression began to form in the ground as the corrugated metal dropped slowly away from the surface. The generator shifted pitch and the metal plate slid sideways, creating an opening on one side that looked down into a black void.

'What's that?' grunted Kulm, stopping and raising his hand for the other two to halt. He rushed back to the data-slate and tapped at it again, halting the metal plate with only a few feet open.

Beltis looked around. 'Where?'

'No, what's that *noise*?'

She listened. At first she thought it was wind, rustling through the trees at the edge of the complex. But then she realised it was too regular. It was the sound of beating wings. She thought of the monsters that had attacked Port Dura. 'We need to get inside,' she hissed, looking around at the surrounding buildings. She glanced at the hole in the ground. 'Maybe we could get in the hangar and shut the hatch until they've–'

There was a loud bang.

Pain exploded in her arm, knocking her sideways. Shots rang out from a nearby cabin, ricocheting off walls and kicking up dust from the ground. She saw more labourers, peering through a broken doorway, before backing away.

'Idiots,' she gasped, gripping her arm and finding it was drenched in blood. It felt as if someone had jammed a hot iron through her bicep. She returned fire and her father did the same, tearing pieces from the cabin.

Semler looked up at the lightless sky, shaking his head. 'You're drawing them to us,' he said. The sound of beating wings grew louder and he turned and ran, sprinting back towards the transitway. He had only taken a few steps when a shadow splintered from the darkness, swooping down to engulf him. Semler screamed, flailing as something locked on to his face.

Beltis aimed at the winged shape and the lumen on her pistol picked it out of the darkness. It was the closest she had come to one of the aliens. It was a disgusting mixture of insect, human and reptile, with a long, flicking tail and wide, leathery wings. Its head was long and crowned with a gnarled carapace, like a helmet. As it turned to face her, pieces of Semler's face tumbled from its mouth.

'My eyes!' howled Semler, still writhing on the ground and trying to crawl away, clutching at his head. Then another shape fell from the darkness, locked its talons around him and flew off. Semler was still screaming as he vanished into the sky.

The tyranid facing Beltis studied her for a moment, then pounded its wings and launched itself at her face.

It flipped in mid-air as auto-rounds punched into its head, then it tumbled back across the ground, thrashing its wings and kicking up dust.

Kulm marched past Beltis, firing at the flailing monster until it lay still, but the air above their heads was now boiling with movement.

Labourers howled and broke cover as tyranids rained down from the darkness.

Kulm turned on the spot, firing in every direction, beset by whirling aliens. He looked like he was in the heart of a cyclone. He spat curses as fast as his gun spat bullets, howling at the monsters rushing around him.

Beltis waved at the opening in the ground. 'Get to the hangar!' she cried, her voice battling against the sound of guns and pounding wings. But her father was too far gone. Rage had consumed him. He was magnificent, facing off dozens of monsters as though it were they who should be afraid rather than him.

Then the tyranids ceased circling and engulfed him, attacking in a storm of wings, turning her father into meat and mist.

She howled, sprinting forwards.

Then they were on her.

Chapter Thirty-Five

THE FORTRESS CITY AT ZARAX
SAMNIUM PROVINCE, REGIUM

'What are they doing?' said Vultis, stumbling over blood-slick rubble.

Baraca was a few feet away, butchering a tyranid with his knife. He hurled the resultant mess to the floor and stood up, gore flying from his blade as he turned, ready for another attack.

Damaris was nearby, wide-eyed and blood-soaked, her sword raised in both hands as she spat curses at the tyranids. She had fought with a fury that even Baraca had been impressed by.

They had killed three of the serpent monsters, but there were more snaking through the walls. The odds had seemed impossible just a few moments ago, but something strange had happened. The tyranids were acting oddly, as though confused. Behind them, through the ruined walls, Vultis saw that the same thing was happening outside – the tyranids had lost their momentum, stumbling to a halt or moving in erratic lurches. Whatever had affected them was intermittent. They would be distracted for a moment, circling in the rubble, then

321

recover and attack the nearest human, before becoming confused again.

There was an explosion of rubble as one of the serpentine tyranids launched itself across the room. Vultis rushed to protect Damaris, but the creature was not heading for her. It attacked another tyranid, latching its jaws around its long, coiled body and tearing a hunk of carapace away, exposing the glistening muscles beneath.

Vultis watched in disbelief as the tyranids fought each other. They grew more frenzied than ever, tearing at each other while others circled mindlessly across the rubble. Outside it was the same – the bipedal xenos were grappling and stabbing each other or firing toxic, barbed parasites at their own kind. Soldiers backed away as the swarm lost its coherency and became a deranged rabble.

Damaris leant on her sword to catch her breath and looked over at the him. 'What is this?' she demanded. 'Have they lost their minds?'

Vultis considered her question. As far as he could tell, most of the tyranids had no minds of their own. They behaved more like puppets, perhaps led by something greater. If they were puppets, could something have severed their strings?

'Vultis.' Castamon's voice crackled over the vox. 'Has it worked? Do you have an answer?'

'Lieutenant,' he replied. 'Our way to the laboratorium has been barred. Tyranids have entered the fortress.'

'You are not even in the laboratorium?' The shock was audible in his voice.

'No, lieutenant. We are surrounded by tyranids. They are in the fortress.'

'They breached the wall, near the north gate, aided by human cultists.'

Baraca grunted in disbelief. 'People helped the xenos in?'

'The cultists acted strangely. I believe they were in thrall to someone or something. They behaved as if they had been hypnotised. But they were killed before I could discover what was controlling them.'

'Lieutenant,' said Vultis. 'We are at the consular villa and the xenos here are attacking each other. Their assault is faltering.'

'That will be Abarim's doing. He devised a way to bolster the shields with his mind. The xenos inside the fortress are now sundered from those outside. But he told me it will not last long. Go now. This is your chance to reach the laboratorium.'

Vultis turned to Damaris.

'I'll show you the way,' she said, her voice husky with emotion. She took a deep breath and climbed through the shattered wall, heading deeper into the building. 'We're close.'

Chapter Thirty-Six

'Can you hear me?' said Valacia. She had crawled under the overturned groundcar and was gripping the woman's hand. 'Avula? Can you hear me?'

Tharro was watching the transitway, staring out into the darkness, looking for movement. At the sound of Valacia's voice, he looked back over at her.

Avula managed to focus on Valacia, giving her a vague nod.

'Look!' said Valacia, hope flashing in her eyes as she turned towards him. 'She hears me.'

Tharro felt a love for Valacia that was almost painful. She was going to die, out here in the hell that used to be her home and she was smiling; smiling because a stranger could still breathe.

Valacia seemed to guess his thoughts. Her expression hardened. 'I didn't stay here to just to die with her. We're getting her out. Stop looking like you're going to cry. Think. What do we do? We're not dead yet.'

He laughed. 'What made you so damned tough?'

'Living with you.' She looked around the ruined vehicle. 'Well? What are we going to do?'

He slapped the buckled chassis. 'We can't move this thing.' He looked at Avula. She did seem to be recovering. She looked more awake by the minute. She had probably just been dazed from the impact. She might even be able to walk if she wasn't pinned down by the roll bar. 'Is this all that's holding her down?' he asked, walking round the vehicle and crouching next to it.

'Yes. I think so.' Valacia looked at him with hope shining in her eyes. 'Can we cut it?'

'We've got no cutting tools.' He looked at the autopistol Jebel had given him. It was a bulky, high-calibre weapon. He felt like he was holding a dangerous predator. He shrugged. 'He did say to use it however I see fit.'

Valacia narrowed her eyes.

'No, I don't mean that. I just wondered if I could use it to shoot that roll bar away. What do you think?'

'But wouldn't the shrapnel…' She lowered her voice. 'Wouldn't the shrapnel kill her?'

Tharro patted the flak jacket he was wearing, then he removed it and rested it over the woman, covering the side of her that was nearest to the roll bar. 'And you could put yours next to her face,' he said. 'Would that work?'

She grabbed his hand and kissed it. 'We'd be giving her a chance,' she said. 'Which is more than she has at the moment.'

They positioned the flak jackets over the woman and she seemed to register what they were trying to do, curling herself into a tighter ball. 'That's it,' whispered Valacia, crouching beside her. 'You'll be fine. We'll have you out in a minute and get you out of here.' Then Tharro waved Valacia away from the vehicle, took a few steps back and aimed at the roll bar.

'Wait!' cried Valacia. She ran onto the transitway, grabbed a piece of buckled metal, rushed back to the wrecked groundcar and wedged it in, near Avula. 'The roll bar might be holding the weight off her.'

Tharro nodded and took aim again.

'Wait!' Valacia said again. 'You've never fired that thing before. You don't know how to use it. Should you try it on something else, first?'

He licked his lips, growing more nervous with every interruption, but he saw the sense of what she was saying. He pointed the gun at the darkness and squeezed the trigger. Bullets rattled out with such force his hand jolted, and he almost dropped the gun. 'Throne,' he muttered. Then he nodded and turned back to the groundcar. 'I know what I'm doing now,' he lied, taking aim at the roll bar. It was inches from the woman, who was still cowering under the flak jackets. If he missed, if the gun bucked in his grip and he hit her, he did not think the jackets would stop the bullets.

He held his breath, waiting to see if Valacia was going to call out again. Then he fired.

Bullets ripped into the door, wide of the roll bar.

Avula gave a cry but stayed still.

He whispered a curse, adjusted his aim and fired again. This time he hit the roll bar. It sheared instantly and he loosed the trigger.

The groundcar creaked and the piece of metal began to buckle as embers drifted near the woman.

'I did it,' said Tharro, laughing with relief.

'It's going to fall!' cried Valacia, running past him back to the groundcar and dropping on her knees beside Avula. 'She'll be crushed.'

He placed the gun carefully on the ground and rushed to help. They grabbed the woman by the shoulders and gently pulled her out. She groaned but did not resist, holding on to their arms as they hauled her to safety. They had only dragged her a few feet from the vehicle when it crushed the metal plate and slammed to the ground, kicking up a cloud of dust.

'Throne preserve us,' whispered Valacia as the woman embraced her.

Tharro stood and watched as the two hugged, laughing and crying. He could not quite believe they had done it. Then, as he watched the darkness, fear jolted through him. 'We have to get out of here. This is the longest we've spent in the open. It might only be a matter of minutes before the xenos catch our scent.'

'Help me then,' said Valacia, and together they lifted the woman to her feet.

'Thank you,' said Avula, still hugging Valacia. Her voice was little more than a croak, but she was able to stand, and as they headed away from the transitway, Avula hanging on to their shoulders, she hardly limped. 'Thank you for staying.'

They made their way back up to the ridge and climbed into the groundcar. Tharro started the engine. 'We can get to Uxama on these side roads,' he said, driving back onto the gravel. 'We won't be as exposed as down there on the arterial route.'

As he drove back into the forest, the groundcar's lights flashed on tree-trunks and creepers and every shape seemed to be moving, making him flinch and curse. Behind him, on the back seat, Valacia tried to clean the cut on Avula's head. 'It's not deep,' she said, dabbing it with an alcohol-soaked rag.

She sounded absurdly hopeful, but Tharro was battling despair. His elation at saving Avula had faded quickly as he thought of Jebel's warning. He and the other labourers would already have reached the hangar and they would take off the moment they boarded the cargo shuttle. 'We might be too late,' he muttered.

'They could have been delayed,' snapped Valacia. 'Besides, what else could we have done?'

Avula sat up and, as Valacia wiped the dried blood from her face, Tharro saw that she was only young, barely out of her teens by the look of her, with dark, wiry hair and sandy, freckled skin. 'You should have left me,' she said quietly, looking at Valacia.

Valacia hugged her and shook her head. 'What would that make us, child? It would make us worse than the monsters. They don't know any better, but we *do*.'

Avula looked unconvinced.

'Valacia's right,' admitted Tharro. 'There's no guarantee that hangar even exists. We've heard half a dozen similar stories on the way here. Everyone claims to know of a way out.' He tried to block out some of the things they had seen over the last couple of days. The behaviour of desperate humans haunted him more than any of the xenos he had seen. It was incredible what people were prepared to do when they were afraid. 'And what right would we have to live if we left you there?'

The girl still looked pained, but she nodded and leant into Valacia as she hugged her.

They drove in silence for a while then Tharro saw lights up ahead. 'They don't look like lumens,' he said, pulling the groundcar over and looking down into an ink-dark valley. There were flashes in the darkness. It looked like lightning, but on the ground.

'It's a fight,' said Avula, leaning forward in her seat. 'Those are las-bolts. And muzzle flashes from stubbers.'

'And that's where we're headed,' said Tharro. 'That's where the chem-works used to be. Jebel has been delayed. Someone must have been guarding the place. That might mean we're still in time to join them on the shuttle.'

'Or someone has turned up looking for the same thing,' said

Valacia. 'That might not be Jebel. Maybe that engineer told more than one person what was down there.'

'What do we do?' asked Avula, looking at him. He felt a rush of panic as he realised that the girl was now trusting them to get her to safety.

'Maybe we should go somewhere else?' he muttered.

'Jebel's no fool,' said Avula. She was sounding surer of herself by the minute. Her words were no longer slurred and she looked from Valacia to him with a confident gleam in her eyes. 'If he thinks there's a shuttle down there, he's probably right. I know what you mean about people offering false hope, but Jebel knew about that too. He ignored most of the stories people spouted. But he was sure about this one. I think there really *is* a shuttle down there. Hidden in the world roots.'

Tharro remembered the confidence he'd seen in Jebel's eyes and nodded. 'He did seem to know what he was talking about. But we can't walk into a gunfight. Firstly, we'll get shot, but secondly, you know what happens when people start making noise like that.'

'That place will be a feeding ground any minute.'

'There's a shuttle there,' whispered Avula. 'I know it.'

'What about if we just get a *bit* closer?' said Valacia. 'We could watch from a safe distance and then see how things play out.'

Tharro shook his head. He was battling waves of terror, but he refused to show it in front of Avula. She had almost been left to die and was now acting as though there was still hope. He looked at the autopistol lying next to him. Then he sighed and nodded. 'I'll get us as close as I dare.'

Chapter Thirty-Seven

THE FORTRESS CITY AT ZARAX
SAMNIUM PROVINCE, REGIUM

Tanaro looked down over the battlements and paused to admire
the scene. The blast at the wall had created rents in the cautery
shield and the tyranids were now everywhere, looping overhead, swarming over the stonework and erupting through the
floors. The fight was horrific, but it was also *glorious*. The Ultramarines of the First Company were gathered on the wall near
the largest hole in the shield. They stood back to back, their
pyreblasters and bolters producing a barrage of light so fierce it
looked like a star was being born in the darkness. Their shots
incinerated everything that came close, and heaped around them
were hundreds of the fortress' human defenders, wounded and
bloody but inspired by the Ultramarines' majesty. The xenos
attacked in frenzied waves but they could not pierce the light,
falling in mounds as they strove uselessly to advance.

Tanaro had climbed up onto a piece of broken canopy, and
for a moment he could do nothing but stare in wonder. It took
all his restraint not to howl in triumph. His men were fighting

with all the pride and skill he had taught them. No, he corrected himself, they had surpassed that. They were more magnificent than he had ever seen them. *The Imperium will mark this moment,* he thought. *Guilliman himself will know what we did here.*

A tyranid swooped from the darkness with an inhuman scream. Conscious of being watched by the crowds below, Tanaro resisted the urge to shoot. He waited until the monster was almost on him before leaping acrobatically into the air and locking his arm around its neck. The impact threw the tyranid off course and it slammed onto the canopy, scrabbling to right itself. He beheaded it with his combat knife, kicked the body from the wall and held the head aloft. 'Thus perish all of the Imperium's foes!' he cried. 'In ignominy and blood!'

Down below, on the wall, some of the soldiers cheered and he saw wounded clambering to their feet, holding their guns aloft in answer. 'Taste the Emperor's wrath!' he cried, hurling the head into the darkness, eliciting more cheers.

He rushed on, climbing up the broken canopy, spotting a route to a ruined tower. He fought off another tyranid as he reached the tower then bolted inside, racing up the spiral stairs to the top. He was seeking a better vantage-point, but as he emerged onto the roof he stepped out into clinging fumes. He made his way to the edge and peered out into the miasma. Castamon had tasked him with holding the walls until Vultis' countermeasures were ready. He needed to be sure his men were deployed in the best location. He shook his head, unable to see anything beyond the walls. He adjusted the magnification of his lenses, but it was useless.

He had decided to leave and search for another vantage-point when the spore-clouds parted. It was only for a brief moment, but it was enough to root him to the spot. The tyranid swarm was still flooding from the forest but there was now a second host, advancing on the fortress from the north. It was even larger than the first – so vast it seemed to have no end. But the thing that troubled Tanaro was the nature of the vanguard creatures. They were enormous, like the monolithic god-machines of the Adeptus Titanicus, only they were formed of glistening muscle and scarred chitin. One of them alone would have the strength to wade through the fortress walls, but he counted dozens, pounding through the darkness, shrouded in clouds of lesser creatures.

As he watched them advance, it occurred to Tanaro that this day might not be remembered for the reasons he hoped. 'Lieutenant Castamon,' he said, opening the vox-link. 'I have news.'

Chapter Thirty-Eight

THE FORTRESS CITY AT ZARAX
SAMNIUM PROVINCE, REGIUM

Vultis stayed close to Damaris as she led the way through a maze of tunnels beneath the city. Some were abandoned and crumbling but most were well preserved.

'Confessor Thurgau has not completely crushed the old faith,' said Baraca, pausing to study a shrine in one of the walls. It contained a sculpture of the Emperor, sprouting from the ground, a gnarled trunk where His legs should have been. There were candles at the base and some of them were lit.

Damaris glanced back, pain in her eyes. She seemed on the verge of saying something, then shook her head and continued.

'Keep moving,' said Vultis, waving Baraca on.

'She is hiding something from us,' growled Baraca when he reached Vultis' side.

'What do you mean?'

'Have you actually looked at her, brother?'

Vultis felt a flicker of irritation. Baraca thought he had no grasp of the human condition, that he was blind to people's emotions, but it was nonsense. 'She is afraid,' he said. 'And grieving for her people.' He thought for a moment. 'And she is brave. She wants to avenge the proconsul.'

'She is ashamed,' said Baraca. 'And her sense of shame deepens every time she looks at us.'

They caught up with Damaris, and Vultis saw that Baraca was right. Her expression hardened as she looked back at them, as though she were in pain. How had he missed that?

They emerged back up onto the streets a few minutes later and even Vultis struggled to make sense of the battle. Most of the street-lumens had been smashed and the aliens were moving in such a frenzied way that he struggled to distinguish one from another. The gun turrets up on the walls were still booming, though, and he saw Sergeant Tanaro striding boldly back and forth on the battlements, spitting fire from a pyreblaster and slapping his battle-brothers on the back as he bellowed commands.

'This way,' said Vultis, spotting the route to his laboratorium and heading off down one of the streets.

Damaris hesitated, hanging back, staring at the nightmarish scrum.

'Make haste,' growled Baraca, waving her on.

Tyranids erupted from the shadows, barrelling towards them. Damaris howled and recoiled, but the Ultramarines strode calmly on as the xenos approached. Then, just as chitin-plated bodies were about to engulf them, Vultis and Baraca finally opened fire. Baraca spilled a river of flame from his pyreblaster, coating the tyranids in burning liquid, while Vultis fired his bolt pistol, splitting skulls and spraying used casings across the street.

The tyranids fought furiously, but then seemed to forget their purpose, turning on each other or leaping at corpses, juddering and tumbling over each other. Vultis marched on, making for a low, rectangular building on the southern edge of the forum. His laboratorium was similar in design to many of the buildings in the fortress – classical and powerful-looking, decorated by thick, fluted columns and a broad skirt of steps.

They had nearly reached the steps when Vultis paused and looked around. 'We are driving them back,' he said, gazing across the crowded square. 'Abarim has granted us the upper hand.' The tyranids were so deranged that even the human soldiers were making short work of them, pouring las-bolts into their contorted bodies and forcing them into retreat.

'On the walls, too,' said Baraca.

Up on the battlements, Sergeant Tanaro and the other Ultramarines were slaughtering the frenzied xenos. Tanaro already looked like he was at a victory parade, swaggering through the violence as though he were invulnerable, which, in fact, he seemed to be. Everyone else was covered in filth and blood, but Tanaro's armour was spotless.

'Have we won?' gasped Damaris, staring at Tanaro in wonder. 'Is it over?'

Baraca laughed.

Vultis shook his head. 'Abarim has only confused the xenos that are within these walls. And he told Castamon he cannot sustain his grip for long. They will soon recover.' He carried on towards the building. 'But he has *given* me time to finish my work. The process is delicate,' he muttered to himself. 'A lull in the fighting will help. Everything must be exactly right.' He continued talking to himself as the three of them rushed up the steps, past blue-and-gold-clad guards, and entered the laboratorium.

Damaris halted in the doorway, looking down at Vultis' collection. 'Holy Terra,' she whispered, staring at the rows of severed heads and preserved foetuses.

Vultis rushed on down the steps. 'Touch nothing,' he called.

He approached his workbench, grabbing electronic devices, transformers and voltaic energy packs. After removing his helmet and placing it on a stand, he quickly arranged the equipment on the workbench, pushing objects back and forth until he was happy with the arrangement. He could feel his predecessors gazing down on him from the books behind him. He had read those tomes so many times that the authors seemed to live in his mind, mentoring him and guiding him as he worked. He knew they would not approve if he began in haste.

'Vultis,' grunted Baraca. 'There is no time for this.'

Vultis nodded and gestured for his servitors to approach. They trundled over, clutching exactly the right tools in their oily pincers, seeming to anticipate his needs by intuition alone. There were preserved tyranid body parts displayed on all the surrounding shelves and tables, but they were old specimens, taken from other warzones. Vultis' attention was fixed on two clear-sided caskets at the centre of the workbench. Suspended in one was the specimen he had captured on the *Incorruptible*. It was rotting, hazed by a cloud of dead skin, little more than a few plates of exoskeleton with claws dangling beneath. 'It is dying,' he muttered.

'Good,' said Damaris, her voice full of bile.

Vultis had forgotten she was there and looked at her in surprise. 'I need both specimens. They must both be alive for the procedure to work.' He waved her away. 'Remain silent while I work.'

He removed the containment canister from his armour and handed it to one of the servitors. The second xenos was in better health than the first. It struggled in the servitor's grip as it was removed from the canister and placed in the empty casket. There was a humming sound as the casket locked.

Vultis studied his captives. Even though they were small and imprisoned, they triggered a powerful wave of revulsion in him. The chamber was lit by fierce strip lumens that revealed every grotesque detail. Vultis had a huge respect for predators. Many of the specimens in his laboratorium were far more impressive, in a scientific capacity, than the humans he was sworn to protect. But when he looked at the two symbionts, he felt only disgust.

He removed his gauntlets and put his hands into holes on the side of the casket, sliding his fingers into gloves that hung inside the box. The specimen attacked instantly, attempting to bite into his hands but failing to puncture the thick gloves.

As he gripped the symbiont tighter, an image flickered across his thoughts. It was so vivid he grunted in surprise. He saw a command chamber, wreathed in perfumed smoke. The walls were draped in banners and the air was thrumming with the power of plasma drives. There was a single, colossal figure in the room, hunched over a stone table, poring over charts and scrolls. Even though the warrior was hazed by smoke, he was unmistakable. It was Roboute Guilliman, Lord of Ultramar and Lord Commander of the entire Imperium. Vultis could name every piece of his primarch's armour and weaponry, from the Armour of Fate, with its layers of intricate filigree, to the huge sword once carried by the Emperor Himself. It should have been a glorious sight, but rather than feeling elated Vultis felt a wave of dread. There was something else in the chamber, something that should not be there, something that radiated insatiable hunger. Dust billowed around the feet of statues and shadows lurched as it approached. And, somehow, the Lord Commander was oblivious. Whatever the threat was, Guilliman was blind to it, too focused on his maps and books to realise that he was in danger.

Then the command chamber was gone and Vultis saw the laboratorium again.

Baraca was staring at him. He removed his helmet with a hiss of escaping air and placed it on the workbench. His face had been repaired so many times he looked like one of Vultis' specimens, but there was concern in his eyes. 'What ails you, brother? You look ill.'

'I saw the Lord Commander.'

He raised an eyebrow. 'You *saw* him?'

Vultis struggled to tell if Baraca was shocked or mocking him. He looked suspiciously at the two tyranids. 'They affected me, Baraca. They altered my thoughts.' He remembered what had happened when Abarim was near the specimen, and he felt a familiar rush of excitement – the same thrill he always felt when he found that facts corresponded to his theories. 'And it must be because they are in close proximity to each other. This never happened when I only had one specimen. Together, they are more than they were individually.'

Vultis connected the two boxes with electro cables and flicked a switch on a transformer. The caskets thrummed with power. The liquid began to glow and the specimens started to shake.

Baraca shrugged. 'These things are just parasites. They feed on larger xenos. Is that not what you said? I fail to see how they can save us.'

'Save us?' hissed Damaris, coming closer again, her voice still full of hate.

Vultis ignored her, continuing with his work, clipping and tightening wires, filling syringes and checking pressure gauges.

Baraca massaged his boulder-like head, stroking his stubbly mohawk. 'If anyone can do this, brother, it is you.'

Vultis nodded but found, to his surprise, that he was struggling to focus. He knew the correct procedure, he knew exactly what to do – how to remove the fat and connective tissue, how to find the right nerves and blood vessels. He had performed countless dissections. But as he tried to begin, his mind kept wandering, returning to the image of Guilliman's command chamber. He could feel something closing in inexorably on the Lord Commander. An assassin. No, not an assassin, a *harbinger*. The name hit him with the force of a revelation. He was watching the Harbinger, hunting the primarch of the Ultramarines just as it had hunted Lieutenant Tyrus on the *Incorruptible*. It had come to kill Guilliman.

Confusion gripped him. 'I feel its thoughts,' he muttered. 'It is so sure of itself.' He looked back at the doors, thinking of the carnage outside. 'All of this is exactly as the Harbinger expected. All part of its plan.'

Baraca gripped his shoulder. The scarred metal of his gauntlet clanging on Vultis' pauldron. 'These parasites are beguiling you, brother. You said it yourself. They radiate madness and lies. You are not like Abarim. You do not have the gift of foreknowledge. This must be another xenos ploy.'

Vultis backed away from the bench, nodding. Baraca was right. He was not a telepath. But perhaps the symbionts were. He felt as though something was trying to reach him *through* them. Their leaders or their hive mind or whatever it was that drove them. He saw the vision again and the feelings of foreboding returned. The Harbinger radiated disdain, as though it considered the Imperium to be a kind of underworld. He slammed his fist on the workbench, rattling the tools, trying to focus his mind. 'You will *not* defy me.' His muscles tensed as anger flooded his body. 'I will *not* fail Castamon.' The thought of the lieutenant gave him balance.

He placed his hands back into the gloves and began working again. Images of Guilliman's command chamber assailed him but he drove them off with Castamon's words, repeating a mantra until it formed a shield. Gripping the symbiont tightly in one hand, he used his other hand to cut away a piece of carapace and then, gently, prised apart the layers of connective tissue beneath. Once he had begun, his confidence grew and the vision faded. Castamon's faith in him was deserved. He had performed so many dissections that he had learned to recognise similarities between even the most divergent species. He probed, pulled and teased. Then he used a mechanised blow-pipe to inflate one of the organs until it became a translucent membrane, revealing smaller shapes pulsing beneath. 'This is it,' he muttered, spotting a brainlike organ he had identified in the first specimen. He clamped a wire to the organ, linking the new specimen to the older one.

'It is done,' he breathed, backing away from the workbench, his pulse drumming.

Baraca frowned at him. 'What is done?'

He gripped him by the arm. 'I think I have linked them. I think I have created a neural network. And, if I have, that would mean I can influence their ratiocination process. I can disrupt the homeostasis of the entire swarm.'

Baraca raised an eyebrow. 'Ratiocination?'

'Their thought process,' he said, frustrated that he had to explain such simple terms. 'If I really can influence it, I can direct them. You saw what happened when Abarim sundered the xenos from their hive mind. They became erratic and ineffectual. I could take that idea much further.'

He tapped the vox-emitter on his workbench and spoke into the receiver. 'Lieutenant Castamon. I am ready to begin.'

There was a moment of static, then a crackly reply. 'Good timing.' Vultis felt a rush of pride as he heard the relief in the lieutenant's voice. Castamon broke off to give out some orders then addressed the vox again. 'Abarim's psychic bulwark is failing. The xenos have regained their senses and are attacking in earnest.

*Abarim is not responding so I am on my way to find him. And
there is disappointing news from Sergeant Tanaro. He has seen xenos
approaching from the north. Which means the Cadians did not hold
Salamis. There must have been some kind of catastrophe, but we
cannot contact the governor. And this new swarm is twice the size
of the one at the gates. We will not be able to repel them all. The
second swarm is almost on us and it is led by Bio-Titans. You must
act now. Without Abarim's intervention, the fortress is being overrun.'*
The channel went dead for a few seconds before Castamon's
voice returned, sounding strained. *'...to your laboratorium, but
they are struggling to reach you. I have sent troops to guard your
doors, but you are not safe. Once I have Abarim, we will join you
and ensure–'* The signal died and would not return.

Vultis drummed his fingers on the workbench. Damaris looked
horrified by Castamon's news and even Baraca seemed troubled,
but Vultis felt elated, dazzled by the ideas whirling in his mind.
The implications of his discovery were staggering. But, for now,
he had to focus on the fastest solution. If he died now, his ideas
would die with him.

He was vaguely aware that Baraca was talking to him, asking
him questions, but he blocked them out and hurried over to
a shelf of medical textbooks, tracing his finger over the spines,
selecting one and pulling it from the shelf. He placed it carefully on the workbench and flicked through the pages, making
a mental note of the instructions. Then he grabbed a data-slate,
looking from the screen to the book and double-checking the
information. 'Hold that,' he said, keeping his gaze fixed on the
book as he pointed to a lever on one of the devices. Baraca did
as Vultis requested. 'And that one,' he said, waving Damaris in
the direction of a lever at the other end of the workbench. She
grabbed it.

The machines were humming and rattling, as though badly

earthed, and Vultis could feel waves of heat radiating from the metal as he gripped a third lever. 'On three,' he said.

'Two.'

He stared at the shapes floating in the canisters, daring them to try to confuse him.

'One.'

They yanked the levers down. They moved easily, clicking on ratchets until the handles were almost resting on the workbench.

The liquid in the canisters flashed white, silhouetting the creatures inside, and there was a loud, voltaic hum from machines under the table.

'Hold them down,' muttered Vultis, flicking switches as he moved his face nearer to the canisters, peering into the liquid as he made adjustments.

A rattling sound filled the chamber. All the nearby benches and shelves were juddering. Every case that contained a piece of tyranid was moving: whether it was a limb or just a claw, all of them were twitching and shaking in their containers.

'It is working!' breathed Vultis.

Baraca laughed as the noise grew. 'Are you making that happen?'

Then the caskets went dark.

The rattling stopped and all the specimens became still again.

'No,' whispered Vultis. He rushed to one of the caskets and shoved his hands into the gloves, feeling for the rotten symbiont. The liquid was now so clouded that he could not see the specimen, but he found it with his hands. As soon as he touched it, he realised the cause of the problem. 'Dead.'

He could not think what to do. This had to work. He had to succeed. Castamon had placed his trust in him. Everything depended on him. Regium. The Sanctus Line. *Everything*.

'Luco,' said Baraca quietly. 'What do you need to do?'

Vultis nodded, thinking back over previous experiments, recalling times a specimen had died during a procedure. 'Of course,' he muttered, filling one of the syringes and injecting the symbiont. At first he felt nothing, but then, to his relief, he detected a faint flutter of life. 'Quickly,' he said. 'The levers. We need to begin again before the symbiont stops–'

There was a loud crashing sound. At first, Vultis thought his machinery had exploded, then he realised the sound had come from the other end of the chamber, up by the doors.

Damaris cried out as the walls caved in, spilling rubble and plaster dust into the room. Cabinets toppled and jars smashed as something rushed into the building.

'The Harbinger is here,' growled Vultis, letting go of the lever and backing away from the workbench. An enormous tyranid stomped into view, stooping to keep its head below the ceiling and trailing a colossal, lashing tail. One side of its face was so badly burned that the workings of its jaw were exposed along with muscles and brain tissue, and its head was topped by three chitinous blades that ripped the ceiling apart as it smashed into the room, causing the whole building to judder and groan.

Baraca drew his pistol and opened fire.

Vultis did the same, but as soon as he began shooting, he realised his mistake. His mind was playing tricks on him. There was not one tyranid but many – pale, chitinous monsters that leapt across the tables. They moved with breathtaking speed, propelled by powerful reverse-jointed legs and lashing out with bone-scythe limbs.

Bolter rounds tore most of them apart, but when the Ultramarines' guns clicked on empty, some of the monsters were still racing towards Vultis and the symbionts.

'Leave them to me,' snarled Baraca, racing to meet them. 'Finish your work.'

He slammed his fist into the first one's face. Ceramite crunched through chitin, splintering teeth and jolting the creature's head back. He followed up with his knife, slashing it sideways through the creature's neck. He cut it with such force that the head came free, filling the chamber with a spray of hissing blood.

He rolled low, gripping the bleeding carcass and using it as a shield as the second attacker tumbled over him in a confusion of thrashing limbs, trying to right itself and turn around. Baraca hammered his knife through its head, twisted the blade and yanked it sideways, cracking the skull and spilling gore across the workbenches. Then he rose and turned just in time to bring the knife up through the jaw of a third attacker, jolting the blade hard enough to split its head vertically before swinging the carcass round and slamming it into the first of the creatures, running from the opposite direction. He lunged and hacked again, finishing off by sheathing his knife, grabbing the final tyranid's head in both hands and snapping its neck.

He dropped into a crouch and whipped out his knife, surrounded by twitching dead. There was a faint hissing sound as the tyranids spilled their toxic blood across the floor, but there were no more attacks.

Baraca stood and walked back over, wiping blood from his face. 'We have reached the end game, brother,' he said to Vultis. 'If you have a move to make, make it now.'

Vultis returned to the book on his workbench, tracing his finger over the lines of text, muttering to himself. 'I thought it *was* working. Why did it harm the specimen?' He tapped something on the page and laughed in relief, realising he had misread one of the equations. He began clicking switches back up. 'Quickly. Raise the levers.'

Damaris and Baraca did as he asked, clicking the handles

back into position. Vultis made some adjustments then nodded. 'Three, two, one, *now.*'

They yanked the levers down and machines growled, flooding the canisters with light.

There was an explosion of noise from the transformers on the desk and then...

And then nothing.

The lights in the canisters died.

Vultis stared at them.

The sound of gunfire drummed outside the doors and he heard soldiers, howling orders and screaming in pain.

'Luco,' said Baraca. 'They are at the doors.'

'I can do this.' Baraca looked surprised by the anger in Vultis' voice. 'I *can* do this,' he repeated in more controlled tones. 'I need to adjust the frequency. I had it right the first time. I just need to make a small adjustment in my calculations.'

The doors rattled on their hinges and the sound of fighting grew more intense.

'I will go out there and help them,' said Baraca.

'I need you here!' Vultis grabbed another book, slammed it on top of the first and began poring over text and anatomical diagrams, mouthing numbers and equations as he read, glancing repeatedly at the shapes in the caskets. What had he missed?

'The second xenos swarm is almost on us.' Castamon's voice was strained and half-drowned by the sound of gunfire. *'They look to be in the millions. Our time is up. Are you ready, Vultis?'*

'A few more minutes, lieutenant. I am close. I just have to–'

'Vultis,' said Baraca, a warning in his voice.

'What is it?' demanded Castamon. *'Baraca. Speak.'*

Vultis glared at Baraca, warning him to remain quiet, but he spoke anyway. 'Luco does not make mistakes, lieutenant.

I have never seen him struggle until now.' He stared at Vultis. 'But there *is* a problem.'

Vultis felt like striking him. 'It will work. I just have to–'

'Is it working now?' interrupted Castamon.

The fury drained from Vultis. He looked back at the books on his desk. 'It will work,' he said, but the strength had gone from his voice.

Castamon was silent for a moment then said, *'That is not enough. Even these walls will not repel Bio-Titans. The fortress is lost. And I cannot let the xenos take this world. If they breach the Sanctus Line here, at its strongest point, they will have a direct route to the Sol System. We need another answer.'*

Vultis planted his fists on the workbench, staring at the books so hard he thought they might ignite under his glare, but however many ways he looked at the problem, he could not pinpoint the solution. He needed more time. It was the only way. But there *was* no more time.

The building trembled as guns roared louder outside.

'This is it,' snarled Baraca, baring his teeth and swinging his gun round from his back.

'Holy Throne,' breathed Damaris, looking up at the shaking doors.

'Luco,' said Castamon. He still sounded calm, as though he were debating a hypothetical situation instead of an imminent apocalypse. *'Don't stay on the path you chose. Stay on the path you need.'*

'What do you mean?'

'If your current course is failing, try another.' Plasterwork clattered down from the ceiling as something slammed into the exterior of the building. Masonry crashed through cabinets and spilled hissing liquids across the floor. *'Could you try the opposite approach? If controlling their minds has failed, could you destroy*

them instead? Could you do as Abarim did, but on a larger scale? Could you use these symbionts to transmit psychic disruption, to sever the swarm's link to the hive mind?'

Vultis took a deep breath and stood up straight, recovering his self-composure. 'Not possible. I could realign their synapses, but my specimens would burn out in minutes. One is already dying.'

The sound of gunfire crackled across the vox and Castamon was silent for a moment. *'Understood. Then what is the solution? We have tried one handle, we must try another. We are outnumbered. We cannot win by strength of arms so we must use something else. You have studied tirelessly since we came here, Luco. You know everything about Regium and this fortress. And your mind is sharper than any I have ever encountered. Forget the neurogaunts. Forget your research. Give me an answer.'*

Vultis was horrified by the idea of leaving his work incomplete, but Castamon's faith in him renewed his determination. He thought back over all he had learned, and then, unbidden, an idea did start to form in his mind. 'There could be a way to stop them. The plasma reactor we engineered for the cautery shields is *unusually* powerful. If we overloaded it, we would create a fission explosion. A thermonuclear blast. It would take out half the province.'

Castamon replied in the same neutral tones. *'Massive civilian casualties. But we would wipe out all the xenos for miles around.'* He paused for thought. *'Still not good enough. The xenos bio-ships would remain in orbit ready to disgorge more swarms. And the tyranids that have already made planetfall on other parts of Regium may be unaffected.'*

Vultis nodded, but now that he was on the trail of an idea, the sounds of battle fell away and his mind filled with facts and data. 'Then we just need a way to magnify the blast.'

Damaris made a strange sound, a mixture of a gasp and a sob, that dragged him from his thoughts. He was about to demand silence when he saw how peculiar her expression was. Her eyes were wide and full of tears. 'What is it?' he demanded.

'It may be nothing,' she said, mumbling. Then she looked annoyed with herself and spoke with more confidence. 'Before Confessor Thurgau came, we had priests of our own – the Keft. They told stories of the world roots – of how they came to be and how they would protect us in times of need.'

'Legends and myths?' Vultis was annoyed that he had wasted time listening to her.

Baraca held up a hand. 'Let her speak, Luco. We have tried science.' Humour flickered in his eyes. 'Perhaps faith can find a way.'

'*Who is in there with you?*' asked Castamon.

'The world roots go deep,' said Damaris, ignoring the question. 'That is not a matter of faith but of *fact*. They have been explored. And legends say they join, forming a chamber at the heart of the world. The legends also say...' She hesitated. 'The legends say that if our world ever fell from the Emperor's grace, He would light a fire in its heart. A fire that would reverberate through the world roots. A fire powerful enough to tear the world apart.' She finished in a breathless rush and looked at the floor, seeming horrified by her own words.

'*Is that the consul?*' demanded Castamon.

'The calefaction pumps,' muttered Vultis. 'She is right. They reach beneath the planetary mantle. The colonists sunk them straight through silicate rock, down as far as the planet's outer core. And there are geoengines in every province.'

'*Which means what?*' demanded Castamon.

'Our reactor is heat shielded,' he continued. 'If we dropped it down a geoengine shaft it would get close to the mantle before it exploded. Perhaps even reach it.' He looked at Damaris. 'I know nothing of the planet's "heart" but the pumps *do* form a planetwide network. And they were designed to *magnify* energy. That was how the colonists terraformed the planet. If we timed the blast right, we could create a chain reaction.'

'*We could detonate the planet.*'

Damaris looked like she was going to vomit. 'Is that the only way?' She looked up at Vultis, her voice shaking. 'What happens if we don't stop them here?'

'*They will feed,*' replied Castamon over the vox. '*They will consume every ounce of Regium's biomass and then they will repro-duce, becoming an even larger threat. Then, having removed this linchpin of the Sanctus Line, they will advance deep into Segmen-tum Solar, consuming countless worlds and billions of people en route to the Sol System. If that happens, the best we can hope for is that Lord Commander Guilliman redeploys his forces to cope with the new threat. If he focuses huge amounts of resources on these xenos, he may be able to stop them, but in doing so he will leave himself exposed on dozens of fronts, allowing Heretic Astartes and cultists to regain ground and tighten their stranglehold. Or if he fails to stop the xenos, they may reach Terra and the steps of the Golden Throne itself. Either way, the future of the entire Imperium would be in the balance.*'

He paused, then said: '*Vultis. Can it be done? Are you sure it is heat shielded enough?*'

Vultis nodded. 'Yes. It only needs to hold out until the reactor is *near* the mantle. That would be deep enough for the blast to radiate through the geoengine network. But not all of the shafts sink straight down to the mantle. Some end at sumps. The tunnels beneath Zarax would be no use.'

'*Where is the nearest usable one?*'

Vultis glanced at Baraca. 'We have just been there. The place where we found the pilgrims. It was only a few miles away.'

'A few miles is a long way through a tyranid swarm.'

'There are tunnels we could use,' said Damaris. 'Routes known only to me and a few others. I know the way.'

The building shook again and there was a chorus of screams from the square outside.

'Then this will be our final move,' said Castamon. *'And we will ensure it succeeds. But we must move now. Abarim is already in the generatorium. We can join him there.'* He paused. *'If that is the consul you are talking to, you should know this: she is a traitor and murderer. She betrayed Squad Gerrus to their deaths and she is awaiting execution.'*

Vultis and Baraca both gripped their pistols, and Damaris backed away.

'Her knowledge of these tunnels buys her a temporary reprieve. But watch her closely.'

Vultis stared at her, thinking of what Baraca had said – that she was hiding some kind of shame. 'The whole squad?'

She looked up at him defiantly. 'I am a fool, but I am being honest. I will get you to that geoengine. I swear it on the Emperor Himself.'

Baraca stared at her. 'We can trust her, Luco. In this matter, at least.'

'We have no choice,' said Castamon.

Baraca rolled his shoulders and raised his chin. 'Someone needs to keep the tyranids busy while you travel to the geoengine. I can make sure I have their full attention while Vultis leads you to the forest.'

Damaris was staring at the door, listening to the screams outside. Vultis guessed her thoughts. 'Your people are already dead,' he said. 'We all are. But we have a final moment. A final chance to do what is right.'

She nodded, but the horrified expression remained on her face.

'Sergeant Tanaro,' said Castamon. 'Zarax is yours. Hold it. Make every life count. We have our solution. We will ensure the hive fleet does not survive the day. But I need their attention to remain focused on this fortress, do you understand?'

'For the Emperor,' replied Tanaro. His voice was even more distorted than Castamon's, but Vultis could hear his pride.

'For Ultramar,' said Castamon.

'Lieutenant,' said Baraca, sounding agitated. 'Do you mean for me to join him up on the walls?'

'No. We must reach the reactor and carry it through miles of tyranid-infested ground. Tunnels or not, I will need you at my side if I am to have any chance of success.'

Baraca looked appalled. 'Tanaro stays? He takes on the entire swarm while I hide in a tunnel?'

'I never marked you down as a glory hound, Baraca. Let Tanaro claim the credit while we deliver the killing blow.'

Baraca's voice was rough with anger. 'A killing blow our enemies will never see coming. A knife in the back. I want them to see my face.'

'No need to worry on that score,' said Vultis. 'The reactor will need to fall a long way before it triggers the reaction. We should have time to emerge from our hole and show our faces.'

Baraca grunted, clearly unimpressed, but he said no more.

'Meet me at the reactor,' said Castamon, then the vox-link died.

Vultis and Baraca locked their helmets in place and grabbed their weapons. Then they all headed up to the doors.

Chapter Thirty-Nine

THE FORTRESS CITY AT ZARAX
SAMNIUM PROVINCE, REGIUM

Castamon was halfway across the forum when he saw Vultis rushing towards him through the battle, followed by Baraca and the traitor, Damaris. The plaza was corpse-crowded and chaotic, and up on the walls it looked like armageddon had already hit. Tanaro and the others were gathered under the canopy, firing into a grotesque, surreal sight. The heat shield was heaped with smouldering carcasses. Rather than accept that they could not pass through it, the aliens had simply kept throwing themselves against the barrier in huge numbers and now they were stacked against it in their thousands. In some places, the weight of the dead was causing the shield to sag and rupture, allowing burning tyranids to haul themselves through and drop onto the walls. Those that fell through the shield attacked with speed and purpose, causing Castamon to pause and shake his head.

While he waited for Vultis to reach him, he tried again to contact the Librarian. 'Abarim?' he voxed. 'What is your status? Why have you stopped shielding us?' There was no reply.

'Well met, brother,' he said, clasping Vultis' arm as the Apothecary reached him.

Vultis and Baraca both saluted, but Damaris simply stared at him in terror. He considered whether there was any way to do this without her aid.

'It was the consul's idea to sacrifice Regium,' said Baraca, seeming oddly protective of her. 'I have no idea what drove her to betray us, but she has now given us our last chance at defeating the swarm. We could wander those tunnels for hours without her to lead us.'

Castamon considered himself a good judge of character. When he looked at Damaris he saw many things – grief, shame and determination, but he did not see deceit. She believed she was helping them. He nodded. 'She lives. For now.' He turned and strode across the plaza with the other three rushing after him. 'I believe Abarim may be wounded,' he told them.

They came to a stop halfway across the forum. A statue had fallen and was lying directly in front of the small mausoleum the Ultramarines were heading towards. There were mounds of dead tyranids piled around it, half-buried in the rubble, their inhuman faces staring up into the darkness. 'This must have been Abarim,' said Castamon, then he rushed on, climbing over more dead bodies, human this time, as he headed into the building.

They passed through the mausoleum and down into the command bunker. Castamon barely registered the piles of weapons and stacks of blinking logic machines. As they raced through the rooms, dead-eyed servitors appeared, hobbling, trundling and gliding after him like mechanical insects.

They had not gone far when he noticed a smell that was different to the foetid aroma outside. This was more like the acrid stink of burned hair. 'What is that?' he muttered.

No one replied. He picked up his pace, hammering access codes as he raced through room after room, heading deeper into the bunker. Finally, he stumbled to a halt as he reached the generatorium and found Abarim. For the first time since landing on Regium, for the first time in his career, perhaps, Castamon was at a loss, struggling to process what he was seeing. At the centre of the room there was a metal casket. The casket was under a glass dome which was linked to machines in the walls by cables. Abarim's hands were *inside* the casket, sunk into the metal. Castamon recognised him by his armour, with its tall cowl around the helmet, but little else of him remained. His body was twisted out of recognition and his face had melted away, leaving just a few fragments of skin on blackened bone. He was the source of the smell. He had been cooked alive. His armour was shaking slightly, making a dull clattering sound on the flagstones.

Castamon stared at the corpse. He had known Abarim for centuries. He knew him better than anyone else. How had he misunderstood him? He remembered the hesitation in the Librarian's voice when they had discussed the plan. He had known this would happen. *How did I not see it?* Castamon had the peculiar sense that his strength was failing. That he was lost. It was not merely his grief, it was also that he felt wrong-footed. He *understood* people, his men, especially. He prided himself on it. How could he have been so blind to this?

'I could have found another way,' he whispered, kneeling by the blackened remains.

'Lieutenant,' said Vultis.

He closed his eyes for a second, then stood. 'Can you salvage his gene-seed?'

Vultis shook his head.

'We will have to disconnect him from the reactor,' said Baraca.

Castamon continued staring at Abarim, playing their final conversation over in his mind.

'Lieutenant,' prompted Vultis. 'We need to disconnect the reactor.'

Castamon let out a long breath and nodded, then spoke into his vox. 'Tanaro. We are going to kill the shield.'

'*Understood, lieutenant.*' Tanaro sounded like he was struggling to breathe.

'Those things will fall into the fortress,' gasped Damaris. 'All those creatures that are stacked against the shield. If you turn it off, they will fall into the city.'

'Muster everyone you have left, Tanaro,' continued Castamon, ignoring her. 'Withdraw to the Citadel of Maxellus.' Then he killed the vox-link and looked at Damaris. 'How far is the nearest entrance to your tunnels? Once the shields come down, we will have limited time before the streets are flooded with xenos.'

'Did you finish filling the Caves of the Rubicassus? That would be the easiest route.'

He shook his head. 'The soldiers were redeployed – sent to join Tanaro on the walls. Some of the cave-mouths are still accessible.' He nodded to one of the servitors that had followed them into room. 'Kill the power.'

The servitor was little more than a ball of metal pincers cradling a human head. It rolled and skittered across the floor, unfolded a metal limb and flicked a switch on one of the cogitators.

The lumen globes burned brighter as energy flooded their circuits. Then Abarim's corpse flopped back from the casket, his neatly severed wrists spilling ash as they slapped onto the floor.

Castamon knelt next to the dead Librarian and placed a hand on his charred armour. He had the feeling that part of him had died with Abarim – that this death was significant in ways he had yet to fathom. He shook his head and stood up, looking back at the reactor. 'Unhook it.'

Another servitor approached. This one was still mostly human – a crook-backed woman with a plasteel plate where her face should have been. She disconnected the cables linking the casket then stepped back.

Vultis and Baraca rushed forwards and picked the casket up between them, each keeping their gun hands free. Then the four of them exited the room, heading back up towards the roar of battle.

Chapter Forty

UXAMA CHEM-WORKS
SAMNIUM PROVINCE, REGIUM

Tharro waved at Valacia and Avula and they rushed across the street to hunker down beside him. They had abandoned the groundcar half a mile from the outskirts of the chem-works and were now creeping through the darkness, dashing from one abandoned building to the next. Most of the structures were little more than roofless ruins but there were signs of recent activity – tyre tracks in the mud and discarded bullet casings glinting in the rubble.

There had been no more gunfire as they approached and the whole complex was deathly quiet, but there was an ominous feeling hanging over the place and they kept to the shadows as they moved deeper within.

'Look at that,' whispered Avula, staring at something lying on the ground up ahead, the colour draining from her face.

'What is it?' muttered Tharro, squinting through the gloom at the dark, crumpled shape. 'Is it a sack?'

'A person,' said Valacia, grimacing.

Tharro felt a wave of nausea as he realised she was right. 'Throne,' he muttered. 'That could only have been done by one of the aliens.'

'And it looks recent,' said Avula, clinging to Valacia's arm. 'Look – the blood is still wet.'

Valacia shook her head. 'Then they're probably still here.'

Tharro glanced at the gun in his hand, wondering if it would be powerful enough to stop one of the xenos.

'But what would they want with a shuttle?' said Avula.

'No,' said Valacia. 'It's not that. Think about it. We saw the gunfire from miles away, so they would have seen it too. They just saw a chance to feed. And if they've finished eating, what reason would they have to stay here?' She waved at the ruined, empty buildings. 'There's nothing for them here. They would have spotted an opportunity, then left.'

Avula stared at the floor, shaking her head.

'Forgive me, child,' said Valacia. 'I wasn't thinking. Were they your family? Your friends?'

'No.' She took a deep breath. 'I met them on the road. Only a couple of days ago. But they were good people. And Jebel…' She frowned. 'He seemed so sure of what he was doing. He was the first person I found who seemed to think there was a chance…' She shook her head.

'There *is* a chance,' said Tharro, trying to sound more confident than he felt. 'If Jebel and the others died, it means the cargo shuttle could still be down there. And' – he found it hard to say the next words – 'if we keep our wits about us and don't start shooting guns, we could reach it without drawing the attention of any aliens.' He felt a rush of pride as he saw how Valacia was looking at him. 'We just need to be as quiet as the grave and we have a chance. Do you know where the shuttle is?'

She nodded. 'Well, I know where the entrance to the hangar

is.' She frowned. 'But Tolophon said he had access codes. How will we get in without those?'

Valacia nodded to the autopistol Tharro was holding. 'That thing seems pretty good at cutting through metal. If there's a lock, we can shoot it off.'

Tharro was not convinced that would work, but he nodded. 'We'll see what the situation is when we get there. *If* we get there.' He edged to the end of the wall. 'No more talking from now.' He looked at the pile of human remains. 'We can't be sure the aliens have gone.' Then he left the cover of the building, crouching low as he jogged towards the next building.

As they neared the centre of the chem-works, the buildings grew larger and more ominous – vast, towering chimneys and cooling towers that threw the place into an even deeper gloom. They also saw more body parts scattered across the ground. Tharro did his best not to look at them, but sometimes it was unavoidable as he almost stumbled into piles of glistening meat. There was still no sign of movement though, and the only sound was the relentless *thump, thump* of alien pods landing in the distance.

They reached the edge of a large, open space where haulers must once have parked and Avula pointed to a dark, rectangular shape in the ground, her eyes shining with excitement. 'It's open,' she mouthed, nodding eagerly.

Tharro thought it seemed too good to be true. If the hangar was open, perhaps the shuttle was already gone? *No*, he thought – if the shuttle had gone, the hangar door would be fully open. He looked around. There were more bodies here than anywhere. There were pools of blood and pieces of meat scattered across the ground, and the remains of a few groundcars that were so mangled it looked like the tyranids had tried to eat those too. But no one was moving. The idea of stepping out into that killing ground terrified him, but he could not imagine the aliens would be cowering in silence, waiting for someone to walk by. The creatures he had seen moved in a voracious, frenzied swarm.

He realised the other two were staring at him, waiting for him to make a move. He nodded and took a deep breath, then, holding the pistol before him, he walked out slowly into the half-light.

The other two followed him, and after a few steps he was sure they were safe. The only thing moving was the weird silt-like gunk that was drifting through the air. Nodding to the others, he scurried across the square to the opening in the ground. It was fifty or sixty feet long but only about three feet wide. He crouched down next to the hole as the others stood behind him, still looking around at the buildings for signs of movement. The gap was wide enough to squeeze through, but it looked like a sheer drop into darkness. There was no way to tell how deep it was.

'Tharro,' said Valacia. She spoke quietly but the word still rang out oddly. 'Listen.' The colour had drained from her face.

He shook his head, frowning. Then he heard it. The thrumming sound of wings. Hundreds of wings. And it was growing louder by the second.

'How did they know we were here?' whispered Avula, pacing back and forth, staring into the shadows.

Tharro struggled to think. Panic threw his thoughts into a jumble as he listened to the sound coming closer.

'Here!' said Valacia. She had rushed to the other end of the opening and dropped to her knees, reaching down for something. 'There's a ladder!'

Tharro and Avula sprinted over to her, and without another word they all began climbing down into the darkness. They had only descended a few rungs when lumen strips blinked into life, revealing a large subterranean hangar.

Tharro laughed in disbelief. It was full of shuttles. There were six, of various shapes and sizes, draped in tarpaulins.

'Can we close the doors?' gasped Valacia as they reached the bottom of the ladder and looked around the hangar. Apart from the shuttles, the place was fairly empty. There was a line of metal fuel bowsers arrayed along one wall, like gleaming sentries, and a stack of void-crates and pallets just to the side of them. On the opposite wall, at head height, there was what looked like a generator, linked to the doors and lights by armoured power cables, and beneath the generator there was a small cogitator on a desk. The machine consisted of a viewscreen fixed to a spherical array of rune keys. At the far end of the hangar, on the other side of the shuttles, there was a pair of large, locked doors.

'Here!' cried Avula, noticing a row of switches near the ladder. She traced her fingers over them, then flicked one down. The doors hummed with current then lurched into life, slamming shut and blocking out the darkness.

'We can't fly out of here with the doors closed,' said Tharro.

'Can you fly a shuttle?' said Avula, eyes wide with excitement as she rushed over to him.

Tharro shook his head.

Avula looked at Valacia and she shook her head too.

The doors above their heads were thick and armour plated, but Tharro could still hear the sound of wings rushing closer.

The three of them stared at each other. Then Avula clenched her jaw and marched over to the nearest shuttle. 'How hard can it be?' She grabbed a tarpaulin and started to yank it free.

'No, wait,' said Valacia. 'That one over there. It's larger.'

'Why's that better?' asked Tharro, trying to keep the panic from his voice.

'Larger means a bigger fuel tank.' Valacia shrugged. 'At least that's what I would assume. And the bigger the fuel tank, the further we can fly.'

'*Where* will we fly?' said Tharro, realising he had not even considered what the destination would be.

'Listen to those wings!' snapped Avula. 'We can work out the details later. First we need to work out how to start the engines. Then we'll open the doors and get miles from those monsters. After that we can decide where to go.'

'Makes sense to me,' said Valacia.

The three of them rushed over to the largest shuttle and pulled the tarpaulin away.

'Throne,' gasped Avula. 'Who put this here?'

'Looks like a rich man's toy,' said Tharro as he studied the hulking polished hull and elegant swooping wings. He saw cargo shuttles regularly, gliding past the agri complex, but they were usually rusted, utilitarian things that looked like they would fall apart in a stiff breeze. This was some other kind of ship entirely, as sleek and powerful looking as a bird of prey. There were even weapons slung under its wings.

The landing hatch was not so different to some of the agricultural machines he used and he easily found the lever. Rather than clattering and banging down, the boarding ramp slid out with a luxurious *whoosh*, revealing the warmly lit glow of the interior.

'We've struck gold,' he laughed, forgetting his terror for a moment.

They rushed up the ramp and into the cargo hold. Beyond that there was a large passenger compartment and then, at the front of the vessel, a cockpit that was larger than Tharro's entire hab-unit. The seats looked like they were upholstered with real leather, or at least something approximating it, and they were stitched with the sigil of a Mechanicus forge world. The flight controls were a fan-shaped array of brass gauges and glossy viewscreens. As they entered the cabin, the controls blinked into life, filling the screens with a storm of luminous binary and causing needles to dance across dials.

They looked at the vast, crowded control panel, then looked at each other.

'I have no idea,' muttered Tharro.

'I used to drive haulers when I was younger,' said Valacia, sitting down in one of the seats. 'And I flew an aircar once. And this is a luxury machine designed for comfort. There's probably some sort of autopilot.'

There was a loud bang outside. Something had thudded against the doors in the hangar ceiling. It sounded like a rock, but they all knew what it really was. They stared at each other as something scuttled and scraped over the doors. Then there was another loud thud as something else landed on the metal.

'We're out of time,' said Valacia, looking at the controls. 'I bet it's this one.' She pulled back some moulded casing and flicked the switch underneath. The cabin was immediately bathed in blinking red light and a klaxon started barking from an emitter somewhere behind them.

'That's not it!' cried Tharro. 'Turn it off!'

Valacia flicked the switch back, but nothing changed. The red lights continued flashing and the klaxon carried on braying.

'Damn it!' cried Valacia, flicking the switch back and forth.

Above them, more thuds sounded on the hangar door. At first they hit in ones and twos, then it sounded like a storm of bodies hammering down on the metal.

There was a low grinding noise as the metal started to give.

Chapter Forty-One

The tunnel lit up as Vultis' bolt pistol jolted in his fist, spitting rounds into a tyranid. The monster exploded, hurling viscera across the walls. It was one of the worm-like species and, as the smoke cleared, he saw the hole where it had burrowed into the tunnel.

Castamon approached the remains with his gun raised, scouring the darkness ahead. Vultis and Baraca were still carrying the metal casket between them, and Damaris was up ahead, clutching a lumen and leading the way. She flashed her light across the tunnel walls, spotting an opening on the left, not far ahead.

'Do we need to find a different route?' Vultis asked, studying the dead tyranid.

Castamon shook his head. 'They are focused on Zarax. Tanaro will make a glorious job of his last stand. He should hold their attention for a good while yet. I think this is just a late arrival that stumbled into us by chance.'

'It might alert the rest of the swarm, though.' Vultis kicked at the slop. 'If they *are* all linked to a hive mind.' He had brought the two canisters with him from his laboratorium and he looked down at them. Since entering the tunnels, he could think of nothing but his failure, playing the moment over in his mind, picturing his notes and equations, trying to spot the flaw in his theory.

Castamon nodded. 'A lone cry of warning might be drowned out by the battle, but we should keep moving. Lead on, consul.'

They pounded on, through burial cairns and tunnels. The Ultramarines were going slower than they would have liked for Damaris' benefit, but she still looked exhausted as she stumbled through the gloom.

Eventually, she stumbled to a halt, leaning against a wall and trying to catch her breath. 'Not long,' she gasped. 'We're close now.'

The tunnel juddered. Pieces of stone and clods of soil drummed down onto the floor.

'Bio-Titans,' said Vultis, looking up at the ceiling as the tunnel shook again. 'They've reached the fortress.'

Castamon nodded and grabbed Damaris by the arm, hauling her down the tunnel.

The next passage ended in a set of tall doors that were inscribed with an image of the God-Emperor breaking up through the ground, sword aloft, roots and tendrils trailing from the blade. 'This is it,' said Damaris, slumping in Castamon's grip.

Baraca took a few steps back and raised his pistol, pointing it at the lock.

'Wait,' gasped Damaris. 'I can open it. Don't damage it.'

He laughed. 'We are about to destroy the world.'

'Humour me,' she muttered, looking embarrassed as she climbed to her feet and pressed her hands against the metal. The mechanism recognised her fingerprints and bolts clanged, allowing her to gently shove the doors open. They revealed a vast, cylindrical hall, networked by dozens of gantries and walkways. It was an enormous shaft, and as she shone her lumen into it, the beam was powerless to reveal either its top or its bottom.

Vultis spotted a ladder fixed to the wall, not far from the platform she had stepped out onto. 'Is that our route?'

She nodded. 'It goes straight down. For miles. To the heart of the world.' Her words echoed strangely down the shaft.

The four of them looked into the darkness below. Then the tunnel behind them juddered again, hurling more rubble from the ceiling.

Vultis nodded to the web of gantries and pipes. 'Does the rest of the metalwork continue all the way down?'

'No,' replied Damaris. 'It's only in these upper levels. After that the shaft is clear.'

'We need to climb down, then,' said Vultis. 'When we reach the last of the gantries, we will head out and position ourselves at the centre of the shaft before we drop the reactor.'

'And then what?' asked Damaris.

'Then we head back up,' he said. 'We should have time to return to the surface and rejoin the battle before the blast hits. The heat shielding on the reactor will hold out a long time.'

'How long?' asked Castamon.

He shrugged. 'Considering Regium's size, it might take a couple of hours for the reactor to reach the outer mantle and become hot enough to detonate. We should have no difficulty reaching the surface in that time.'

Castamon looked down at Damaris. 'You have done what you promised. We have no need of a guide from here. If you wish, you can return to the surface now.' He nodded to the sword on her back. 'Perhaps you could put that thing to good use.' He shrugged. 'Or you can stay here and wait for the end.'

'You aren't going to shoot me?' she whispered, shaking her head.

He studied her. 'I will never know why you did what you did but–'

'I never believed you,' she said, staring at the floor. Her voice was little more than a whisper. 'About the xenos, I mean. I thought it was all just propaganda. I thought you were a lie.'

Castamon was silent for a moment and Vultis wondered if he would finally execute her. But when he spoke, there was no anger in his voice. 'A weapon does not lie.'

She frowned, confused, but said no more.

Baraca shrugged. 'When that blast hits, you will know you struck a blow in the Emperor's name. No one can ask for more. You can be at peace.'

'At peace?' She shook her head. 'Not until I see that reactor fall. I'm coming down there with you.'

Castamon continued looking at her for a moment. Then he turned, grabbed the ladder and started climbing down.

The reactor was heavy enough to slow Vultis and Baraca, and Damaris looked as though she might collapse at any moment, but Castamon rushed ahead, quickly disappearing into the darkness. As he climbed, Vultis recalled songs and legends he had learned about the world roots. Scenes and words circled in his mind until he felt like he was descending into a mythical abyss – a place where gods and daemons vied for dominance and the trials of humanity were insignificant. The sounds of battle grew even more distant and, gradually, the heat began to rise. He pictured Guilliman's command chamber and he felt the presence of the Harbinger, closing in on its prey. Even here, way beneath the ground, the tyranids were muddying his thoughts and confusing him.

Finally, they reached a gridded metal platform that stretched out across the entire shaft and below which there was no more metalwork. Castamon was already waiting, out at the centre of the platform. As they left the ladder and rushed towards him, he took out his bolt pistol and fired into wire mesh, punching a hole through it. The report of the gun echoed strangely around the shaft as he holstered it, dropped to one knee and took out his combat knife, cutting at the metalwork.

By the time Vultis reached him, Castamon had almost made a hole large enough to drop the casket through.

Vultis and Baraca knelt next to him, cutting at the metal, but Damaris hesitated, looking up into the darkness. She shook her head, muttering to herself.

'What is it?' demanded Vultis, still cutting as he looked up at her.

'Someone's coming,' she muttered, frowning in confusion. 'Someone I've seen before.'

Vultis was still battling to shake his visions of Guilliman's command chamber. He nodded. 'I feel it too.'

Baraca stopped cutting and looked up. Then he laughed oddly.

There was an explosion of breaking metal. An enormous tyranid dropped from overhead, smashing through the pipes and gantries and landing on the platform. The monster was so large that its weight rippled through the platform, causing it to buckle and tilt.

The reactor slid away from the Ultramarines, rattling down the slope, heading away from the centre of the platform and juddering towards the tyranid.

Supports and cables snapped as the network of gantries began to come away from the walls. Girders screamed and sparks billowed through the darkness.

Damaris howled.

Vultis felt no surprise as he recognised the monster. He felt as though their journey through the tunnels had been building to this moment. One side of the tyranid's head had been burned by an explosion, leaving a mass of scabs and scar tissue, but it looked at him with a calm intensity, quite unlike any other xenos he had faced. This was not a mindless eating machine. It was the Harbinger. And the recognition in its eyes was somehow obscene.

Damaris screamed and tried to crawl away, but the platform was still tilting her up, threatening to hurl her into the monster's grasp.

All three Ultramarines opened fire, managing to steady themselves on the listing platform. Vultis and Castamon used their bolt pistols, punching holes in the monster's chest, while Baraca took his pyreblaster from his back and spewed flames, engulfing the monster's head.

The Harbinger screamed along with Damaris and the sound raked through Vultis' mind. Blood rushed from his ears and nose.

Damaris began sliding down the slope towards the Harbinger.

The Ultramarines advanced calmly, still firing, driving the tyranid back towards the walls.

'The reactor!' cried Vultis. The casket had slid right across the platform and was now near the tyranid's hooves. The creature knew why they were down here. Vultis could feel it. It *understood*. While the rest of the swarm had fallen for their decoy, attacking Tanaro at the fortress, this creature had seen through the ruse. And it had come to stop them.

'Covering fire!' cried Castamon, then he sprinted across the juddering platform. He leapt a dozen feet into the air, hammered his combat knife into the monster's thigh and yanked it sideways, tearing flesh and exoskeleton.

The Harbinger screamed and slumped as Baraca and Vultis rushed forwards, knocking it back with another barrage of shots.

Castamon clambered quickly up the Harbinger, grabbing handholds as if the monster were a rock face and drawing back his knife to hammer it into its chest.

The Harbinger grabbed him, wrenched him from its body and slammed him into the wall, striking with such force that his helmet smashed and blood exploded from his armour. Then it hurled him at Baraca and Vultis.

Baraca leapt over the lieutenant and rushed at the tyranid's wounded leg, driving his knife into the wound Castamon had opened.

Vultis dropped onto his knee and continued firing, pinning the Harbinger to the wall.

Castamon lay in a crumpled heap, blood rushing from his ruined helmet, but Vultis continued firing, trying to protect Baraca. As he fired, Vultis felt again that he had entered a world of gods and heroes. Courage and anger surged through him. The Harbinger considered them vermin. He could feel the disdain radiating from it.

Damaris clambered to her feet and stumbled across the platform, trying to follow Baraca, drawing her sword from her back and gripping it in both hands. 'You will not defile the world roots!' she cried, her voice hoarse. The hole at the centre of the platform had been ripped wider by the arrival of the tyranid and Damaris teetered at the edge, almost falling, before she managed to right herself and skirt around.

The Harbinger turned and looked directly at Vultis. It ripped Baraca from its leg and hammered him repeatedly onto the floor with a crack of splintering bone and ceramite. Then it dropped him and began limping across the platform, still staring at Vultis.

Damaris held her sword aloft and howled in wordless defiance.

Vultis rushed forwards, but the Harbinger batted him aside with ease, sending him tumbling off the edge of the platform into the bottomless dark.

Baraca hauled himself to his feet, blood pouring from his armour as he ran at the monster from behind. Damaris was nearby, gripping her sword, crouched into a battle stance and looking up at the Harbinger, looking for a place to strike. Castamon was dead and there was no sign of Vultis.

The monster's tail lashed out. Damaris hacked through it, severing some of the armour, but it flicked back and ripped her chest open, flinging her backwards.

Baraca felt a wave of peace wash over him. This *is my time*, he thought. In his darkest moments he had known doubt, wondering if he was destined to spend eternity seeking a purpose that did not exist. But now he saw that he had been right to wait. Right to endure. His life had led to this.

He grabbed the reactor in his arms, and, as the monster stared down at Damaris, he leapt unnoticed at its ruined leg, gripping on to the torn chitin with one hand and hanging on to the reactor with the other.

He hit the tyranid with such force that it fell sideways, screaming in surprise. Then Baraca, the tyranid and the casket fell through the gaping hole, plunging down the shaft.

Baraca roared as he fell, exultant. This was the death he had been waiting for. A death without fanfare. A death that would *matter*. But it was more than that. He knew Vultis would have laughed at him, but as Baraca fell, he saw something spiritual in what had happened – a symmetry that was loaded with significance. It was thanks to the local religion that they had originally found this place. And it was faith that had prompted Damaris to talk of the world's heart. Baraca began to see links and causality, meanings beyond science. Then he loosed the casket and fought, plunging his knife into the Harbinger.

Damaris grinned ferociously as she watched them vanish into the darkness, Baraca still stabbing the tyranid as they fell. 'For Vela,' she tried to say, but blood filled her mouth, drowning the words. Then she lay back on the sloping floor. Each breath she took was weaker than the last. Her lumen blinked and went out, and as the darkness closed in, her pain faded and she felt calm. She wondered what Vela would say if she were there. Probably something crude and inappropriate. The thought made her smile, and when her heart stopped, the smile remained on her face.

Chapter Forty-Two

THE FORTRESS CITY AT ZARAX
SAMNIUM PROVINCE, REGIUM

A screaming sound knifed through Sergeant Tanaro's ears. He could hear nothing else. He thought for a moment that he was blind as well as deaf, but then he realised it was just blood, clinging to the eye-lenses of his helmet. He wiped the blood away and climbed to his feet. He was standing on a mound of corpses in front of Castamon's once glorious citadel. Everything was either broken or breaking. The walls were tumbling. Buildings were exploding. Towers and pillars were crashing to the ground. Hundreds of soldiers and civilians lay dead around him, and with a rush of outrage he realised that his battle-brothers were also slumped in the pile, their armour rent and steam rising from their insides.

Beyond the piles of dead there was an ocean of inhuman faces. There were tyranids everywhere he looked. They had broken off from their feast and come in their thousands to gather round him. They knew he was their final obstacle. *No,* he thought, smiling. They *thought* he was their final obstacle. 'Courage and honour!' he roared, holding his pyreblaster aloft. His hearing returned and he revelled in the power of his own voice. Then he staggered, punch-drunk, across the bodies towards his foe.

His smile broadened as he saw people dragging themselves from the wreckage and marching at his side. Most of them were just civilians, clutching borrowed weapons or shards of splintered metal. All of them were bloody and broken, but they stood with him, and when he charged they charged with him, howling and screaming.

He doused the front lines of tyranids in promethium, creating a wall of dazzling fire. Then, with the tank empty, he placed one foot on a corpse, removed his helmet, shook his hair from his face and opened fire with his pistol, punching bolter rounds into the burning host. People fought and died all around him, rushing in from every direction, looking up at him with awe and admiration as he held the tide of xenos back.

The tyranids fired living projectiles into his chest, punching through ceramite and filling him with toxins. He howled, reeled backwards and finally crashed down into the gore, struggling to rise as parasites burrowed into him. The toxins made his head spin and his hands slipped in his own blood. *One last shot*, he thought, gripping his pistol with trembling fingers, but his hearts were labouring and he could not rise.

He heard the tyranids scuttling slowly towards him, moving in for the kill. He was proud to realise that they were hesitant, unsure if it was safe to approach him.

Then a woman appeared in front of him, frail and bloody, her clothes in tatters. There were lines down her cheeks where she had been crying, but she was not crying now. She looked proud as she held out her hand.

'You can't lift me,' he gasped, taking her hand in his. 'Too heavy.'

'Courage,' she said, her voice full of conviction.

Tanaro realised that, incredibly, she *was* managing to lift him from the ground. Then he realised why. People had gathered all around him and placed their hands on his armour, hefting him up from the dead.

'Honour,' he said, as they managed to right him.

Then, as one, they charged.

Chapter Forty-Three

Vultis watched Baraca fall to his death. He felt no sadness for his brother. Baraca had done what he always swore he would do. He had chosen his moment and he had made it count. But Vultis felt sadness for himself, that he would not spend his final moments with his friend.

He was clinging to the platform by a single hand, but that posed little difficulty. His grip was strong and his armour was still intact – the servos and fibre bundles allied with his natural strength made it easy for him to swing his other hand onto the ledge and haul himself up.

Damaris was lying a dozen feet away. Her body had been torn open and she was sprawled in a pool of blood, clearly dead. But, as he walked over to her, he saw that she had a peaceful smile on her face. She had shown unusual courage fighting the norn-emissary known as the Harbinger. She had offered up her life and her world to stop the tyranids. He found it hard to believe she had really betrayed Gerrus. Perhaps there was more to the story than Castamon realised. 'May your god be with you,' he said.

He looked around for Castamon. He was lying on the far side of the platform, near where the tyranid had first landed. His head had been pulverised and, like Damaris, he was surrounded by blood. He had no doubt what Castamon would say if he were still alive. He would see this as a victory. They knew their duty and they performed it well. But Vultis still felt a wave of sadness as he approached the body. Vultis found people unreliable and unpredictable. They did not correspond to the laws of nature that he knew so well. Even his battle-brothers were driven as much by their emotions as by reason or fact. But Castamon had been different. He saw things clearly. And he had taught Vultis to do the same.

It was only as he crouched down next to him that Vultis realised his mistake. Castamon's head was still intact. It was only his helmet, destroyed and lying at an unnatural angle, that had given the impression his head was crushed. Quickly, he used an attachment on his backpack to connect with Castamon's battleplate. The auto-senses were still active, and he smiled as he saw that Castamon still had a pulse. Both his hearts were still beating. He was unconscious but it was self-induced – triggered by his suit's medicae functions. He was dazed but alive. The medicae systems had slowed his pulse to protect him from trauma. It was similar to the biologically triggered response that had saved Vultis when he had escaped from the *Incorruptible*. The memory reminded him of something Castamon had said to him when he'd come to in the medicae facility. *Thanks to your foresight, we now have a specimen to examine.* He looked at the containment canisters fixed to his belt and the shapes inside. He had been *so* close. The others had doubted him, but he was sure he had been on the cusp of granting the Imperium an incredible weapon – a way to stop this happening again. The reactor would halt the invasion of Regium but there were other tyranid swarms spreading across the galaxy, other fleets that might also be heading to the Sanctus Line. And, with Regium gone, the chain would be broken.

He checked Castamon's vital signs again. There was damage to some of his muscles and ligaments and several broken bones, but his body was already trying to repair the worst of the damage. And there was nothing that looked fatal, for now, at least. He disconnected from Castamon's armour and began pacing around the platform. *This is a mistake,* he thought, drumming his fingers on the canisters. He couldn't take this to his grave. He *had* to get word to the rest of the Chapter. But what could he do? The reactor was racing towards the planet's core. He thought of Baraca. If he were here, he would not let logic be an obstacle. If he did not accept it was his time to die, he would find a way to live.

Vultis sat next to Castamon, scouring his thoughts for a way to choose his fate rather than have it thrust upon him. Pieces of metal were still tumbling down around him, pinging off the walkways overhead. He looked over at the ladder. There was still a way back to the surface, but that would only give him a chance to die in battle as the swarm descended on him. There were tunnels, too. He had seen them when they were climbing down. More of the world roots, as Damaris would have called them. But he had no map – no way of knowing where they led.

He triggered his suit's auspex and found that, down here, away from the atmospheric seeding on the planet's surface, his suit's auxiliary systems were working well. The tunnels gave off no heat or energy signals, though. He could only identify the nearest parts of the network. He had no idea where the tunnels led. He tried the suit's audio filters. He scanned dozens of frequencies and found nothing, but something made him persevere. He discarded a few sounds, recognising them as tyranid activity, but then he noticed a faint signal that was different from the others. It was a repetitive noise that was reverberating through the ground, pulse-like. Absurdly, he thought of the things Baraca had told him about the local faith – tales of spirits living deep beneath the ground, shadows of the Emperor guiding the dead to rest. He shook his head, trying to focus, still hounded by the visions that were trying to confound him. He adjusted the audio filter, homing in on the sound, and realised it was a warning klaxon. It was somewhere above him, not far away. He adjusted the filter again and realised that, beneath the klaxon, there was a humming sound. It sounded very similar to the sound of an engine, the kind used by a voidship.

A sense of fatalism gripped him. He was not *meant* to die down here. The symbionts had to be preserved and weaponised. It was his fate. He had never felt like this before and it was exactly the kind of mysticism he would have ridiculed Baraca for, but down here, in the vision-haunted darkness, it seemed to make sense. Besides, what other option did he have? He could wait down here to die or try following his instinct.

He used the medicae equipment on his backpack to give Castamon a shot of stimm serum. 'Lieutenant,' he said, once the serum had taken hold. 'Can you hear me?'

Castamon groaned and his eyelids flickered. Vultis removed the shattered pieces of helmet and wiped some of the blood away. Then he put his arm under him and helped him up. To his relief, Castamon not only stood but managed to open his eyes too. He tried to speak but there was too much damage to his throat.

'Save your strength,' said Vultis. 'I only need you to walk.'

Castamon grunted and Vultis began to lead him across the

broken platform, back to the ladders. When they reached Damaris and the hole in the floor, Castamon hesitated. 'We did it,' said Vultis. 'And Baraca dragged that thing down with him.' Castamon closed his eyes. Then he allowed Vultis to lead him on.

They reached the ladder and, without prompting, Castamon began to climb. Not long after, Vultis spotted the tunnel they needed and helped Castamon off the ladder, letting the lieutenant lean on him as they headed down another passageway. After a while, Castamon shrugged him off and began to run. He lurched like a drunk but refused any offer of help.

'We still have work to do,' said Vultis a while later, as they headed up a slope, back towards the surface.

Castamon tried to speak but failed, grimacing at the effort, so he nodded instead, gripping Vultis by the shoulder before stumbling on.

Chapter Forty-Four

Avula screamed as the hangar doors buckled and split. Dozens of shapes were pounding against the other side and the frame had almost come away. 'They're in!' she howled.

The shuttle's engines were howling like they were about to explode, but no one could work out how to turn the things off. The klaxon was still barking and was now accompanied by several others, but however Tharro and Valacia pounded at the controls, nothing would silence them.

There was a crashing sound behind them as the doors finally gave way. Snarling, thrashing monsters tumbled in from the darkness, slamming onto the floor. Their anatomy was revealed in gruesome detail by the hangar lights.

Tharro grabbed his autopistol, cursing as he rushed back to the landing ramp and stepped out of the shuttle. He fired, rattling bullets into the nearest tyranid as Valacia appeared at his side, shotgun in hand. 'Wait!' she gasped, gripping his arm and lowering his gun.

Darius Hinks

'What are you doing?' he demanded, then he understood. The tyranids were crashing down to the hangar floor, but none of them were getting up. They were wounded, all of them, ripped apart by gunfire, their carapaces shattered and bloody.

More fell from the darkness, hissing and spraying blood as they toppled downwards and bounced off the walls. A few tried to crawl towards the shuttle but they quickly collapsed and lay still. Tharro realised that he could hear gunfire outside.

A final tyranid thudded to the ground and then there were no more. The last one to fall was still alive and it tried to rise, but Valacia strode down the ramp and fired the shotgun, tearing its head off and sending it sliding across the hangar floor.

Tharro looked up at the opening. 'Is that it? Is that all of them?' He edged down the ramp and stood next to Valacia, pointing his pistol at the rectangle of darkness overhead.

She laughed nervously. 'I think, maybe, it was.'

Something rose from the shadows and Tharro fired, rattling bullets into the night.

'Hold your fire.' The voice was deep and amplified.

'Is that a man?' gasped Avula, appearing at Tharro's side and looking up at the figure. 'Is that you, Jebel?' she called out. 'Tolophon?'

The figure stepped closer until the hangar lights illuminated him from beneath. It was an Ultramarine, or, at least, Tharro *guessed* it was an Ultramarine. He had only ever seen grainy pict-captures of the off-worlders. The armour design was definitely as he remembered but the Ultramarines in the picts were glorious, clad in immaculate blue armour. This warrior was drenched in blood and filth and his armour, which seemed to have once been white, was rent out of shape. There were pieces of sinew dangling from his gauntlets. He looked like he had been dragged through a charnel house. He studied them for a moment, gore dripping from his helmet, then looked at the shuttle.

'Did *you* do this?' asked Avula, nodding to the butchered tyranids.

The Ultramarine ignored her question. Then he gestured to the shuttle. 'I have to leave.' He walked back into the darkness, then reappeared carrying another Ultramarine. This one looked even worse, as if he had been chewed in the gears of a great machine. He was barely conscious, swaying as the first Ultramarine led him to the ladder and began helping him down. When they reached the hangar floor the Ultramarine in white helped his comrade across to the landing ramp.

Tharro, Valacia and Avula backed away without question. Even in such a dreadful state, the Ultramarines radiated unquestionable authority. It was only as they began clanking up the ramp that Tharro realised what was happening. 'Wait!' He tried to sound more confident than he felt. 'We found this. You can't leave us here.'

The Ultramarine in white turned to face him.

Tharro felt just as terrified as when he faced the xenos. The Ultramarine did not look like a saviour. He did not look noble. He looked like a blood-caked war engine. Tharro took a step backwards, shaking his head, looking at the huge pistol locked to the warrior's belt.

For a painfully long moment, the Ultramarine said nothing. Then he nodded. 'Find a space and keep out of my way. We leave now.' With that he strode off into the ship, taking his wounded brother with him.

Tharro looked at Valacia, battling the urge to weep.

She embraced him and Avula in a fierce hug. None of them could hold back their tears of relief and they leant on each other as they entered the shuttle, sobbing and praying as the ramp began to rise.

Chapter Forty-Five

'He's stable,' said the medicae officer, speaking to Vultis from the opposite side of the observation deck. She was young, only twenty or so, and she looked like she had only recently been posted to the augur station. Her uniform was dazzlingly clean and looked starched enough to crack. She was also terrified. She had not managed to come within twelve feet of Vultis since he had docked the *Barbalissus*.

He had placed Castamon in a state of induced catatonia to speed his recovery, so he already knew the lieutenant was stable, but the woman clearly wanted recognition for her diligence. He nodded.

She hesitated and seemed to expect more of him, so he tried to think of something else to say.

'And the three civilians?'

'Recovering well,' she said, seeming pleased by the question. 'Their physical wounds were superficial and their lungs are clearing.' Her expression darkened. 'But they've endured a great trauma.' She shook her head. 'I've asked them if they want to discuss it, but they seem unwilling.'

Vultis nodded, pleased to hear it. He had ordered his three passengers to say nothing of the events on Regium until he gave them permission. They would soon be leaving the augur station on a pilgrim vessel, bound for the shipyards at Gabris. From there, he would be able to contact Chapter command and inform them of the invasion through official channels. They would decide how to explain what had happened. Until then, he had no intention of spreading panic.

'And *your* injuries?'

He shook his head.

The woman hesitated a while longer. She was clearly desperate to prolong the conversation, to ask him more questions, but he turned back to the oculus, making it clear he had no more to say.

He heard the woman leave, but a few minutes later more people began filing onto the observation deck. It was a group of Chartist officers, along with their ratings and menials. They stared at Vultis, giving him an awkward mixture of bows and salutes. Then they hurried over to the large domed oculus. They were clearly excited about something.

'There!' cried one of the officers. 'I've never seen a meteor shower like that.'

Lights were flickering into view across the void, flashing like clusters of shooting stars.

'It can't be a meteor shower,' said another officer, speaking in a pompous voice. 'Meteor showers are debris hitting atmosphere. This station *has* no atmosphere.'

'What is it then?' demanded someone else, but no one answered and they all fell quiet as the lights doubled and tripled until an incredible light show was billowing across the heavens.

'It's beautiful,' said someone. Vultis wondered if they would still feel that way when they learned that the lights were Regium, blasted into dust and scattered across the void. So many had died. He struggled to comprehend it. The decision had been made and enacted in such a short space of time that he was still coming to terms with the magnitude of it. He pictured faces in the lights: Tanaro, Abarim, Damaris, Thurgau and Karpova. Then, finally, he thought of Baraca, which reminded him of what he had been doing before the medicae officer interrupted him. He picked up his pauldron and continued scoring a line into the ceramite, chipping and scratching at it with his knife. It would be the first of many such lines. 'Not my time to die,' he said, hearing Baraca's voice in his head. Some of the Chartists looked over at him in confusion but he ignored them.

As he worked, Vultis played a scene over and over in his mind. It was the moment on Regium when he had failed to control the symbionts. He had been close. Some minor detail had eluded him, that was all. As soon as he and Castamon reached somewhere safe he would demand tools and a space to work. The people of Regium had made the ultimate sacrifice but it was, at best, a stalling tactic. The Great Devourer never stopped. And now it had broken the Sanctus Line. There was a crack in the dam. More tyranids would be on their way. He had to make the sacrifice worth something. He looked at the canisters fixed to his belt.

The other worlds in the Sanctus Line had to be warned.

He *had* to find the answer.